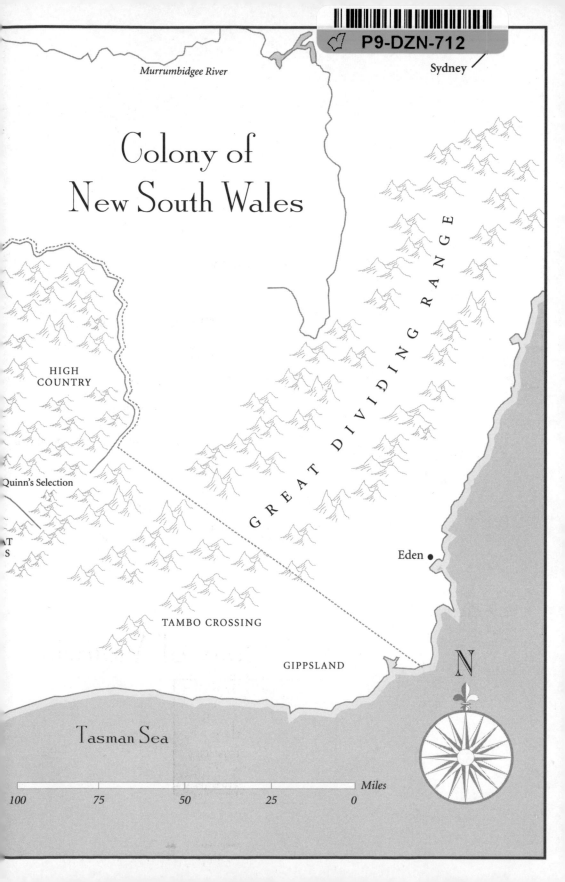

Murrumbidgee River

Sydney

Colony of
New South Wales

GREAT DIVIDING RANGE

HIGH
COUNTRY

Quinn's Selection

AT
S

Eden

TAMBO CROSSING

GIPPSLAND

N

Tasman Sea

Miles

100   75   50   25   0

True History
of the
Kelly Gang

True History of

the Kelly Gang

Peter Carey

faber and faber

First published in 2000 in Australia by The University of Queensland Press, Brisbane
First published in Great Britain in 2001
by Faber and Faber Limited
3 Queen Square, London WC1N 3AU

Printed in England by Clays Ltd, St Ives plc
© Peter Carey, 2000

The right of Peter Carey to be identified as author of this work has been asserted
in accordance with Section 77 of the Copyright, Designs and Patents Act 1998

A CIP record for this book is available from the British Library

ISBN 0–571–19216–5 (hbk)
ISBN 0–571–20408–2 (pbk)

2 4 6 8 10 9 7 5 3

for Alison Summers

The past is not dead. It is not even past.

WILLIAM FAULKNER

True History
of the
Kelly Gang

BY DAWN AT LEAST HALF *the members of the Kelly gang were badly wounded and it was then the creature appeared from behind police lines. It was nothing human, that much was evident. It had no head but a very long thick neck and an immense chest and it walked with a slow ungainly gait directly into a hail of bullets. Shot after shot was fired without effect and the figure continued to advance on the police, stopping every now and then to move its headless neck slowly and mechanically around.*

I am the b————y Monitor, my boys.

The police had modern Martini-Henry rifles yet the bullets bounced off the creature's skin. It responded to this attack, sometimes with a pistol shot, but more often by hammering the butt of its revolver against its neck, the blows ringing with the clearness and distinctiveness of a blacksmith's hammer in the morning air.

You shoot children, you f————g dogs. You can't shoot me.

As the figure moved towards a dip in the ground near to some white dead timber, the police intensified their attack. Still the figure remained erect, continuing the queer hammering on its neck. Now it paused and as its mechanical turret rotated to the left the creature's attention was taken by a small round figure in a tweed hat standing quietly beside a tree. The creature raised its pistol and shot, and the man in the tweed hat coolly kneeled before it. He then raised his shotgun and fired two shots in quick succession.

My legs, you mongrel.

The figure reeled and staggered like a drunken man and in a few moments fell near the dead timber. Moments later a crude steel helmet like a bucket was ripped from the shoulders of a fallen man. It was Ned Kelly, a wild beast brought to bay. He was shivering and ghastly white, his face and hands were smeared with blood, his chest and loins were clad in solid steel-plate armour one quarter of an inch thick.

Meanwhile the man responsible for this event had drawn his curtains and was affecting to have no interest in either the gunshots or the cries of the wounded.

At dark a party of police escorted him and his wife directly from his cottage to the Special Train and so he neither witnessed nor took part in the wholesale souveniring of armour and guns and hair and cartridges that occurred at Glenrowan on June 28th 1880. And yet this man also had a keepsake of the Kelly Outrage, and on the evening of the 28th, thirteen parcels of stained and dog-eared papers, every one of them in Ned Kelly's distinctive hand, were transported to Melbourne inside a metal trunk.

Undated, unsigned, handwritten account in the collection of the Melbourne Public Library. (V.L. 10453)

His Life until the Age of 12

National Bank letterhead. Almost certainly taken from the Euroa Branch of the National Bank in December 1878. There are 45 sheets of medium stock (8" × 10" approx.) with stabholes near the top where at one time they were crudely bound. Heavily soiled.

Contains accounts of his early relations with police including an accusation of transvestism. Some recollections of the Quinn family and the move to the township of Avenel. A claim that his father was wrongly arrested for the theft of Murray's heifer. A story explaining the origins of the sash presently held by the Benalla Historical Society. Death of John Kelly.

I lost my own father at 12 yr. of age and know what it is to be raised on lies and silences my dear daughter you are presently too young to understand a word I write but this history is for you and will contain no single lie may I burn in Hell if I speak false.

God willing I shall live to see you read these words to witness your astonishment and see your dark eyes widen and your jaw drop when you finally comprehend the injustice we poor Irish suffered in this present age. How queer and foreign it must seem to you and all the coarse words and cruelty which I now relate are far away in ancient time.

Your grandfather were a quiet and secret man he had been ripped from his home in Tipperary and transported to the prisons of Van Diemen's Land I do not know what was done to him he never spoke of it. When they had finished with their tortures they set him free and he crossed the sea to the colony of Victoria. He were by this time 30 yr. of age red headed and freckled with his eyes always slitted against the sun. My da had sworn an oath to evermore avoid the attentions of the law so when he saw the streets of Melbourne was crawling with policemen worse than flies he walked 28 mi. to the township of Donnybrook and then or soon thereafter he seen my mother. Ellen Quinn were 18 yr. old she were dark haired and slender the prettiest figure on a horse he ever saw but your grandma was like a snare laid out by God for Red Kelly. She were a Quinn and the police would never leave the Quinns alone.

My 1st memory is of Mother breaking eggs into a bowl and crying that Jimmy Quinn my 15 yr. old uncle were arrested by the traps. I don't know where my daddy were that day nor my older sister Annie. I were 3 yr. old. While my mother cried I scraped the sweet yellow batter onto a spoon and ate it the roof were leaking above the camp oven each drop hissing as it hit.

My mother tipped the cake onto the muslin cloth and knotted it.

Your Aunt Maggie were a baby so my mother wrapped her also then she carried both cake and baby out into the rain. I had no choice but follow up the hill how could I forget them puddles the colour of mustard the rain like needles in my eyes.

We arrived at the Beveridge Police Camp drenched to the bone and doubtless stank of poverty a strong odour about us like wet dogs and for this or other reasons we was excluded from the Sergeant's room. I remember sitting with my chilblained hands wedged beneath the door I could feel the lovely warmth of the fire on my fingertips. Yet when we was finally permitted entry all my attention were taken not by the blazing fire but by a huge red jowled creature the Englishman who sat behind the desk. I knew not his name only that he were the most powerful man I ever saw and he might destroy my mother if he so desired.

Approach says he as if he was an altar.

My mother approached and I hurried beside her. She told the Englishman she had baked a cake for his prisoner Quinn and would be most obliged to deliver it because her husband were absent and she had butter to churn and pigs to feed.

No cake shall go to the prisoner said the trap I could smell his foreign spicy smell he had a handlebar moustache and his scalp were shining through his hair.

Said he No cake shall go to the prisoner without me inspecting it 1st and he waved his big soft white hand thus indicating my mother should place her basket on his desk. He untied the muslin his fingernails so clean they looked like they was washed in lye and to this day I can see them livid instruments as they broke my mother's cake apart.

Tis not poverty I hate the most
nor the eternal grovelling
but the insults which grow on it
which not even leeches can cure

I will lay a quid that you have already been told the story of how your grandma won her case in court against Bill Frost and then led wild gallops up and down the main street of Benalla. You will know she were never a coward but on this occasion she understood she must hold her tongue and so she wrapped the warm crumbs in the cloth and walked out into the rain. I cried out to her but she did not hear so I followed her skirts across the muddy yard. At 1st I thought it an outhouse on whose door I found her hammering it come as a shock to realise my young uncle were locked inside. For the great offence of duffing a bullock with cancer of the eye he were interred in this earth floored slab hut which could not have measured more than 6 ft. × 6 ft. and here my mother were forced to kneel in the mud and push the broken cake under the door the gap v. narrow perhaps 2 in. not sufficient for the purpose.

She cried God help us Jimmy what did we ever do to them that they should torture us like this?

My mother never wept but weep she did and I rushed and clung to her and kissed her but still she could not feel that I were there. Tears poured down her handsome face as she forced the muddy mess of cake and muslin underneath the door.

She cried I would kill the b–––––ds if I were a man God help me. She used many rough expressions I will not write them here. It were eff this and ess that and she would blow their adjectival brains out.

These was frightening sentiments for a boy to hear his mamma speak but I did not know how set she were until 2 nights later when my father returned home and she said the exact same things again to him.

You don't know what you're talking about said he.

You are a coward she cried. I blocked my ears and buried my face into my floursack pillow but she would not give up and neither would my father turn against the law. I wish I had known my parents when they truly loved each other.

You will see in time your grandfather were a man of secrets and what he said and done was different things though for now it is enough to know my mother had one idea about my father and the police the opposite. She thought him Michael Meek. They knew him as a graduate of Van Diemen's Land and a criminal by birth and trade and marriage they was constantly examining the brands on our stock or sifting through our flour for signs of larceny but they never found nothing except mouse manure they must have had a mighty craving for the taste.

Nor was your grandmother as unfriendly towards the police as you would expect if solely instructed by her testimony she might of wished to murder them but would not mind a little drink and joke before she done the deed. There was one Sergeant his name O'Neil my mother seemed to like him better than the rest. I am talking now of a later time I must have been 9 yr. of age for our sister Kate had just been born. Our father were away contracting and our small hut were more crowded than ever now there was 6 children all sleeping between the maze of patchwork curtains Mother hung to make up for the lack of walls. It were like living in a cupboard full of dresses.

Into this shadowy world Sgt O'Neil did come with queer white hair which he were always combing like a girl before a dance he were v. friendly to us children and on the night in question he brung me the gift of a pencil. At school we used the slates but I never touched a pencil and was most excited to smell the sweet pine and graphite as the Sergeant sharpened his gift he were very fatherly towards me and set me at one end of the table with a sheet of paper. My sister Annie were 1 yr. older she got nothing from O'Neil but thats another story.

I set to work to cover my paper with the letters of the alphabet. My mother sat at the other end of the table with the Sgt and when he produced his silver flask I paid no more attention than I did to Annie & Jem & Maggie & Dan. After I made each letter as a capital I set to do the smaller ones such were my concentration that when my mother spoke her voice seemed very far away.

Get out of my house.

I looked up to discover Sergeant O'Neil with his hand to his cheek I suppose she must of slapped him for his countenance were turned v. red.

Get out my mother shrieked she had the Irish temper we was accustomed to it.

Ellen you calm yourself you know I never meant nothing in the least improper.

Eff off my mother cried.

The policeman's voice took a sterner character. Ellen said he you must not use such language to a police officer.

That were a red rag to my mother she uncoiled herself from her seat. You effing mongrel she cried her voice louder again. You wouldnt say that if my husband were not gone contracting.

I will issue one more warning Mrs Kelly.

At this my mother snatched up the Sergeant's teacup and threw the contents onto the earthen floor. Arrest me she cried arrest me you coward.

Baby Kate woke crying then. Jem were 4 yr. old sitting on the floor playing knuckles but when the brandy splashed beside him he let the bones lie quiet. Of a different disposition I begun to move towards my mother.

Did you hear your mother call me a coward old chap?

I would not betray her I walked round the table and stood next to her. Said he You was busy writing Ned?

I took my mother's hand and she put her arm around my shoulder.

You are a scholar aint it he asked me.

I said I were.

Then you must know about the history of cowards. I were confused I shook my head.

Next O'Neil was bouncing to his feet and showing the full hard stretch of his policeman's boots said he Let me educate you young man. No said my mother her manner now completely changed. Please no.

A moment earlier O'Neil had a stiff and worried air but now there was a dainty sort of prance about him. O yes said he all children should know their history indeed it is quite essential.

My mother wrenched her hand from mine and reached out but the Ulsterman ducked behind the 1st set of curtains and emerged to prowl in and out and around our family he even patted little Dan upon his silky head. My mother were afraid her face was pale and frozen. Please Kevin.

But O'Neil was telling us his story we had to quiet to listen to him he had the gift. It were a story of a man from Tipperary named only A Certain Man or This Person Who I Will Not Name. He said A Certain Man had a grudge against a farmer for lawfully evicting his tenant and This Person etc. conspired with his mates to kill the farmer.

I'm sorry said my mother I already apologised.

Sgt O'Neil made a mocking bow continuing his story without relent telling how This Certain Man did 1st write a threatening letter to the landlord. When the landlord ignored the letter and evicted the tenant This Certain Man called a SELECT MEETING of his allies to a chapel in the dead of night where they drank whisky from the Holy Goblet and swore upon the Holy Book then he said to them Brothers for we are all brothers sworn upon all thats blessed and Holy. Brothers are you ready in the name of God to fulfil your oaths? They said they was they swore it and when they done their blasphemy they descended upon the farmer's house with pikes and faggots burning.

Sergeant O'Neil seemed much affected by his own story his voice grew loud he said the farmer's children screamed for mercy at the windows but the men set their home alight and those who escaped they piked to death there was mothers and babes in arms the Sgt would not spare us either he painted the outrage in every detail we children were all silent open mouthed not only at the horror of the crime but also the arrest of the Guilty Parties and the treachery of This Certain Man who betrayed all he had drawn into his conspiracy. The accomplices was hanged by the neck until dead and the Ulsterman let us imagine how this might be he did not conceal the particulars.

What happened then he asked we could not answer nor speak nor did we wish to hear.

This Certain Man kept his life he were transported to Van Diemen's Land. And with that Sergeant O'Neil strode out our door into the night.

Mother said nothing further she did not move not even when we heard the policeman's mare cantering along the dark road up the hill to Beveridge I asked her what was meant by This Certain Man and she give me such a clip across the ears I never asked again. In time I understood it were my own father that was referred to.

The memory of the policeman's words lay inside me like the egg of a liver fluke and while I went about my growing up this slander wormed deeper and deeper into my heart and there grew fat.

Sergeant O'Neil had filled my boy's imagination with thoughts that would breed like maggots on a summer day you would think his victory complete but he begun to increase his harassment of my father rousing him from bed when he were drunk or fast asleep he also needled and teased me whenever he seen me in the street.

He would mock the way I dressed my lack of shoes and coats. I were all knees and elbows and shy of any comment I couldnt walk past the Police Camp with my friends without him calling out some insult. I pretended to be amused for I would not give him the satisfaction of seeing blood.

It were during Sgt O'Neil's hateful reign we heard Mr Russell of Foster Downs Station was to sell off a great mob of bullocks and cows in calf also a famous bull he was said to have brought from England for 500 quid. It were a much bigger event than we was accustomed to in Beveridge just a straggly village on a difficult hill reviled by all the bullockies between Melbourne and the Murray River. 1/2 way up the hill were a pub and blacksmith and portable lockup then farther west a Catholic school. That hill were too much effort even for the bitter winds which turned around and come howling back towards our hut below. West of the road the water were salt. Our side had good water but it were still known as Pleurisy Plains. No one ever come to Beveridge for their health.

The sale changed all that and suddenly there was squatters and stock agents come to visit even a veterinarian from Melbourne all these strangers set up camp beside the swamp between our place and the hill. There was gaffing & flash talk & grog drinking & galloping up & down the Melbourne road it were good as a circus to us boys to hang about the boggy crossing and see the fancy riding. Day by day Jem and me run the long way to school to see what new tents were set up at the swamp. We was on tenterhooks awaiting the beasts but it were not until dusk on the day before the Auction we heard that particular mournful bellowing on the wind it were a mob of cattle being driven over a track they did not know.

I told Jem I was going to meet them.

Me too.

We wasnt finished tending to the pigs and chooks we did not care our feet was bare the ground were hard and rocky though we was used to it and run right through the Indian corn. Said Jem We'll be whipped.

I don't care.

I don't care neither.

We had just gained the swamp bulrushes when the beasts come into view flooding down the smooth green hill of Beveridge like a breaking wave it were the gleaming wealth of all the nations pouring down towards us and the water. Cor look at them blacks said Jem.

Of the 7 stockmen 5 was blackfellows they rode ahead of the coming storm with flash red scarves round their necks and elastic sided boots upon their feet. Said Jem Look at them boots.

Damn them I said. Yes damn them said Jem we was raised to think the blacks the lowest of the low but they had boots not us and we damned and double damned them as we run. Soon we gained the rutted ruined Melbourne road where we passed Patchy Moran he were 16 yr. old rawboned and lanky but we was faster any day.

Wait you little b————rs.

But we wouldnt wait for Patchy or no one else splashing through

Boggy Crossing to the splintery top rail of the yard. Moran made no comment on our victory but lit himself a cigarette and the leftover beard of tobacco fell in glowing cinders to the earth. Look at them effing niggers.

We already seen them.

I heard the rattle of a bridle and turned to see my father's tormentor had ridden up behind us Sgt O'Neil had his stirrup leathers so long the iron could be held only with the tip of the toes it were the English fashion. His horse was 17 hands he thought himself high and mighty but if you had give any of us boys a pony we would of left him in the dust.

Patchy Moran said Look at them niggers Sergeant did you see their adjectival boots how much would that cost do you reckon Sir boots like that?

O'Neil did not answer but leaned forward in his saddle looking down at me beneath the visor of his shako his eyes as watery as a jar of gin. Ah young Kelly he said.

Hello Sergeant said I so accustomed to his teasing that I thought Moran's remark about the blackfellows' boots would lead to comments about my own bare feet. Said I thats a mighty bull they got by Jove we heard he was worth 500 quid.

Said O'Neil I just saw your father. I knew from his lazy drawl he had something worse than shoes to hurt me with. He said I just seen Red Kelly galloping across Horan's paddocks dressed like a woman can you picture that now?

I couldnt see the policeman's expression in the failing light but he spoke so very conversationally. Patchy Moran laughed but stopped midbreath I looked towards poor little Jem he sat on the rail staring grimly at the ground his brow furrowed in a torture of confusion and my friends gone v. quiet around me.

Pull the other one Sergeant.

Your father was seen by Mr McClusky and Mr Willett and myself he was wearing a dress with roses on its hem can you ever imagine such a thing?

Not me but you can Sergeant its the very thing you just done.

You watch your lip young fellow do you hear? When your father saw us he galloped away down the north face of Big Hill. He can ride I grant him that but do you know why he would go that way?

No.

Oh said the Sergeant he was off to be serviced by his husband I suppose.

I leapt upon his high armoured boot I tried to twist him off his saddle but he only laughed and swung his horse around so I was almost crushed against the fence.

Thus were the great day destroyed. I told Patchy Moran I did not come to see a nigger show Jem said he did not want to see one neither. We walked home together through the dark. We did not say much but was very melancholic. She'll strop us won't she Ned?

No she won't.

But of course our mother had the razor strop laid out ready on the table she hit my hand 3 times and Jem once. We never told her what O'Neil had said.

I doubt I had the courage to repeat O'Neil's slander to my father but I were anyway denied the opportunity for he had departed once again to shear the fat merino sheep for Mr Henry Buckley of Gnawarra Station. As it were spring he should of been engaged on his own land but couldnt afford it and on the way to Gnawarra he nearly died.

A vicious Sydney black by the name of Warragul had gotten a mob together made of the remnants of different tribes my father had done nothing against Warragul but when he arrived at the Murray River near Barnawatha a shower of spears sailed out of the bush and struck his donkey dead beneath him. My father dragged his carbine from its saddle holster and by careful use of his remaining powder were able to keep Warragul's mob at bay until dark. Then he retreated into an abandoned hut he barricaded the door and windows and so imagined himself safe but in the early hours of the morning he woke.

The roof were on fire and the hut surrounded by shouting savages.

He used the last of his powder to shoot into the faces of blackfellows who was peering through the gaps between the logs but when the powder were gone he had nothing more to look forward to than death and begun to say his prayers while the blacks thrust their spears through the gaps. The roof were already burning falling in lumps when Father paused from praying long enough to realise the spears was only entering from the front. He removed the barricade from the rear window and with the blacks keeping watch on one side of his funeral pyre he made his way out the downwind side thereafter hiding in a hollow log for 2 days before he were discovered by Mr Henry Buckley himself and thus finally delivered to Gnawarra.

At the time my father had been battling for his very life Sergeant O'Neil's slander spread about the Catholic school the source of this contagion being Patchy Moran.

I cautioned him. You say that one more time I'll whip you.

Patchy Moran were a good foot taller his voice broken like a man. Said he You are an adjectival tinker you can't give me orders.

And with that he punched me in the temple so I fell.

Regaining my feet I faced him again he hit me hard enough to push the pudding out of me. I were bent over wheezing to get my wind back he called out I were a sissy and the son of a sissy. He seemed a giant all hair and pimples I thought he soon would kill me but I closed with him on the barren ground beneath the peppercorn tree and then by skill or luck I got round his dirty neck and pulled him to the ground. How he hollered to be brung down how he kicked & bucked & twisted rolling me amongst the tree roots and the gravel. I felt a red hot sting on my back and rolled him over. There were a bull ant also fastened to his pimply neck.

I wouldnt let him go not even when I felt a 2nd bite myself I hope you may live your life without a bull ant bite for it is worse than any wasp or bee. Patchy howled in my arms cursing and pleading but I held his shoulders to the earth as he thrashed and drove his tormentors into greater fury still.

Take it back.

He bawled the snot run down his lip.

Take it back.

He said he would not take it back but in the end he couldnt tolerate the pain he cried Damn you damn your eyes I take it back. Brother Hearn heard his blasphemies so did 16 other scholars standing by the schoolhouse door observing us. No one said nothing they stood v. quiet and watched Patchy Moran rip off his shirt and britches the girls all saw his private skin.

I were soon ill from my great number of bites but no one said no more about my father from that time.

I thought my problems over and I once again imagined there were never a better place on earth than where I lived at Pleurisy Plains. I could not conceive a better soil or prettier view or trees that did not grow crooked in the winds. I were often in the swamp it were a world entire with eels and bird eggs and tiger snakes we tried to race them along the Melbourne road. Then one mild and dewy morning I went out to find some worms and discovered my younger sister Maggie seated on a cairn of them brown pitted rocks the ancient volcanoes had throwed around the plains of Beveridge. Our father often had us busy tidying the earth in this manner. This particular pile of rocks was in a thistlepatch near our back door and Maggie were using it as a throne while she squeezed milk from the thistles onto her warts. She asked would I please squeeze some on a difficult place behind her elbow.

I were very fond of Maggie she were always my favourite sister as true and steady as a red gum plank. As I set down my worms and dripped the white sap over her warts she warned she had found something I would not like.

What?

You'll have to move them rocks.

I already moved them once.

You better do it again.

There were no more than 8 rocks Maggie helped me roll them to one side and I discovered the freshly broken earth beneath.

Its something dead.

It aint nothing dead.

From down amongst the thistles she produced an old gooseneck shovel with a broken handle.

I took it from her hand and dug until I uncovered something hard and black it were 3 ft. × 2 ft. It were also deep so I levered and jemmied and soon dragged a battered tin trunk out to the light of day. It were inside that trunk I found the thing I wish I never saw.

It were a woman's dress v. soiled along the hem the roses was exactly as Sgt O'Neil had said. There was also masks made of red paint and feather I hardly seen them it were the dress that made my stomach knot a mighty anger come upon me.

I heard our sister Annie calling and I whispered I would kill Maggie if ever she mentioned what we seen. Her dark little eyes welled up with tears.

Annie were demanding I bring firewood she come down the path in a mighty fret with her thin shoulders hunched forward and her hands upon her hips. If youse don't come now you'll get no adjectival dinner.

I split the wood all right but then carried it back to the thistlepatch and made a fireplace from the rocks.

What are you doing? You can't do that you know it aint permitted.

Just the same she give me the matches I asked for. She were a worry-wart she retreated back to the doorway while I burned the horrid contents of the trunk. By the time she come back I were poking the last bits of dress into the flames.

She asked me what I were destroying but all us children had suffered from O'Neil's story and she knew the answer to her question well enough.

Said Annie You better bury that trunk. Her face were pinched her mouth set with worry she were only 11 yr. old but she must of already saw her future it were written on her face for all to see.

A 2nd time she ordered me to hide the trunk so I dragged it down the back and shoved it under the lower rail of the horse yard.

You can't do that.

I pulled the trunk through all the manure into the middle of the yard.

You'll get the strop said she.

I never doubted it would be worse than that and when our father come ambling up the track 3 days later I awaited my thrashing it were as sure as eggs turn into chickens.

At 1st he didnt see the trunk he were surveying his crop of Indian corn doubtless pleased he had not been speared or burned and had money in his pocket. But finally he saw his broken secret lying in the air and while the little children all run around crying for him to dismount he stared silently down at the blackened trunk his eyes small inside their puffy lids.

Where's your ma?

Baby Kate took ill she's gone to Wallan to the Doctor.

My father dismounted and then carried his saddle and bags into the hut I were waiting by the door to get my punishment but he never even looked at me. After a little while he gone up the pub.

I lost my own father from a secret he might as well been snatched by a roiling river fallen from a ravine I lost him from my heart so long I cannot even now properly make the place for him that he deserves. Forever after I unearthed his trunk I pictured him with his broad red beard his strong arms his freckled skin all his manly features buttoned up inside that cursed dress.

Up to that point I had been his shadow never losing a chance to be with him. In the bush he taught the knots I use to tie my blanket to my saddle Ds also the way I stand to use a carpenter's plane and the trick of catching fish with a bush fly and a strip of greenhide these things are like the dark marks made in the rings of great trees locked forever in my daily self.

I don't know if my mother realised what were hidden in the trunk she never said nothing and it were left to lie in the middle of the dusty yard and when it rained the horses drank from it.

A rich man driving his buggy past our home might see the tin trunk in the yard and the pumpkins growing on the skillion roof but he would never imagine all my father's issue the great number of us packed behind the curtains breathing the same air snoring farting blind and deaf to each other as a newborn litter.

I had long taught myself to be deaf to my parents' private business but after digging up that trunk I would stay awake at night listening to my mother and my father talking.

I learned not a thing about the dress I discovered it were land my parents whispered about and in particular the Duffy Land Act of 1862 it gave a man or widow the right to select a block between 50 and 640 acres for £1 per acre part payable on selection the rest over 8 yr. My mother were for it but my father were against it he said the great Charles Gavan Duffy was a well intentioned idiot leading poor men into debt and lifelong labour. He were correct as it happened but when my mother abused my da for cowardice the terrible turmoil in my heart were somehow soothed. Only a simpleton she said would try to farm 20 acres like my da were doing. I thought yes you must be a mighty fool.

This debate about the Land Act were life or death and my mother enlisted her family who was presently our neighbours but in the midst of buying land far away in the North East.

The Quinns was purchasing 1,000 acres at Glenmore on the King River they was Irish and therefore drunk with land and fancy horses all the old hardships soon to be forgotten. The Quinn women come visiting with soda bread and surveyor's maps the men was tall and reckless they cursed and sang they fought anyone they did not like and rode thoroughbreds they could not afford to buy. My uncle Jimmy Quinn were a man by now there were a dreadful wildness in his eyes like a horse that has been tortured. The Quinns would of tossed my father down the well if they had seen the dress but they chivvied and joked and finally prevailed upon him to sell everything he owned in Beveridge he got a total of £80.

But when my da finally had the cash put in his hand the thought of giving the government so large a sum were more than he could bear and when the new owners arrived to take possession he borrowed a cart and shifted us to rented land on the outskirts of the township of Avenel. So while my mother's brothers and sisters went on to farm 1,000 virgin acres at Glenmore my father transported us 60 mi. to a district of English snobs and there to my mother's great outrage he slowly pissed away the 80 quid on rent and booze. I were his flesh and he must of felt me draw further away but he were proud and did not try to win me back.

The question of our lost opportunity were now always present my mother could not leave it alone my father would sit solid in his chair and quietly rub the belly of his big black cat. I am thinking now of one night in particular when he broke his silence.

Your family arent bad fellows said he at last.

If you're planning to speak ill of them you can stop right there.

Oh I aint got nothing against them personal.

Of course not they was always good to you.

I'm sure the land will do the job. Them rocks aint nothing but the land can't touch this land Ellen.

And us with no meat but the adjectival possums.

We aint got beef its true.

Not even mutton.

But do you notice we aint got no police? Now thats an interesting thing I wonder why that is do you imagine your family is as lucky up at Glenmore?

Oh no not this again.

Well you must agree the Quinns attract the traps as surely as rabbit guts will bring the flies.

My mother shrieked a plate or cup were dashed against the wall.

Well Ellen said he I know you're very low about your farm but I would rather die than go to prison.

You great galoot no one wants to put you in prison.

So you say.

No one she cried her voice rising. Are you mad?

And why was the traps always visiting us do you imagine?

You have been a free man 15 yr. they don't want you back again.

The Quinns bring attention its the truth.

O you adjectival worm.

My mother were now sobbing Maggie also I could hear her little rabbit noises on the far side of the curtain. Then my mother said my father would rather his children starve than take a risk and beside me Jem pulled his pillow tight across his ears.

The land were very good at Avenel but there were a drought and nothing flourished there but misery I were the oldest son I thought it time to earn my place.

There were no dam or spring upon our property each day I took the cows to water them at Hughes Creek. In a good year it would of made a pretty picture but in the drought that creek were no more than a chain of sandy waterholes. It were across this dry river bed that Mr Murray's heifer calf come calling out my name I were very hungry when I heard her and knew what I must do. I had never killed nothing bigger than a rooster but when I saw the long line of the heifer's crop above the blackberries I knew I could not be afraid of nothing. Her eye were a little wild but she was a poll Hereford and very sleek. I later heard that Mr Murray had made a great investment on her and poddied her with corn and hay which must be true for there were no feed in any of his paddocks and although he owned 500 acres his stock was out grazing on the roadsides finding what nourishment they could. I did not care I bailed her up and led her down the creek into a thick stand of wattles with a clearing in the centre. She did not like the rope around her neck she fought and bucked and would of done herself a damage had I not bound her hind legs and tied them to a wattle trunk. She began to bellow terribly. Soon she were trussed up like a Christmas chook but I had no pity nor did I have a knife. I ran up through the scrub to fetch one from the hut. Inside my mother were occupied trying to plug the spaces between the slabs with clay and straw so I took the carving knife from beneath her very nose she never even noticed.

Said she Theres one of Murray's beasts caught down the creek.

You must be mistaken.

I can hear it bellowing from here.

I said I would attend to it and let her know.

Within the year I would of learned to kill a beast very smart and clean and have its hide off and drying in the sun before you could say Jack Robertson but on this 1st occasion I failed to find the artery. I'm sure you know I have spilled human blood when there were no other choice at that time I were no more guilty than a soldier in a war. But if there was a law against the murder of a beast I would plead guilty and you would be correct to put the black cap on your head for I killed my little heifer badly and am sorry for it still. By the time she fell her neck was a sea of laceration I will never forget the terror in her eyes.

And this is how my ma found me with the poor dead creature at my feet and my hair and shirt soaked with blood and gore.

We have beef I said we'll feast on her.

But my words was bolder than my upset heart and I were very pleased she relieved me of the bloody knife I didnt know what next to do having not the faintest idea of how to butcher the heifer and yet not wanting the privilege to go elsewhere. My mother took my gory hand and led me across the dusty paddock to the hut and after tying up the dogs she ministered to me with soap and water all the time berating me and saying I were a very bad boy and she was angry with me etc. etc. but this were for the benefit of the other children who was listening at the door and watching through the chinks between the logs. My ma cleaned me so very gentle with the washer I knew she must be pleased.

Of course Annie could be relied upon to tell my father what I had done before he even got the saddle off his horse. He had been delivering butter to people with English names a job that always put him out of temper so when Annie showed him the dead beast he come inside to give me a hiding with his belt a mark on my leg I carry to this day. When it were dark he took a lantern down by the creek and skinned and butchered my beast and carried the 4 quarters back across the paddock one at a time and then burned the head and hung the hide and cut out the MM brand so none could accuse us of stealing Murray's heifer. He salted down what meat would fit into a barrel and the rest he ordered my mother to cook at once.

All through this Annie would not speak to me even Maggie kept her distance but very late that night we had a mighty feast of beef and I noticed it were not just my excited brothers who ate their fill.

2 days later I were sent home from school at lunch time to collect my homework which I had forgot again I found a strange bay mare tethered beneath our peppercorn tree it had VR embroidered on the saddlecloth in silver Victoria Regina. I knew it were the police. I entered the hut and my father were sitting in his usual chair watching a lanky fair haired Constable spreading out the heifer's hide across our table.

Come on John said Constable Doxcy putting his hand right through the hole where the brand had been. John we know whats missing here.

As you can see said my father I slaughtered a cow and made a greenhide whip.

Ah you made a whip.

Correct my father said but did not protest or struggle against the accusation.

So be a good fellow will you John and bring me the whip.

My father did not say nothing he did not move he stared at the Constable with puffy eyes.

Perhaps you never made a whip at all.

O I must of lost it.

Must of lost it.

I'll bring it up to you soon as I find it.

More likely it were the brand John. Did you cut out Mr Murray's brand?

No I made a whip.

Did you ever hear of Act 7 and Act 8 George IV No 29?

I don't know.

It is a law John it says that if you duff another fellow's heifer then you're going to go to adjectival gaol and you can bring me any adjectival whip you like but unless it can fill this hole exactly John you're going in the adjectival lockup. We don't like Irish thieves in Avenel.

I can't bear prison my father spoke as plainly as a man who don't like Brussels sprouts.

Well thats a shame said Doxcy as he moved towards him.

I done it I said I thrust myself forward.

I put my hand on Doxcy's hard black shoulder belt and he rested his hand upon my arm.

You're a good boy Jim said he.

I'm Ned I done it.

The policeman asked my father Is this so?

But my father would say nothing he were like some creature drugged by spiders.

I turned back to Doxcy demanding he arrest me and he laughed ruffling my hair and smiling a foolish sentimental smile.

Pack up your things John he said to my father you can bring a blanket and a pannikin and spoon.

I done it I said the brand were MM I done it with the carving knife.

Shutup my father says his eyes now alive and angry. Shut your gob go back to school.

Thus were Father taken from me handcuffed to the stirrup iron of Doxcy's mare.

In the days before our father were imprisoned we Kelly children would walk to school along the creek but now we took a new path through the police paddock where the lockup stood. Apart from this stockade the paddock had no feature other than a dreary mound of clay which marked the grave of Doxcy's mare. Even this miserable sight my father were denied for there was not one window in them heavy walls. At 1st we would shout out to him but never got any answer and finally we all give up excepting Jem who run his hands along the frost cold walls patting the prison like a dog.

I dreamed about my father every night he come to sit on the end of my bed and stare at me his puffy eyes silent his face lacerated by a thousand knife cuts.

I were so v. guilty I could never of admitted that life without my father had become in many ways more pleasant. Only when his big old buck cat went missing did I frankly tell my ma I were pleased to see it gone.

Do not misunderstand me our lives was far harder for his absence. The landlord provided no decent fences so the mother and her children was obliged to build a dogleg fence 2 mi. long to save our cows from impounding. In any case our stock would still escape the fines was 5/– for a cow 3/– for a pig. This we could ill afford. Our mother were expecting another baby she were always weary yet more tender than before. At night she would gather us about her and tell us stories and poems she never done that when my da were away shearing or contracting but now we discovered this treasure she had committed to her memory. She knew the stories of Conchobor and Dedriu and Mebd the tale of Cuchulainn I still see him stepping into his war chariot it bristles with points of iron and narrow blades with hooks and hard prongs and straps and loops and cords.

The southerly wind blew right through the hut and it were so bitter it made your head ache though it aint the cold I remember but the light of the tallow candle it were golden on my mother's cheeks it shone in her great dark eyes bright and fierce as a native cat to defend her fatherless brood. In the stories she told us of the old country there was many such women they was queens they was hot blooded not careful they would fight a fight and take a king into their marriage bed. They would have been called Irish rubbish in Avenel.

Our mother grew bigger. We boys laboured beside her in the garden it were a good loam soil and we was set to improve it further. That 1st winter we had parsnips and potatoes only. We had to sell the wagon and 2 horses but kept our small herd of dairy cows. We produced 2 lb. of butter per day but rarely had anything except lard for our own bread. Jem and I tramped into town and back delivering the butter on foot walking right past our father's lockup not calling out to him no more. Each day I waited for the night to fall who can imagine from where happiness will come?

On the 5th of August 1865 I come home in the loud dripping dark. It had been raining already for a week the creek were a river roaring so I did not hear Mother's cries until I were at the door. I picked up a shovel and inside I discovered her lying on the earthen floor. When she saw me she sat up and explained she was beginning to have her baby. The handy woman were already gone to Hobbs' Creek for another birth so my mother had sent Maggie to borrow the Murrays' horse and ride to fetch old Dr May. That were 2 hr. previous and now the pain was very bad and my mother feared Maggie had been thrown off the horse or drowned crossing the creek.

Annie were the oldest but of a nervous disposition she had chosen this occasion to have the gastric fits. So while my mother laboured Annie vomited into a bowl beside her. I helped Mother onto her bed which were made from 2 thick saplings set into the wall and a piece of jute bag suspended between the shafts. Thinking her darling Maggie dead she cried continually. Jem were just 7 yr. and Dan were only 4 yr. they was both disturbed to see their mother in such distress.

In the hours that followed she could find no comfort or relent finally directing me to place a quilt over the table which she climbed upon at the same time instructing us all to go back behind our curtains. Dan begun bawling in earnest the table were revealed to be too short and my mother could not lie down as she had planned. Little Jem tried to help and were shouted at for his trouble. Mother instructed me to come and hold her hand then squatted on the table it had one loose leg my father had neglected to repair. The light were very poor just the one tallow light burning but I could see my mother's pain and were vexed I could do nothing to please her. She asked for water but would not let me go to fetch it. She cursed me for a fool and my father for abandoning her. All the while we expected the doctor but there were no sound from outside not even a mopoke nothing save a steady rain on the bark roof and the thumping of flotsam in the flooding waters of Hughes Creek.

All through the endless night I stood at her side and with every hour her cries and curses got wilder in the end Dan and Jem just fell asleep.

Around 4 o'clock Mother got herself once more onto the table and I thought the baby were finally coming but she swore at me and would not let me look. I heard a high thin wail like a lamb and knew my sister were arrived but she told me keep my back turned and find her best scissors in her tin box and then to put them in the flame of the fire. I done as ordered.

I heard her shifting on her table she gave a little cry of pain then she spoke more tenderly. All right come on here and see the little girl.

My mother sat on the table holding your Aunty Grace to me. She were a little foal a calf her eyes were wide her newborn skin glistening white and bloody nothing bad had ever touched her.

Cut says Mother cut.

Where I asked.

Cut she said and I saw the pearly cord going from her stomach down to the dark I shut my eyes and cut and it were just as the old scissors crunched into the flesh that Maggie led Dr May into our hut and there he saw a 11 yr. old Irish boy assisting at his sister's birth. He seen the earthen floor the soot black scissors the frightened children peering out from behind the curtained beds and all this he would feel free to gossip about so every child at Avenel School would soon get the false idea I seen my mother's naked bottom.

After the old drunk checked my sister with his instrument he handed her to me and attended to my mother. Don't drop her lad said he it were not likely I held our precious baby in my arms her eyes so clear and untroubled. She looked me frankly in the face and I loved her as if she were my very own.

By the time he finished doctoring to my mother it were dawn a luminous grey light filled the little hut and all the world seemed bright and new. I were happy then.

Said she Go tell him now.

I'll go later.

Go now.

But I did not wish to leave my new sister with her soft downy black hair and her white white skin how it glowed like a sepulchre inside that earth floored hut. Go tell your da he has a little girl.

So as the Doctor ambled his groggy way along the track I cut across through the wet winter grass. There were a low mist lying across the police paddock lapping the edges of my father's solitary gaol. I approached the logs they was always damp and stained green with moss and mildew they give off a bad smell like dog shit in the rain.

You got a girl I yelled.

The magpies was carolling the lories screeching and fighting in the gums but from the walls of the lockup come no sound at all.

Her name is Grace.

No answer the prison were silent as the grave but then I seen a movement from the corner of my eye it were my father's big buck cat standing on the mound where the mare were buried. The cat looked at me directly with its yellow eyes and then he arched his back and swished his tail once more as if I was no more than a robin or a finch. I threw a stone at him and went home to see my sister.

Soon all the scholars at Avenel School heard of my role at the birth. They never dared venture nothing to me but Eliza Mutton said something to Annie it made her most distressed. Them scholars was all proddies they knew nothing about us save Ned Kelly couldnt spell he had no boots Maggie Kelly had warts Annie Kelly's dress were darned and fretted over like an old man's sock. They knew our pater were in the logs and when we come to school each day they learned from Mr Irving that all micks was a notch beneath the cattle.

Irving were a little cock with a big head and narrow shoulders his eyes alight with finer feelings he did not wish to share with me. It took the whole year until September before he would appoint me ink monitor by then he had no other choice for everybody with an English name had taken a turn. I cannot now remember why I desired such a prize only that I wanted it a great deal. When my time came at last I vowed to be the best monitor that were ever born. Each morning I were 1st to school lining up the chipped white china inkwells upon the tank stand then I washed and returned them to their hole in every desk.

Monday mornings I were permitted to also make the ink climbing up on Mr Irving's chair and taking down the McCracken's powder from the upper shelf it had a very pungent smell like violets and gall. I measured 4 tblspn. with every pt. of tank water it were not a demanding task but required I get to school by 8 o'clock.

It were on account of this I saw Dick Shelton drowning.

In my desire to avoid the lockup I had walked to school along Hughes Creek which were very swollen from the spring rains all sorts of rubbish piled up in the current 1/2 burnt tree trunks broken branches fenceposts a drowned calf with the water rushing across its empty eye. From the opposite bank I seen a boy edging out into the water. At the time I thought he had a fishing rod but later I learned he were using a pole to pick up the new straw hat that were swept into the flood and caught up in a jam. He stepped into the creek the black water drove up his legs he were no more than 8 yr. old.

I hollered Go back but he never heard above the thunder of the creek. There were a bed of twigs like a lyre bird mound he tried to jump onto. Then he were gone.

Never one to wait I were swimming in the flooded creek before I knew it the water so fast and cold it would take your breath like a pooka steals your very soul. It were v. rough sweeping me violently down into a wide pool you would not credit the power of it. I glimpsed the boy's white face young Dick Shelton knew himself a goner and no more for this world. I got his arm but we was washed on down together more under than above the flood.

50 yd. down the creek has a dogleg where the proddies swim in summer. The pair of us was driven close to the bank against an old river red gum submerged in flood. It were slippery as a pig but I were able to gain sufficient purchase to drag his drenched and soapy body back from that other world where he had imagined himself consigned.

Though the little chap were 1/2 drowned I got him upon my back he were crying and vomiting and agitating a great deal. He wore boots but my own feet was bare as usual I set off straight through the bush towards the Royal Mail Hotel where I knew his father were the licensee. It were a sharp and rocky bit of ground I chose.

The yardman at the Mail were a failed selector named Shaky White he were burying night soil in the scrub when he seen us coming and he started hollering Missus Missus Jesus Christ.

An upstairs window in the pub flew open a woman screamed a moment later Mrs Shelton were running down the yard towards her son but even in her great emotion she never ignored the Catholic boy and I were taken into her hotel and given a hot bath in a large white tub. I had never seen a bathtub until that day it were a blessed miracle to lay in that long smooth porcelain with all the steaming water brought to me by Shaky in 10 buckets I never saw so much water used to wash.

Then Mrs Shelton brought her older son's clothes to wear while mine was laundered they was soft and had a very pleasant smell. I would of given anything to keep them but Mrs Shelton didnt think of making that offer instead she put her plump arm around my shoulder and led me downstairs saying I were an angel sent by God.

In the dining room I discovered a merry fire and a man in a 3 pce. suit doing great damage to a plate of eggs and bacon but apart from him the room were empty. Mrs Shelton sat me at a table near the fire it were set with shining silver knives & forks & cruets & salt & pepper & a sugar bowl with a curved spoon. I knew my mother would have liked it very much.

Mrs Shelton asked would I prefer cocoa I said yes she asked would I like a breakfast and presented me with a menu. I never seen such a thing before but soon I got the gist of it and used it well. I had begun the day with bread and dripping now I was ordering lamb chops and bacon and kidney it were very tasty. There were carpet on the floor I can see the pattern of the red roses to this day. Mrs Shelton wore a bright yellow dress and a gold bangle on her wrist she wept and smiled and stared at me all the time I ate she said I were the best and bravest boy in the whole world.

Mr Shelton had been in Seymour overnight but soon arrived in his wagon and rushed into the dining room in his muddy gumboots and oilskin coat. He tried to give me 1/2 a crown but I wouldnt hear of such a thing.

Mr Shelton were tall and broad with long side whiskers and his thin straight mouth would of looked mean were his eyes not so bright and brimming.

Is there nothing you wish for boy?

Nothing.

It were not true I would have liked a dress for my mother but I didnt know how much one would cost.

Very well said he then let me shake your hand.

I took his hand but confess that I were not nearly so noble as my speech suggested. I walked to school in my nice borrowed clothes and a pair of shining pinching boots I were so disappointed I were sick at heart.

The following morning a buckboard drew up at the schoolhouse Mr Irving were always fearful of inspectors he got suddenly nervous as a quail.

Wipe clean your slates he commanded while trying to make some order of his pigpen desk. He were fast with multiplication but very queer and jerky in this crisis and now it didnt help him that his head were big for he couldnt reckon where to hide his fret saw.

To Caroline Doxcy he said Go to the window see if it is a gentleman with a case. Smartly smartly Caroline.

He has a parcel.

Yes but does he have a satchel?

Oh Sir it is only Dicky Shelton's father.

Mr Irving were a king amongst children and didnt like visitors to his castle so he was out the door before the publican could enter. We could hear their voices clearly.

Damn it Irving roared Mr Shelton I'll do what I adjectival like.

The door banged against the wall and Esau Shelton burst inside with the odour of stale hops and raisin wine they was his constant friends.

Ah children cried he granting us a rare sight of his teeth.

Mr Irving come following behind rubbing his big pale hands together and telling us unhappily that we must listen to Mr Shelton.

Now look here little children said Mr Shelton and he placed his brown paper parcel amongst the litter on the teacher's desk. My son Dick nearly drowned yesterday did you know that? No? My Dick would be in heaven now were it not for someone in this very room.

The scholars now began to crane their necks and look enquiringly around and Annie seemed she might die folding her hands in her lap and staring ahead with glassy gaze. Jem were 7 yr. and so copied what his older sister done but my barrel chested Maggie never feared it were she who raised her hand.

It were my big brother Ned.

The blood rushed to my face.

Correct said Mr Shelton v. solemn please come and stand up here Ned Kelly.

I knew he were going to give me the brown paper parcel I had no doubt it contained the respectable clothes I always wanted. As I rose I caught the eye of Caroline Doxcy she smiled at me the 1st time ever. I put my shoulders back and walked up to Mr Irving's platform.

Mr Shelton bade me face the class then shut my eyes there were the crinkling of the paper the smell of camphor and the smooth feel of silk against my cheek.

I thought thats women's stuff it were a dress to give my mother.

Open your eyes Ned Kelly.

I done as ordered and saw his little slit of mouth all twisted in a grin and then Eliza Mutton and George Mutton and Caroline Doxcy and the Sheltons and Mr Irving staring at me with his wild bright eyes. I looked down at my person and seen not my bare feet my darned pullover my patched pants but a 7 ft. sash. It were peacock green embroidered with gold TO EDWARD KELLY IN GRATITUDE FOR HIS COURAGE FROM THE SHELTON FAMILY.

At the very hour I stood before the scholars in my sash the decapitated head of the bushranger Morgan were being carried down the public highway—Benalla—Violet Town—Euroa—Avenel—perhaps it would be better had I known the true cruel nature of the world but I would not give up my ignorance even if I could. The Protestants of Avenel had seen the goodness in an Irish boy it were a mighty moment in my early life.

If these events made a big impression on my own young mind they made an even bigger one on Esau Shelton. What phantoms haunted his top paddock I have no way of knowing but it is very clear he could not stop dwelling on how his son were nearly dead and the more time that passed the more he felt the agony. He had been previously known as a tight lipped b————r not suited to his profession but now dear Jesus he could not be shutup and must offer endless accounts of young Dick's rescue to every bullocky selector or shearer who come to prop up his long bar. He never considered the embarrassment his emotions might be causing others it were his own peace of mind he sought.

Not many nights after I brung the sash home to my mother I were woken by the low growling of our kangaroo dogs and then detected the faint odours of stale hops.

Then come a most distinctive whisper from the night Mrs Kelly Mrs Kelly might I trouble you?

My mother replied with that hiss so particular to the mothers of young babes. What is it you want Mr Shelton?

But what is it you want Mrs Kelly?

My mother stayed silent but I could hear Mr Shelton scraping the mud off his boots as if he were intent on entering regardless.

What are you thinking Mrs Kelly?

What am I thinking? And any of her children would of recognised the dangerous rise and hook on its last word. Mr Shelton she said I'm lying here wondering who might be adjectival fool enough to wake my baby.

Beg pardon Mrs Kelly I'll come back tomorrow.

I don't want you back tomorrow Mr Shelton. She rose from her bed and knocked the pegs from the door and I watched through the curtain as the big smelly man shambled to the table and begun to noisily arrange his pipe and tobacco amongst our dirty dishes. He appeared pretty much a wreck as far as I could judge.

Mother wearily pulled her possum skin around her shoulders and waited impatiently for her guest to speak he was tongue tied and required a v. loud impatient sigh to get him rolling again.

Mrs Kelly said he at last your boy has given me back my son.

We know that Mr Shelton just tell me what is bothering you.

Its the sash he admitted.

I thought please Jesus don't talk about the sash I valued that reward more than anything I ever owned but my mother had taken a shocking set against it on account of her opinion the Sheltons should have offered money.

The sash?

I'm thinking.

Go on Mr Shelton she encouraged.

Frankly it just don't seem sufficient.

There were a very long silence.

Would you like a cup of tea Mr Shelton?

No Mrs Kelly there is nothing you can offer me.

Some oatcake?

I just ate.

Would you take a brandy to settle your digestion?

Mrs Kelly you're a woman who lost her husband just like I nearly lost my son.

Don't cry Mr Shelton they aint neither of them exactly dead.

Thats it Mrs Kelly that is what my wife has pointed out to me. I have the power to bring Mr Kelly back to you.

Though I couldnt see my mother's face I did see her back shiver like a cat with ringworm.

How do you mean?

Mr Kelly is in the lockup you'll forgive me mentioning it.

It is a private subject.

I made an enquiry of Constable Doxcy.

That aint your business Mr Shelton.

You'll forgive me he says it is a matter of £25.

But my mother did not want her husband back. Oh no she cried I will not let you.

But I must Mrs Kelly I am bound to it.

Mr Shelton it is a lovely sash you give our Ned but if you don't watch out you'll spoil him. He's a good boy but very headstrong and don't need no encouragement to take more risks he's lucky he didnt drown himself.

But surely you aint saying you wish his father left in gaol?

No cried my mother I'm saying you shouldnt make a fuss of my boy.

But you would not object to your husband being freed?

Dear Jesus cried my mother what sort of woman do you think I am?

What else could she say? One week later her husband walked back into her life. We was seated round the table eating tea when he come and stood behind me. I twisted in my seat but didnt know whether to rise or what to say.

Get out of my adjectival chair.

I squeezed down the long bench and my father took his place he rested his freckled forearms on the table and asked my mother the baby's name. I could not take my eyes off the arms all puffy white and sweaty like cheese wrapped up too long in summer.

Grace as you know.

How would I know?

I sent Ned to tell you.

Again my father turned his eyes on me and I felt he were looking into my heart at all the sins I committed against him and he pushed his stew away telling my mother to give him what money she had hidden. I thought she would say no but she emptied her sock and give him all she had and my father walked back out into the night. We was all very quiet after he were gone.

You may think it strange that a man can survive transportation and the horrors of Van Diemen's Land and then be destroyed in a country lockup but we cannot credit the tortures our parents suffered in Van Diemen's Land—Port Macquarie—Toongabbie—Norfolk Island—Emu Plains. Avenel lockup were the final straw for your grandfather he did not speak more than a dozen words to me from that day until his death.

Once he worked with us putting in the oats but he no longer liked the light of day and mostly remained inside the hut. By late spring the following year he were so bloated you could hardly see his eyes was lost and lonely and angry in the middle of his swollen face. We moved around him as if he were a pit too deep to fall into. Dr May come and told us he had dropsy and we paid a great deal of money for his medicine but there were no improvement and our father lay on his crib he could hardly raise his head to sip the rum.

Mother and I now did all the ploughing we seeded 20 acres but it were too late in the season. One day at noon it were a hot December day the sky were blue and the magpies carolling my mother returned to the hut then come straight back out to fetch me.

Come she said come now.

We entered the hut together our bare feet caked with soil our hats already in our hands and there we saw our poor da lying dead upon the kitchen table he were bulging with all the poisons of the Empire his skin grey and shining in the gloom.

I were 12 yr. and 3 wk. old that day and if my feet were callused one inch thick and my hands hard and my labourer's knees cut and scabbed and stained with dirt no soap could reach yet did I not still have a heart and were this not he who give me life now all dead and ruined? Father son of my heart are you dead from me are you dead from me my father?

His Life

Ages 12–15

Red-and-white-striped cloth booklet with red-and-blue-marbled boards (6½" × 7½" approx.). First page inscribed "To E.K. from your own M.H." Comprising 42 pages completed in red ink, 8 pages in faint pencil. Dust soiling along edges. Several 1" to 4" tears without loss of text.

An account of the family's arrival at the district of Greta and a visit from their Uncle James with a very full description of his subsequent arrest for arson and his sentencing at the Autumn Assizes. A brief report of Ned and Jem Kelly's life as agricultural labourers in the service of Ellen Kelly's sisters. Mrs Kelly's selection of land at Eleven Mile Creek is narrated with considerable enthusiasm. Also includes unflattering portraits of Anne Kelly and of various suitors of Mrs Kelly.

Now were your grandpa's poor wracked body finally granted everlasting title to the rich soil of Avenel and your grandma left free to reveal her passion for the Duffy Land Act once again. There were now no one to contradict her or call her a fool certainly not us children. We knew the Quinns had gotten 1,000 acres at Glenmore on the King River and that is what we wanted too even Dan who were the most distressed by our father's death.

In the hot summer evenings following the burial my mother gathered her brood about her. It were not Cuchulainn and Dedriu and Mebd she talked of now but the mighty farm we would all soon select together she said we would find a great mountain river and flats so rich no plough were needed we would plunge our hands into it and breathe the fertile loamy smell and be neighbours with our aunts and uncles once again and break wild horses and sell them and grow corn and wheat and raise fat sleek cattle and all the land beneath our feet would be our own to walk on from dawn to dusk ours and ours alone.

We did not talk about our father knowing our very excitement were an insult against his memory and his soul were within each soul of ours and would be for every moment of our lives and there would never be a knot I tied or a rabbit I skun or a horse I rode that I did not see those small eyes watching to see I done it right.

There was 60 hard crabholed miles between Avenel and my aunts Kate and Jane. The very small children rode in a borrowed cart together with our chooks in baskets & pots & pans & blankets & axes & hoes & 2 bags of seed my mother sitting up on the bench driving with baby Grace at her breast.

We older ones had charge of the cows and the dogs it were our job to catch the pig when he escaped though we never minded on account of we was going to a farm. Doubtless my mother had the same idea but when we finally arrived at the township of Greta we discovered our uncles had been put in gaol and the aunts and all their children was living in a de-licensed hotel. Once a palace of the gold rush it was abandoned now like a grand old ship beached on the wide brown plain it seemed the height of luxury to me.

There was 13 bedrooms and wide hallways such as I had only previously observed in Shelton's hotel and my cousins Tom and Jack and Jack Jr and my sister Kate run up and down and around in merry misrule.

If my mother were disappointed she never showed it she were always singing with her sisters and riding around the country with her father and brothers deciding which land she might finally select. My aunts must of been very poor but in memory it were a time of plenty and there was duck and chook eggs and fatty mutton with potatoes. Aunt Kate were 4 ft. 10 in. and skinny as a greenhide whip she made what my father called BRUITIN and the Quinns called CHAMP it is potatoes mashed up with a great lump of butter. She had a vegetable garden and she improved the soil so well it could grow anything we pulled up onions 12 in. across it would astound you to see what the land could produce in them days.

I had not been in Greta 2 wk. when I found an unbranded horse I broke with considerable assistance from Jimmy Quinn who did not have the T burned in his hand like old Ben Gould but he were already a famous thief and there was people in Greta said he'd sold his soul to the Devil. Be that as it may there were no better judge of an animal I ever met and never a man who could trick him with an unsound horse or a cow whose horn rings had been fixed up for sale with the clever aid of a file or burning iron.

Jimmy were already 1/2 mad from his numerous incarcerations wild and foul mouthed and violent but always very patient and kind to me and he didnt laugh when I said I were leaving school in order to be a selector. He said a 12 yr. old boy could do very well at buying and selling horses on the side and he helped me break several more unbranded horses so by the time my 13th birthday come around I had a small breaking yard and thought myself an expert in the matter. Some horses I traded and give the proceeds to Mother to help buy our land. I were later given several sheep which I increased by breeding until the flock was 18 strong.

When the older men in the district went off shearing at Gnawarra my brother Jem and I done the same at home me working the springback shears with Jem standing ready with the tar pot to dress their injuries. So you can see I had become a very serious boy it were my job to replace the father as it were my fault we didnt have him anymore.

I were sitting on the old hotel veranda when Dan come running white faced across the paddock he were 6 yr. old and would not tell me what it was had frightened him but he grabbed me by the sleeve and dragged me back from whence he come.

What is it?

I looked in the direction we was heading the little red strips of cloth my mother had torn for St. Brigit were fluttering from the wattles across the street.

Is it a snake?

In the distance was the Warby Ranges but where we walked the country were v. flat and the grass straw white and ankle high I kept my head down looking for the snake.

There he is.

I couldnt see nothing.

Up over there.

In the middle distance I made out a figure emerging from the shadow of a single gum tree and at 1st I thought it human but then observed that broad and careful walk and noted the way the square head were set so high and proud the stiffness in the arms which he held out from his belt. I crossed myself.

Its him.

I took Dan's hand walking slowly forwards all the time I were wondering why my father would return and what message did he have. Then we come closer and I begun to see some dreadful damage had been done to him he had been melted in the fires of Hell his shoulders sloped his legs was bowed his nose were drooping at its end. But when I were the length of a cricket pitch away I could see the deadly bloating were all gone the misery smelted from him his eyes a lively blue. My da was now a humorist.

You are Ned said he his tone were most familiar.

My hair were prickling on my neck.

And you are Dan?

Dan gripped my hand he would not answer.

Well boys I am your Uncle James and I am hot and thirsty and my horse is in the pound in Beechworth.

My father's eyes was private he had took his dreadful secrets to the grave but this man had no secrets and when I introduced him to the kitchen he couldnt hide his brotherly affection for my mother kissing the women and hugging the children all except Dan who were still agitated and hung back in the doorway. Tiny Kate Lloyd give him a jar of water and Mother made a cup of tea and when that did not slake his thirst he thought a tot of rum might do the trick. He proved a very lively fellow to have about the premises he were curious about everything and forever sniffing at horses' necks children's hair or crumbling yellow box leaves beneath his melted old red nose.

My father had been a stubborn ironbark corner post you could strain a fence with 8 taut lines and never see it budge but it didnt take a day to realise Uncle James were dug too shallow or placed in sandy soil. Everything about him were on the skew his arms and shoulders and eyebrows was all crooked. Just the same he made a v. amiable impression on his nieces and nephews and none were more taken with him than Dan who hung on his every word. He had a mighty hoard of stories and Dan brung me every one in turn Uncle Jim could sniff out gold and Uncle Jim knew where there were a reef and Uncle Jim knew where there were a herd of unbranded thoroughbreds hidden in a fastness in the bush.

From the day our da died Dan had worn that hurt and angry look he carries to the time of writing but in Uncle James' shadow he were once again the grand little chap that helped me deliver the butter in Avenel.

Uncle James ate like a horse and the women was happy to feed him. The 1st morning he declared himself too shagged out to work but the 2nd day he went out into the bush with a sledgehammer and a bag of wedges and split fenceposts until dark. That night the sisters was very pleased they filled his glass and their own as eagerly. Then one thing led to another and by the time Sunday come he were chasing my mother around the house in broad daylight and the cows was not milked and I could hear them setting up their fuss. I attended to them while Maggie did the pigs and chickens though she complained there were a great deal too much adjectival laughter coming from the house. Afterwards I washed my hands I heard my mother run laughing to her room. It were by this time almost dusk.

My mother locked her door behind her but Uncle James were not offended and he fetched a chair from the kitchen so he might sit outside her door and sing to her.

> *Here comes Jack Straw*
> *Such a man you never saw*
> *Through a rock*
> *Through a reel*
> *Through an old spinning wheel*
> *Through a bag of pepper*
> *Through a miller's hopper*
> *Through a sheep's shank bone*
> *Such a man was never known*

I did not immediately understand the song but my aunts was calling out their comments from the kitchen and soon enough it dawned on me that Uncle James were no different from Sgt O'Neil or any of them men who come knocking at my mother's door.

> *Here comes I Jack Straw*
> *With a stick in me hand ready to draw*
> *I had 14 childer born in one night*
> *And not one in the same townland*

Then I hated him. I were 13 yr. old my head didnt reach the lowest point of my uncle's sloping shoulder. Not able to beat him man to man I told him if he come with me I would pour him a big jar of poteen but he were deaf as a dog in the middle of a war and would not be diverted from his lechery.

You put your dirty stick away my mother called.

Uncle James' beard parted in a grin. My stick is spic and span.

I did not want to hear no more I pulled my uncle towards the kitchen. Its Grandpa Quinn's poteen I said.

He must of had a quart already for he swung a freckled arm and knocked me against the wall then he spoke directly to my mother's door.

Begob I'll put that stick inside your little stove.

I would not permit him to speak thus to my mother so I ran and climbed right up him clamping both my hands onto his beard and then twisting his head like I seen my father bring down calves at branding time. With all my weight on his great hairy head I struggled to settle him.

You mutt he cried striking me across the head so hard I landed on the floor I were winded the sparks flying like blowflies inside my brain.

Then my mother flung wide her door. You leave him alone you effing mongrel.

Whoa Ellen whoa now. He tried to take her by her forearms but she easily broke his grip. Said she I aint a horse.

I rushed him from behind and punched him in the kidney but he swatted me away and pushed my mother back into the bedroom and there he tried to throw her on her bed.

No you aint a horse. You is a bouley maiden.

I knew what this meant as did my mother. The bouley maiden is the cow which will not take the bull. She leapt up at him like a windmill and she were scratching and slapping his face and chest so I took the lower 1/2 from knees to kidneys and when he would not retreat I punched him in the bawbles. He were not our equal he fell he rose he tripped and tangled on himself and backed in defeat towards the kitchen.

Later I saw my uncle sitting on the front veranda it were that time of evening when my aunts would try a little poteen it were not quite dark and the currawongs was still crying in the mournful gloom. When the light were gone everyone come inside to eat the stew but Uncle James would not sup with us and in the end we was all so miserable and sorry to see him sad that Mother sent Danny out to ask him in for a drop of pudding.

We waited a good time but Dan didnt come back. Out on the veranda I found my little brother holding my uncle's horny hand both of them was glued together in their malevolence. Neither of them would speak a word to me.

In my dream I were in Hell with endless heat and choking even waking I could not escape the terrors. The room were filled with smoke my brother Dan had disappeared so I opened the door to the hall and saw nothing but smothering fumes. Then Dan come running lost and terrified and coughing and bawling for his mother. I told him stop bawling or he would die of it. I shook Jem awake.

The Kelly girls was accommodated in the next room so bringing Dan along I picked up little Kate and hollered to the others they must flee. Annie needed no 2nd bidding she went flying up the hallway like a white chook in her nightie. Maggie wore nothing but a pair of bloomers she tried to rescue Dan but he wouldnt leave my side though his skinny chest were shook with coughing. We once more entered the infernal hallway as my cousins come running past reporting the back of the house were all on fire. We caught up with Annie at my mother's door it were locked we would need an axe to break it down. Then thank God my mother come out. She tried to give Grace to me so she could return for her tin box. I don't know what were in that box no more than scissors and reels of cotton but I do know she would of died for it. I ordered her to take the children and I would rescue her treasure from her room. With some difficulty I found the box but by then the smoke were too hot and thick in the hallway so I retreated to the room where I discovered the window sash were jammed. Thinking I would die I budged the sash enough to squeeze out into the night air. It were a beautiful night the moon high the summer paddocks white as snow.

Looking for my mother I discovered instead my Uncle James gazing blearily at the burning laundry wall he were staggering drunk and careless of the flames licking all around him. I tried to lead him away but his eyes were shining and he pushed me violently against the chest. Stumbling I saw him pitch his drink into the fire but even witnessing the rush of flame I were slow to understand his glass were full of paraffin. My uncle were burning down the house and did not care who knew it. Now he rushed off into the dark and come back with pine palings to pitch into the blazing laundry.

Having no time to worry what damage he might do me I ran at him head down and as he were now v. drunk I tipped him over as easy as a sleeping cow. He cursed me and limped off again into the dark then returned with more fuel so I picked up a handy length of lead pipe and approached him swinging it above my head. The old arsonist could do naught but retreat before me.

The windows was cracking suspended in a rage of heat. I picked up the tin box to give chase but lost him as the entire west wall dissolved in flame. I opened the door to the chook house but it were too late the rooster and his wives was lying dead upon the earth our dairy cows come fleeing past me their big eyes was dancing with reflected fire.

Finally I found Mother out on the road and all the children safe beside her. I give her the tin box just as Constable Sheehan rode up with his pyjamas visible beneath his uniform.

So what is happening?

It were a very stupid question anyone could see the roof were about to fall. The policeman jerked his head at the stranger who was standing on the road with my frightened brother Dan captive in his freckled arms.

Who's that?

This is James Kelly says my mother. He has burnt our effing home down or words to that effect.

The following day our family were dispersed like ash upon the wind my mother taking the littlies 20 mi. away to the town of Wangaratta where she hoped for some type of job. Me and Jem was left behind to work as labourers for our aunts.

Before imprisonment our uncles had selected land out at Fifteen Mile Creek and now there were no choice for their wives but move out there immediately and set to clearing and fencing and performing all the back-breaking tasks which are the poor selector's lot. Jack and Jimmy Quinn come to assist their sisters get back on their feet and it were them that built the hut we was to sleep in. True they was kind enough at nighttime when the grog was talking but they was very hard men and brooked no laziness around the property. My brother Jem were only 9 yr. old and brung back homework every night from Greta School but were still required to split the firewood and carry pollard and mash for the pigs and many other chores too numerous to mention. We could do no more than curse and swear beneath our breath we had not come to the North East to work as slaves but to possess our own land we could walk on from breakfast until we saw the last kookaburra marking its boundary across the evening sky. We left Avenel expecting we would soon have sleek black cattle and big rumped long necked horses I had imagined them horses most particular in the picture they would make thundering across our plain.

Our aunts was not unkind neither and kept saying our mother would soon make some money but then admitted she were taking in laundry in Wangaratta so we could no longer sustain our hopes.

O how I did hate James Kelly for stealing our destiny from us and I would lie on the hessian bunk with my brother's bare feet in my face and him and me would comfort ourselves by inventing gruesome punishments for our uncle scalding him and flogging him and dragging him behind a speeding horse. My daughter you will grow to count the days till it is Christmas morning and then you will know exactly how Jem and me reckoned the time to the Autumn Assizes when James Kelly would be assigned his fate.

The Assizes was held in Beechworth. There were much higher country to the south and east but no one could see that from Beechworth for there the law did sit in pomp and majesty and there were no higher place than its own elevated opinion. Of course the town fed off all the sweat and labour of the miners and the poor selectors on the plains below but in those grand stone buildings they could bankrupt or hang you as they pleased. They had a courthouse & prison & hospital plus 4 banks & 2 breweries & 15 hotels.

It were here I reunited with my mother as she descended from the Wangaratta Coach she wore a bright blue silk dress and a bustle and a mighty hat that towered above her head. I were most surprised to see how prosperous she looked.

You grown out of them britches she said.

I didnt understand how she could profit so well from laundry but knew better than to question her directly. In any case we rushed to court and I entered that cool limey building like it were a church my hat removed my head were bowed. I had not seen a Judge until that day and when we was told to rise I done so. When he come to the bench I never knew he would be my enemy for life I seen his wig and his bright red robes and he were a Cardinal to my eyes his skin all white and waxy as if he were a precious foreign object kept contained in cotton wool.

Justice Redmond Barry looked down on the crowded court with hooded eyes we all went quiet even the Lloyds and Quinns could feel his power to harm them.

The traps then brought up Uncle James from the cells he were all skin bone and misery as pitiful a creature as a plucked cockatoo and when he caught my eye he flinched away. It were not so easy to keep hating him when he were called into the dock.

My mother then give her information speaking her mind even when the Judge told her not to. After she were finished the Judge listened to Cons Sheehan read aloud from his notebook. Then the Judge addressed Uncle James and asked did he wish to say anything in his defence.

I will marry Mrs Kelly.

But do you have anything to say in your defence?

Yes I will marry her.

And that is all?

Yes your honour.

Then I will pronounce sentence. Justice Redmond Barry took a square black cloth and placed it over his head.

Mother were now moaning I thought she were upset by this proposal but then I heard the Judge say that Uncle James were to be taken away and hung until dead and I watched the old boy's mouth open and saw his tongue flick around the corners. His frightened eyes looking out towards us we watched in horror while they took him down.

When we come out of court the women was weeping but Jem and me was silent sick with shame to have our wish come true.

After the death sentence my mother were red eyed and the worse for drink she caught a night coach back to the rented rooms in Wangaratta and what them rooms was like I cannot say. A mother can have no secrets in a settler's hut she cannot so much as break wind and all her children must hear what she has done but now she were far away from Fifteen Mile Creek and no longer could I guess her life. I were told she took laundry and perhaps she did but I am sure she only did what she must do. She had a mother and father and brothers and sisters but in the end she were a poor widow and she had 7 children and all of them was alarmed and unsettled by their lives. Dan peed his bed and Annie's bones ached at her knees and when she run they made a click. Nor were I too shy to tell my mother the misery that come of being her sisters' slave.

I didnt know I had grown 2 in. and thought my Aunt Kate were boiling my clothes too hard for they now was cutting into my crutch and tight across my chest but all I knew were that an unpaid Agricultural Labourer went hungry and weary from dawn to dusk.

I were sitting in the outhouse at Fifteen Mile Creek one August morning that is 4 mo. since Uncle James were sentenced I heard a rider approaching at a gallop but I didnt think much of it for all the Quinns and Lloyds was flashy riders they was lairs and larrikins and they would put on a show or jump a fence as soon as blow their nose. I sat in the stinky dark and did my business listening to the horse trot round the hut and a woman's voice hooing hahing and then I heard my name being called impatiently. I were peeved that I could not get a moment to myself

I come stumbling from the dunny tugging at my braces as my buttons would not do up no more.

It were my mother wheeling around me the morning sun behind her I saw her dress were some fancy silk or satin it were a new and brilliant red. Land ho she cried.

She wore no hat but her black hair were braided and her face flushed and her black eyes bright and she sat astride her handsome chestnut mare with her skirts rucked up to show her smooth bare knees. Land ho she cried we got our land.

I looked to the new dairy and saw skinny Aunt Kate and buxom Jane they was standing at the door and Aunt Kate were frowning and Aunt Jane were smiling to see this vision of their sister splendid as a queen. Just then Jem come mooching out from behind the woodheap where he had been hiding but seeing the visitor he run up to the mare he got a grip on the horse's kneebone between his big toe and his 2nd toe and with that stirrup he sprung upon our mother's lap. He had missed her company very bad.

I asked what were the rent and she kissed Jem on his head and neck then wheeled her horse around. No rent she cried it is selected I give the money order to the Land Office last night at 5 o'clock it is our own own land my darling boys.

Where Ma where is it?

You'll see she cried for we're off to live there now.

Today?

This very adjectival minute.

I had never thought I would be happy again but a 1/2 hr. later having give Jem my saddle I were galloping bareback towards our destiny. I were still only 13 yr. and my mother were a young woman not much over 30 and she thundered past us through the cutting tearing down the white clay track with a low fog wrapped around her knees. Then we come along by the narrow little creek the blades of sunlight falling through the foliage and there were a hut surrounded by a stand of dead white ringbarked trees and I seen the slab wall and the rough battens and the steam rising off its damp bark roof and I could not know that this were the very site where you would one day be conceived.

My 6 yr. old brother Dan raced out its open door he had no clothes upon his lower self and sturdy laughing Maggie were behind him and they chased towards us through the sun drenched mist and then I knew this were my home my heart were bursting I jumped off my horse and scooped the laughing naked boy into my arms.

My mother's selection were 3 mi. from Greta it bordered the Eleven Mile Creek from which the district takes its name. Section 57A was one of 5 blocks of roughly equal size it were lightly timbered near the track but soon the bush were very thick all flat and clayey then elevating slightly to the south running up between the 2 arms of Futter's Range in a wide basin.

88 acres were less than I had imagined though my mother chose it not for its acreage but for the great commercial advantage of having a hut already constructed and adjacent to a public thoroughfare. The morning Jem and I arrived she had already set up a barrel of brandy and purchased 2 doz. clear glass bottles and a gross of corks she were in the way of running a little shebeen. Of course it were illegal to sell grog without a govt. licence but she must do what she must do and this were the only way to fund the improvement of a property all still unfenced and uncleared.

I caught Dan and helped Maggie get his britches on while my mother give Jem the reins and went in the hut. Next thing I knew the red dress were gone and replaced by a shirt and pr. of men's trousers tied up with rope. She then said we must all get to work and help her build a cockatoo fence to keep the dairy cows contained of a night. Once that were done we could bring the little herd across from Fifteen Mile Creek and begin to have income from our butter which were bringing 2/– per lb. at that time.

I had not been on the land 2 hr. before I had felled a mighty gum tree the parrots squawking with alarm and a baby possum dead upon the ground. My sisters Kate and Grace buried it beside the creek but neither my mother nor the older children had no time for sentiment we all was slaving even Annie despite her never liking to get her hands dirty.

At the end of the day the fence were still not completed but my family had witnessed my new strength and they knew I could be the man. I were v. tired as anyone would be. I didnt do none of the children's chores and sat in the last of the sunshine using the wet stone on my axe. Annie should of been busy with her mother but instead called to me she found a yabby in the creek. I told her to fetch a bit of bacon rind and a length of string we took it down to the creek and I instructed her how to tie the bait I were not surprised she didnt watch.

Tell her not to sell the grog.

I saw there werent no yabby nowhere that she had practised a deception in order to speak to me alone.

They'll arrest her for the grog she said and then they'll send us to the industrial school. This were typical of her she were always the same.

Jeez Annie take it easy.

But she put her hand upon my sleeve and twisted it. We need a cove said she.

What for?

To marry her says she to save us.

Annie Annie do not fret.

Fret my foot. Are you stupid?

Fair go Annie. Didnt you see how many trees I dropped? Don't you know I can catch a yabby if there is one. I'm as good a shot as any cove you know. We will make a mighty farm here Annie.

She snorted I looked at her thin and bitter mouth and were reminded that my older sister could never see no hope or good in anything it werent her fault it were her nature.

You're only 13 said she. You don't know nothing about life.

Annie herself knew nothing except to fear every ant and spider but I didnt say nothing cruel to her. We had our own land and even when the sun went down and it turned out our mother had forgot to purchase matches and we must therefore retire to our dusty cribs with no more to fill our stomachs than a mixture of uncooked flour and creek water I still remained what is called an OPTIMIST and when our mother lay on her crib romancing about all the fine cattle we soon should own I seen no cause to doubt her.

Thus did time pass very happily through the winter and spring of 1868 I received a new blue shirt and corduroy trousers in a parcel my mother were given by Father Wall in Benalla these clothes belonged previously to a man knocked from a horse when nightriding. He were 18 yr. old when he died but his trousers fitted v. well.

My mother dug up my father's bluchers these mighty boots was studded closely with nails and though the leather were cracked and hard I fast softened them with lard & mutton fat & Venetian turpentine a recipe given me by Mr Holmes a contractor. They was still a mite too large but when stuffed with fresh grass was not at all uncomfortable and as for their weight I never minded any load I carried in that 1st spring season at Eleven Mile Creek.

After dropping 3 trees in a day I could still find time to break a horse and while these 1st products was a little hard mouthed my younger brothers and sisters soon was riding to the school in Greta. Also I presented to Mother a handsome mare a thoroughbred with a touch of Arab. Once she rode it to mass in Benalla where the police tried to pretend it were stolen but having no case they was afterwards 1/2 hearted in pursuing it.

The spring rains begun early in September they was good and steady by the end of October the weather got gradually warmer and the cows proved productive in their new pasture. The police troubled us no more than they did other poor settlers in the district.

Annie's chest were growing very womanly but she remained a baby so far as I could see with hardly a week going by when she didnt suffer some alarm that the police was about to raid us and carry our mother off to Melbourne Gaol.

I heard a horse said she one moonlight December night you could smell the perfumes of summer the dust and eucalyptus in the air. Theres some b————r skulking around the hut she said.

Maggie said it were the new gelding causing trouble she were positive.

Its the adjectival police cried Annie I know it is.

I learned early that these alarms was best settled before my mother and Annie began going at one another. I were the man and it were therefore me who rose out of his crib to put them heavy bluchers on but even as I done so Annie were hissing like a goose about the brandy not being hid away. My mother told her shut her gob. Knocking the pegs out of the door I stepped out into the night.

There in the moonlight stood a man he were holding a specially tailored carbine in his right hand he wore a belt outside a bearskin coat which also held 2 big bright revolvers. I asked him what he wanted.

The man did not answer directly he were broad shouldered spade bearded and heavy jawed his black bearskin coat reaching down to his knees. This is a lonely place said he at last.

From inside the hut I heard a scraping sound as my mother armed herself with the hearth shovel. The man stooped to pluck some thistles and fed them to his horse I could clearly see he were a creature of his own design his white moleskins shone in the moonlight like robes in a stained glass window.

I told him if he had a shilling I would bring him out a good sized glass of grog.

And who might you be sonny Jim?

Ned Kelly.

You're a little young to be running a shebeen Ned Kelly.

I help my mother Sir.

Do you now?

Yes Sir I do.

The visitor smiled at me and tied the reins of his horse to the veranda post. Tell your mother that Harry Power is here to see her.

The mention of this famous name set off a violent scuffling within the hut I heard Annie cry Mother and my mother say Shutup.

One minute later I followed the great Harry Power inside the dark little hut. My mother by then were out of bed sitting at the table in her bright red dress. Please come in said she as if there was 100 candles burning.

My mother were reluctant to produce a light but the visitor fossicked around in his pockets and once some balls and percussion caps was removed he discovered his box of lucifers and then our tallow candle were ignited and the flickering shadows filled with children's eyes. We all witnessed the bushranger lay his carbine on the table it were a terrifying weapon its bore were almost one inch the stock 1/2 cut away the barrel severely shortened. I waited to hear my mother tell him he must take the murderous thing outside but she never spoke a word against it and when he said he would appreciate that jar of brandy he were promised by the boy she slipped behind the curtain to personally fetch him what he wished.

Harry Power swept the balls and caps into his big cupped hand putting the caps in his left pocket the balls in the right then he leaned back in the chair looking frankly up at all the staring eyes. Do you know who I am?

I were behind his shoulder so he couldnt look at me but he frightened

Gracie and Maggie they hid theirselves. Annie and Dan was staring boldly through the gaps in the curtain the little boy's big black eyes was popping to see so legendary a creature his older sister's lips was twisted up with scorn.

I'm Harry Power the bushranger.

When Annie did not soften the famous head begun to turn towards me but suddenly I were shy and shed my bluchers and crawled up to my musty crib. I found Annie in the gloom her arms folded tightly across her little bosoms it were very clear that Harry Power were not the type of cove she wanted for our mother. But the ma were not unhappy I could hear her dancing step as she come back from the skillion. 1st I heard one glass set down then the clink of a 2nd. A little bit of what you fancy Sir.

Harry Power asked my mother did she remember him it were hard to hear for Dan and Jem was whispering.

Oh yes Mr Power I remember you very well.

You know my present circumstances?

You escaped from Pentridge on Wednesday or so I heard from Tom.

He's an adjectival bushranger Jem whispered to Dan now shut your gob and go to sleep but Dan crawled back across me into Annie's bed where he were not welcome neither. Get off me you little b————r go to bed.

In a moment Dan were barrelling back to Jem he were most excited Jem Jem he's got them concertina leggings on his boots. Shutup said Jem.

Shutup you little b————r cried my mother but it done no good Dan were a wombat charging back to Annie's bed where I followed him myself then our mother begun asking about Uncle James then even Annie wished to listen she relented of her vicious kicking. The whole family was still much occupied with the fate of Uncle James.

Aye he were there said Harry Power the sword of Damascus is hanging over him. I seen a lot of condemned men in my time Mrs Kelly and they is all different. Do you recall Ryan and Evans? They made a chemical concoction to murder Evans' wife.

He aint condemned whispered Dan tell him thats wrong tell him our uncle aint condemned no more.

We is appealing you idiot said Annie then my mother shouted I'll get the adjectival strap to you I'll lay it across your legs Anne Kelly I swear I will.

Harry Power paused to gaze up into the dark. I were on good terms with Ryan he said at last. After his sentence he couldnt eat at all poor blighter but your brother in law is more like Evans who always took great solace from the nosebag.

James were always an adjectival glutton.

Mrs Kelly now you know that aint polite.

He's already ate 20 quid of mine to pay his solicitors and he still aint in the clear. I don't know why we don't let the b————rs hang him.

Well what is called gluttony in one man is a healthy appetite in someone else.

My mother leaned back on her bench and crossed her arms.

She don't like him whispered Dan and at 1st he appeared to be correct my mother's expression had now turned v. hard.

I have a fellow's normal appetites Mrs Kelly.

Annie give a groan she pulled a pillow across her head and commenced to kick at us again.

But said Harry I have been so denied the satisfaction of one of them that I envy any cove what can eat as freely as James Kelly. I have a stricture in my bowels said he.

Annie come out from under the pillow hissing into my ear that I should put Dan back into his bed but I were watching Harry remove his big thick hobble belt twisting it to illustrate the exact nature of the stricture and I seen how this demonstration made my mother soften it were a very rapid transformation that he extracted from her Is that so my mother said.

Later I would watch Harry do this so frequent that I were no longer amazed at the uses to which he could put his bowels but this 1st time were a wonder to see the glow in my mother's eye and the angle of her head displaying a very powerful female sympathy. Would a little bacon tempt you Harry?

It would damn me Ellen.

Do you fancy lamb?

I dream of lamb said Harry Power I like it very pink and tender.

He licked his lips delicately and my mother gazed at him distractedly she asked him what of beef?

The very same.

They went through a list of every known animal and I found the conversation both confusing and disturbing and I saw the way my mother took the belt when Harry offered it and how she rolled it neatly and then smoothed it on her lap. I had been very taken with Harry Power but as he looked at her neck and bared his teeth I didnt like him not at all.

Excuse me I called.

O Holy Jesus my mother cried.

Does Mr Power think Uncle James could be got off being hung?

Harry Power glowered up at me. What is it boy?

Its Uncle James Kelly. We never wished him hanged.

Harry took the belt back from my mother wrapping it once more around his girth he seemed very out of temper.

The trouble with your Uncle James is that his solicitor is a famous fool.

That had a sharp effect upon my mother she did not like to hear this low opinion of how she spent her hard earned money.

Harry's tumbler were not empty but she suddenly picked up both the glasses and removed them to the skillion.

What would you have me do she called.

Zinke.

Whats that?

A solicitor in Beechworth he's the boyo for us Zinke's your man Ellen.

When she come out from the skillion her hands were empty her eyes were hard and black as buttons. Zinke!

But just as she come to the precipice of her famous temper at that very moment Harry Power extended his hand seeming to caress her palm then withdrew again leaving her as peaceful as a broody hen.

You give this to Mr Zinke said he and he will get James Kelly put safe and sound where no rope can attach to him.

I could not see the 10 gold sovereigns from the foot of Annie's crib but certainly heard my mother crying and saw her seize the cove's broad and damaged hands and cover them with tears and kisses. In a settler's hut the smallest flutter of a mother's eyelids are like a tin sheet rattling in the wind.

Angry bunions swollen veins it were a queer thing to see a stranger's big flat feet sticking out the bottom of my mother's blanket next morning and to be honest I will confess I would much prefer that she invited no new husbands to her bed but seeing as I couldnt have this wish then I preferred old Harry Power. No woman was ever the worse for knowing me he told me once and even allowing for his feet and bowels he were far superior to the other coves who come trotting along the heat hazed track to see the widow e.g. Turk Morrison from Laceby and that natty Englishman Bill Frost. Old Turk liked to sing love songs to my ma but Bill sat at our table bashing her ear about how to overcome the lack of rain. He were nothing better than a boundary rider but imagined himself a mighty expert on matters agricultural he said the Australians did not farm the land correctly they was low and ignorant etc. etc.

Bill Frost dressed the squatter and wore his hairy brown tweed coat right through the worst of summer which is why Annie were in favour of him but I were insulted by his ignorant opinions it drove me mad to see my mother fall under his spell.

O yes Bill is that so Bill etc. etc.

My hands was blistered bleeding I could chop down 5 trees in one day and you might imagine it would shame a man to see a boy labour thus but Frost never picked up an axe or dropped a single gum that I recall. Instead he give me his ignorant opinions advising me to spread manure across the paddocks or warning it were no benefit to burn crop stubble unless the rain should follow shortly.

And that were the great virtue of Harry Power for he didnt give a tinker's fart if we seeded St. John's Wort or tried to cross a bush rat with a wallaby. He would arrive by night and leave early in the morning always bringing a present and if he had robbed a coach he would bring a gold fob watch or a sapphire ring and if he had held up a tavern he would bring a cask of rum or some rancid banknotes and it were left to us to improve the property any way we wished with no argument or contradiction.

But Bill Frost never brought nothing more useful than the local rag it were named THE BENALLA ENSIGN and he and my mother would pore over the cattle prices and cluck their tongues over the ignorance of colonial farmers and I took this very personal.

Alex Gunn were another suitor that were clear the 1st time he appeared on the track from Greta township it were a hot smoky Sunday the sort of day when all your throat is caked with dust the flies crawling in your ears and up your nose holes. I were in the cow yard when a lanky rawboned rider come through the muddy creek up past the hut to where I were trying to persuade our sick jersey cow to taste water from a bucket.

That cow has got a bald spot said the stranger.

I knew that already said I.

You know what will fix it?

We been putting butter on it.

What you need is some Ellman's Balsam have you any Ellman's?

I don't know.

He remained in his saddle staring down at me he had blue eyes and sandy hair and a v. sunburned face he were under 28 yr. much younger than my mother. I thought he were going to criticise something else but finally he brought his horse to keep the sick cow company. Later I saw him walking towards the hut he had bowyangs tied around his bandy legs.

I turned back to my cow when there were a mighty crash a heavy branch fell from the grey box and bounced off the roof of the hut and dropped amongst the chickens who was more or less undamaged. That grey box were often losing branches we was accustomed to it but the visitor were very loudly shocked at such a dangerous tree so close to human habitation. If this were for my benefit it were wasted there was other things to do around the place but soon he located the widow at the cow-bails and gathered her children round him as if in training to be their father.

As I come upon them I heard he were instructing them about the grey box a species of the family eucalyptus so he said it were famous for killing people with its branches. He claimed they called it widow maker in tribute to the men it struck down in their prime.

We aint worried I said.

The stranger glanced at me before turning back to my mother. Might I trouble you for a loan of your axe he asked.

She don't have no axe said I.

He had a little broad hooked nose like a parrot he looked at me along it best as he were able.

Ned said my mother you can bring Mr Gunn your axe. She put one hand round young Dan's shoulder and stroked Annie's head with her other and I could see my sister were as pleased with this candidate as she had been displeased with Harry Power. But I wouldnt permit him to be my da so I told him where he would find an axe if he cared to look himself.

O I'll fetch it Annie said she sauntered over to the hut everybody following and gathering to witness the astonishing sight of Alex Gunn sharpening an axe. When that show were done he split some shingles my mother watching like she never seen such a feat before.

I left to attend the pigs though it were not my job and once I finished I seen the suitor had cut some notches up the grey box using the shingles perhaps 30 in. apart to make a series of steps up the main trunk.

Now he were set to perform the wonder of dropping the tree but then Annie were sent out to bring him inside and by the time I had cleaned myself down at the creek I found him invited to feast on roasted kangaroo. That night he slept on the table that is very close by my mother's bed. He was up twice in the night and each time I were there to fetch him the lantern.

Next day Alex Gunn departed and Harry Power returned it were like an adjectival railway station he give my mother a sapphire she were very grateful at 1st but they spent a good deal of the afternoon drinking then quarrelled in the middle of the night so he went away.

The next day I dropped 3 very big river gums without no assistance and also shot 4 cockatoos which I plucked and gutted. Annie made cockatoo pie for our supper I admit it were very tasty.

The next time Harry come back he presented my mother with a freshly slaughtered ewe he had shot it in the head and up the backside though he did not explain how this occurred. He stayed the night and left early.

By design or accident Alex Gunn returned almost immediately afterwards he smelled of pomade and he brung a new hemp rope he received more gratitude for that 2/– rope than Harry got for his sapphires. With the others I watched as he carried the rope up the tree I hoped he fell and broke his adjectival neck. 30 ft. or so above our chooks he secured the largest overhanging branch which he cut and lowered to the roof. My mother made such a fuss about how she admired him she had Annie cook him lamb's fry from Harry's ewe. When the fry were cooked it must be eaten so dark came with no more than one branch removed from the grey box.

Gunn slept on the table each time he rose I were awake and by his side I was an adjectival terrier.

My mother and I spent the following week sawing up the river gums I had previously felled then we done the best we could to roll and lever the bigger logs to one side. The leaves and lighter branches we pulled into piles so as to burn them once they was all dry it were a mighty endeavour but none of this made a topic of conversation within our family. All they wished to discuss was Alex Gunn.

A week later he brung hoops and dolls also silk scarves for Mother and Annie. To me he give a Bowie knife I thanked him but didnt pay very much attention because we had a paying visitor a boozy old bullocky who were playing me at draughts. I suppose Alex Gunn must of promised to complete his tree on the morrow for I definitely heard Annie tease him saying he would end up as the man in the moon who were sent there by God as punishment for chopping wood on a Sunday.

He said the story made no sense to him at all.

Annie said that he need only step outside she would happily show him the man in the moon with his axe and dog and the bundle of sticks on his back.

Crowning my draughts piece I come back dealing death to the bullocky's pieces I didnt notice them return until I heard Alex talking to my ma.

Mrs Kelly said he I wonder would you like a stroll as well.

Certainly said my mother. She put down her darning and walked out into the night with Alex Gunn.

I asked Annie What game does he think he's up to?

For answer I got only a strange smile while the bullocky jumped 4 of my pieces thereby winning himself a crown. Which is where the game were halted for my mother now come in through the door she were arm in arm with Alex Gunn both of them was beaming.

Annie put down the darning. Her cheeks was pink her eyes bright as she looked at me but even when my mother made a clear announcement I were too discombobulated to take it in. It were some moments before I understood my skinny sister was to marry Alex Gunn.

I had thought myself full growed but now I seen the truth it were a mighty shock I were trying so hard to be a man I had kept myself a child. Looking at my sister I saw how her cheeks glowed her bosoms pushed out against her blouse I blushed to think the things they would now be allowed to do together.

His Life at
15 Years of Age

59 octavo pages all of high wood-pulp content and turning brown. Folds, foxing, staining and minor tears.

An account of a poor Irish wedding party at Emu Plains. Contains interesting details of the author's apprenticeship to Harry Power, together with claims that this arrangement was not to his liking. A primer in the geography of North Eastern Victoria. A rare description of the outlaw Power pursuing his trade, and a full (if fanciful) explanation of the source of a successful squatter's wealth. This document is typical of the collection in that it contains accounts of numerous fights. It concludes with the author's first experience of a prison cell.

Annie and Alex Gunn's wedding party were at the Oxley Hotel I were 14 yr. old and there was girls my age but I did not know how to dance and once I won the long jumping and the 1/4 mile gallop I were bored. Everywhere there was untended children running wild but I were waiting at the kitchen doorway with nothing to do than wonder how long it would take to get the dinner served. From this doorway I also could observe my mother in her bright red dress with bustle she were dancing with a ferret faced fellow in a checked tweed coat I refer to that ignoramus Bill Frost. My mother had just won the Ladies 1 Mile Handicap and were v. bright and happy until she spied me watching. Then she abandoned her Englishman and sought me out.

Come said she lifting the hem of her fancy dress and drawing me out through the steamy slippery kitchen into the hotel veggie garden where my Uncle Wild Pat the Dubliner were lying blotto under the tank stand. Not a glance did my mother give Wild Pat but escorted me down between the dunny and the compost heap and there she asked me bluntly how I liked her dancing partner.

I don't mind him.

Then it would be a favour if you quit glowering at him. You look 1/2 mad.

I cannot help my face.

She seemed to weigh this answer but she were a woman and I could no more imagine what she were scheming than I could conjure up the thoughts of a Chinaman.

So what do you reckon about old Harry Power?

O I prefer him Ma no question.

You think he's the better man?

Strewth yes.

Then you would help me with Harry?

Yes Ma anything at all.

Once more she became bright and happy kissing me on the forehead saying I should wait by the side of the hotel. She needed me to spend some time getting to know Harry better.

You mean we will have a yarn?

More in the nature of a ride.

I had arrived at the wedding in my da's old bluchers they was much softer now thanks to Mr Holmes' mixture but were no lighter or quieter than before I therefore had hidden them beneath the floor of the hotel. Imagining I would be with Harry an hour or less I left them there.

I heard Power's heavy footsteps on the veranda before I seen him. There were a type of crooked stair from the veranda down to the track but now overgrown with wisteria vine which tripped him causing him to fall almost at my feet. As the famous bushranger rose before me I almost failed to know him he had been a prince but now all his bones was taken out. Never having seen a man brought down by love I didnt recognise the condition.

A kingdom for my horse he cried he were v. drunk with bloodshot eyes the whites gone yellow. I led him down the rutted track to the paddock where he 1st spotted his switchtailed mare then a poor piebald pony laden down with packs and saddlebags. He took the mare or more truly threw himself upon her mercy.

Indicating a 3rd horse what they call a WALER he told me it were his and I should mount. It were a lively animal 2 yr. old I didnt mind this order in the least.

Bill Frost were meanwhile on the back veranda dancing with my mother it were his great specialty. He bent her to him springy as a sapling she were whippy and dangerous but Bill Frost had patent leather dancing shoes he were most excited by his prospects.

Power turned his head away from this torment we passed at an amble staring earnestly out towards the west.

The boy imagined the famous bushranger knew where he were going but when the pair had rode an hour or so beyond Moyhu the man reined in his horse to ask where they was. The boy were come beyond the limits of his world and said so plainly.

Said the boy Perhaps we should be getting home now.

The man cursed him for a fool then turned cantering into deeper wilder country the boy didnt know what to do but follow.

Let me give you a very rough idea of the territory it is not an easy bit of land to learn so 1st I will give you a simple picture you must imagine a great wedge of pie with a high ridge around its outer crust they call that ridge the Great Dividing Range.

At the apex of the wedge is the river town of Wangaratta and you might imagine the Ovens River running along the eastern side of the wedge. It would be simplest to say the Broken River makes the western side of the wedge thats a lie but never mind. The King River is more obliging cutting right down the centre of the wedge to join the Ovens River exactly at Wangaratta. Next you must imagine the pie slopes up from Wangaratta where the land is very flat. It were near here in Oxley that Annie were married but the boy and the grisly man spent the afternoon travelling to higher elevations along the centre of the wedge. By late afternoon having left the limits of selection they poked up a long winding ridge and by early evening they was definitely entering big country. At last they picked a path down a densely wooded gully to a mountain stream.

What river do you think this is asked the man his voice still slurred his eyes was red and baleful. When the boy said he didnt know where he were the man again cursed him for a fool soon they both were dismounted the pair of them quarrelling the man's voice a low and dirty grumble the boy's squeaking like a broken organ pipe. Then the man were drawing in the gloomy dirt with his broken fingernail saying north were that direction the boy said it were another he were very keen and earnest and no matter what cruel things had happened to him he were still so young and trusting and did not understand he were an apprentice sitting an examination he would be well advised to fail.

Then we won't be home tonight?

Home my arse.

That question answered the man revealed he brung but 3 bottles of rum and nothing to eat save a bag of weevily flour so when the moon rose the boy went off alone and shot a possum thus proving his usefulness a 2nd time. Back in camp he found only darkness the bushranger were lying on his back and snoring. The boy shook him but did not succeed in waking him until the fire were lit and the food cooked.

That night the boy were very cold indeed he kept the fire burning while the man snored and farted in the dirt like a kangaroo dog he had an oilskin coat the boy had none his feet was cold and already swollen from 1/2 a day of riding with no boots. The boy missed the comfort of his brothers and sisters he would of give anything to be back up in his crib breathing that warm familiar fug.

The dew began falling not long after midnight the boy couldnt sleep and long before the calls of the whip birds finally echoed round the damp and misty dawn he resolved to flee home that very day he bore no malice to the man. Rising he found the flour and picked out many weevils then he made johnnycakes with strong black tea and as he done this particularly well it were as bad a mistake as shooting possum for thus he sealed his fate.

The boy and man was breaking their fast sitting side by side on a log when between mouthfuls the boy announced he could find his own way back to Eleven Mile Creek. There was no reason to imagine the man would stop him and indeed he done nothing more than quiz him about the tracks and ridges. The boy were clearly correct for the man topped up his pannikin with tea and give him an extra spoon of sugar.

Just the same said the man Eleven Mile Creek aint your concern no more. In other words he were telling the boy he could not go home.

The boy did not appreciate this were more than an opinion he earnestly explained he were sorely needed at home that Jem werent yet strong enough and it were himself alone who felled the trees. He told the man that Bill Frost were very determined and bound to move in under the mother's blanket and he reckoned that would be very bad for both the travellers.

The mention of Bill Frost made the man very thoughtful he blew into his tea and warmed his whiskers in the steam. It aint Bill Frost's adjectival farm he said.

No road the boy agreed.

It aint his adjectival farm no more than mine.

The man looked around that gloomy little clearing in the wattles it were all the home he had. The boy thought it very sad that the man could grow so old and still have no place on earth to call his own. He said he hated Bill Frost and would do all he could to keep him from his mother's blanket.

I aint no farmer young'un I'm an adjectival bushranger.

It aint so hard to learn to farm.

The man's painful bloodshot eyes stared out beneath the shadow of his hat then suddenly he grinned and give the boy's knee a mighty horse bite it hurt a great deal but were kindly intended.

Let me give you some advice Ned. Never had he used the boy's name before. Do you know who were the previous incumbent on your selection?

His name were Mr Peasey he defaulted.

No he effing hung hisself from that old grey box he jumped off the adjectival roof and they didnt find him till the crows ate his adjectival eyes and 1/2 his adjectival brain. Forget your mamma said he. There aint no happiness for neither of us at Eleven Mile Creek.

The man threw the remains of his tea into the fire and began to set his kit together rolling the rum bottles up inside his oilskin coat.

The boy asked But still you'll take me home?

My hand and word to you said he but he did not commit as regards when the promise might be paid.

The boy walked down the horses to remove their hobbles then saddle them and even as the 2 riders and their packhorse finally set off south he imagined they would soon cut down a spur to the west but the country got higher and craggier and the boy seen the man were in no hurry to honour his pledge.

When stopping by a creek to boil the billy the boy showed how his feet were swollen and declared he couldnt continue he must turn back.

Don't worry I'll buy you boots.

I don't need new boots I got bluchers back down home.

Eff the effing bluchers I'll buy you adjectival effing elastic sided boots.

And so the boy were persuaded to follow the great melancholic rump of the man's mare all the way to Toombulup where naturally there were nowhere to buy boots only a broken down shanty the boy were permitted to sleep on its back veranda except he couldnt as the mosquitoes was bad all night long the drinkers roared and boozed and 2 men fought each other on account of a dog being called a runt. When cold dawn arrived at last the boy quietly saddled up the Waler and were about to mount when he received a mighty thump in the middle of his back it sent him falling to a heap upon the rutted track. He turned to discover the source of this malice were the man.

I give you my hand and word said he I'll get your effing boots now get back inside before I knock the effing bark off you.

He grasped the boy's arm escorting him back onto the veranda where he roughly bound his swollen feet in a freshly torn curtain. After each had drunk a cup of sour milk they set off down into the wild bush called the Wombat Ranges. The boy never knew he were being taught the path of his life.

2 days later they was on the plains below with the boy having his 1st view of Myrrhee Station. As they cantered the quails rose out of the grass there was black falcons tiny ground larks the wheeling pink galahs turning silver grey against the morning sky. The winter rains had not yet come and the grass were still as pale as straw but the boy marvelled at the wealth and power of all those endless acres owned by just one man.

Finally the pair come to Wangaratta if the boy had known his horse were listed as stolen in THE POLICE GAZETTE he might of felt different but he were very excited to come to so big a town they stabled their horses at Lardner's Countryman's Hotel it were like a wedding cake 2 storeys high with grand wrought iron along a high veranda. The boy said he were sure they would not permit an Irish boy to enter also his bandaged feet was filthy but the man clapped a hand around his shoulder and marched him up to a fancy desk and there ordered a room for both.

Yes Sir Mr Power says the fellow. The fugitive from Pentridge Gaol were not at all upset to be known by name the opposite. The fellow behind the desk give him a big key with a number on it but the man were in no hurry to use it he 1st took the boy out to the street to remove his bandages and wash his feet with water from the horse trough.

Now said he I promised you some proper boots.

The boy could think of no finer thing but knowing how much boots cost he said he'd rather spend the money on a present for his mother and for this received a powerful clip across the back of the head and then were hauled by the ear across the road to what they call a GENERAL STORE.

Soon the boy were sitting in a purple velvet chair with a cove in a suit and fancy collar attending him yes Sir no Sir Mr Power Sir.

This lad will be wanting a pair of elastic sided boots with Cuban heels.

Very good says the cove taking one of the boy's dirty aching feet to measure very careful with a tape.

Soon he come back with a brown cardboard box marked ARTHUR QUILLER & SON and when the lid were lifted the boy did not dare believe what he saw nestled in the bed of pure white tissue. The cove placed the box on the floor then went away and while the boy were still wondering what he was meant to do the cove returned with a pair of woollen items.

My darling girl your father never knew what he were looking at for he never wore socks in all his life. He sometimes put grass inside his bluchers it had served him well till now. The cove showed him how to arrange the sock correctly and it were a wonder of a thing just to see it turn the corner at the heel. You must not laugh at him for being so simple.

When the cove offered the elastic sided boots the boy pulled them on his feet still painful but them boots was soft and supple as a lady's glove. Lord knows what expression he showed but both the bushranger and shopkeeper was grinning at him and the boy begun to laugh out loud.

And there is your father standing 2 in. taller than he had ever been he were particularly happy.

That night Harry sprung for a mighty feed in the dining room at Lardner's Countryman's Hotel you never saw the likes. There were a crystal cruet and lumps of sugar in a silver dish the twist in Harry's bowels was v. bad but I were hungry so he watched me eat roast beef and Yorkshire pudding then pancakes which the waiter set afire before my eyes. I don't know what it cost but there were no extra tariff for a bath it were superior even to the Sheltons' tub in Avenel for you only had to turn a spigot and steaming water poured forth without relent. I soaked until my skin were wrinkly as a prune.

I was woken in the middle of the night Harry were crashing around drunk and when he fell onto his bed I did not mind the snoring. It were my final night as his apprentice tomorrow I would be home again telling my family everything I seen. In the dark I checked beneath the bed to feel the boots and in the morning I wore them very proudly to a breakfast of porridge and kedgeree a bottle of black sauce on every table.

Our horses was fed and watered by a fellow called an OSTLER and when I come out to find the dear old Waler all I had to do were put my new boot into the stirrup it was a crisp clear morning not yet 8 o'clock we rode together out of Wangaratta at the end of habitation there were a sign pointing home to Greta.

Here I bade Harry farewell I were the oldest boy there was work to do at home I told him the Land Act was a b————r of a thing they would take our land away if we did not comply.

Well I'm a b————r too said Harry Power and you must comply with me.

But you give your hand and word that I could go home.

Very well then give me back them boots.

Very well I pulled the boots off and hurled them on the track then I turned the Waler's head for home but Harry were very fast for his weight he was suddenly upon the ground holding my horse by the bridle I didnt care just dug my heels into the Waler's flank but the Waler wouldnt budge he knew who were the master in every way.

This is my horse said Harry Power.

I swung down off the saddle saying I did not need his adjectival horse I would walk home in my socks and if he wished the socks then I'd go barefoot he could not prevent me.

He said he would not advise me to return home as my mother would be angry.

I laughed out loud I said he were a liar but was unsettled to notice something akin to sympathy were showing in his yellow eyes. You come with me he said its what your mater wants and all you got to do is hold the horses.

What you're saying don't make sense said I. My ma can't run that selection by herself the government will take our land off her.

Well your ma has other sources of support it seems.

How do you mean?

He shrugged unhappily and seeing his sadness I knew he meant Bill Frost the boundary rider and then I believed him. I were poleaxed. My father were lost just 2 yr. before and I didnt deserve to lose a mother too not even if I had offended her she should not cast me out.

Harry were holding out the boots to me and in the end what was I to do?

Soon I were following the bushranger down south once more following the King River towards the higher country. There was a crisp refreshing breeze and the sky was pure and blue but I were now a boy without a home my mood lower than the water in the King and all the land around me seemed set to share my feelings. Where forest had been cleared the grass were eaten to the roots the soil beneath a dry grey sand and every time I seen a cockatoo fence or a ringbarked tree or any signs of a selector's labour then I felt a great grief rise up my windpipe.

We rode all day late that afternoon Harry chose a camping place just off the track it were nothing but a dusty little knoll with scant feed for the horses. He began to make himself a mia mia such as the blackfellows build from saplings and fallen bark but soon lost patience with it kicking it apart so it were left to me to go deep in the bush to peel a great green sheet of stringybark. So were a shelter properly constructed. Next I shot a kangaroo then butchered it and took the ramrod from his carbine threading on the meat fat lean fat lean fat just as my da had taught me. I were very low.

Harry praised the mia mia he said the roasted meat were delicious but in the night he found his bowel were v. badly twisted he went out into the bush I heard him cry every foul word you could imagine thus must the outcast cry in Hell.

There were sheet lightning but no thunder I slept very badly thinking how Bill Frost stole my land. Picaninny dawn were dry and dewless I woke to such a pain of homesickness that I cooked Harry johnnycakes and brung him his billy tea before giving him any particular attention. He had his 3 pistols and carbine laid out on the horse blanket and were measuring gunpowder from a patent flask.

Now look here young Kelly.

As he rammed home the ball and wadding I observed his general shine his beard were washed his eyes were peeled and lively. Now see here we'll get you a nice gift to take home to your mamma.

I thought he were referring to the remaining kangaroo meat.

Let Bill Frost shoot her an adjectival kangaroo.

Harry lay down his pistol he stood and tied a red handkerchief round his thick neck he said we was about to do something Bill Frost could never do. Jesus boy he said thrusting his pistol in his belt I'll send you home an effing hero.

You said she don't want me home no more.

No I never said that.

Not liking to have my feelings played with I asked what my mother really said he pushed me away I shoved him in the chest and faster than the human eye he snatched his hobble belt out from his pants and brought it cracking down around my naked arm.

You want a lashing lad said he begob don't you never do that again.

I wouldnt let him see how much it hurt.

Now said he you go take off the hobbles and saddle up the horses then you'll get them packs onto the pony.

The pain was bad it were a considerable effort not to cry I said I would not be his slave but it were a weak rebellion and he knew it. He threaded his belt back into his pants then took a steel comb from his pocket and begun to preen himself. And you'll effing do it tomorrow said he and the day after that and you'll be effing proud to do it too you aint some barefoot Irish mutt no more you're Harry Power's offsider.

You said she didnt want me home no more.

By the 5 crosses I'll whip you till you can't sit down now listen when I talk to you you'll break up that mia mia and pack the camp then you'll keep them horses all quiet and steady and watch the show.

I don't know what show you mean.

Harry didnt reply but I were soon aware of the thundering of hooves from the direction of Whitfield he urgently buckled up his coat thrusting 3 pistols in its belt.

The show is called Dick Turpin said he then strolled down to the track his hair was oiled his grey beard combed and he stood astride the centre of the roadway with his sawn off carbine in his hand he were the very picture of a bushranger.

I listened to a coach labouring up the last of the hill the driver shouting the whip cracking. Just hold them horses Ned cried Harry. A moment later a bright red coach come round the bend my heart were pounding in my chest all my anger suddenly abandoned. Bail up cried the famous Harry Power taking a pistol from his belt and firing it into the air then our packhorse reared and lurched dragging me 1/2 across the clearing towards the road and while I struggled I heard the coach brakes bite in a great screaming noise of steel on wood and my Waler reared and whinnied.

The air was filled with dust and panic. Throw down your gold I'm Harry Power.

I calmed the packhorse and the Waler but my own blood were stirred something awful. Throw down the effing gold cried Harry and I knew we would be rich and were v. happy.

There aint no adjectival gold said a dirt dry voice I peered out through the wattle fronds and seen Hiram Crawford's gleaming Yankee Coach still rocking on its queasy springs a tall thin stick of colonial driver were staring down through the settling dust.

Harry pointed his one inch muzzleloader directly at the driver's shirt. I will blow your effing innards out.

But the driver were a Beechworth man named Coady he were one of them fools so frequent in the bush he'd rather die than be impressed by anyone he spat a wad of baccy juice down on the dust. There still won't be any adjectival gold said he hello mate watch out this fellow thinks he's Harry Power.

This 2nd remark were addressed to a lone rider who come ambling around the corner from the other direction.

Who might you be demanded Harry of the newcomer.

I'm Woodside from Happy Valley.

Well Squatter Woodside you is being bailed up you will take the bag of gold from this driver here and throw it at my feet.

I told him said the driver there aint no adjectival gold.

I'm Harry Power cried Harry and I say there is.

I don't care if you're the Duke of Gloucester said the driver there aint no gold mate and no amount of hollering is going to change that.

Eff you roared Harry firing the muzzleloader by design or accident decapitating a crow which had been innocently loitering by the road. The explosion alarmed my nervous packhorse so severely that it now went plunging out onto the open road with me clinging to the reins scratching my face in the wattle all I could think was I was now marked as a robber a woman inside the coach were staring directly at me.

I persuaded the horse back behind the screen of wattles then cleaned the mess of bloody bird off my new boots and by the time there were an opportunity to assess the progress of the holdup the mailbags was all lying on the road their sides slit open Harry kneeled beside them enquiring of their contents.

You might be better off to try the parcels suggested Mr Woodside his helpful attitude perhaps produced by the fear that his horse might be taken from him. It were a very spirited and well bred beast.

There is only 2 parcels said Coady but thats registered mail in the blue bag I must say the last cove to stick me up was well satisfied with what he found in there.

Give me the parcels.

But they was a disappointment the 1st containing lace and the 2nd an English clock the discovery of which produced a bout of threats and curses against that country and what Harry would do to the English when he had a moment free he must of scared the panties off the passengers for now they begun shouting there was a Chinaman amongst their number this celestial gentleman were pushed out onto the road he stood before Harry Power clasping a carpetbag.

You a miner?

The Chinaman were certainly a miner his physique very close to Power that is v. broad with sturdy legs.

No miner I givee money 10 shillings he dug into a purse and removed some coins he held them up to Harry.

Gold demanded Harry he thrust his empty carbine in his belt then drew a Bowie knife which he opened with his teeth he advanced on the Chinaman with the pistol in his left hand the knife in the right.

The Chinaman were very brave a credit to his race. 10 shillings you take.

Blast your yellow heart cried Harry lunging out with his dagger.

The Chinaman danced deftly away as Harry sliced the carpetbag and lo it were as if it were a bag of wheat or seedpod a great harvest of glass marbles poured forth onto the road there was agates & cat's eyes & bloodreels & twisters & lemon swirls & tombowlers & glass eyes spilling out and rolling still amongst the dust beneath the horses' hooves. Of gold no trace.

Bad bad howled the Chinaman I kill you b-----d but Harry kicked him in the shins and drove him back inside the coach at gunpoint.

There Harry somehow lost his spirit for he never even got the other passengers and once the coach and the squatter was sent on their different ways Harry called me out onto the road to show me all the marbles spread across the hard dry earth.

There you are lad help yourself.

These will make me a hero?

Harry's hand went to his belt but of course it supported his pistols and he could not easily withdraw it as before.

Just pick up the adjectival marbles he said wearily I did so and that was the moment by the law I made myself a bushranger as well.

I were but 14 1/2 yr. old no razor had yet touched my upper lip but as I cantered after Harry Power my pockets crammed with marbles I were already travelling full tilt towards the man I would become. Harry rode in the old style leaning so far backwards at the jumps that he must of born the mark of the crupper on his spine. For my part I rode with short stirrups standing at a gallop leaning forward when jumping the fallen timber. We was Past & Future we was Innocence & Age riding very hard till Whitfield where we relieved a poor selector of a bucket of oats. All through the middle of the day we pushed the horses up the track to Toombulup we never saw a soul not even at the shanty where Harry had tore the curtains. Here we cut down through the bush into the Wombat Ranges and slowed our pace considerably as the horses was tired and the bush v. dense there was more and more wild ravines the mighty white gums they was saplings when Jesus were a boy. Not until almost dusk did we amble into a shallow valley with a little creek but 18 in. wide and on its banks amongst a field of bracken stood a drear and eyeless hut constructed from thick logs. The crows were cawing and in that mournful light it give me a bad feeling straight away.

Home said Harry.

The hut were as hard and dark as a govt. lockup with its lack of windows it looked very weak and as easily preyed upon as a blind worm. Hobbling his horse Power set the poor beast to grazing in the bracken then asked what did I think of the place.

I told him his horse would be useless if he didnt provide it better feed. There were no warning of his response a blinding whack across the head.

You will learn said he staring at me with his red and yellow eyes you will learn to leave your awful ignorance behind then you will see I know more about feeding horses than if you survive to be 100 which I doubt you will. This little hut is a thing of beauty do you see that yet?

I do I do.

You are a liar you don't yet know what it can do for you but you will wash your mouth with soap and water and say to me Harry you let me off that day when I were ranting like a mongrel about things I knew nothing of.

Yet for all the pain he caused his tone of voice were becoming almost kindly although arriving at the door he did pronounce one more lecture.

Let me tell you Your Ignorance said he I have been hunted by every trap from Wangaratta to Benalla and Beechworth besides and none of them can find their way around the Wombat Ranges.

Then he struck his lucifer upon his shoe and the dreadful looking hole were thus illuminated it were airless with the sour evidence of mice who have found food and blankets and think themselves in a position to begin a family.

Harry set about making his camp in what I would soon know were characteristic fashion kicking aside old grog bottles shaking a dead baby bush rat from inside a folded blanket then he reached up into the dark space between the walls and ceiling beams to find some candles.

This here is Bullock Creek my friend and I will tell you now it won't never betray you. I know all your mates are fine fellows but there aint one that cannot be purchased by the police when the price is right and women will grow weary of you farting in their beds and dogs make good company but then they die. This old hut said he has timber 2 ft. thick do you know what that means?

It is slow to rot?

Harry then drew his pistol from his belt I were expecting him to show me where to hang or hide it but instead he fired there were a bright flash a deafening roar and with my ears still ringing he held the candle and showed where the lead was swallowed.

Its bulletproof said he now is that not an effing wonder to your eyes? We might be Ali Baba do you know the tale? Briefly Ali Baba had a cave and had to put up with the inconveniences. It is very hard to find a dry cave where you can also light a fire and the chimney draws decently in all weathers but this hut is a fortress you can hold off an army if they ever find you.

There is people who will say Harry were a mighty bushman and some like my mother would say he werent a bushman's bootlace and it is true he could not feed himself or even clean his teeth but he had more bolt-holes than a family of foxes he had secret caves and mia mias and hollow trees throughout the North East of the colony of Victoria and I were destined to sleep in all too many of them.

And here you grasp a new aspect to his character for there were a squalor of debris yes but only at the surface and in the dark corners of

Bullock Creek you'd find tallow candles & canned sardines & flour & gunpowder all neatly packed. Above Reedy Creek he had a crib cunningly wrought from green saplings and tin and burlap.

Some of these boltholes was newly established but there were no other that he trusted so absolutely as this evil place on Bullock Creek where he showed me his secret weapon 2 cwt. of oats in 2 steel drums.

Here Your Ignorance said he you may feed the horses. So I fitted them with their nosebags and they was very happy then I cooked the old b————r a sweet mottled johnnycake which he praised. He called me a good boy and I were pleased to see this gentler character and I were also happy and for a while forgot Bill Frost had thrown me off my own land.

When the dishes was washed I asked him would he tell me the story of Ali Baba.

I'll do better said Harry you sit over there where the wall slopes in a little and I will tell you the story of how James Whitty got his acres. I done what he directed while he stuffed his pipe full with smelly tobacco and then he lit and tamped it with his hard black thumb.

This all happened he said on account of a bag of marbles like the ones you gained today.

At this mention I let out a sudden bitter laugh.

Harry paused for a moment I thought he would beat me but he did no more than wag his pipe.

You listen young'un said he and we'll see who is laughing at the end. When Mr James Whitty arrived in Beveridge he were as poor as your da and ma he had not a pot to piss in but one dark rainy night the Devil appeared as he were riding home along the adjectival Melbourne road.

Is this a true story?

Shut your hole and listen if you doubt the Devil then you've no more nous than James Whitty neither did he credit it at 1st. Did I say it were raining?

You did.

Rain and wind and he were probably 1/2 shicker as well he had been drinking at Danny Morgan's Hotel so when he hears the Devil talking he thinks its Eddie Wilson or Lurch O'Hanlon or one of them but he couldnt hear no horses so he rides up the hill listening to the Devil who I suppose were flying through the air beside old Whitty's ear.

Did he have an Irish voice?

What do you mean?

When the Devil spoke were he Irish?

Jesus boy just listen to the tale for soon the Devil appears before him so Whitty asks what does he want and the Devil says why nothing not a thing. Thats good says Whitty because I want nothing from you no road and puts his spur into the horse's flank meaning to ride on but a horse has not the power to pass the Devil she will not budge. You are wrong says the Devil when you say you want nothing off me because there is something you want off me awful bad and with this he produces a leather purse and offers it to Whitty.

It were marbles?

Don't interrupt said he Whitty don't cast the purse away from him even though it were the Devil done the offering. Whats in here then he asks the Devil.

Its marbles says the Devil.

Says Whitty what would I want with a bag of adjectival marbles?

The Devil tells him he has only to throw one of them marbles through a certain window and he will be granted any wish he cares to make.

Being a farmer Whitty's a hard one with a bargain so his 1st question is about the cost.

Well says the Devil it is by way of being free. For as long as you live I collect naught. The price will be payable only upon death which will be of no concern for you. Fair enough says old Whitty that sounds very nice but what if you can't give what I wish? Then there is no charge says the Devil but there were never a wish I could not grant. Here take this purse and if ever you want something you can throw one of the marbles through the window of St. Mary's Church in Beveridge.

I know that church Harry I been there.

Hadnt Whitty's own children been baptised there? Said Whitty to the Devil them are stained glass windows in that church one for every station of the cross. Yes said the Devil thats the church I mean and so they shook hands.

What were the Devil's hands like?

Cold and slimy but thats not the point at all for pretty soon old Whitty found himself coveting a choice bit of river frontage though with no hope of getting it on account of the villainy of the squatters and their stooges. So one dark night he rides into Beveridge and throws his marble through the 1st window he takes the nose off Jesus Christ Himself and the broken glass hardly hits the floor inside before the Devil come out from one of them miserable pine trees the priests all like to plant about their churches. The Devil couldnt be happier he asks old Whitty what it is he wants and Whitty says he wants a particular grant of land telling the Devil the parish and the lot number which the Devil writes down in a blue lined exercise book. Very well says the Devil go to the Post Office next Thursday afternoon.

5 days later Whitty goes to the Beveridge P.O. and theres the title to the land he wanted all right and proper in a brown govt. envelope O.H.M.S. so all is hunky dory as far as Whitty is concerned and for him there is no looking back. For 11 yr. he gets whatever land he wishes until he has 10,000 acres and 3 famous Angus bulls. For all this he has broken the window of Simon the Cyrenian and the one of Veronica wiping Jesus' face and the stripping of His clothes and the nailing of the Saviour on the cross.

But finally he is struck down by pleurisy and he gets in a terrible panic and confesses all to the wife and weeping and hollering he is going to Hell and nothing can be done. Lucky it is for him but his wife is a Tipperary woman and therefore very capable. Stop snivelling says she and tell me have you got any marbles remaining. Just the one says he I could not bear to damage the body in the tomb. Very well says she getting him out of his bed and into the dray and off they go to Beveridge him coughing and shaking with his rattle. They come down that hill so fast you would think the horse a runaway but no. At the church there is some doubt as to whether the dying man has the strength to break the Ascension but he makes a good shot in spite of everything and takes the Lord out through his Sacred Heart. Soon as this is done the Devil appears as pleased as punch for he has been hearing this rattle these last 4 hours. So says he I see you are ready to come to me. Not so adjectival fast says old Whitty you owe me one more wish you b————r. Suit yourself says the Devil but to judge from that cough you'll be mine before the day is out. We'll see about that says Whitty if you can't grant my wish why then I'm bound for Heaven. If I can't grant your wish says the Devil you're a man more clever than I know you to be.

Well said Harry the Devil were correct enough but didnt reckon with Whitty's wife who were hiding behind a nearby hydrangea bush and when Whitty makes his last request of the Devil its to ask for what the wife figured out. Did I say she were from Tipperary?

You did.

She were from Tipperary as clever as a fox she told her husband what to say.

Said Whitty to the Devil I want you to make honest men of lawyers.

Now as you know the Devil is a coal black thing and he does not have skin but scales so when he hears what Whitty asks those scales turn pale the colour of this ash here. I can't do that says the Devil. O you must says Whitty. I can't says the Devil if I did that I would be idle from one week's end to the next and never a coal to warm myself.

That is the story Harry told me in the bolthole in the Wombat Ranges. At the time I assumed Mr Whitty must of passed into the next world but I were mistaken as before too many years were passed I had the pleasure of meeting him at the Moyhu Races but that as they say is another story.

Annie's wedding were in April and now we was near the end of May so the rains had come and the injured country were turning green. As we travelled place to place about our business I seen docks and dandelions emerging in much of the newly cleared land. Had I been in my rightful place I would of recruited Jem and Maggie and even Dan to work with hoe and hand until the pest were defeated for a dairy farm cannot afford the flavour of the dandelion. Many a wet autumn night I fretted Bill Frost had neglected this particular work and I lay in a mia mia or hut or cave swearing that night were my last with Harry but in the chilly morning found myself once more collecting blackberry roots and boiling them to make the infusion for his bowels. Once more I would scour the battered frying pan with river sand once more endure those whispering lies the deceitful mouth glistening with breakfast juices offering promises of gold what spoils I would take home when the time were come.

So I were still Harry's offsider when he robbed the Buckland Coach on the 22nd of May and I were that nameless person reported as Power's Mate who dropped the tree across the road I held the horses so Harry could go about his trade.

Bail up he cried that day. Bail up you effing b-----d.

As chance would have it the coachman had heard this speech before you may recall his name were Coady a lanky fellow as dry and sarcastic as they come.

Well look who's here said he dropping the reins into his lap and reaching straight away for his tobacco pouch.

Harry were standing on a cutting some 6 ft. above the road.

You mongrel he cried and slid down the cutting on his backside waving his pistols in the air. At the sight of this charging dervish Coady quickly changed his tune and by the time Harry were beside the coach Coady's baccy pouch had been replaced by his purse which he held out ready to deliver. Harry didnt count the contents only threw it on the ground to collect later.

Get down cried he get down. You too he told the passenger beside Coady this were a stocky butcher his striped apron still visible beneath his oilskin coat.

All I've got is 10/6 said the butcher holding out the coins in his square white hands I changed my last quid to buy the coachfare.

Harry took the money anyway. All out he cried you is being stuck up.

The coach door slowly opened and out come 2 females and a young boy. The older of the females were a plump matron of some 30 yr. she unclasped her purse to produce a 10/– note and 3 florins.

Thank you Ma'am says Harry dropping the money into his pocket I'll take that pretty necklace too.

The woman had been previously excited about the prospect of being bailed up but when she seen she were to lose her jewellery her face fell she bowed her head so the boy could unhook her necklace. I were wondering she said as she watched her treasure disappear into Harry's pocket I were wondering could I have a shilling back I'll need to send a telegram.

He must of give her more than a shilling for her face brightened considerably and she made a little bow.

This emboldened the 2nd female who said she had no money at all though she would gladly give it all if she did.

The boy then stepped forward and gave threepence.

I were watching this scene in some despair for I could see little good would follow from this robbery but as Harry give back the boy his threepence I witnessed a rider trotting up the road. She were a very well dressed young woman riding sidesaddle on a chestnut mare 16 hands a white blaze on its forehead 20 guineas would not buy you such a creature. Harry had promised me a new animal for the Waler were gone lame.

Bail up I am Harry Power.

O Mr Power said the owner of the horse I am sorry to disappoint you but I have come out without a farthing on me.

In this you will say she were behaving no different than the other women except her voice were different her accent were all Englishified in other words she took a certain tone.

Dismount roared Harry.

Would you assist me please says she.

Assist your adjectival self says he.

She did so rather smartly and in a moment were standing beside her splendid horse her face v. red with embarrassment.

Now aint it wondrous strange said Harry addressing all the gathered passengers aint it very queer to see a filly like this in the company of an empty purse. I do believe that is the queerest combination since the Queen of England took an adjectival German to her bed.

With respect said the butcher.

Shut your gob butcher.

But the butcher were a plucky chap and he jutted his chin at Harry and continued.

With respect this is Miss Boyd she's a poor schoolteacher she aint got 2 bob to rub together.

Jesus butcher you think I am a fool?

I heard you never robbed the poor.

Poor! Look at her adjectival saddle man a saddle like that is worth 14 quid. Since when does poor women have 14 quid saddles?

Not unless.

Unless what? You should be very careful butcher talking back to Harry Power is a dangerous occupation.

I aint talking back said he but his colour were rising and he planted himself opposite the bushranger with his legs astride I'm just pointing out that saddles like this is often won in raffles but perhaps having been elsewhere you were not aware.

Elsewhere?

I read you was away.

You mean PUT AWAY you mongrel.

No offence but I heard you was in prison I know that aint your fault but they are raffling saddles only recent like.

Even from my distance I seen Harry were uncertain he couldnt tell were he being gammoned or no.

Well said he what about the horse did she win her in a raffle too?

At this crucial moment come a loud cooee from up the road there then appeared one more punter a tall red headed Irishman with no other wealth apparent but a walking stick cut from ironbark root. Harry had him turn his pockets out but they was empty too and the traveller were then sent to stand with the other prisoners gathered around Miss Boyd and that horse I was now imagining my own. I were expecting Harry to effect this transaction when a Chinaman arrived also on foot followed shortly behind by a dairyman from Whorouly who were riding a poor & broken nag of no use to anyone. Harry robbed them both apologising as he done so with his little speech about how he were forced to crime I will not trouble you with it here.

By the time the celestial handed over his money Harry had taken a grand sum of £3 while Coady had lit a little fire beside the track and there were now a total of 9 prisoners huddled around the flames all waiting to see how they would be disposed of.

Now said Harry to Mrs Boyd will you swear on the Bible that you is the teacher?

She eagerly performed this perjury as were later reported in THE ENSIGN for she were Miss Phoebe Martin Boyd the niece of a wealthy squatter a valued customer of Allan Joyce the butcher.

I swear on the Bible of King James.

Very well said Harry it aint my business to rob a poor teacher I'll take the lead horse off the coach.

It were one of those days where nothing will go right. The lead horse were not prepared to be his servant so Harry chose the brown sniphorse that is the offside wheeler from the coach. It were a serviceable enough animal but broken in its spirit.

And it were the selection of the sniphorse which resulted in my being seen by Dr J.P. Rowe the squatter from Mount Battery Station.

May 23rd fell cold and dark there were no moon. I stood on the front veranda of a shanty in the Oxley shire but it gave no protection from the bitter wind the heavy rain were in my face and splashing off the muddy floor. I did severely miss the sweet dry fug of my home but I were still Power's unpaid dogsbody ordered to keep the watch for policemen although God only knows how the traps could of reached us in this torrent the King River Bridge were 2 ft. under and groaning in the current. I were v. tired and fed up with my life.

The poor sniphorse off the Buckland Coach were sheltering with me under the veranda she had been fired on by the squatter Dr Rowe and were now wounded. It were Harry's fault there were no reason to take her from that dull and honest coachhorse life her great heart pounding on the daily climb up the mountains the drear cycle of ceaseless labour must seem sweet enough to her now. She had taken the bullet high in her shoulder and when she cooled would certainly be lame for good. Thence only death a sledgehammer between her blindfolded eyes such is life.

Inside the shanty were much laughing and singing the shadows flitting across the curtains. Harry Power were dancing I heard not a word about the bunions he otherwise were whingeing about night and day. I never knew a man to make such a fuss about his feet. Feet & bowels never ceasing bowels & feet. My 1st job each soggy morning were to find them blackberry roots for his bowels thank Jesus he ministered to his smelly bunions by himself. He had a red string with 7 knots he must wind in a particular way around his inflamed joint then recite the following:

> Bone to bone blood to blood
> And every sinew in its proper place

The sniphorse pissed forlornly on the muddy floor I could smell bacon frying inside the shanty but none had been sent out to me. I were working myself into a temper on this point when the door swung open it were Harry Power holding a red hot coal in a pair of blacksmith's tongs. Beside him come the landlord's big chested wife she had narrow hips like a boy and very pretty hands in which she carried a sugar bowl. She were tipsy laughing pretending to fall against the famous bushranger.

Hold the horse Ned Kelly said he I did not thank him that he used my name in front of witnesses. Only 2 days previous he had caused Dr Rowe of Mount Battery Station to clearly see my face. We was lying on the rock above his paddock looking for a more spirited replacement for the sniphorse. Rowe were a cunning old fox he crept up beside us and let off a shot which kicked up the dust in front of my nose. I would of surrendered there and then but were more afraid of Harry than of the squatter thus we made this mad rush riding 2 days into the face of the storm arriving on this veranda drenched to the bone I were whipped and cut across the face by myall scrub my lip consequently swollen as if I had been thrashed.

Now the landlord's wife give Harry Power the sugar he sprinkled it onto the red hot coal.

Hold the effing horse he says to me.

I took the bridle while Harry encouraged the smoking coal to pass over the horse's wound I had seen this remedy practised by the Quinns and Lloyds but Harry were drunk so he placed the coal too near the skin I could smell the burning hair. The 1st time she were burnt the horse kicked but the 2nd time she reared and I couldnt hold her she broke through the bark roof of the veranda. Of this damage to the shanty Harry seemed oblivious. There he said that'll fix you girl. That were a lie because the ball were buried too deep it had gone to a place no smoke could reach.

To me he said he would soon send out some tucker.

I'll come inside said I.

O you will will you?

There aint no point in watching here I said unless the traps is coming in an adjectival ship.

For answer I got a mighty clout across the head I took a swing back at him. This he would not brook he grabbed me by the bawbles.

You want to fight me boy?

No Harry.

While the landlady watched he squeezed my bawbles till I could not help but cry out with pain and having wrung that humiliation from me he turned his back and took his girlfriend back inside. I calmed down the frightened horse swearing this would be my last adventure with the famous Harry Power.

By and by the door opened it werent Harry the stranger were more like a farmer with his powerful sloping shoulders and heavy arms but he bore no greater burden than a glass of liquor which he offered though I never liked the smell.

Too strong for you boy? He were a so called HANDSOME MAN a neat beard framing his naked face. You want some lemonade in it?

He were watching me very close a smile playing round his lips so I sipped to show I could of drunk it if I wished.

Your ma is very partial to that drink I'm sure you know it.

I might.

Very partial said he.

All my childhood there were always some man thought he could tell stories about my mother he rested his back against the veranda post and grinned. You know Bill Frost?

I admitted the connection.

Thats a chap who is awful partial to his rum and cloves. He made it sound so dirty I were embarrassed laying my face against the mare's cold wet neck and stroking her but still the man would not cease.

You been absent from home a little while I hear.

It were not his nosey business where I been I did not say nothing.

Perhaps you aint heard your mother's news.

I werent going to be drawn by his familiarity.

Your ma has been busy baking said he.

Thats good.

Good for Bill Frost he said for he's the chap what put the bun inside her oven.

My fist went up into his gut before I knew what I were doing I felt his very entrails part to accommodate my hand and smelled the air push out him it were sour as week old pollard mash he were a big fellow 12 or 13 stone but he staggered back with his mouth open like a Murray cod. I hated him I spat in his face pushing him out in the rain he stumbled and I rode him like a pig down into the mud and out into the woodpile as he wailed and hollered out for help I cried I would kill him if he ever said her name again.

From the corner of my eye I seen the door open and Harry come across the veranda his great bull neck thrust forward he were keen to damage me. The sniphorse recognised her torturer and let out a high whinny pulling violently against her reins which I had tied to the veranda post. Harry Power stooped for a stick of firewood I saw it in his hand I did not care.

The post give way at the floor as the horse backed out into the rain pulling the pivoting pole along while Harry Power begun to whale into me with the firewood belabouring me about the kidneys I did not feel a thing instead I got the Handsome Man's arm behind his back his face down in the mud.

The horse could not escape but were bucking and kicking in a fright-ful manner her hooves was death her eye panicked white no one dare go near. It were her made me release the gossip not a bit of Harry. They both watched as I spoke to the poor trembling creature she permitted me to untangle her and then lead her down into the yard.

The downpour meanwhile increased it were very loud but could not prevent me hearing Harry Power apologising. Enough light spilled from the shanty for me to see the Handsome Man were seated bowlegged heavy with mud as if he had fouled himself. When I come back from the yard he retreated he would never speak so casually of my mother again. When I turned to Harry his thumbs was in his belt beside his guns.

Come here said he.

He's going to shoot me I thought but followed. One minute I were a warrior the next stumbling down into the rainy dark like a poor scouring beast on its way to slaughter explain that if you will. I come down the side of a steep gully beyond even the pale yellow illumination from the shanty here Harry put his hand upon my shoulder and I stopped. I could feel the water flowing around my ankles it might as well been around my heart.

Give me the boots.

I obeyed and felt the gluey wet clay puddle at my feet at length understanding that he had gone away. I were dismissed.

My mother were sitting up in the hut at Eleven Mile Creek she had already covered the fire with ash to keep its life for the morning but now something kept her from her bed and she remained seated on a low 3 legged stool her legs out straight her large hands resting on her pinny.

Mother were still a handsome woman her hair as glossy as a crow's feathers the light of the hearth dancing in the sheen. She could of gone to sleep but instead she were brushing her hair again and when 200 strokes were done she started braiding and when the braid was woven she pulled it into a bun and now her head felt tight as a drum and she could not go to bed. She remained before the ash banked fire and her children filled the hut with their cold breath the mice rustling in the wall behind the pasted layers of THE BENALLA ENSIGN.

When the rain relented it were very quiet nothing louder than the tatt tatt of the leaking roof above the table but my mother's handsome head tilted listening to something else. She says it were worry about the level of the creek that finally drew her outside not nothing superstitious. She knocked the pegs out of the door then picked up the lantern and in her long nightdress walked through the dead ringbarked gums they was ghosts of trees their sappy trunks now dry as bones. The kangaroo dogs was silent but circling on their chains.

As my mother held up the lantern I were many miles away limping along the road in stolen boots I could see no more road than a smudge of charcoal in the blackness.

My mother picked up her hems coming down to inspect the flood her bluchers leaden with mud and manure but all that were soon washed clean off them for the creek had risen rapidly insinuating itself across the track to claim the oats.

It must of been after midnight when I left the road now travelling through grasslands my hands ahead of me no idea where on earth I stood. My mother returned to the hut but still did not take her bed. When she imagined hearing Mr Pawson's goat bleating she once again knocked the pegs from the door and went outside with the lantern. There was no goats to be heard or seen.

She were about to go back inside when she seen a shadow at 1st she thought it a savage but looking hard she made out an old white woman wearing a red dress.

Are you lost dearie my mother called but the woman paid her little mind she were no taller than the pigpen which is to say less than 3 ft. in height.

Who do you want called my mother all the skin on her body raised in bumps her braided hair straining against the fright of her scalp.

No answer.

Who are you? But she knew already it were the Banshee she retreated to her door so her children would be safe behind her.

Who do you want?

The Banshee made no answer my mother had been told from her youngest years that you must not interfere with the Death Messenger and she knew of the man whose hand were burnt and the one held against the wall of his cottage all night long and she knew an hour's luck never shone on anyone who molested a Banshee but she were in another country far from where the Banshee should of been so when she held up her lantern then the Banshee turned away and give a kind of shiver as you see in them with bad tempered natures. She were an ugly old crone but now she revealed her long and golden hair which she set about combing as if to soothe herself. My mother knew all the stories of the comb she knew the bone comb & steel comb & comb of gold & now she witnessed the dread implement move through the hair and knew the thing to do were get into bed and shut her eyes but my mother were a Quinn and this were not her character.

You tell me who you want my mother shouted.

I were far away walking across the grassy flats knowing nothing of what was transpiring but I can locate the time exactly as you will soon see.

Said my ma Its Ned aint it? Its my little Neddy that you want.

The Banshee didnt answer so my mother took up the splitting axe Jem had left laying against the door and she swung it in both hands like a Scotsman then sent it whooshing through the dark towards her.

At this very moment I were north of Crooked Crossing as it were called. I heard the Banshee cry. It were not what they say it were not like a vixen fox but a dreadful shriek that would turn a strong man's bowels to water it filled the whole vault of the heavens. I lay down on the dark earth with my hands across my ears feeling the clay quiver beneath me and even when the noise were gone I didnt move but lay on the cold ground as it sucked the warmth out of my blood. I did not move until the dawn when I stood up I were stiff and grey as if I myself was turned to clay. I went to the end of the gully where Tom Buckley lived he had built a pitch roof over the hollow stump of a giant gum and thereby constructed a very pretty house. I opened the door it were very dark a miner's cottage with many shelves and everything in its proper place all except the owner who I immediately saw lying in the middle of the floor one leg folded underneath. He were dressed in the uniform of some foreign king I don't know why. The uniform were very old and Tom Buckley dead an old bachelor and no wife or child to mourn him. Not knowing what to do I borrowed his horse and set off for home as fast as I could go.

When our brave parents was ripped from Ireland like teeth from the mouth of their own history and every dear familiar thing had been abandoned on the docks of Cork or Galway or Dublin then the Banshee come on board the cursed convict ships the ROLLA and the TELICHERRY and the RODNEY and the PHOEBE DUNBAR and there were not an English eye could see her no more than an English eye can picture the fire that will descend upon that race in time to come. The Banshee sat herself at the bow and combed her hair all the way from Cork to Botany Bay she took passage amongst our parents beneath that foreign flag 3 crosses nailed one atop the other.

In the colony of Victoria my parents witnessed the slow wasting of St. Brigit though my mother made the straw crosses for the lambing and followed all Grandma Quinn's instructions it were clear St. Brigit had lost her power to bring the milk down from the cows' horn. The beloved saint withered in Victoria she could no longer help the calving and thus slowly passed from our reckoning.

But the Banshee were thriving like blackberry in the new climate she were with us when ice were on the puddles and when all the plains from Benalla to Wangaratta was baked hard as Hell. Even when the bush quivered in a eucalyptus haze the angry flies droning without relent the Banshee would not go home and her combs was at different times reported in Avenel and Benalla and Euroa and beneath the new bridges on the Melbourne road.

When I heard the Banshee wail I never doubted what it were and once on Tom Buckley's pony I galloped home all the time praying no one in my family had been took. I tore a switch from an Ovens wattle and drove the gelding brutally the golden blossom broke and lay like salt across his bleeding flanks.

It were a shock to finally see the home I had dreamed of so many lonely nights for now it appeared v. small its bark roof swaybacked all around it broken grey tree trunks some standing others fallen. It were a wet winter morning the creek raging there were low grey cloud and a threatening cold wind off the mountains. I witnessed a great kind of desolation such as I had not remembered there were not a crow or magpie not a butcher bird sitting on a fence. In the silence I were certain the Banshee had been about her deadly business and I pushed the horse along the flooded track fearing for Mother's life.

The creek were too high for the pony so I removed the boots and walked across the fallen log it were still our only bridge.

The dogs begun to bark then I saw our Gracie she were 4 yr. old and running screaming from behind the pig house it were a moment before I realised she were larking. Then come our broad strong Maggie calling Gracie Gracie I'm going to tan your hide.

And then Jem come up from behind the peppercorn he had grew 2 in. since I seen him last he were broad and strapping his feet were bare and muddy his dark eyes gleaming to see me home again and I knew no one were dead.

My mother followed walking with her left hand rested against her stomach the way a woman does when another heart is beating in her womb. This were Bill Frost's improvement nothing else. No bridge no more land cleared and the pastures filled with docks and dandelions it broke my heart to see them yellow flowers.

My mother said Where's Harry?

All around our feet was abandoned logs the mother and son once cut together with the crosscut saw.

And how is Harry said she is he well? She did not demonstrate none of her feelings towards me. In truth she had been more forthcoming with the Banshee.

Old Tom Buckley's dead he's lying in the middle of his hut.

She crossed herself then put her hands on both of my shoulders feeling that all my bones was solid and correct. She smiled at me. You've got strong aint ye?

You'll see.

What will you do Son?

I come home to work around the property.

My ma began to silently shift the metal pins around her hair.

I won't argue with Bill Frost I said if thats what you're worried about I won't glower at him or nothing.

Gracie wrapped her arms round my legs and were picking at my bowyangs.

I'll be his right hand man I said all I want is to work about our property.

But my mother now were looking away to the smudgy grey horizon it were obvious she saw nothing useful there.

Well what about the old Harry?

I don't think thats no concern of yours said I.

Is Harry nabbed is that it?

No he aint nabbed I come back home I should of thought that would make you happy.

Is there a warrant out for you as well?

I come back home I said the adjectival pasture is filled with dandelions and docks no one cleared nothing while I were gone.

My mother sighed and shook her head Dear God Jesus save me.

I said I aint in trouble.

Jesus you don't know nothing about my problems Son.

Well anyone can see you aint done nothing to meet the requirements of the Act.

My mother looked around her property you could not deny it were a sad and ruined sight no new fencing not a single acre claimed.

They'll take away your lease said I.

At this my mother suddenly turned upon me slapping me fiercely about my ears.

Where's my money she cried where is my adjectival money?

Gracie let go my leg I felt her melt away.

I came home to help.

I know you b————rs stuck up the Buckland Coach. You stuck up Reed Murphy's Station too your sister read me all the papers.

The bushranging aint as profitable as you'd expect.

You aint got nothing for me?

Nothing.

Then what am I to do my mother cried.

I come home to help.

You can't come home I paid the b————r 15 quid to take you on. You are his apprentice now.

The mother and the son stood separate in the middle of the home paddock the chooks all droopy and muddy the pigs with their ribcages showing through their suits the waters of the Eleven Mile already receding leaving the spent and withered oats lying in the yellow mud. The son felt himself a mighty fool he'd been bought and sold like carrion.

At breakfast next morning my mother continued to speak despairingly she were exhausted with her life she said and seeing I had brung home no money she did not know what she would do.

Bill Frost now were occupying not only my mother's bed but also my father's chair he were so smug his ruddy face shaved smooth and glistening with salve I asked what he could think to help our property.

Give it back to the blacks he said then burst out snickering no no the blacks don't want it give it to the Irish just joking Ned thats a very good question and it just happens I have the answer here. He pulled a crushed envelope from his back pocket I thought he were about to produce the latest cattle prices but the envelope contained a piece of brown and yellow cloth. Said he This is your mother's salvation Ned it is what I promised her when I asked her for her hand.

Hand? I never heard no mention of this before I looked to my mother but she had set the baby on the ground all her attention taken by the scrap of cloth.

What is it Bill she asked.

This item is worth 4 times as much in New South Wales as it is here in Victoria. Frost looked around the table as if he were a magician we should all admire.

Do not tease me Bill.

He released the cloth into my mother's hands. All I have to do is row this across the Murray River and its worth 4 times what I paid for it. Now don't that beat churning butter Mrs Kelly?

My mother caught my eye a sharp triumphant look. It must of been the smuggling she were always attracted by courage and now wrongly imagined she had found her equal in that quality.

As for me I did not glower or nothing but when I saw my mother give Bill Frost the butter money I suggested to young Jem he come outside. As we left the front veranda I picked up 2 axes and once behind the cowbails advised my brother that we must do the labour which the boundary rider had no taste for. It were this or we would surely lose our land.

Jem were only 9 yr. old but he listened to me v. serious his brow furrowed his dark eyes never left my face and when he understood my strategy he said he were damned if he planned to go back slaving for our aunts then he cut his hand upon his axe and I done the same. We mixed our blood together and proclaimed an oath he said I do swear to be true to my captain or corrovat until death.

It were a Sunday and Bill Frost were not required at his employment but soon he left the property.

Might as well begin said I.

We made our oath beneath a mighty ironbark it were 8 ft. across as old as history its bark so black and rough it were like the armour of a foreign king.

Might as well said Jem then spat upon his hands and laid his axe into the brutal bark the flesh were sour and red we removed it in great glimmering slabs Jem's axe were 5 lb. I rested often so as not to shame him.

I could of dropped 2 normal trees before dinner but this one were a grandfather we both worked throughout the day the flies was in our open mouths our hands black and sappy we ate no tea neither but continued on until the light were sucked from the sky it were then I heard a creaking sound.

If you have felled a tree you know that sound it is the hinge of life before the door is slammed.

A tree falls slow and fast on the one hand it takes forever and on the other it is swift as a guillotine. I called to Jem to flee he stopped to look back and still I can see his handsome dark eyes his puzzled brow. Then there come a very small tearing noise like a single sheet of paper being ripped apart and I reached and pulled Jem's head close to my breast. The ironbark went. It fell like a whole empire collapsing its crown crushing into the adjacent grey box I heard the sound of a thousand bones breaking all at once. The trunk bounced into the air and shot back on itself passing us with all the weight of God himself He travelled like a cannon an inch beside my ear.

Our mother had noticed the ringing axes all through the day but until my shout she imagined it were our neighbour Bricky Williamson. Now she felt the earth shake she come running through the dusk and Maggie & Dan & Gracie strung out behind her they was the flesh of her flesh in order of their birth. They was shouting and fighting through the fallen canopy my mother tore her way between the branches she almost stood on top of us. She never wept but now lay down upon the darkening earth shaking us with her sobs her fat salt tears upon our dirty faces. Feeling the child in her belly I pulled away to help her to her feet.

My mother blew her nose. We was brave boys v. good she said she would henceforth assist us in our labours.

I were the man now so I told her we all knew she were with child I said we would look after her and make her farm successful she could depend on us.

I had not known I would say this nor had my brothers and sisters but when they heard my speech they come to my side vowing also to look after their mother. Dan were 7 yr. old he couldnt lift an axe without making a danger to himself but he made his vow all solemn and my mother thanked him. No one said nothing about Bill Frost or Mother's hand.

At night the man himself returned to find me sitting in da's chair he didnt say nothing but hurried to my mother in the skillion.

My mother said O let him be. After that it were all whispers but when Bill Frost brung his plate to sit amongst us he wore a smirk upon his ruddy face. So said he spooning gravy and potato into his mouth You boys is going to clear 10 acres is that so?

My colonial oath Jem said.

Well thats a great shame said Frost.

Now hush Bill my mother said they been good boys they is a great help to me.

Bill Frost had a most superior attitude a way of tilting his head up while turning down the corners of his mouth. Now he give his look to Jem saying I thought you'd rather be living in a big house in Melbourne and attending the Melbourne Cup.

You aint doing that said Jem.

O aint I just?

And what will happen to us asked Maggie who were playing with a doll made from a thigh bone wrapped up in a bit of gingham cloth. Would you go away and leave the rest of us?

No my mother said we aint leaving no one.

But said Bill I thought they had a plan to continue as selectors at Eleven Mile Creek I must of misunderstood.

You understood as good as gold said Jem.

So then your future is pretty much written and you will do a little cattle duffing like your uncles and you will be put in gaol and that will be the end of you except when the wind blows from the south you might stand near the window of your prison cell and hear the sound of the racetrack down at Flemington.

Jem said nothing but his head were bowed and I knew he were trying not to cry so I asked Bill Frost politely not to frighten him.

Said he Jem knows me he knows I'm joking.

I looked at Jem his eyes was pooled but he shook his head not wanting a fight he feared I would be sent away.

In any case said Bill Frost its my home and I'll talk to youse kids any way I want.

It aint your home said I.

Now hush said my mother.

Frost turned on me saying it certainly aint your adjectival home and you can get out before I throw you out.

At this I placed my hands on the table and looked him hard in his weak little eyes. So you'll throw me out Bill I asked putting down my spoon and making as if to rise.

He did not say nothing but I swear he understood my character for the 1st time. O Christ said he can't a man eat his adjectival tea.

Nothing were ever said to note this moment as remarkable but never were there any doubt about what transpired between us.

Hard days followed the butter money were all taken and not a skerrick of income generated by the alleged 60 bolts of cloth. By September the milk had gone up into the cows' horns which meant bread and water for our breakfast. There was many disturbances at this time not all of them related to Bill Frost or where he sat at table.

Annie's husband Alex Gunn were charged with stealing sheep I now understood that Alex were as kindhearted and steady as a furrow horse where women and children was concerned. He were known to nurse a sick babe or ride through a rainstorm to fetch medicine galloping 2 hr. to Benalla and 2 hr. back arriving with hail damage down his arms his broad back bruised blue to yellow like a lady's dress. In Benalla Court I swore on the Bible he bought these sheep from me but my words made no difference and they gaoled him just the same.

Jimmy Quinn were arrested for stealing from a Chinaman and also went to gaol then Sergeant Whelan rode out to tell my mother there was witnesses who'd swear she sold illegal liquor and if she didnt quit that business he would lay a charge and finally old man Quinn died.

I come out one morning to find a long lantern jawed boy sitting on the woodpile sharpening his axe so I asked what the Hell he wanted he said his name were Billy Gray and my mother had hired him to help me grub the stumps. By this I learned my mother knew no profit would come of them bolts of cloth. I told Billy Gray he were not needed and he went away.

Bill Frost were now absent more frequently and my mother oftentimes too tired to work as hard as previous but we laboured into the spring with axe & mattock & horse & fire and my mother even borrowed a pair of bullock from old Jack Dyer so me and she could spend a morning grubbing stumps with their reluctant assistance. Bill Skilling then arrived he were a miner from Gaffney's Creek 29 yr. old and very strong indeed. My mother employed him then I dismissed him although unlike Billy Gray he would not leave.

The mudeyes in the creek the emperor gum moths round the lamp at night and every other breathing thing told us it were time to be sowing seed so every day we rose earlier and went to bed later I were dreaming of trees and stumps without end. I were determined that we would have a farm but I saw it as only a madman does it were a phantasy so green it were never possible in such geography a grand homestead a creek flowing all through the drought and not a single smouldering windrow no dead and ringbarked trees. So often were I labouring in the bush that only by a roll of dice were I present when the Chinaman Ah Fook come wandering down the track.

My sister Annie Gunn were back living with us while Alex did his 3 mo. she were pretty much unhappy all the while but that day she brung us picnic dinner and so we had gathered by the creek at the place where the track passes our selection.

My mother sat amongst the riverside grasses on an upturned bucket her belly big and heavy her eyes sunken with a weight of doubts and she squinted back into the hard light at the smoky paddocks which no bolt of cloth would ever save her from. It were October which is when the big rains should come but already she could feel the summer smell the puddles drying and see the ground baking hard around the tree stumps.

It were she who 1st saw the Chinaman coming through the glare predicting what he wanted while he were still 50 yd. away. In court Ah Fook claimed he were a poultry hawker but there is no such thing as a hawker of one thing as they are jacks of all trades from corsets and opium to lead pencils for the littlies. He also said he had asked for water and that were his 1st perjury because he begged a dram of whisky and my mother would not supply it.

You give me.

No I don't do that no more.

Ah Fook made the grunt the Chinaman will make it is a kind of hum in their throats. He looked us all up and down but when his eyes lit on me he took a step forward and held out his hand and my hair stood on end to see what was in his paw a 1/2 dozen marbles they was agates & cat's eyes & bloodreels & twisters & lemon swirls & tombowlers & glass eyes. Were this the Chink we robbed before I did not know.

We got no time for games said I.

Boy got plenty time he said then pushed the marbles at me so I knocked his hand away and the marbles spilled onto the ground like quondong seeds.

Pickee up said he.

You going to be ordered by a Chinaman Annie asked me.

I aint said I and sat back down to take the plate of boiled eggs as Annie passed them.

The celestial were meanwhile looking down at his marbles then up at me and across to my mother. He very bad son said he.

Arrah nonsense my mother said he is an adjectival good son.

He very bad son the Chinaman said then took me by the ear hoping to make me pick up them marbles.

I now believe he intended no more than to give a gift but it were a grave misjudgment on his part trying to force a Kelly so I knocked him in the gullet. Continual fighting were the way of the world in them days just watch the birds in the gum blossoms it is still the same. Dan kicked the Chinaman's leg while Jem picked up the fellow's own bamboo and struck him severely on and about the head. When the poor b————r rose I kicked again then the marbles burst from his person as from a broken pod.

Regaining his feet he were surrounded by Kellys and he dare not move.

Barley called my mother all right quit it come and give him back his toys.

But we would not go barley and it were Mother who picked up all the marbles and give them to their owner.

But now Ah Fook folded his arms across his chest. I report you b————rs said he I report to police you adjectival devils.

Now now my mother said fair is fair my Ned meant no offence.

You crazy Irish devils you try to kill me.

No no says our ma they're just boys.

But Ah Fook suddenly wrested the bamboo pole from Jem's grasp leaping backwards with the pole raised like a sword.

Now you hang on a mo said my mother you just wait right here.

Calmly turning her back on the bristling fellow she walked back to the hut. The Chinaman stayed with his pole held high as if about to smite us but we was not scared. I had an axe Jem a mattock and when we picked up these implements and made a circle round him he must of thought his end were come.

Soon our ma came back from the hut holding in her hand a generous jar of grog. This will be after improving you.

The Chinaman sniffed at the grog. He put down axe said he then I drinkee.

I laughed then put my axe down as the Chinaman took the jar. When it was empty my mother gave him a 10/— note.

You would consider that fair but when this were all transacted the perfidious celestial walked into Benalla swearing to the coppers I had robbed him of £1. Sgt Whelan came out with 2 troopers the following day when he dismounted I imagined he were just checking for stolen brands as was the custom.

Are you Ned Kelly?

Yes I am.

Then I am arresting you for Highway Robbery.

At Benalla Barracks Sgt Whelan dismissed the Constables and escorted me through a dark narrow passage containing 3 black doors their surfaces studded with black bolts the last of these swung noiselessly and my fate announced itself in a sad and manly perfume of musk and piss and unwashed skin. Stepping inside I discovered an uneven floor of worried earth also a single window v. small and deep high up in the wall.

This is your new selection said Sgt Whelan and I knew I were finally in that place ordained from the moment of my birth my eyes were adjusting to the light I were studying that iron cot beneath the window thinking it not as bad as I had feared.

Hold up your hands lad. His tone were fairly friendly.

I turned to him so he could fiddle at my handcuffs with a bunch of keys.

You know what you is charged with sonny? The chosen key didnt seem to fit. You heard the charge clear enough?

I did.

All his attention were on my handcuffs. Ah theres the little blighter said he as the manacles come off. Did I know he asked me what were the penalty if I were convicted.

No.

It is death by hanging you little eff.

Many more times would death be pronounced over me but on this 1st occasion I were least prepared I could hear some boys playing cricket in the yard across the road also the regular chink chink chink of a nearby blacksmith at his forge. My legs must of give way beneath me but I didnt realise I were sitting down till I felt the crib's cold hard cleats behind my knees.

Then I heard the mongrel laugh I couldnt see him properly no more than the white of his teeth the reflection in his big bug eyes but as he laughed I knew him weak and thus were comforted.

I know you is Harry Power's offsider said he and if you help us nab him then we'll let you go before tonight.

I made no comment.

Stand up!

I obeyed and received a sudden blow in my stomach which winded me but in the pain and airlessness I seen the truth and hope. He wouldnt of hit me if he were going to hang me.

Stand up he cried again. Now what do you answer me?

You never asked me nothing.

He hit me once again but I could endure much worse than this without succumbing for I were raised on stories of Irishmen being tortured and would not go home a traitor.

Said he I'm going to call for an interpreter for the Chinaman. You could be here for a month or 2 while we find someone suitable.

I thought you was hanging me.

And so of course he hit me again giving a comfort he did not intend for with every blow I were reminded that I would not die.

When he finally locked the door on me I were very hurt but still able to climb up on the crib and here there were sufficient light to see the yellow bruises surface slowly on my sallow Irish skin. I watched them like clouds changing in the spring sky thinking of my father and what horrors he endured in silence.

Yet the greatest torture in that cell were not the walloping not the threats of hanging it were the vision of my family working without my assistance I knew myself better off than them for I had fresh yeast bread and jam there were barley and mutton soup for dinner and delicious stews for tea each one better than the day before.

Finally on the 11th morning a strange pale fellow in a high winged collar come into my cell he were tall and stooped and his voice were high.

Edward Kelly he asked peering into the gloom. For Jesus Christ's sake how old are you?

I am 15.

Well I am Zinke said he giving me his hand which were very limp and damp. I am 28 yr. old and I have been retained as your solicitor.

I told him there were no money I could not afford to pay him.

Well I would be very worried if you could.

My mother's got no money neither.

I am instructed said he that if you are not released by teatime I am to pull a rabbit out of Whelan's arse and make him eat it raw.

Harry's paying?

Shush boy I never consort with escapees do you understand?

Yes Sir.

And nor do you.

No Sir.

So speak quickly young fellow for we have just 1/2 an hour until we face the bench.

PARCEL 4

His Life at
16 Years of Age

National Bank letterhead as in Parcel 1, 44 pages of medium stock (8" × 10" approx.). A few finger smudges or stains in text but otherwise very neat, as if produced in domestic circumstances.

The author's confession of having made a threat to murder. A narration of the events following Bill Frost's abandonment of Mrs Kelly and the author's subsequent reunion with Harry Power. Description of a journey on horseback through bushfire. The shooting of Bill Frost. A character portrait of Harry Power and a detailed explanation of the factors leading to the robbery of R. R. McBean. An account of the two offenders' journey across Mt. Stirling to Gippsland and of the author's disillusionment with his mentor.

Arriving back on our selection at teatime I discovered Bill Frost sitting in my chair with a big plate of mutton stew in front of him and it were bring me this & give me that but I embraced my sisters thus preventing him being served. They hugged me crying my mother smiled at me but she were busy bandaging Dan's finger. Bill Frost were calling bring me this & give me that but I held the girls around me and he had to vacate the chair in order to get his own potato.

The moment he stood I sat down in my chair so when he returned he had no choice but move his mug and spoon to a new position the girls was most amused. Soon all except Bill Frost was eating happily but he would rather use his mouth to criticise me for my own imprisonment. You got to consider Ned said he them lawyers' bills is a terrible burden on your mother.

Dan spilled his milk it flooded across the table dripping through the planks onto the children's knees so my mother started for the skillion.

Jesus Christ said Bill Frost sit down will you Ellen?

My father would never have spoke to my mother in this way but Ellen Kelly did not rebuke Bill Frost it were a terrible thing to see her bullied by so weak a man. No need for anyone to worry about them lawyers' bills she said she wrung a rag into a bucket.

Why Ellen said he slyly I never saw you so carefree about 5 guineas.

My mother wiped up the milk. It were 4 guineas Bill.

Ah 4 guineas! Only!

My mother sat down picking up the tea pot she found it empty so she stood once more without complaint and threw the leaves out the door and went to the fire to pour fresh boiling water in the pot. Bill Frost watched her all this time.

Who paid them 4 guineas? He were looking at me as he spoke I thought what a weasel I would like to pull his beaky nose.

Who said it were paid? said my mother the tea were yet to brew but still she filled her cup. Thats how I knew he had her shaken.

Bill Frost turned his lizard eyes upon the cup. Said he I hope you aint been accepting gifts from Harry Power.

My mother sipped tea in silence Bill Frost peering sideways at her like a chook about to peck a cabbage stalk.

Eat up Ellen.

My mother's stew had a skin from waiting for the spoon so long. She ate as ordered.

I suppose you think I'm an ignorant sort of fellow Ellen.

Frost's tone had turned so poisonous I began to rise in my seat but Mother quickly placed her hand on the boundary rider's hairy wrist. I would never think you ignorant dear.

As for me I could not stomach this conversation and left my food in favour of the air outside. Jem and Dan quickly come along and Jem and me was soon teaching the little fellow how to hit a ball with a stick. Dan were a fierce and determined little b————r he would not give up until the darkness beat him.

That night I woke to hear my mother crying and Bill Frost talking very low. I spent a lifetime learning not to see or hear what werent my business but when Bill Frost called my mother Harry Power's whore I could not be deaf no more. As I rose from my crib I felt Maggie's hand upon my arm she tried to restrain me but when I rushed from behind my curtain she come with me.

Don't call our mother bad words she said she were no coward.

Shutup go back to sleep.

Apologise I said or I will break your nose.

As Frost rose slowly to greet us I realised he were blotto I were not sorry for this handicap he had a longer reach. I'll apologise he said his voice were very slurred he kneeled and took my mother's hand.

Bill Bill no Bill please.

I beg your forgiveness Ellen said he for everything I ever said or done without exception. Them was his words but there was such an air of threat and nastiness about him I could not predict what he might do next. Ah Ned said he and he held out his hand but even as we shook his dull pale eyes was filled with malice. I thank you Ned yes I thank you most sincerely.

With that he took his hat and stepped out into the night my mother calling piteously after him.

Maggie Maggie fetch Bill back.

Maggie wouldnt budge so my mother turned to me her cheeks was wet and shining.

Don't go Maggie said.

You effing get him cried my mother if you don't do nothing else for me do this. You go get him and say you're sorry. We'll starve without his wages.

Then we heard a horse galloping full tilt down the track my mother collapsed onto the floor in great torment.

He's the father of my babe cried she.

Very well I said I'll fetch the mongrel.

There was a good moon so I found him easy enough he were no longer galloping but walking his horse in the direction of his employment.

I told him my mother had asked me to apologise and he would be wise to give her that impression. For my own part I could only say that if he ever abandoned her I would come and shoot him while he slept.

I saw his reptile eyes in the moonlight staring at me. He didnt say a word but together we turned riding slowly back towards my home.

The next morning was like nothing never happened it were unseasonably hot my mother took a hair of the dog but Frost declared he had a hankering for shooting kangaroos there were a big grey b————r he had his eye on we sometimes saw him come right down to the creek beside the hut. My mother were poorly she said it was too adjectival hot for shooting anything but Bill Frost went ahead cleaning his fowling piece his eyes was bloodshot but that were normal he didnt act like a man threatened with murder the night before.

Jem and Dan and me went with him along Futter's Range the twigs and leaves snapping like bone beneath our heavy bluchers. We found the kangaroos awaiting us in the shade of an old river gum they watched us approach not knowing the part we would play in their history.

On our return I helped Bill Frost salt down a great quantity of meat my mother's eyes was dark and apprehensive. The night were airless Bill Frost announced that his employer Mr Simson wished him to draft a mob of cattle down to the Haymarket in Melbourne so when he went to work on the morrow he would be away from us for 7 days. This were in no way unusual he had done it many times before.

In all the leave taking on Monday morning my mother were a little too jolly running to the cow pasture to get a dandelion for his shirt she were teasing him about all the fine ladies he would see in Collins Street but once he were on the track towards Laceby she took straight to her bed.

I come to her side she said her life was gone to smash she knew Bill Frost would not return.

I thought she would get over it but as the days passed her spirits did not improve soon she could barely eat her eyes was sunk deeper in her head I could not guess what she were thinking. Neither could I bear to see her misery it were a torture worse than any I could imagine worse than prison in Benalla certainly.

7 days my mother lay on her back with her hands resting on her womb. Bill Frost were due back on the 8th day but when we finally heard a horse come through the creek she never stirred and it were me that ran out into the light to discover a v. lively stallion ridden by a wispy sort of boy.

He trotted on towards me he wore short pants his legs no thicker than the handle of a hoe. Ah thought I Bill Frost has sent a message.

Are you Ned he called. His naked feet was a good 10 in. long so I looked up into his face to see what sort of being this were he had a worn out little face his blue eyes very faded the kind you see in the children of old fathers.

I asked Are you from Bill Frost?

For answer he offered a brown envelope held out with fingers which was long and slender as little sticks.

Inside the envelope were a letter and a crisp new one pound note I assumed were from Bill Frost it were only when I read POWND FOR MA. GO WITH BOY that I understood I were being summonsed by Harry Power.

Jesus! I were so disgusted that I picked up a broken demijohn and hurled it out into the yard.

It aint far said the boy.

If he were at effing Greta it would be too far.

Its further than Greta the boy admitted.

To Hell with him.

I opened the note and read again POWND FOR MA I had vowed never again to serve Harry Power.

Whats he effing want?

I don't know said the boy don't the note say?

I read the note a 3rd time POWND FOR MA it were only then I began to think that Harry were very soft on my ma I thought he would do anything to help her.

Wait here I told the boy I won't be 1/2 a mo.

Inside our hut my mother were lying in her crib with all manner of coats and dresses and blankets piled on top of her. From this nest I removed an old brown oilskin coat that were my da's I put it on.

Ma I'm going to bring Bill back to you.

My mother give me a smile but it were very weary she hardly had the strength to make it. We had a crooked old fowling piece only good for frightening sparrows and this I slung round my back then found some balls and 4 percussion caps and a powder flask which was easily accommodated in the big pockets of the coat. Finally I kissed my mother on the cheek and give her the pound note.

This is from Harry Ma he's going to help me find Bill.

Dear Harry said my mother dear silly old b−−−−r.

Having kissed my mother once more I found Maggie and told her my plan then without no waste of time I saddled up my mother's bay. All the while the stallion were sniffing and snorting he could not wait to leave the boy spoke to him in a soft sweet voice.

Then straight away we was at a gallop I were a horseman myself fearless as any youngster will be but that other boy were an adjectival wonder he led me down 2 steep escarpments that took my breath away God Jesus save us to think of the things we did when young.

We went through Greta in a cloud of dust cutting across country through Oxley and Tarrawingee and along the way I shot 2 good sized rabbits with the fowling piece the boy was v. queer he did not often speak but he said I were a good shot and in turn I told him I never knew a better rider than himself. After 2 1/2 hours riding we came to a very pretty farmhouse by a track the yards was neat and well made a barn and a shed for chickens and housing for the pigs and the fenceposts was all mortised. This was where the boy lived though he did not tell me that. When we went inside the house the floorboards was polished and there were a room set aside specially for eating it had white curtains on the window a jar full of roses sitting on the table.

In a 2nd room of chairs and sofas I presented the rabbits to the boy's mother she were very pleased removing them straight away into the kitchen with the promise she would stew them for our dinner.

I asked where were Mr Power they said he would be along directly but I waited a long time and Harry did not appear and the boy started jumping chair to chair around the dining table it were a very queer game and I could see his mother were frightened of him she would not stop it. Often he touched the ceiling with his strange thin fingers although later I thought I must of imagined this for the ceilings were 13 ft. high.

After a long time a v. pretty girl come along she was perhaps 14 that is 2 yr. my junior but already showing a womanly shape and she folded her arms across her chest when she saw me looking at her. Having sisters of my own I knew to look away.

After a time she asked would I like to see their cattle. She could show me a valley she said where there were no drought. She had long dark hair and bright and lively eyes so I thought I might as well I followed her across a sandy creek then up a rise we climbed up great shelves of granite to the rocky top below which were a sheltered hollow with grass so green it were beyond belief I could of lived there all my life. The small herd of cattle were all fat and gleaming it is always such a lovely thing to see proof of what contentment the colony might provide if there is ever justice. I asked how old her brother were she said he werent her brother then I asked where Mr Power were she said not to fret he would turn up bye and bye. She said her name were Caitlin.

She held out her hand so I could help her off the rock and her hand were very warm and she led me down a steep wall she knew the way but seemed to need my hand to guide her. Soon we come across the source of all the greenery it were a spring seeping from the rocks it were cool and dark with ferns growing from the crevices. Here we sat together side by side I were very happy for a while.

The people at this house turned out to be particularly kind. The mother shown herself a mighty cook she soon give us steamed pudding with jam sauce and yellow custard I never seen such a treat in all my life. I were 1/2 way through my 2nd helping when the door swung open and there stood Harry Power Esq. He had shaved his beard off it were disturbing to see his naked phiz revealed the jaw too long the mouth would not give a smile unless compelled to. It was such a hard square head as you see in prisons it were made by hammering and burning.

Come out the back he said I want a word with you Ned Kelly.

On the back veranda Harry were holding out my elastic sided boots. When last I saw them boots they was muddied and sodden but the old wombat had been to work on them and that surprised me mightily for he had a great aversion to menial labour. If this were meant to be apology or payment he did not say but he had scraped and oiled and dubbined them until they was soft as a lady's purse.

Here said he tossing them to me I reckon you forget these when you run away.

I looked into his hard old face but did not see the slightest flicker.

There was nothing for me to do but sit down to pull the boots on. My feet must of grown for now they pinched my toes.

Comfy?

Yes Harry.

You can try them out with bringing round my horse.

I were pledged not to take his orders no more but fair is fair I did require his assistance in the matter of Bill Frost so I went to the paddock hunting down his poor old switchtailed mare then I found his saddle abandoned on a stile and did the duty he required of me.

Where's your own nag he said when I come back. Jesus lad the light is wasting.

I didnt say goodbye yet.

Eff goodbye said he you go and get your effing horse.

I walked back down through the thick green pasture and found and saddled my own horse but still did not mount though I could feel Harry's growing fury at my dawdling. I suppose it were the girl that done it to me for I walked slowly up towards the house admiring all the neat fencing and the fat black cattle making their way from the river to the bails. Of course Harry were already mounted his gleaming pistols stuck plainly in his thick brown belt. His pipe were clenched in that long strong jaw he had previously hid beneath his beard.

Get on the horse said he.

He did not understand I were now too old to be talked to in this manner I made no move until I saw he was about to welt me then I spoke.

My ma needs your help.

Ah said he and everything about him changed.

Bill Frost is bolted to Melbourne. My ma is awful upset.

He almost smiled. You reckon do you?

Yes I reckon.

Harry pulled his pipe in 1/2 then blew a long stream of thick black spit out the stem. He seemed v. pleased as he always were when about to prove another man a fool.

Well said he now here is the latest. Bill Frost never went to adjectival Melbourne.

He's there I know it.

By the 5 crosses he aint.

By the 5 crosses he is.

By the powers of death he aint. He is at Peter Martin's Star Hotel in Wangaratta and he has been there all this week not 10 mi. away.

You seen the b————r?

Maguire had the pleasure.

I don't know Maguire.

Well you tried to murder him at Oxley the night you lost your boots but apart from that its true you don't know a tinker's fart about him. Maguire has seen our Bill and reports the man is having a great old rort him and his new sheila Brigit Cotter.

I never heard of her.

Well when the man aint shagging her he's in the public bar entertaining all the punters with how Ned Kelly threatened to shoot him. O I see you blush. He is making an adjectival fool of you with that story by now it is knowed by everyone in Wangaratta.

It were a sweet spring evening now but I had reason to recall Bill Frost's lizard eyes in the moonlight it had been a dull malicious way he stared at me.

That is why I sent for you said Harry.

Its exactly why I come said I we was both thinking the same thought.

O I doubt it son I really do.

He's a dreadful mongrel but she's very bad without him. I need to bring him back.

No said Harry his voice were almost gentle that is the scheme you wanted when you was ignorant but now you know that Frost has been

unfaithful to your ma. He has a new donah and you know what he is saying about your own self.

He's a b—————d but my mother has a baby coming.

We can look after your ma said Harry but 1st you have to attend to
Frost you aint got a da to tell you this so let me do the honour you cannot
let him make a jackass of you.

There aint nothing I can do.

O aint there?

What he says is right I did say I would shoot him if he bolted.

He makes out you are a coward is that right too? Are you a coward?

Don't say that Harry. You know I aint.

Then you know what you must do.

I looked into them hard old eyes and saw the deed that lay ahead of
me it were a horror no one could wish but now I knew there were no
choice.

Yes I know what must be done.

Leaving the dusk in the valley we had just regained the sunlight on
the crest when we was violently confronted by a horse and cart it come
swinging round the corner with a short old fellow standing on the buggy
seat like something in a circus he had a clay pipe clenched between his
teeth and his whip were roiling a great cloud of dust pushing it down
the road ahead of him. We only just escaped his path but then he saw us
he whoaed up and when the confusion were all settled I realised it were
Mr B. I will use that initial although it is not the right one for he were a
poor selector known to both of us. His wife had passed away not long
previous.

Mr B. had finally pulled up 1/2 way down the hill so I called a greeting
as I rode towards him but he would not answer I reckoned he were cutting me. He spoke only to Harry using his 1st name many times as if
proud to be as friendly with him as he were disdainful of myself. His
information were that Bill Frost had departed Wangaratta for Beechworth and when I realised Mr B. had flogged his swaybacked nag into the
ground for the sole purpose of bringing Harry the news I began to see the
size of event I had precipitated.

When Harry opened his purse in order to reward him Mr B. swore he spat and said Harry were his mate he would be insulted to take money for the service.

Mr B. were a poor man his shirt were ragged his boots patched with pitch and twine but he had to make his speech and Harry did not mind listening not at all. Finally the old selector accepted the money and returned the way he had come his cart horse had thrown a shoe and was limping badly.

As the poor pay fealty to the bushranger thus the bushranger pays fealty to the poor.

We turned our horses ambling back down the hill we was now in no hurry to reach our destination my reason will be obvious enough but as for Harry he wished to enter the town late at night because there was 2 Constables in Beechworth with a hankering to make their reputations with his neck.

We was passing the little farmhouse where I had been so well entertained when Harry asked what I thought of the boy Shan and I answered he could ride as well as any boy I ever saw. Then Harry told me that it were his strong suspicion that Shan were not a human boy but a substitute that had been left.

It were that time of day when the light is high up on the ridgetops while down in the valley floor everything were what Scots call the gloaming all the crows and currawongs very melancholy. Harry said there were a couple near Tipperary that had a child which were taken in the night. The so called CHILD left in its place were very strange with a wasted appearance in its eyes you could see that it were very old indeed. The parents was afraid of it and would not argue with it and it could break a plate or climb around the thatching without them daring to contradict it. Harry hadnt seen this substitute child himself but his mother knew him she said the boy had the ability to be in many different places in the one time. He liked to sew and while this were a strange occupation for a boy no one would make jokes at his expense. The wonder of his village he were often about in the woods or nearby towns then inside his cottage sometimes at the same minute he were also in the fields. At the cottage he sat by the fire working on a patchwork cloak it were quite outstanding and no one could explain where he got such colours from. There were a red in particular which were like the red you find in a stained glass window and there was no red about his mother's garments in the whole house not the smallest skerrick.

People come paying their respects to the parents but they really come to see the cloak to watch the boy's fingers as he sewed no one never seen the like of it before. The fingers was so very long and nimble they were like the fingers of a monkey bending as he sewed as if there was no bones at all but as for the design itself people complained it were almost impossible to get a good look at what the boy were up to.

Time passed his brothers and his sisters growing older with children of their own but the boy didnt age a day although some thought his eyes grew paler no one could imagine how a simple cloak could occupy him for such a length of time.

Then one day the mother goes to the priest saying that the boy had a question that wanted answering and would the Holy Father call on them at such and such a time. The priest come to the house where he found the boy were waiting by the fireplace and the boy straight away asks his question which were as follows.

Would he go to Heaven yes or no.

The priest looked at the boy at his strange washed out eyes his long thin fingers and he did not wish to offend him nor did he wish to lie.

At last he spoke he said I can promise you that if you have a drop of Adam's blood in your veins you have as good a chance as I.

And if not says the boy.

Then said the priest you will not go to Heaven.

And with that the poor creature let out an awful kind of shriek he dropped his patchwork on the floor and run away. He were never seen again but his parents kept the needlework for many years after. It were a picture of the Holy Mother with her Babe and everyone who seen it reported it were very fine.

It were now almost dark I asked Harry did he ever see this needlework he said his mother had been shown it on the eve of the very day she were transported. I asked him did he believe in the fairy stories and his answer were he had heard so many from his mother he concluded their only purpose were to frighten the young people to keep the boys away from girls but now his mind were changed. He thought there might be something to them after all.

The horses were ambling v. slow it were hard to see the track at this time I asked Harry what it were that changed his mind but he give no answer. When I asked had he seen a Banshee he remained silent so I didnt ask him no more but my mind began to dwell on dark things as we travelled north towards Bill Frost and my heart were heavy with foreboding.

It were no more than 15 mi. from Beechworth that we smelled the cursed odour of burning eucalyptus I said there were a bushfire very close Harry said I were mistaken the fire were far away. When we come across Hodgson's Creek there was black leaves falling from the sky but still Harry refused to be diverted and it were not until them leaves begun to show the crimson fringe he finally called a halt. I would not have to be a murderer or so I thought.

Wet your kerchief said Harry placing a bottle of water in my hand. Tie that hanky across your mouth and schnozzle.

So we pushed on towards the murder and you can rightly say I would of proved my manhood better by turning back to Greta but on that fateful night I were caught between my 15th & 16th yr. and in my wisdom thought I had no choice but accompany Harry Power. I followed the old wombat through the dark the smoke now stung my eyes without relent. My horse didnt like it neither she froze with her head up her ears flickering back and forth. I would not whip her but lay along her quivering neck speaking comfort to her. Harry led us off the road but I knew he could not see no track no more than I could. Edging forward carefully along a ridge we come onto a saddle where we might of expected to glimpse the distant lanterns of Beechworth but instead found only choking smoke it were brown and yellow illuminated by a glow like the inside of a baker's furnace. There were no sight of flames but the wind were rising from what I took to be the east. My horse quivered she felt the doom in front of her and I spoke to her and told her she were my good girl I would never see her hurt but in truth I were lost and could not see the moon or stars. We begun working our way along the contour but the wind only grew hotter. Twice Harry's mare frighted and reared up in the dark and I imagined him also lost but in this I did him an injury for he succeeded in guiding us cunningly around the conflagration that were no mean feat of bushmanship.

From above Reid's Creek we finally attained a clear hill from which we could view the main front of the fire which were running the ridge to the north east coming almost to the edges of Beechworth itself. The native pine were blazing the apple gum and scrub alight the fire come roaring up our flank forcing us down into the Woolshed Valley beside Reid's Creek. In dense smoke we nearly trampled a lone selector with his children all done up with scarves around their faces going off to fight the fire. There were one boy he were no more than 5 yr. old wearing his father's flat grey hat and his eyes was fearful in his lantern light. I said we should help them save their fences.

Harry looked back over his shoulder he said fences get rebuilt he would not stop. I felt a very bad conscience to see that family disappear into the smoke thinking of my own family imagining my mother at that moment with her hands across her belly the baby quickening in her womb. God willing one day I would tell that baby the story of the apple gums exploding in the night the 1/2 mad kangaroos driven down before this wrath into the township of Sebastopol.

In the same desolate valley we found a group of Chinese still working their sluices by lantern light. The white miners had quit these diggings years before but the celestials was sifting through the leftover mullock they would never rest not even fire could drive them from their labour. The earth here were like a mighty firebreak all ripped apart like a creature slaughtered its skin pulled back its guts torn out by dogs it were like a battlefield no quarter given. This certainly were not our original destination but through this hellish scene did the young murderer ride and soon he come upon a rough little hut outside which a number of Chinamen was engaged with a game of mahjong on a wide wooden plank. These was hard looking fellows all dried out and salted down for keeping.

Well heres a sight said Harry.

I thought he were referring to the gamblers but in fact he were staring at a familiar splayfooted grey mare hitched to a post.

O thats a pretty horse said he although she werent at all. Do you recognise the mare sonny?

No.

It belongs to himself said Harry he were smiling once again.

I said I didnt think so but it were a lie. Foul fortune had brung us to our quarry's door.

Said Harry Go look see what type of iron its wearing.

I picked up the right rear hoof but already knew them shoes would be most distinctive having a small protrusion on the wall of the U.

I gave Harry the thumbs up but my stomach were in turmoil. The Chinks was staring as I lowered the hoof and nothing seemed real to me no more. Harry whispered I should find a dark place so I might prime my fowling piece so I went behind the hut and when I come out Harry were giving money to the Chinese the 1st time I seen witnesses bribed before a crime were done.

Then standing at the door of the rough hut with my fowling piece at my hip I were ready to break the 6th Commandment.

No he is behind you.

I turned and saw an even more lamentable habitation than the hut a sad and dirty tent and across its filthy fly were a yellow rope from which were suspended a sign reading PRIVATE and beside which were a lantern of torn red paper hanging from a bamboo pole.

Harry winked unloosing the yellow cord so the sign dropped to the ground. When he pushed me forward I had no clue I were walking into a brothel the outside of the tent were streaked with grey and mildew but the skin won't predict the inside of a fruit.

I swear the 1st thing that struck me were the woman had no rump on her yet there were so many 1st shocks all rushing in at once. She were naked as were Bill Frost he knelt before the tart like a man at church and when he heard me enter he rose to his feet and what could I do but raise the gun.

Get out I told the tart go on missy.

The tart's almond eyes was v. angry but she pulled a black silk gown around her shame and done what she were ordered. Frost would not cower from me. Come on he said and held out his sunburned arms his parts was there for all to see. Come on said he give me the adjectival gun before you do yourself an injury. He stretched his long arm towards the barrel and feeling the wall of the tent behind me I knew I could retreat no farther. I cocked the gun.

Shoot me if that is what you effing want. Do you want to spend your whole stupid life in gaol?

I didnt know if I could kill him or not yet I saw I must and I shouted he were a cheat and a liar and I were aiming the gun when a voice come from the dark.

Don't make a murderer out of the boy.

Is that Harry Power?

You know it is.

Then call your adjectival dog off Harry.

I overheard what you said about him spending his life in gaol so here I am. I'm what they call the substitute.

And with that Harry Power pushed into the tent he had his heavy American repeater in his hand. This fearsome weapon he now pointed directly at Bill Frost's temple and I were too apprehensive of the murder to feel v. much relieved. Holding the pistol in his left hand Harry took a hold of the fellow's private parts with his right.

This is a very nice bit of sausage Bill.

O Jesus Harry said Bill Frost he now were frightened and who could blame him Harry were a terrifying man without his beard you could see the cruelty in his cheekbones the anger in his mouth.

But this pizzle has been very troublesome to you Bill.

No Harry. Barley. Fair's fair.

You know it is a big vein delivering all the blood to this pizzle but you would know that Bill for you're a highly knowledgeable sort of chap. Don't they call you Yesbut? Yesbut Frost? Yes but I know better aint that it?

Harry then cocked the Colt.

When I shoot it there will be an awful lot of bleeding Bill.

No Jesus Harry.

Ned would you kindly pick up Bill's boots.

But Bill had come to visit the tart in his dancing shoes I picked them up they was so light and dainty the soles as thin as paper.

Please Harry I'm sorry whatever I done.

Say sorry to the young'un not to me. Ned please remove a shoelace thats the boy.

What are you doing?

Now Bill it is very important you use a tourniquet.

I did not know this word neither did Bill Frost I could see it alarmed him worse than anything before. A what? What are you saying?

You don't know what a tourniquet is? Thats one for the books Yesbut but yes you'll bleed to death without one and that will be your own adjectival fault so pay attention Bill you tie that lace round your pizzle. I could do it for you but I need one hand to hold the gun.

Bill Frost's face were normally a ruddy red but as he tied the dainty shoelace to his member it were grey as a corpse.

You've been a bad boy Billy said Harry Power.

Bill Frost's chest were shaking crying hard he gasped O Christ Harry please will you please just let me off.

Yes but can you promise you won't never slander young Ned here.

I will yes he were crying loudly now the tears running down into his beard.

Will what?

Will promise.

Yes but will you also promise to provide £1 per week for the upkeep of Mrs Kelly's baby?

I will yes I would of anyway.

Then you is let off cried Harry knocking him on the head with the butt of his pistol.

Harry would later claim to regret he had hit Bill Frost but it werent the hitting which then made it all go wrong. The problem were Bill Frost he were proud as a billy goat and once the terror were removed all he could think were how the story would be told around the district. He could not bear the shame. Now his eyes was wet with tears his lips all swollen as he kowtowed but withdrawing from the tent I seen his large and violent shadow as he sought the means for his revenge. I called to Harry but Bill were already rushing us his howdah pistol in his hand.

You mongrel Power cried he.

I fired my musket from the hip I thought I missed but when he staggered against the lantern I observed his hand pressed to his gut the black blood flowing like jam between his fingers.

It were February I would not be 16 until December.

With that single shot I was once again bound as Harry Power's apprentice he woke me at dawn in the stables where we was hidden by his friends. Already he had been out and around the streets.

Bill Frost has carked it he said he has bled himself to death.

Now it is many years later I feel great pity for the boy who so readily believed this barefaced lie I stand above him and gaze down like the dead look down from Heaven.

The traps is out for you sonny Jim.

I asked if there were a warrant sworn against me and for answer he opened up his ivory handled clasp knife then dug his hand into his coat pocket to produce a length of butcher's sausage still hot and shining from the pan. He passed it to me with the knife his eyes was alive with emotion I mistook for sympathy.

Here eat some breakfast poor tyke.

Reminded of Bill Frost's pizzle I shook my head and Harry took the sausage back.

I don't want you to worry said he but there is a mob of troopers recently left for Eleven Mile Creek they think they will arrest you there.

I never showed my terror only asked again were there a warrant sworn.

My hand and word to you said the old rogue I'll not rest until I see you safe.

I said I would be hung no question.

You'll be safe said he if you fetch me a bucket of ashes quick and lively.

He must of been delighted to see how obedient I were become. When I carried him the pail he commenced blackening his great long jaw and neck instructing me to follow his example. He rubbed the filthy ashes over his big wide nose around his pouchy eyes he said this will make you a good citizen my little feral fellow.

When we both had muck all across our skin he ordered me to give the horses a good feed of oats then to bring some water from the well. I were a rabbit in his snare but did not know it yet.

All night the hot north wind were blowing through the town filling my nightmares with murder and smoke and iron wheels rolling along the road below but now the wind had dropped the streets was deadly quiet. As Harry and me started up Ford Street on horseback a single pedestrian come limping towards us carrying a pole on which hung a burnt bit of hessian he had been using to beat the flames. He looked up at us his face were black with smoke and soot his eyes well bloodshot.

Morning said Harry.

Morning mate.

The fire were all in the west so we frauds headed south ambling our horses down the centre of Church Street. 2 females rode a cart filled with milkpails in the direction of the fires.

God bless you boys they cried.

God bless us murderers the old ham raised his hat he couldnt be happier. Soon we passed that solid stone edifice wherein Bill Frost supposedly lay dead I couldnt help but cross myself I were so ashamed and sorry and I slumped there in the saddle with my eyes cast down upon the mane.

Soon we was on the Buckland road and thence drifted onto the kangaroo pads that ran like quicksilver throughout the dry bush and along these we passed silent as blood itself. Thus like chiggers we twisted our way deep into the country till finally we come down the ridge to that old hut at Bullock Creek eyeless in a field of bracken.

No one shall ever catch ye here said Harry.

I am painted as such a criminal but it seems to me I were so young and gullible that Harry Power could play with me almost any way he wished. I believed him when he said I were safe in the Wombat Ranges but when he announced we would be better in the Warbies I never lost my trust not even when he took me to more populated areas in the hills behind Glenrowan or into hotel bars where there was police in uniform.

He knew I were badly shaken by the murder but he never showed me no sympathy only the opposite he were blithe as a sparrow continually mocking the dead man calling him Yesbut or Bill Frot which means to rub your private parts or so he claimed. By the campfire he would perform a very vulgar imitation of Bill's Waltz for which he thrust his big square backside out into the dark.

Many is the moonlit night he left me alone with nothing but a single shot muzzleloader with only 2 percussion caps and not until much later did I hear from my Maggie she were always pleased to see a bright moon for it were on those same nights old Harry come riding down from the Warby Ranges to court my mother. The 1st night he boasted that he had shot Bill Frost for treating her so bad. Soon he done Bill's Waltz it made her laugh and I must admit the old deceiver raised Ellen Kelly from her bed before he took her back to it.

He were a dirty liar it were his great hobby and profession he done it continuously like another man might pick his nose or carve faces on a bit of mallee root just to pass the time. He easily made my mother believe I were gone travelling in New South Wales but he told me the troopers was camped out at Eleven Mile Creek waiting to arrest me. What a web he wove. He said he were observing the cops and would report when they was gone away. Of course I believed him for he were all that stood between me and the noose and I willingly held the horses for his constant robberies every night I bagged a kangaroo or a possum or some bush pigeons I never served him the same tucker 2 nights running. He were as lazy as the dog that rests its head against the wall to bark but I didnt grudge him so at different times I fed him Murray cod or yabbies or a snake. I also chopped the wood tended the horses and shoed them regular. If the night were warm I would dig 2 shallow trenches to hold our sleeping bodies then across this little grave I staked out mosquito nets. This service were not all caused by my good nature for I knew that when this activity ceased my mind would hurry back to that night of murder it would picture the Chinese woman with no rump Bill's black blood spilling through his fingers.

Every now and then Harry announced that things was hotting up and we should clear out to the Wombat so again I trusted him even though I come to dread them times at Bullock Creek for once there he could abandon me alone for 2 wk. at a time I suppose he returned to court my mother but I were left in solitude and my thoughts was very troubling. With hoe and scythe I cleared the bracken from around the blind walled hut so when the rains come the grass were much encouraged. I panned for gold and made a cockatoo fence also caught and broke a brumby mare but none of this ceaseless activity could still my mind I were v. guilty for having killed the father of my mother's child.

Yet the truth is neither a boy nor a horse and not even Harry Power can suppress it forever not with cunning or abuse not even with the great weight of his mighty arse. I got my 1st glimpse of the situation one morning as we travelled through McBean's Kilfeera Station on the way back to the Warby Ranges. McBean were not only a squatter but a powerful Magistrate so on his land I had learned to follow the creeks and gullies those low lying areas the soldiers call the dead ground. It were a 2 day journey and in the morning of the 2nd day we was on the northern edge of McBean's station having feasted on one of his jumbucks the night before. We come cantering up out of a deep and narrow valley and nearly tangled with a rider passing the other way. We was so close I could smell molasses on his horse's breath and as I wheeled around my stirrup clashed with his. His horse reared while mine stumbled but neither of us fell. The rider had such a spit and polish shine to him I were immediately sure he were police in mufti then as we both swung away I saw Harry raking his spurs fiercely along his horse's flank and suddenly the strange rider were coming after us. He were tweed suited and heavy gutted he might have been a

Superintendent he were waving his hat at us. Hey Bill he hollered hold up Bill.

Harry might of continued safe enough but he did not. Bill he cried who the eff are you calling Bill?

The stranger kept his temper answering pleasantly I'm sorry mate. His full cheeked head were broad but he had a sharp little nose his quick black eyes now searched Harry's face very carefully.

Your face aint like Bill's but you sit a horse pretty much the same. You know Bill Frost? They call him Yesbut? I aint seen him since he come out of hospital.

Thus did the truth appear but in a lightning flash like a fish jumping at the evening rise and by the time I saw it there were nothing left but ripples. By then Harry had dragged his American repeater from his belt and aimed it directly at the stranger's breast.

Confound your impertinence he roared.

Easy on mate said the horseman. I didnt mean you no offence. You don't resemble Bill at all.

Mate cried Harry I aint your adjectival mate and I'll teach you how to talk to a gentleman. Take your watch out of your pocket then get off your horse and tie your watch to the bridle God damn you.

Once the cove obeyed Harry circled around to his horse to untie the watch from the bridle. He lifted the instrument beside his ear and made a show of listening to it. Said he This must be a very costly item.

Now I don't know who you are Sir.

I'm Harry Power you adjectival fool.

Then you are a famous man said the fellow and your reputation precedes you.

Harry couldnt keep the pleasure off his shining razored face he folded the golden chain into his palm then dropped the prize into his jacket pocket.

They also say you are a fair man said the cove I've heard songs sung about you.

I never heard no song and I doubt Harry had neither but his face increased its shine he said thats true I am as you describe.

That watch was my father's said the man so why not come up to the house and I'll give you money instead.

I am fair said Harry but I'm not effing stupid and I know there aint no house near here except Kilfeera homestead.

Thats the one said the cove.

And you are R.R. McBean I suppose smirked Harry and that gelding the famous Daylight.

I am. He is.

Harry werent expecting that so to hide his astonishment he rode around the cove's horse as if planning to purchase it. He were in deep manure he knew he were up the proverbial creek without a paddle.

Well Magistrate McBean it is very nice to make your acquaintance but now you better get walking before I put a lead plug in your big fat arse.

That aint wise.

You're right but I aint wise.

The Magistrate then turned to me his eyes was black as ink a fellow could of drowned in them. You don't wish to be associated with something so foolish do you lad?

I said nothing.

Let me keep my horse at least.

Said Harry you aint got a horse that I can see.

You would steal my horse?

You aint got a horse repeated Harry.

Are you sure you would not care to reconsider this Mr Power?

I was never a great one for reconsidering.

Very well the Magistrate said and he turned on his heels and began the long angry walk across his dusty paddocks.

Dismounting from his own mare Harry got on the squatter's horse.

What was that about Bill Frost?

Nothing.

He said he seen Bill Frost.

No he never.

I knew what were said and yet I never encountered such a bald faced lie before and thus I doubted myself. When Harry dug the spur into his new horse I followed him back to the so called SAFETY of Bullock Creek.

That night we camped at Tatong but Harry wouldnt let me make a fire we ate canned beetroot then later on I heard him groaning perhaps it were his bowels perhaps he now were considering what a very stupid thing he had just done. When I woke to the clear metallic notes of magpie &

bellbird I discovered Harry sitting hunched over on his rolled up swag when I approached him I saw he were winding up his new gold watch he paid it a v. fussy kind of attention and once assured it were ticking fast enough he threaded the gold chain through his buttonhole and patted it in place.

Does it keep good time?

He did not look up.

Will I light a fire?

When finally he raised his eyes I could see he lost his nerve.

Perhaps it is time for some new country he said.

Where?

Gippsland.

If you know the precipices the razorback ridges and treacherous shale of the mountains between Tatong and Gippsland you will have some geologic measure of his fear of R.R. McBean. In fact he were not alone I were also very sorry McBean had seen my face.

Said he Our little absence will give this matter time to be forgot.

So I never lit no fire that morning nor the next we pushed our horses quietly up through the Wombat Ranges to Toombulup where we procured a 2nd packhorse and thence to the town of Mansfield where I were sent to buy flour and sugar we had eaten so much beetroot our piss were red as blood.

Departing Mansfield we also left behind our old familiar wedge of territory and when we come out by Merrijig on the Delatite River the south wind were in our faces we looked upon the waving meadows of kangaroo grass and the high wild country and Mount Buller waiting like a scaly beast kneeling on the earth.

The 5th day of our flight were clear and cold with sufficient wind to bring the dead timber crashing down around us as we poked up along a chain of ridges. At day's end we arrived on a high and windy saddle where all that grew were dwarfish white trunked gums and scrappy khaki bushes that lay low amongst the mountain rocks.

Now you can light an adjectival fire.

The wind made the hunting very easy I bagged a wallaby he never knew I were there. That night we ate roast meat and Harry did not complain about his bowels. Perhaps he missed my mother's company I cannot say after we ate we was silent on our blankets looking out across the mighty Great Divide I never seen this country before it were like a fairy story landscape the clear and windy skies was filled with diamonds the jagged black outlines of the ranges were a panorama.

You're going to ride a horse across all that.

I know.

He laughed and he were right I knew nothing of what lay ahead.

See that there he pointed. That is called the Crosscut Saw and that one is Mount Speculation and yonder is Mount Buggery and that other is Mount Despair did you know that?

No Harry.

You will and you'll be sorry.

It might be hard country but I were not afraid I went to sleep in starlight I woke to hail with the horses kicking and bucking in their torment the 2nd packhorse had gone missing it took me 1/2 the morning to walk him down. Then commenced the long and treacherous trip to Tambo Crossing following steep and dangerous routes known only to thieves and wombats it took 5 more days and all but one of them cold & wet.

With our arrival at Tambo I were farther from my home than I had ever been. We soon found McFarley's Tavern its floor were mired with mud and liquor the drinkers was crowded and stinking like wet dogs in a haycart some was there by choice but some had been trapped by rising waters of the Tambo amongst them was bitter mouthed selectors and laid off shearers and knee faced underdogs with their eyes red from fallen sawdust. The air were as sour and sullen as you might expect from a crowd of drunk unhappy men and I did not like to be a foreigner amongst them.

While Harry moved to slake his thirst I stood by the open doorway in the better air and I could see the roaring Tambo its waters so red with dirt you could claim a farm from every gallon. This side of the river were a small paddock overcrowded with the customers' horses pushing & biting & fretting at each other in the rain.

So then I were about as far from Eleven Mile Creek as you could hope to get I seen a rider ambling up the track his horse were a grey mare with a slightly splayfooted gait. He wore a low brimmed hat and a long mud splashed oilskin of an English style and like his horse looked pretty much done in. The rider took off her saddle as if he planned to stay a while then turned the horse into the muddy barren paddock. How queerly familiar were that bandy gait as he walked wearily towards the tavern.

Meanwhile Harry presided over the bar with his bearskin coat undone his pistols showing. Quick I whispered come quick. When he seen my excited face he must of had a premonition he immediately took refuge in his stolen watch fiddling with the chain and flipping open the case to stare a good long time into its face.

Its him I said.

Harry closed the watch and dropped it in his fob pocket then smoothed the golden chain across his dirty waistcoat.

I'll be there directly sonny Jim.

But then Bill Frost were in the open doorway so there were no denying him.

This cannot be cried Harry Power.

Bill Frost saw us both his complexion paled to match the colour of his naked English arse he reached into his pocket for his howdah pistol.

We heard you died said Harry quickly.

By what cause? Frost never moved his eyes off me.

By shooting I said. Harry's hands was resting on his belt adjacent to his American repeater.

What mongrel told you that said Frost his attention still on me.

Harry heard you died said I he heard you bled to death from my gunshot.

Harry Power is a liar said Bill Frost and even you should realise that for Christ's sake. I seen him twice at the adjectival hospital then once at your mother's when I come to get my stockwhip just look at him he's effing winking at me now.

I turned on Harry he were grinning like a dog.

Take a joke.

He's been servicing your mother said Bill Frost.

Take a joke.

You dirty liar I cried I were beside myself I were never so deceived or cheated in all my livelong days you dirty effing liar I did not care what I said to him.

But Harry Power could not afford having a boy speak to him thus he therefore pulled his Colt .31 revolver from his belt and pressed it to my head above the ear.

Now the quiet descended all around me I looked into Harry's eyes they was dead and pale as a curtain.

Better apologise he whispered.

I'm sorry Harry.

Louder.

Sorry Mr Power.

You was mistaken.

Yes I were mistaken.

He removed the barrel back from my skull uncocked the action and now he dared to grin and clip me across the head the fool he did not know me.

I returned his smile laying my left hand on his shoulder he were a big hard man I could feel the heft in him but as I were no longer afraid I punched him in the bowel. When he doubled over I brought up my fist into his throat a dreadful noise then come out of him and I took his revolver off him and pushed it against the back of his square head I could see his dirty scalp showing through his thinning hair. My hands was trembling I asked him did he wish to live or die.

For answer the famous Harry Power collapsed upon the boozy mire gasping like a great fat Murray cod I ripped the gold watch off him it tore a lump of his waistcoat which were still attached to its chain when I threw it on the ground.

I'll kill you I cried.

My blood were boiling but I could not kill instead I shot the rich gold watch and it leapt and spun its very innards the wheels and springs spilling out as the drunkards all fled in a tangle to cower in the shadows of that muddy room. Putting the weapon in my belt I turned and walked out into the rain.

That night my dear mother dreamed about me she could correctly describe the horse I mounted outside McFarley's Tavern she knew it were a dappled grey she knew I were in danger but did not know the threat were Harry Power. Walking towards the holding yard I glanced back to the shanty and observed Power were once more on his feet his right hand resting on his big American repeater. I did not touch the Colt .31 but climbed the fence where the famous Daylight were busy making a nuisance of himself with the fillies he were a very handsome horse with a good barrel a long strong neck and I resolved to have him as payment for my services to Mr Power. The mares now headed him away from the fillies while I saw from his bloody flanks they had already kicked and bitten him as punishment but this were no bad sign of character to me. As I come up with his bridle he turned his bum to me but if he had intended to kick me he soon changed his mind and tried to bite my leg instead.

A crowd of men was watching from the veranda of the shanty I saw Bill Frost clap his hand upon Harry's shoulder only to be pushed away. I won't say my heart werent thumping but I deserved that horse I knew it and I took him for a ride in the rain and once he had snorted and pigrooted a little I let him know my mind were open as to his character. All this time Harry Power & Bill Frost continued their study of me each one as cunning as an outhouse rat I should of watched them every instant but this were not possible so I carried the weight of their hateful old eyes upon my back. Tethering Daylight to the fence I found our packhorse she were still full laden I helped myself to Power's best waterproof sheet also some tea a few potatoes and a lump of cheese. These provisions I placed in a gunnysack while I were more or less hidden by the stock.

I climbed the fence with a horse blanket rolled up beneath my arm and the gunnysack across my shoulders I seen Harry had set his American repeater at the danger position which is in the middle right above his fly. I tied the blanket over Daylight's pommel and then at last I mounted.

It made no sense to shoot me but Harry had a dreadful pride in fact the river were so loud I cannot say for certain that he didnt fire as I departed only that when trotting round the hillock at the bottom of the track I were still alive. The clean clear rain poured off my hatbrim as I cantered beside the flooded Tambo and now I could enjoy my fine new companion fully. The sight of his ears flicking back and forth the freckled grey neck bobbing in front of me the mane bouncing in time with his stride all this soon conspired to put me in a very happy frame of mind.

Gitup I told him and my God he gitup very rapid he had a heart like a house he swam the flooded river to clamber up the crumbling bank and then the very track were flying under us a mighty beast he were steaming snorting game for anything. We was both free of Harry Power and now might go whichever way we chose whether home through the mountains to Harrietville or to Siam to see the King there were nothing we couldnt do.

Up at Doctors Flat the rain finally relented and I fell in with 2 old miners who was as evenly matched as a pair of unwashed china jugs they was both spade bearded no more than 5 ft. tall the rogues. Sucking on their yellow pipes they told me I were mad to think to cross to Harrietville for that required me to come down the Fainter Spur. When they understood I were not to be dissuaded they said I should write down my will on the inside of my oilskin for there was bad fogs after the rain and a great deal of shale and they predicted Daylight would fall from the Fainter and I would die. I were not afraid I asked them to show me the way so they laughed and said I should follow the same track used by Bogong Jack when he ran his stolen herds up into New South Wales they drew me a map in the mud. Thus educated I cantered off along the trail.

By nightfall I were back in high grand country the air hurt the inside of my nose though it were sweet pain to me the skies once more v. clear and I found myself a spot amongst a stand of snow gums and lit a fragrant fire inside a log. It were very cold indeed I give Daylight the blanket but in the night it were so frigid I took it back and perhaps on account of this he chose to pay me out. In the morning he were absent without leave.

Having hobbled and belled him I knew he could not of gone too far so I took my time to bake 2 of the potatoes and brew some tea for breakfast. After washing my face in the icy stream I begun the search but not until almost all the morning were spent without the slightest tinkle of his bell did I begin to see my situation were v. serious having little food and a very long walk ahead of me in country I did not know. Climbing up a long rocky ridge sometime around noon I found myself in a great wide dish of plain cut through by a narrow rocky stream the grass were green and sweet in marked contrast to the parched earth down around Eleven Mile. Following the stream for signs of the gelding I come upon a shepherd's hut amongst a stand of snow gums. Its roof were very high pitched for the winter snow it had a stone fireplace which were most unusual in the bush. I called cooee but it were long abandoned the walls was rough adzed slabs but inside some houseproud shepherd had plastered the slabs with mud then papered the walls with pages of THE ILLUSTRATED AUSTRALIAN NEWS not glued all higgledy piggledy but v. neat. It were like walking inside a book I couldnt stop to read but there was many pictures of the war the Yankees fought between themselves the ships with guns the battle plans and every page were dated from 8 and 9 yr. previous. The hut were large and dry and orderly its bunks constructed to accommodate 6 men I thought how happy I would be to live in such isolation but there were no food and it were clear I would now be walking all the way to Harrietville.

Back at the campsite I were stuffing my pockets with whatever I could find for the ordeal when I become aware of a slight movement in the scrub. Having heard kangaroos thumping in the night I swiftly primed the Colt and aimed it where the branches shook. At the very moment the trigger clicked to its 1st pressure point Daylight decided he had had sufficient fun with me and he shook his long grey head the bell rang and he pushed his nose enquiringly out of his hiding place.

You adjectival b−−−−−d I shouted.

He were so very sorry he said walking out into the clearing to hobble around me his bell ringing constantly it were hard to credit his deception but there is no doubt the whole business were intentional for his head were very low in apology. I told him he were a rogue and a scoundrel this cheered him up no end he come up and nosed me it made me laugh I could not help it. From this time we was great friends and I talked and joked with him continually. He brought me down the Fainter but never once baulked or stumbled on all that dreadful descent.

That night we made camp not far from Harrietville I apologised that I must tether him for the night.

As he had had no decent feed for 2 days now I didnt push him on the 3rd we travelled by slow and roundabout paths so even while passing through the township of Bright I were never directly on a public road. Soon we was back on them tracks so beloved of Harry arriving at Glenmore at mid afternoon of the 3rd day and it were here I learned from Jimmy Quinn I had not escaped from nothing. The cops had arrested my uncle Jack Lloyd he were falsely charged with the theft of McBean's heirloom watch and gelding but it were worse than this for the traps was now hunting my cousin Tom Lloyd for my role in the robbery.

His Early Contact
with Senior Policemen

Of generic stock, 20 ruled pages (9" × 12" approx.)
roughly torn along left-hand margin. Blue ink with
damp stain in lower margins.

*The author's return to Eleven Mile Creek, and
a claim that the family attempted to restore the
stolen horse to Magistrate McBean. A description
of his arrest by Sgt Whelan and imprisonment
at Benalla. Kelly's growing reputation confirmed
by the arrival of two superintendents The manu
script contains allegations of both corruption
(the police) and perjury (R. R. McBean). £500 is
offered to reveal Harry Power's whereabouts. The
author is transported to Melbourne where a
meeting takes place with Commissioner Standish.
An account of a night spent in the cells at Richmond Depot.*

Tom Lloyd were my own age we had raced sticks down the flooded creeks and wrestled in the dirt and once we staged a famous galloping contest from Greta to the Winton swamp I would never permit him to be punished for my crime. Thus my return to my own district were v. melancholy for I knew there were nothing to do but surrender myself to the police.

It were night when Daylight and me come past the ruins in Greta where the old hotel burnt to the ground and though it were not warm the sweet scents of the dark clung to me like cobwebs there were no smell of ashes anymore only of gum leaves and freshly turned earth I could smell mad Michael O'Brien's 15 pigs the rich sour sawdust from Mrs Danaher's new veranda. There was neither stars nor moon but as I finally come down Futter's Range a 1/2 hour later there were a fine rain carried in the south west wind and although I couldn't see a thing I heard a bandicoot with its snout in the leaves beside the track. No dogs barked I thought this very queer.

Twice Daylight were spooked and I pushed him on he moved only v. reluctantly and then a shower of sparks burst from a chimney to my left and thus I discovered that I were 100 yd. from my home. In that moment of illumination I also seen the bulky shadow of a tall horse the rider dressed in white it were my own mother waiting God knows how she knew I were drawing near but she give me a great start she put the heart across in me.

As I rode through the creek the dogs stayed mute but I heard my mother's dear familiar voice both rough and tender at its centre.

Is it you?

Its me.

I heard the rattle of her horse's bit but could not see her it were pitch black.

Said she I have a good strong mare for you my darling boy and theres cheese and pickled meats in this here gunnybag.

The traps are looking for me I said I were strangely relieved to say it.

Some silly b————r bailed up old McBean said she and now the district is crawling with police like a bull ants' nest. They is camping on the Fifteen Mile and they is camped in Greta they're here each morning before sun up knocking on my door. They're looking for your cobber Tom Lloyd but will lag anyone who aggravates them. I hear they is getting the stick from the higher ups in Melbourne.

Ma this here is McBean's horse I'm riding.

My mother did not respond.

Ma it were Harry Power and me that did the crime.

Harry told me you was in New South Wales.

Harry said a lot of things that wasnt true Ma.

Well all the more adjectival reason to take this horse. You give me McBean's nag I'll lose it fast enough.

Theres more to say Ma I come home to tell you I shot Bill Frost. It werent my business to shoot Bill I'm more sorry than anything I can say.

Harry done it he told me.

Harry's a bigger liar than any of us could ever credit.

There were a long pause I couldnt see or feel my mother's thought.

Is the saddle stole too she asked.

Its got McBean's initials on it.

Where is the watch I hope you aint got that.

Harry has it whats left of it.

Then you leave both horse and saddle then take this mare of mine and get off up the Wombat.

Well Ma I can't let Tom do my time.

O Jesus Ned do you think the Lloyds would do as much for you?

Dismounting I tethered Daylight at the fence and finally my mother followed me inside our hut.

Our 2 kangaroo dogs was kept inside to prevent them warning spies of my arrival so now they scampered out into the dark. Once we was inside my mother's distress were exceedingly clear but she turned her hard white back on me and kept her feelings between her and the fire.

It were after midnight when I entered but one by one my brothers and sisters emerged from behind the curtains. Maggie were the 1st of them smelling of clean earth and boiled milk she led me by the hand to meet our new sister Ellen. Bill Frost's daughter were no bigger than a loaf of bread she lay asleep in a fruit box on the table if ever dross were turned to gold then here she was.

In this bitter hour when my mother knew I would not flee from punishment she instructed Maggie to spread our best tablecloth then when Kate crawled out of bed she ordered her to fetch the willow plates from their hiding place. She sent Dan to scrub his filthy nails while she herself lit 4 good beeswax candles spacing them evenly along the span setting one place for each Kelly as if to Christmas dinner. So did the yawning children sit at table as my mother unpacked the groaning gunnysack she had prepared for my flight.

When Maggie saw all she had baked for me now laid out she began to cry and then Gracie were weeping as well and Kate looked as if she would at any moment join the chorus so I told them all about old Daylight's pranks and how I nearly shot him for a kangaroo.

Kate and Gracie enjoyed my story greatly they ate their plum pudding and was soon back in bed asleep. Dan said he were not a girl he would not sleep he would stand guard for me but v. soon his head were falling and I laid his ferocious little 8 yr. old body upon his crib.

Jem pledged to take McBean's horse up to Winton and leave him tethered near the pound so I went outside to say goodbye and I told Daylight I would never forget him he were the bravest horse I ever rode. Coming inside I saw my mother had placed a parcel in the middle of the table it were wrapped in white tissue paper so I thought it must be baby clothes. Only as she unfolded it before me did I recognize the 7 ft. green sash Mr Shelton give me so long ago in Avenel. TO EDWARD KELLY IN GRATITUDE FOR HIS COURAGE FROM THE SHELTON FAMILY.

Put it on she said her eyes was fierce and brimming. I done what she wished and when I had girded the sash around me I sat down once more and then my mother sat by my side and took my hand and stroked my wrist. Thus we waited for the cruel morning when we would harvest the bitter crop sowed on our land by Harry Power.

At dawn I were arrested by Sgt Whelan then taken from my family and escorted in pouring rain into Benalla I had no notion of the forces stirred against me. I knew I had helped steal the horse and timepiece from the Police Commissioner's friend but understood so little of that class that I couldnt imagine so much as McBean's feather pillow. I were a plump witchetty grub beneath the bark not knowing that the kookaburra exists unable to imagine that fierce beak or the punishment in that wild and angry eye.

The cell were the same as previous and I expected Whelan to bash me as before but he done much worse for the moment he took away my sash and belt and bootlaces he sent news to Police Commissioner Standish dotdot dashdash and soon the name Ned Kelly were spoken out loud inside the Commissioner's rooms 100 mi. away in Melbourne and before the day were over Supt Nicolson and Supt Hare were ordered to Benalla to interrogate me and so up that rotten crabholed Melbourne road the 2 higher up policemen sped. They was oil & water chalk & cheese the differences not at all disguised by their flash jack uniforms. It rained all the way across the Great Divide them sitting inside the coach with their silver laced caps in their laps. I were 16 yr. old and had no idea of their approach.

On Tuesday May 10th after a meal of bread and water I were brought in handcuffs from my cell to a room at Benalla Police Station I were very surprised to see them 2 officers I smelled their power as distinctive as a lady's perfume. It were the dapper handsome Hare who done the talking whilst sturdy old Scots Nicolson looked out the window he seemed more interested in how the farrier were filing the teeth of Sgt Whelan's horse.

Hare were broad shouldered and posh spoken he sat grimly behind the cedar desk trying to frighten me with his blue English eyes he recited a list of robberies which I were alleged to have done with Harry Power.

He asked me what I said to that.

I told him he better tear up that warrant for my cousin Tom Lloyd.

He cleaned out his pipe with a queer silver instrument he might of been a surgeon. He used a silver studded leather pouch to hold his baccy he said he would arrest Tom Lloyd and keep him forever if he so desired he also said Tom Lloyd had been harboured by my mother so her selection could now be taken from her under the Land Act of 1865.

You got no evidence of that said I.

He answered he would gaol my mother if he so chose and all my brothers & uncles & cousins and he did not care if we should breed like rabbits for he would lockup the mothers & babies too. When he stood up it were like seeing a tapeworm uncurl in your presence the length of him were sickening to see he were 6 ft. 3 in. even 6 ft. 4 with dainty feet.

I'll make you regret you ever laid eyes upon Mr McBean he said and left the room.

Nicolson were left behind he seemed old and weary much kinder than the Englishman. He asked how many acres my mother had and once I answered him politely he criticised the Land Act and said it were a crime to use good cattle country for the wheat. He asked me would I like my bracelets removed and I thanked him and he give me a chair confiding in me that Hare were a spiteful b—————d I should not of gone against him. You should give some information for your own protection said he just a little would do the trick. I know old Harry is your mate.

Power aint my mate I said he is an adjectival mongrel.

So much the better said he.

But I aint a fizgig I said and I won't shop no one to you b————rs.

At this he jumped up and rushed at me I raised my fists in protection but he suddenly turned away pretending a great interest with the scenery outside the window. We sat in silence for a while then he winked at me this strange old bird I didnt know what to make of him.

I heard your mater is in a friendly situation with Mr Power he said at last.

Harry Power is a liar and a thief said I my mother won't see him no more I warrant you.

He peered at me with sleepy eyes. Well then says he how would you like to see all your charges thrown out of court?

I already confessed to Sgt Whelan he wrote it down I signed it.

Sgt Whelan is famous for losing paper son he winked again.

He would manage to lose the warrant for Tom Lloyd?

O I do not doubt it said he. You just give me a little taste of what you're offering and he will lose young Lloyd's warrant and the 1st of the 6 charges against yourself. Is that fair or aint it?

I then gave him certain information it were nothing much. Later that day he come to my cell to tear up Tom's warrant in my presence. So is the law administered in the colony of Victoria.

Early next morning Hare & Nicolson went to my mother she did not care for anyone's opinion but were still embarrassed to be discovered butchering a possum.

I thought you were Mrs Power these days said Nicolson that is what we heard.

You effing well heard wrong said she putting the possum in the meat safe where their eyes could not feast upon it.

So you havent been keeping company with Harry?

No I aint.

Well thats a considerable pity said Nicolson for you just missed a chance to make a very handsome sum.

500 said Hare.

5 quid? My mother could not help showing a certain degree of interest. You are offering me 5 quid?

500 Mrs Kelly.

Faith what for?

For introducing us to Mr Power.

Hare produced a carefully folded issue of THE POLICE GAZETTE and offered it to my mother she could not read as the smirking b−−−−−d would of known.

My mother washed her hands before she took the paper.

Lord Heaven help us she stared at the page and then returned it. Will the government give me £500 for flatfooted old Harry Power?

I cannot imagine why you would deny yourself the profit.

Then you're as ignorant as a heap of dog manure cried my mother her voice so loud she woke her baby Ellen.

Mrs Kelly there are children present you must think of the example you are setting them.

The example I would give my children said our mother is that nothing is as low as trading a man's life for money now get off my land before I put the dog on you. That kelpie has a taste for eating horse droppings but I warrant he would prefer a fat policeman's arse.

Hare and Nicolson then went on to visit Uncle Jack Lloyd he were released from gaol the day before and while we do not know what were said it is pretty clear Jack did not chase them off the property.

The Superintendents never mentioned the £500 to me they provided other incentives for betrayal. They brung McBean as witness to Benalla Court where I watched in astonishment as the squatter swore on the Bible I were on no account the boy that robbed him.

Said Nicolson Just watch what we can do if you cooperate.

The following day we was all in court when Hare and Nicolson once more played with justice they pushed it pulled it made it hop & jump and the Crown withdrew 2 more charges.

Feeling obliged to offer something more I described our journey across the Great Divide down to Tambo Crossing. I claimed Harry were planning to flee the country from Eden on the coast of Gippsland.

They wrote down what I said.

Next day there was legal argument I could not fathom. Finally the Magistrate put me on remand to be took to Kyneton but when the Superintendents returned my sash and belt they transported me to Melbourne instead. They give me a curried egg sandwich which I ate in the coach while Hare and Nicolson drank their brandy and smoked their cigars. I asked them what would happen next but they would not say and I never showed them I were afraid.

I expected to be transferred directly to Franklin Street in the cold blue stone citadel of Melbourne Gaol but instead were taken to a mansion in a Toorak street the night were filled with the sweet aroma of burning autumn leaves. Nicolson swung open the grand wrought iron gate Hare rung the bell and a handsome Constable in uniform appeared like he were a butler then I seen a mighty Turk rug stretching out before me it were blue and vermilion no one in my family could of imagined such a lovely thing I could not credit I were permitted to walk on it in my boots but Hare escorted me along its entire length and finally we come into a large room where gentlemen in long black coats was playing billiards they had ribbons and medals on their coats I could not predict what bad thing would happen to me here.

You did not catch your fox then Superintendent?

I have the pup Sir.

Ah I see said a tall gentleman and he smiled at me and I saw the hurt and harm in him he were slim and dapper but his sharp teeth was crooked and stained as old piano keys.

So you are Ned Kelly he asked me obviously he knew and there were no point in a reply.

The prisoner will answer the Commissioner.

I am Ned Kelly said I and the room went quiet.

You stole Mr McBean's watch.

For answer I said I heard McBean swear on the Bible that I had not robbed him and I were sure a Magistrate like him would not commit a perjury.

This Commissioner had not liked me at the start now he liked me even less. Well Ned Kelly said he I suppose you play a fair deal of billiards up at Eleven Mile Creek the men behind him was sniggering I said there were not a game I could not play and as for billiards I reckoned any boy who could shoot a running rabbit would do well enough with a white ball and stick.

Ignorance makes you very cocky said he.

Just give me one of them sticks.

It is called a cue.

Give it to me then you'll see which one is ignorant.

This come out as ruder than intended and raised his eyebrows very high. O dear says he what will we do with him?

Whip him Sir. Thrash him etc. etc.

Very well said the Commissioner I'll play you billiards and if you win I will release you from all charges.

I said that were very fair the gentlemen was still sniggering they thought me v. stupid they did not expect I had a sense of humour.

But what if you lose Ned Kelly?

Then you can have my handcuffs.

The sudden laughter did not please the cove at all. If you lose he said you will forfeit Harry Power.

I answered I did not trade in human flesh and the Commissioner's face went very red said he I should thrash you severely.

I said I were not a coward and would fight him man to man if that were what he wished.

He then spoke so very close I could smell his dinner he said he would dearly love to burst my spleen but the dignity of his office forbade him touching criminals his spit were wet upon my face and there were a blaze showing in his eyes it were the fury of weak men.

Supt Hare then brought in the Constable from the front door announcing this individual had volunteered to be the Commissioner's nominee in other words the poor Constable would fight in his boss's place. The gentlemen began immediately pushing the furniture back against the walls they rolled the rug back to mark a square in billiard chalk upon the floor.

The Constable were 6 yr. my senior he had the advantage in both weight and reach but when he come out into the ring I struck him on the temple very hard. His head jerked back I felt the pain right through my arm but knew when I seen his eyes that his distress were greater. He ducked and shuffled very prettily but landed no decent blows so the audience began to barrack him for being a coward he were amiable and handsome but he had no taste for pain. When he come in again I got inside his reach landing to the neck the selfsame punch I give to Harry Power. My present opponent staggered holding his hands up to his injury. I then delivered the postscript at which he doubled over on the floor but the gentlemen would not let him off.

Get up man get up and fight.

Trying to finish him as humane as possible I struck him on the temple and he fell and knocked his head violently upon the skirting board his eyes was closed shut no one called for him to rise. Indeed the room become so very quiet and sour you could smell the shame as the Englishmen turned back to their brandy or remembered there was pretty ladies waiting in another room. As for me I were the winning dog but I got no prize I were put back in my bracelets then transported to Richmond Police Depot. And that were the extent of the Police Commissioner's interrogation.

Supt Nicolson ordered the Duty Sergeant to provide an extra blanket but then he went away leaving me to the charity of 2 turnip faced Irish Constables who did not even seem to know my name. They give me no blanket just pushed me into a dark wet courtyard where I caught a whiff of chaff & manure I therefore thought they planned to lock me in a stable.

By lantern light I were relieved to see 2 empty cells side by side then I reminded the Irishmen to bring the blankets but they said they was not my effing servants and they thrust me in a cell. The floor were stone not earthen though the smell of fear and disinfectant were most unpleasantly familiar. Some time afterwards one of my gaolers returned reporting there was no blankets for all the bedding were sent to Coburg for disinfecting.

I were still wearing my moleskins and red shirt the same light clothes in which I had been taken 5 days previous I were so cold my teeth were rattling like old Fratelli's wooden dummy and my green sash proved little comfort to me here.

A very long time passed until finally a bright light showed under the door I shouted I were cold.

No reply.

God help me mate whoever you are.

Swear on the Virgin you will not jump me said a voice.

I were promised a blanket said I.

Stand back against the adjectival wall.

Thinking they was going to bash me I stiffened up the sinews but then the door swung open and there stood the handsome Constable I had earlier defeated he were as pretty as a saint in a Holy Card the shining all around him his arms was full of blankets.

Swear on the Virgin you won't jump me said he his face were beastly bruised the skin all were broken on his brow.

I swear on the Virgin.

Spit twice.

I done it.

Good man said he delivering his burden to my cot. I fell upon the blankets straight away they was scratchy and smelled strongly of camphor but never were a rough embrace so comforting and kind.

My name is John Fitzpatrick said he.

Ned Kelly.

I know he said placing his lantern on the floor then unwrapping v. carefully the newspaper from around a bottle which he swigged before wiping and passing to myself. I confessed I did not drink.

You aint too young to start.

Don't like its taste.

Good show said he placing his treasure gently beneath the crib then solemnly smoothing out the newspaper it had been wrapped in.

If you jump me it would be the finish of my employment you must not do it.

I won't jump you no road.

Spit he said.

I spit.

Spit twice.

I done so again.

Good show he said smoothing the newspaper once more. I've been 2 months in this racket it aint perfect but its better than Mount Egerton. I could not bear that place again.

He now folded the paper in 1/2 upon his knee then 1/4 and 1/8.

You know Mount Egerton he asked mournfully.

I don't.

Here he said and producing his dagger he sliced the paper along the folds. I thought this must be something to do with Mount Egerton but I were wrong.

Its to wipe your bum he said you stick it on that nail there. Thats the spirit. Now could you find room for a little govt. meat?

Whatever he were going to say about Mount Egerton was now forgot he cut the string on a 2nd parcel to reveal a whole leg of the Commissioner's lamb then sat beside me on the cot and cut me hunks of pink meat it were cold and the fat v. crunchy and I thought him the best policeman I ever met and said I were sorry to have caused him a damage.

He said I were the best adjectival fighter he had ever engaged and being the Welterweight Champion he should know. He said he liked the adjectival moment I offered to whip Commissioner Standish and would gladly suffer any number of beatings to see that look I put on the b─────d's adjectival face.

Dear daughter I know your mamma kept many newspaper clippings relating to the so called KELLY OUTRAGE if they aint been burnt by now you will be able to consult the photograph of this Fitzpatrick's younger brother Alex it were him who introduced me to your mother. In the photograph Alex shows you his strong legs and big hands but his mouth is the size of a rabbit's bum. The man who came to my cell were a more expansive spirit and he lit a cigar he had stolen from the Commissioner's table. He prayed to God each night he said to keep him forever from Mount Egerton. He swore if I looked into his eyes I would see the district's dreadful naked hills reflected back. I saw no hills only a generous soul and I can only say I liked him.

I asked why he would take this risk on my behalf.

Listen to me Ned said he you are a good and plucky boy you are straight as a die as far as I can see. But these officers will squash you when they don't need you which will be very soon I promise.

You cannot know that.

Mate it will happen by tomorrow I spit and swear it.

You can't know that.

Shutup shutup I adjectival spit and swear it they make us servants at their adjectival dinners even though that aint permitted by the rules those b————ds do not care they are the bosses of the effing colony. Shutup and listen to me Ned you're acting like I did before I come down to Melbourne I had no adjectival clue I were wine waiter at a dinner where the Commissioner had the table set with naked ladies there were one in every chair.

No.

My colonial oath you don't know who these b————rs are.

Naked completely?

It were at that moment we heard a cough nearby.

He whispered there must be a prisoner in the other cell but I knew the other cell to be empty. Shutup said he hurriedly wrapping the lamb.

When he squeezed my arm he were suddenly a man 6 yr. older and not the chap I had knocked to the ground and he put his mouth near my ear and spoke very rapid.

When they don't need to be nice no more you'll see their damn colours.

I made to draw away. Shutup he said pulling me back they'll declare your mother A Person Not Suitable then they'll annul her lease. They don't want your family in the district thats what they said I heard it Ned I see you don't believe me but I aint no liar.

A liar he were not but at that moment I couldnt tell if he were friend or foe.

Harry Power will be betrayed day after tomorrow.

So you say.

Listen its true they have offered a man called Jack Lloyd £500 reward and he is sucking on the bait. Soon they'll set the hook then Harry Power will go to prison. You might as well get the reward they don't want your evidence they just want you to point the bone.

Then he picked up his bottle and his lantern. Pass me the bottle through the hatch.

It were very dark inside the cell I done as asked.

I aint no liar said he and he were gone leaving behind only the blankets and the smell of grog.

Marvellous Melbourne so they call it in the newspapers.

Perhaps if I were a Chinaman I might of had the sense to betray Harry Power without no shame I cannot say but we Irish was raised to revile the traitors' names when I were a child and they wished to make me hate my own father they said he were A Certain Man.

At Beveridge Catholic School we learned the traitors better than the saints so at 5 yr. of age I could recite the names John Cockayne Edward Abby even poor Anthony Perry who finally betrayed the rebels after the English set his head alight with pitch and gunpowder. Likewise but contrary I knew the names of the Athy blacksmiths Tom Murray and Owen Finn they would not betray the rebels though they was flogged and tortured the whole town echoing with their screams.

Though Harry Power used me v. poorly I could not betray him. Through that long dark night at Richmond Depot I imagined we would all be badly punished for my refusal but when the cold dawn come and the reward were declined no one threatened me with nothing and I were too relieved to think it worrisome or strange.

Back in Benalla 2 days later the charges against me was all dismissed and I were given the Queen of England's kind permission to freely walk the 13 wet and windy miles to our selection.

I had been a prisoner for 3 weeks but Mother did not greet me upon my return she slid her straining spoon along the top of the saucepan then scraped the rich yellow cream into a small brown bowl.

I asked her whats the matter do I smell?

She would not answer yes or no so I walked out on the veranda Maggie were approaching from the dairy but when I waved she pretended not to see me. Soon she were on horseback riding out towards Bald Hills.

There was many tools on the veranda including my old sledgehammer its handle smooth and familiar as my own skin I found my wedges in a canvas bag hanging by a nail from the roof. Knowing useful labour were awaiting I carried these items out behind the cowbail where I discovered nothing but laziness and neglect the rank weeds growing right around the previously cut up logs.

Very soon I heard a horse coming down the track upon its back was Dan 9 yr. and Jem 11 yr. Though I stood in plain sight my brothers played blind and it were thus clear I had committed some grievous offence against my family. I rolled one of the logs clear of the weeds then I set a little #1 wedge and drove it home.

Jem returned alone he brung our father's 6 lb. sledgehammer I stepped back so he could drive a wedge.

I don't blame you Ned no road who could adjectival blame you.

For what I asked.

I seen his dark eyes filled with considerable emotion.

You know.

I don't know nothing.

We know you dobbed in Harry Power.

And that were how I learned Power were finally arrested he had been taken by old Nicolson at his bolthole above the Quinns.

They say you was taken down to Melbourne Ned.

Yes I were but I never dobbed old Harry.

They say you was brought to the Police Commissioner then you come back to lead the traps to Harry.

Its a lie.

Aunt Kate knew before it happened Ned she come and told us what you was intending. She said you would be released in return for leading the traps to Harry. And then Harry were lagged and here you is released as prophesied.

I ran back to the hut shouting from the doorway that my mother should accuse her effing sister not her son. My mother were deaf she wouldnt even look my way.

Your sister Kate is an adjectival liar its her that sold Harry to the traps not me.

My mother charged slapping me violently about the head I retreated before her. Get out she cried get out I cannot bear the adjectival sight of you.

I removed myself to the veranda but still she kept on coming.

Judas she cried.

Judas? I picked up a shovel.

Yes Judas.

It were the worst thing ever said to me. Stand I cried don't take another step.

She were still furious but I held her favourite weapon many is the time I saw her swing that shovel I were trembling like a horse thinking her an unnatural mother to believe a sister before her son.

It were Uncle Jack Lloyd betrayed Harry I cried. I swear it by this blessed iron.

My ma shook her head her disbelief blowing such a draught upon my rage I swung the murderous shovel hard against the wall and the red gum handle split in 1/2 and I picked up both pieces and each of them as deadly as a pike they was bright red and hard as railway sleepers.

Damn you I told my mother.

Gracie screamed she grabbed me round the waist. Do not hurt your ma.

Them Lloyds sold Harry for 500 quid!

O Lord! My mother sat suddenly upon the step holding her hand across her mouth. She recognised the price thank Jesus.

I freed myself from Gracie's grasp and returned to my sledgehammer but hard work did not calm me quite the opposite I were even angrier that my ma should have judged me so poorly and my hands was shaking and my feelings jumping like a slice of bacon on the pan. The timber now had lain in the air for a year so though the bark were wet and slimy the heartwood were well dried the grain straight and true I remained v. hungry all afternoon.

More than food I yearned for your grandma to apologise for her injustice it were not till dusk that finally she made her visit she told me I done a good job with the rails.

You're a good son said she and we stood side by side looking out across the cold green winter paddocks to where the cows was bunching at the fence much bothered by the inconvenience of their milk.

PARCEL 6

Events Precipitated
by the Arrest of
Harry Power

12 pages (8½" × 9½" approx.) consisting of 6
envelopes opened to provide room for text. Old
stamps partially removed, envelopes addressed to
Mrs M. Skilling, Greta, Colony of Victoria. The
exceptionally small hand is nonetheless recognisably
Kelly's.

*The common belief that Kelly has betrayed Harry
Power provokes conflict in the extended family.
He confesses to having tricked his uncles Pat
and Jimmy Quinn into a fight with Constable
Hall with dire consequences for Pat Quinn. A
falling-out with Constable Hall. Author delivers
an insulting note and package to a Mr and Mrs
McCormick, is arrested by Hall and sentenced to
three years.*

My mother knew I were no traitor but she were alone of all her sisters except the guilty Kate Lloyd and of course it were Kate with husband Jack who had most reason to spread this slander so wholeheartedly. Soon all my aunts and uncles hated me but Uncle Jimmy Quinn and Uncle Pat Quinn was easily the most upset they insisted I should be flogged.

My daughter please understand I am displaying your great uncles in a bad light they was wild and often shicker they thieved and fought and abused me cruelly but you must also remember your ancestors would not kowtow to no one and this were a fine rare thing in a colony made specifically to have poor men bow down to their gaolers.

Were I a fat squatter with his children safe asleep in bed I would have the time to tell you sentimental stories of the Quinns by birth or marriage and it is true that Wild Pat the Dubliner played the accordion at my ma's shebeen that Uncle Jimmy had a beautiful voice it would make you cry to hear him sing the Shan Van Voght. This very man who now began calling me c––t and traitor had been very kind when I were a child.

But them is stories to be saved for happy days and this was dark nights with Jimmy and Pat my constant tormentors for they was ashamed to think their own relation had betrayed the mighty Harry Power. Criminals by any code their horses was sleek and black they were pirate kings or so they thought Jimmy were the taller one he were a good looking b––––r with deep hooded eyes. Wild Pat were not so handsome his side whiskers grew fat as rosebushes his mouth were v. mean. This pair would sit on the veranda at O'Brien's Hotel and barrack me whenever I rode past Ned Kelly were a fizgig a lying traitor he should be wrapped in barbed wire and rolled into the Winton swamp.

Until Harry's arrest I were well regarded in that district but now people was crossing the street to get away from me no one would employ me.

At home it were very quiet no customers come to our shebeen no relations arrived to ease our poverty. I existed in a silent agony where my so called CRIME could not even be whispered. I were so lonely I wrote a letter to thank Constable Fitzpatrick for the lamb and blankets and I explained it were not the police who were punishing me for refusing the reward it were my own family.

Needing an address I called by the new Police Station at Curlewis Street and I found Cons Hall behind his desk all 16 stone of fat and no more popular than me. He addressed an official envelope to Fitzpatrick and sealed my own letter within he would take no money for the postage.

He said he had heard I were looking for work.

I said no one would employ me to do so much as bury a dunny can.

O I think we can do better than that he said then offered the job of constructing a split rail fence for a horse paddock it were 5/– a day which were v. good money.

Going on the traps' payroll made me fair game but I were already reviled as a turncoat I could not see my reputation disimproving but I were wrong. On my very 1st day of employment Harry Power were sentenced to 15 yr. hard labour and once this harsh punishment become known I were more actively sought out.

One wet bitter Monday afternoon the wind were coming in squalls and the sky were black as dye bleeding from a widow's weeds as Pat and Jimmy Quinn came along Curlewis Street they was full of harm in their long brown coats their hats pulled down across their eyes. At 1st they didnt cross the fence but sat on their horses watching me work and when the rain come back they turned towards the pub. I hoped that were the end of it but a few hours later they was back racing up and down Curlewis Street this were Furious Riding in a Public Place and the great 16 stone Cons Hall were on the veranda until he suddenly remembered he had pressing business inside.

Seeing this cowardice Jim and Pat lifted the slip rail and ambled into the police paddock coming close to where I now were chiselling the mortises they circled me like wedgetails waiting for a beast to die.

I could not believe Hall would tolerate this flagrant trespass but there were no movement from inside the station and Jim and Pat got bolder making the circle tighter all the time taunting me as a defector and a spy. Pat said I should come down to the pub to take my flogging there were no escape and every poor woman married to a drunkard must know the foreboding those encircling men brung to my young heart it were not the prospect of pain itself but the dark sick feeling what comes beyond hope of self defence. Soon Cons Archdeacon returned from patrol he didnt say nothing to my uncles only slid a govt. rifle from his scabbard as he removed the slip rail. My uncles said nothing neither but ambled insolently past him heading once more towards the pub.

When the coast were clear Cons Hall come out to pay me wages but would not look me in the eye he smelled of wine and had difficulty calculating what sum I were owed.

He asked were I going to the dance in Oxley.

I said I had to go down to O'Brien's to fight Pat and Jimmy Quinn as they was slandering me.

Until this moment Hall showed a great dull and greasy sort of lethargy such as derives from sitting on your backside with the blinds pulled down eating dry biscuits and drinking Millawa wine but when he learned I had to fight the Quinns his manner changed entirely.

No cried he no that aint fair.

When I seen his wet eyes shining in the gloom I could imagine how he must of felt caged in his office by his own fear. How often that afternoon he had come to the door only to find himself too afraid to take them on.

O Ned cried Hall we can't have this.

I knew he were a liar and bent in every possible way but when he said this I liked and trusted him.

Said he Constable Archdeacon is returned so now theres 2 of us and we'll arrest them if they touch you I swear we will.

I knew he wouldnt stand a chance of arresting them at the pub the crowd would not let him. Sharing the same thought he said You start something thats the thing to do.

Its already started said I.

Just start something then run back up here thats all I ask. Them Quinns is bullies but this will be their Waterloo. Hall had previously been inclined to treat me like his servant but now he picked up my axe carrying it up to the veranda.

Constable Archdeacon he hollered.

To me he said O we'll teach them b————rs a lesson Ned they can't insult the Queen and walk away.

As he went inside to prepare for battle I rode slowly down along the yellow puddled track to O'Brien's it were dusk and a whole row of hurricane lamps was hanging from the front of the pub so I easily found my uncles Jimmy and Pat they was standing by the roadside drinking with a cove called Kenny. I rode my horse straight at Jimmy then I swung around and knocked him hard he did not fall but lost his balance and his beer.

Why in the name of Jesus did you do that?

Find out why don't you.

Jimmy then leapt on me dragging me off my horse but I escaped to remount Kenny got hold of my bridle I kicked the b————r in the ear reining my horse away to set off full pelt back for the Police Station.

Kenny and my uncles was in hot pursuit shouting they would tear off my bawbles they would have my guts for garters. I jumped down running into the station where Hall and Archdeacon was standing side by side their thumbs stuck in their belts.

Go on said Hall get out the back.

I went as ordered but didnt wish to miss the spectacle so I come out to the front veranda and I were witness to a mighty stoush. Cons Hall had pulled Jimmy off his horse and was struggling to handcuff him. Then Wild Pat rode down on Hall with a stirrup iron he unbuckled from his horse he were swinging it like a mace. I called out but it were too late the stirrup iron smashed down on Cons Hall's head he fell like a bullock in the abattoir. Cons Archdeacon then attempted to finish cuffing Jimmy but Pat rushed him with the stirrup he were ready to phrenologise again.

Stave in his effing skull cried Jimmy.

I come up behind Pat as the stirrup iron whistled past my ear.

Let him go cried Hall to Archdeacon he were staggering to his feet. Let the b—————d go he shouted pulling me backwards by the shirt collar. Thus all 3 of us withdrew into the station. There were great chaos as the policemen attempted to find fresh balls and powder while all the time the blood were streaming down Hall's porkish face upon the floor the desk the logbook and by the time they found the key to unlock the munitions cabinet my uncles and their mate was gone.

It don't matter said Hall they is up to their neck in manure for this.

. . .

When the following Thursday Jimmy and Pat was brought to the musty little redbrick court in Benalla I were witness for the Crown and my mother come to watch me give my evidence. On her left sat her worried sister Margaret the wife of Pat the Dubliner on her right were fierce Kate wife of Jack Lloyd the traitor. Blood is thicker than water so when it were time for me to speak I could not betray my family to the police not even if the mongrels deserved it. I therefore told the court that Cons Hall had asked me to provoke a fight so he could arrest the Quinns I thought this would get the charge dismissed.

Instead the Judge threatened to put me away for perjury he said my Uncle Pat were a murderous swine he were guilty of the charge and would be taught a lesson.

Aunt Kate rose to her feet calling out that the fight were incited by police.

Shutup said the Judge or I'll send you down to Pentridge too.

She sat down after which the Judge sentenced her brother in law Pat Quinn to 3 yr. for the gash on Hall's head at this Margaret began to bawl and my Aunt Kate rose again but quicker than she could speak the Judge give 3 mo. to her brother Jimmy.

Outside on Arundel Street the crowds dissolved before me and even my own mother disappeared only Cons Hall came forward to seek out my company.

I said I were sorry but could not help betraying him for family reasons.

He smiled and patted me on the back it were only later I realised this were to make my friends and family hate me all the more. Speaking very whispery he said he could not help it either but before the year were out he would get me locked in Pentridge Gaol.

Thus commenced a very poor time for us on our selection no more did my mother look up expectantly at the sound of an approaching horse her gaze darting out along the misty track to see if this were Bill Frost or that were Jimmy Quinn or Harry Power arriving with a new blue dress or a pocket filled with beer soaked currency. No more did I wake in the small hours to dancing and bagpipes and wailing big boozy men in oilskins boasting about their horses in the dark. The Lloyds did not visit no more our land were poor our purse were empty and many is the night we sat before the fire with no food other than what I shot. Once again my mother began telling stories as she done when our father were in gaol.

I had grown the brave beginning of a beard but were not too old to hear the tale of Conchobor and Dedriu and Mebd or the one of Cuchulainn in his war chariot bristling with ripping instruments and tearing shafts and how I wished I had some equal defence against the world. My mother told these tales the firelight shining in her eyes and every space inside the hut were taken by a ready ear and beating heart. We was far happier than we knew.

One morning looking out the skillion window I spied this little fellow walking up the track in mud thick gumboots a leprechaun could be no smaller he were roughly 5 ft. tall but broad of shoulder with a high forehead a spade shaped beard and a rolling gait you knew could carry him a 100 mile. While he stamped the yellow mud off of his boots I recognised him as Ben Gould the hawker the letter T were branded on his hand and his cart filled with bolts of cloth and dresses and hats and elastic sided boots in sizes 6 to 12. Now this cart were bogged on our land so he asked could he pay sixpence a day board until the ground were dry enough to pull it out. What a mighty sum that now seemed and Jem were sent into Greta with the 1st instalment he raced back with a pound of sugar and that may seem a strange thing to have 1st on our shopping list but I hope you have never lived without a grain of sugar. Sugar were just the thing it always cheered us up no end and so it did on this occasion. But Gould were even better. He were a very funny man and he come to us with what we needed his vim his verve his eyes was all creased he shut them every time he laughed.

Had we looked deep into Ben Gould we would of seen a familiar fury at the centre of his soul for though he were not Irish he carried the same sort of fire I mean that flame the government of England lights in a poor man's guts every time they make him wear the convict irons.

On that 1st night he were the easiest fellow alive he were particularly friendly towards me but best of all he made my mother laugh it were a miracle that hawker caused to bring the tears of laughter to her cheeks once more. Even Dan lost that tight and pinched appearance his cheeks growing rounder Jem's forehead smoothed and our little Kate who suffered from the bronchitis all that wet and weary month now climbed out of her curtained crib to rest her happy head against my chest.

The following morning the clouds was gone all the sweet green earth were steaming like laundry in the sun. I woke to Ben Gould's laughter he were standing on the veranda in his singlet and braces his toes was sticking out his socks.

Roll up cried he roll up.

I had not set the fire so there were not yet no boiling water but my ma arose in great good spirits all the children tumbling after. This were not how mornings started as a rule.

Roll up ye adjectival Kellys.

I come outside discovering my brothers and sisters shivering in their nightgowns staring out through the mist to see what could be so amusing on that boggy track. On the other side of the fence were a broken old mare a mangy swaybacked creature perhaps 5 yr. old but she were being harried by a young gelding and she were frisking every which way as if she were the prettiest thing you ever saw.

You know said Gould thats adjectival old McCormick's cart horse I knew I recognised her.

We never heard of McCormick but soon learned he and his missus was hawkers like Mr Gould himself.

This rotten looking mare said Ben Gould is proof positive of the rule that a horse will end up like its owner or should I say the wife.

I knew I should set the fire but there were a change in Ben Gould's face that kept me waiting.

McCormick were a keeper at the Demon said he.

He meant McCormick had been a warder in the savage prison of Van Diemen's Land. He said Mrs McCormick were a Derwenter she had been his prisoner.

Then he turned to me saying You better take the adjectival mare back lad or they'll have Cons Archdeacon here saying that you duffed it.

I said the police knew me better than to think I would steal a bag of glue.

Don't be always arguing lad take the adjectival mare to the township. The McCormicks is camped there you'll see their wagon it has the name wrote on the side.

He aint going my mother said.

Oh?

Jem will go said my mother my Ned is staying away from Greta at present.

Ah I see said the little fellow looking at me long and hard he made me most uncomfortable.

So Jem took off on the horse while my mother and Gracie seen to the milking and I lit the fire so Maggie could cook our breakfast. The 1st johnnycake were not yet in the pan when I witnessed a couple come at a very fierce pace up our track splashing across the creek and when they reached our hut they both jumped down like the troopers in the song.

McCormicks!

Mr Gould leaped up to repel them his wide little body blocking the doorway me standing right behind.

Nice of you to give my horse back said the man he were a lanky Irishman with blaming eyes his mouth were the size of a fish's arse.

Ben Gould said it were very nice of us indeed. He pushed slowly forward forcing the McCormicks to step back down onto the boggy ground.

After you had worked it cried the Missus.

No one worked your adjectival horse said Gould the boy just returned her free of charge. It were effing nice of you to let him walk back thats a nice lesson to teach him for his kindness.

You worked it said Mrs McCormick She were a young woman she had small sharp teeth like a Murray perch. You worked it don't change the subject.

Why work your horse said I when we got 20 horses here as good or better.

Now the perch teeth turned on me. We know who you is said she.

Missus I never saw you in my life.

You're Harry Power's mate and you betrayed him and is known to be a thief from here to Wangaratta. You worked my horse you adjectival larrikin.

Ben Gould picked up a bullwhip which were hanging from the veranda. Well said he it is a great shame you can't stay.

We aint leaving cried Mrs McCormick.

Gould become a total stranger his creased eyes went hard as stone and without once taking them off the McCormicks he laid the bullwhip out along the path. I'll thrash ye he cried.

And with that he leapt down to the earth when he cracked it the lash sprayed stones & wood chips threw them violently across the roof down into the chook yard there were a mighty cackling and rush of feathers.

We aint leaving said Mrs McCormick but her husband had the better sense dragging her by the arm back to their horses and off they rode.

My brothers and sisters thought this v. funny but the McCormicks had set off something powerful in Gould's heart he strode up and down the veranda with the profanities pouring from him he could not stop. Soon he wrapped up a pair of calf's testicles writing a note to say McCormick should tie them to himself before he shagged his wife.

Here said he run these into town for me.

I had promised my mother not to risk Greta but I set off anyway. As the McCormicks was not in their camp I left the gift where they would find it.

There was now several respectable weatherboard cottages built amongst the flat and peaceful paddocks and in one of these lived Mrs Danaher an old Irish woman she called out she had a message for my mother. I therefore sat awhile with Mrs Danaher I ate her bitter tea cake and drank her strong black tea.

As I finally rode homewards the Derwenters spied me from the veranda of O'Brien's Hotel.

We're going to report youse cried McCormick he were standing with a great mob of drinkers this doubtless made him very brave.

We'll summons you for that adjectival parcel.

I called back I could summons him for slander if I wished I said neither Gould nor me had stole their effing mare.

Then Mrs McCormick come rushing down the steps wielding a bullock's shinbone she must of picked up on the way. Mr McCormick followed behind her shouting out I were despised by everyone in the district he said I were a coward and were hiding behind my mother's skirts.

At this insult I dismounted. Mrs McCormick then struck my horse on the flank with her impertinent weapon and the horse jumped forward and as I were holding the rein it caused my fist to come into collision with McCormick's nose and he lost his equilibrium and fell prostrate. Tying up my horse to finish the battle I seen Cons Hall descend from the pub like a glistening old spider gliding down from the centre of its web.

He asked me what the row were about. I told him I were being slandered.

The McCormicks fetched the parcel then Constable Hall unwrapped the testicles and read the note I never will forget the smile that come across his face. Did you write this he asked but I could not betray Ben Gould and so I did not answer.

For this crime I were immediately arrested and placed in the Greta lockup where I received neither bread nor water. Next day I were brought to court where Jack Lloyd Sr give evidence that he had seen me ride a horse over Mr McCormick and that was how my uncle paid me back for the imprisonment of Jimmy and Wild Pat Quinn.

I were sentenced to 3 months for hitting Mr McCormick and 3 additional for the testicles and bound to keep the peace for one year. Across the crowded court I held my sad old mother's eyes. She knew better than I did what lay ahead.

I were 17 yr. old when I come out of prison 6 ft. 2 in. broad of shoulder my hands as hard as the hammers we had swung inside the walls of Beechworth Gaol. I had a mighty beard and was a child no more although in truth I do not know what childhood or youth I ever had. What remained if any were finally taken away inside that gaol boiled off me like fat and marrow is rendered within the tallow pot.

I were released out into Ford Street on a sunny March morning I took shanks' pony home to Eleven Mile Creek but I were bound by court order to present myself to the Greta police. Thus I were compelled to lay eyes on Cons Hall once more I come into the station & found him gorging himself on a curried egg sandwich his desk were littered with chopped up lettuce.

What can I do you for said he finally looking up from his feast.

I have to report to you said I.

And who would you be when you're at home?

That is where I understood the changes prison had made for the arresting officer no longer recognised the lad within the man.

Why I am Ned Kelly.

He had lettuce in his beard there was flies crawling on his filthy desk how could I have ever trusted such a being. He told me I were a fool if I thought I had escaped my punishment he promised he would gaol me again the moment he had a chance.

Is that all?

Yes you is dismissed.

Resolving to avoid him in the future I went down the track to my mother's selection and there I soon met Wild Wright a friend of my brother in law Alex Gunn's. Wild was in possession of a very pretty chestnut mare white faced and dock tailed she had a very remarkable brand M as plain as the hands on the town clock. Soon this mare went missing and we spent the day looking but in the end Wild said he might as well borrow one of our mares and I could keep his until he returned to swap them back. He never informed me that his mare was someone else's property.

Shortly thereafter I was travelling to Wangaratta I seen his mare by the road I caught her. Several days later I was riding her back through Greta when Cons Hall hailed me saying there was some papers I needed to sign in relationship to my bond. As I were dismounting the great oaf caught hold of me and thought to throw me but then slipped and landed on the broad of his own back. I should have put my foot across his neck and taken his revolver from him but instead went to catch the mare she had galloped away.

Hall raised his revolver he snapped 3 of 4 caps but the Colt's patent refused the gun would not fire. When I heard the snapping I thought I were a dead man I stood until Hall came close the pistol shaking in his hand. I feared he would pull the trigger again so I duped and jumped at him and caught the revolver with one hand and himself by the collar with the other.

It were only then he cried out the mare were stolen and he were arresting me for horse stealing. I did not believe him and I tripped him and let him take a mouthful of dust I could of done worse but were bound to keep the peace. Hall still had his gun but I had learnt a thing or 2 in Beechworth Gaol and I kept him rolling in the dust until we got to the spot where Mrs O'Brien were erecting brush fencing outside the hotel and on this I threw the big cowardly policeman. I chucked him on his belly and I straddled him and rooted both spurs into his thighs. He roared like a big calf attacked by dogs and I got his hands at the back of his neck and tried to make him let the revolver go but he stuck to it like grim death to a dead volunteer.

He called for assistance to some men who were looking on I dare not strike any of them on account of my bond. These men got ropes tied around my hands and feet and then the great cowardly Hall smote me over the head with his 6 chambered Colt.

When my mother and sister Maggie came to Curlewis Street to find me they could trace me by my blood in the dust the same blood which spoiled the lustre on the gatepost of the barracks. That night Dr Hastings put 9 stitches in my head.

Next morning I were handcuffed with a rope running from the links to my legs to the seat of the cart.

In Wangaratta Court they swore their lies against me Hall claiming to know the mare was stolen by information in THE POLICE GAZETTE but the report of the stolen horse was not gazetted until April 25th that is 5 days after Hall tried to murder me.

In Wangaratta they charged me with horse stealing but here is another curious thing I had been in Beechworth Gaol on the date the mare were stolen and they could not convict me of horse stealing then or ever.

Instead they found me guilty of receiving a horse not yet legally stolen and for this I was given 3 yr. Hard Labour my last hope of youth was stripped away I had never kissed a girl but were old enough to be a married man.

No one else got punished as severe as me. Wild Wright had took the mare but his sentence were only 18 mo. and as for Hall who tried to murder me he had no penalty except being transferred away from the district.

I was returned to the cells of Beechworth Prison and here the turnkeys stripped me and shore my cut and bleeding head while heaping me with threats & insults but even a green log will burn when the heat is high enough. Many is the night I have sat by the roaring river the rain never ending them logs so green bubbling and spitting blazing in a rage no rain can staunch.

PARCEL 7

His Life Following His Later Release from Pentridge Gaol

Linen-bound pocket diary (3" × 4¾" approx.) of 50 pages. On the endpapers there are 6 drawings of people, trees and fences, the quality of artwork somewhere between doodling and drawing. Dust soiling along edges. The small publisher ticket of "J. Gill, Jerilderie" is pasted to the address panel, which dates the composition after February 1879.

Although concluding with a rather wistful recollection of two years during which he was employed at the Killawarra sawmill, these pages concentrate on a few turbulent months in 1874, the time between his release from Pentridge Gaol and his celebrated boxing match with "Wild" Wright.

In the middle of my 1st yr. as prisoner my mother were dealing with the difficulties of a widow's life she were standing on a chair with a hammer in her hand attempting to affix a sheet of tin to deflect the cold rain from her back door. She had just hit her thumb the 2nd time when she become aware of a stranger standing by the horse paddock observing her. He were an old fellow in a terrible raggedy coat & raggedy trousers and my mother thought he were a swagman and took pity to beckon him over then she fetched a cup of flour so he might make himself a little damper. She give him the flour wrapped in a cone of newspaper and only then did she discover the object of her charity were a v. stinky old man his wool coat tanned with his own urine the smell of the process made worse by the rain. Just the same the old boy were as proud as a prince telling her she could keep her flour he had no use for it.

Then what are you needing uncle?

I wouldnt be sorry to get a drop of the brandy said he.

Brandy were threepence the slug my mother told him so.

But I have no more than tuppence the old man said.

If its tea you was wanting my mother said I'd supply it and sugar with it.

Said he The fact of the matter is I am a rat charmer.

Thats very nice but do you want the flour or not I can't stand here all day discussing it.

I'll give you my 2 pennies said the old fellow and also the benefit of my rat charming.

I have no rats.

Thats for me to know.

What do you mean by that you stinky old galoot do you think I do not know my own house and what is in it?

Never you mind what I mean my name is Kevin the Rat Charmer and that is a name you won't be forgetting in a hurry I will send a plague upon your shebeen.

Will you now?

I will begob and ye will be praying to the Virgin that you had relented of your penny.

And with that he turned away. If he had a swag it were hidden somewhere up the track for my mother never seen it and if he had baby rats riding in his pocket they was cleverly concealed for my mother detected nothing astir on his person. He were just a stinky old man in a woollen coat he went off down the muddy track to the creek then cut down in the direction of Winton. She never saw him again but he were correct that she would remember the name of Kevin the Rat Charmer for many a day.

That very night the plague come into the hut with rats in the flour and inside the walls and over the bodies of the children they was screaming in the night it were a terrible business. The rats brung the diarrhoea that sickened our beloved baby Ellen she who were fathered by Bill Frost.

My mother sent her young children out to fetch the rat charmer to each she give a bottle of brandy so whoever it was that found him should make up for her offence. Away they went to the 3 towns Dan to Beechworth & Jem to Benalla & Maggie & Kate to Wangaratta but although Kevin the Rat Charmer were well known in them places they could locate neither hide nor hair of him.

Returning to Eleven Mile Creek that evening they found their mother praying to the Virgin with their baby sister lying dead and cold beside her in the basket. Next day the carpenter at McBean's Kilfeera Station made a coffin whilst Jem and Dan dug the grave beneath the willow their sister were just a poor little thing 14 mo. old but still had to be dug very deep on account of the wild dogs.

That were not the end of it.

Jem fell prey to headaches so my mother took him in a pony cart to Glenmore where Aunt Margaret Quinn shaved his head then placed a mustard poultice on it he could never bear anyone to touch his head thereafter. There was many other afflictions there was warts there was boils that could only be drawn by a hot bottle placed direct upon the skin and then my married sister Annie had her horse stolen as a result of which she fell into the hands of Cons Flood.

When she later seen what the Constable were up to my mother brooded on his name asking herself were not a Flood also a plague? Flood were a tall man with bloodshot eyes they say the raven will bleed from the eyes when it mates. My sister were Mrs Annie Gunn but the Mr were in prison and Cons Flood were soon bleeding from the eyes and soon he got my sister with child.

Meanwhile her husband and I was breaking rock together in the outer yard of Beechworth Prison he had dark circles beneath his eyes his body bent as if he were carrying a millstone on his shoulders. When the priest come to tell me my sister died giving birth he didnt relate the precise circumstances but Mother always believed it were the stinky man's curse that killed our Annie & left us with Flood's child and for this she took all the blame onto herself. When Jem were convicted of cattle theft my mother said this also were the plague.

One morning in the summer of 1872 my mother were 42 yr. old she had 2 sons in prison also 1 brother & 1 uncle & 1 brother in law. 2 of her beloved daughters was buried beneath the willow tree and God knows what worse were on the way. On this bleached and dusty morning she and Maggie was staking tomatoes when a stranger come and asks her for a jar of brandy. This one were an American tall and wiry with a small beard hooded eyes and a little smile working behind the cover of his mouth as though he found the world so very droll but were not permitted to tell you exactly what the joke might be. Like the stinky man he claimed to have no money only a cheque he couldnt cash until Benalla.

Maggie began to act sarcastic towards him but my mother suddenly turned v. passionate against her. Listen to you girl said she anyone would think we had no adjectival charity. Go on said she and bring the gentleman his drop.

I am to serve him asked Maggie astonished her muddy hands upon her strong broad hips.

What would prevent you?

Well said Maggie do you mind that? But she done as she were told and my mother went back to staking the tomatoes. For a long time she believed the rats didnt depart until Maggie donated George King that glass of grog.

When 3 yr. had been cut out of me I were set loose once more into the world to see what I would make of it. Having no horse I walked the 20 droughty mi. from Beechworth down across the plains of Lurg and 8 hr. later I approached my previous life only to find it altered beyond hope the creek had changed its course and nature it now were no more than a chain of muddy water holes. The grand old black wattle had dropped while the big red gum at the bottom of our track were 20 ft. taller. There were also a new holding yard built with split rails the timber still new and yellow then I seen my mother come out of the hut with a newborn in her arms I thought it must be baby Ellen but then recalled baby Ellen were dead and buried beneath the willows.

Here was my mother's 1st words to me.

You won't cause trouble Ned.

I looked in her arms and could not understand what babe it was.

Don't you worry about me said I looking back to the horse paddock where there were a number of v. fine horses also a tall young man he were no more than 20 odd yr. of age. How he stared at me never taking his eyes away not even as he removed a saddle and settled it across the top rail of the fence.

We had a plague my mother said her hair were showing grey she had on a bright new dress I thought were much too girlish for her age.

I asked her Who is that young fellow?

That's George King.

Who's he?

I couldnt marry him until you got here Ned I made him wait till you was arrived.

I watched George King climb the fence. It disgusted me to see his age he were young enough to be myself.

My mother fed George King's new baby the same breasts had given suck to me 20 yr. before she were a young girl then the prettiest figure on a horse my father ever saw. Now she sat in a small chair by the window while the new incumbent stretched his great lanky legs from the table nearly to the hob his Yankee boots was yellow with higher heels than a Cuban more like a fancy woman's shoe. Once she burped the baby my mother passed her to G. King and he lay a towel upon his chest so his nice yellow sweater would not be spoiled with vomit. My mother then sat there a foolish smile upon her face and watched how tenderly he played with the baby's toes and fingers.

Dan arrived very excited to see me out of prison he were a man now or so he thought he were 13 yr. old with a smudge of hair on his top lip pimples on his nose his hair were wild his clothes was flash he preferred 2 shirts one atop the other and the straw hat he kept in place with a strap beneath the beak. No sooner had he shook my hand than he wanted me to ride to Wangaratta and meet his sweetheart. I told him I wanted a quiet life he said I had come to the wrong adjectival address for that then he took a swig of brandy from George King's cup and George winked at him I could see they thought themselves the Lords of Misrule they had grown to be great mates together.

After teatime I politely asked King to take a stroll there were still some light in the summer sky the air all purple and malty so we sat upon the fence he had constructed on our land and I informed him I shot Bill Frost after he had abandoned my mother.

He rubbed his beard but made no response.

I asked him how he planned to support his baby.

At that he bared his white teeth at me saying he planned on having many children and he had a very fine scheme which meant he had no fear of feeding any of them. He asked me Do you want to hear my scheme?

I did not say nothing. The gloom come down around.

Would you prefer to shoot me?

I felt so sad I couldnt speak.

Ned do you know this squatter McBean?

Too adjectival well.

He's got some pretty handsome horseflesh aint he? What say you and me escort said horseflesh across the Murray into New South Wales & then we get them impounded & then we buy back from the pound.

So my mother had chosen herself another flash talking b————r he were no better than Bill Frost with his bolts of cloth.

Are you going to assist me said he or will I have to turn to Dan?

You do that I said and I really will shoot you.

Well I aint eager to be shot.

It were properly dark now the stars was glittering the 1st night sky I had seen in 3 yr. the air were hot and northerly.

If you want some advice I said I would not eff around with Mr McBean.

Fair enough says King you've just got home you shouldnt go exerting yourself.

But later that night when the littlies was all asleep I realised he were stalking me like an old goanna looking for a way into a chook yard. He scratched his beard he smiled a lot and my mother watched approvingly as he tried to reel me in.

I said to her You come with me outside I want to talk to you about the pasture.

I led the way out into the night she following obediently when we was almost at the creek I turned to face her I had been away 3 yr. there were so much in my heart not least that I had come home with plans to save our farm.

Ma you've changed.

I'm happy said she but I'm sorry if that aint to your liking.

Why would you want to sic McBean onto me? You know he'll put me back again.

I thought my mother silent then but after a time had passed I realised she were weeping. When I put my arm around her she shook herself free. You don't know nothing about my adjectival life she said you don't remember what its like to live here with the adjectival squatters impounding every adjectival chook and heifer they can snaffle and the traps always knocking on my door hoping to take away my children. He pinched an adjectival saddle she said.

Who pinched what saddle?

Dan the silly little b————r were trying to make some money for his ma. There is no future here she said I can't make sufficient from the grog and now he's stole a saddle and they'll lag him for it.

I told her I were planning to breed some horses but she didnt seem to hear me. I said I would be at Eleven Mile Creek long after George had bolted.

For that she slapped my face. Shutup she cried and look around you. Look at his fences is they the work of a cove who plans to bolt?

The posts are grey box they'll be eaten out inside 4 yr. Our da would not use grey box no road. It were only ironbark or red gum for him.

I could not endure it cried she stooping in the dust and scooping it in her hands and rubbing it in her hair and on her face. I would rather die than spend another minute with your precious da.

She run back to her boy husband as for me I remained a long time under the stars in the very place I so long imagined whilst locked in my blue stone cell but all the dreams which had comforted me in prison was now turned to manure beneath my boots.

By lunchtime next day I had found a job as a faller for Mr J. Saunders and Mr R. Rules' sawmill near Killawarra some 20 mi. from home moving that afternoon to the men's hut beside the log yard.

It were most relaxing to enjoy the freedom of the air the absence of threats and quarrelling.

All my life all I wanted were a home but I come back from Pentridge Gaol to find the land I had laboured on become a stranger's territory. George King were welcome to it I didnt care but there was also 30 thoroughbred horses which was my rightful property so when I discovered they was missing I sent word to my mother asking what she done with them. I learned they was stolen and the thief were beyond the law he were Constable Flood of Oxley. That injustice put me in a rage nothing would ease but danger I now craved it like another man might lust for the raw burn of poteen.

As luck would have it I already had the correct employment a faller's job were perilous it was slippery in the rain always very risky in the wind. 1st we cut notches in the trunk then fitted 8 in. boards into them to make a kind of staircase and here we worked 12 ft. above the earth. My workmate J. O'Hearn were a married man so when the tree were about to go he jumped down and run off leaving the bachelor to deliver the final blows. The danger made me forget my wrath for a moment but once the defeated tree lay ruined on the forest floor then my black mood would flood back and I would brood on how my life and land was taken from me. Thus like an idiot I spoiled my own freedom brooding day and night and this were like a lathe for it shaped the thing that were brooded upon and soon enough the object of all my separate unhappiness had taken the single form of Wild Wright his thick neck his quizzical lopsided brows. I had a great passion to knock him in the jaw to beat him to the dirt it were he who had knowingly left me with a stolen horse. It were soon clear to me that I would have no peace until I seen him punished I begun to make enquiries regarding his whereabouts.

I continued to stay clear of Eleven Mile Creek but my mother come to see me bringing a tin of shortbread I knew how much butter she sacrificed to bake me that. We sat together on the steps of the men's hut & when I asked if she seen Wild Wright she understood my reason and lied to me saying he were up in New South Wales.

My mother had such dark and lively eyes she were ever full of tricks but also laughter. We had always liked to argue about horses a subject reaching back before the ancient Romans my mother holding v. strong opinions of blood and breeding which was our normal field of conversation but on this particular afternoon she led the subject to the mighty bloodline of McBean's thoroughbreds she confessed she couldnt keep it from her mind how much money would be made if they was stolen.

I told her she might as well go back to Eleven Mile if thats what she come for.

She held my hand to her lips saying it were her son she come for and she missed me very bad.

I did not trust her I told her Dan were her son too.

What you mean by that?

Don't talk Dan into duffing them horses.

Faith what sort of mother do ye think I am?

You're Mrs Adjectival King as far as I can see.

She rode away upset leaving her fancy biscuit tin behind while I went back to brooding on Wild Wright and all the damage that had resulted from my imprisonment.

Wild were a friendly enough cove when the sun were shining but he were a big b————r and would kill anyone who looked at him 1/2 wrong. His brother Dummy Wright were as good as his name for he were a mute and when Dummy were mocked by others Wright would be murderous in his defence. I therefore began to make a habit of ridiculing Dummy to me mates at the sawmill it were a poisoned bait I lay out for my bear. In my sleep I dreamed of Wright I could feel my hands shattering as I crushed his jaw his brow his nose it were no pain but a kind of ecstasy. Tom Lloyd were my best mate then & ever and I confessed to him the pleasure of my dreams. He said I were lucky they was dreams since Wild Wright would kill me awake he were 5 stone heavier.

Tom were son to my uncle the traitor but he himself were plain as a brick & steady & serious. It was Tom who said we should build up a new herd to replace the stolen one it would all be straight and honest with nothing on the cross. And it were them horses that slowly brung me back to life God has made no other creature so beautiful there is no feeling to equal the surging of a good horse galloping across the plains.

I didnt wish to hear about what transpired at Eleven Mile Creek but as there were no escaping gossip I soon learned that G. King had found my mother an Arab mare I thought this a mistake for 2 reasons 1st that an Arab will turn a mob of thoroughbreds into time wasting scoundrels 2nd that the horse were certainly duffed and I feared my mother and her baby would be sent to prison.

I decided it healthier to leave the district and giving notice at the sawmill I travelled 200 mi. to a similar job in Gippsland but the forests there were damp and dreary my mood plunged even deeper into rage and gloom. My father and mother now appeared to me every night in dreams my father's face lacerated with a 1,000 cuts I knew I done this then I saw that woman's dress in the dreadful tin trunk in Beveridge and I cried out and woke my workmates with my horror.

Returning to the North East I discovered Tom Lloyd now had 2 of our mares in foal that were the best thing to happen in a long while so I began to cheer up and think once more about the future. One Saturday I were riding across the plains at Laceby that is 1/2 way between Killawarra and Eleven Mile Creek. It were winter the clouds was grey and smudgy with distant rain the light were fading fast. In that melancholic landscape I seen a female on an Arab she were riding at full gallop. No woman on earth could ride like my mother it were thrilling to behold she rode with her back straight her stirrups long her skirts rucked up to show her knees. She made the girls at the Killawarra Races seem all milksop babes.

Mother always liked a race and now I chased her across the plains into the myall where she veered off heading for the Warby Ranges. In the low foothills she briefly disappeared beneath a rocky rise. The rabbits had made a great mess here the earth were riddled with their holes but since the rider would not slacken her pace her horse soon stumbled. When an Arab stumbles it does so properly standing on its head and rolling on its back and by the time the rider gets to his feet the Actress is out of sight and heading home for dinner. But my mother did not rise.

I dismounted and run towards her my heart racing I were sure I killed her.

But it were not my mother. It were a dark haired boy clad in a dress! This creature were no more than 18 yr. of age breathing hard his chest rising and falling but I were so riled I might of bashed him badly if he were not so small and dark and bandy legged. Once I had dragged him to his feet I did no more than slap his face. The dress were over the top of a shirt and moleskins there were mud on its breast and hem.

I told him he were a horrid thing and administered another slap he were not afraid he spat at me. The dress aside he had made no effort to make himself a female indeed he were doing his best to grow a beard. He had an old firelock in his belt and he were regarding me so fiercely with his possum eyes I thought I better retrieve the gun before he did us both a damage.

I asked him why he wore a damn dress he looked so adjectival ugly. Then I took his firelock throwing it some distance.

He said the firelock were his father's and I should not do that.

I said his father would throw him down the well for dressing like a girl.

He dared laugh at me to spit blood at my feet then ask me were I still blowing about fighting Wild Wright.

Shut your gob you horrid thing you don't know me.

You're Dan's brother said he and you shook my adjectival hand at the Wangaratta Races.

I remembered him then a little dark haired jockey his name were Steve Hart.

I told him I would let him off because he were Dan's mate but if ever I saw him in a dress again he would be rendered into sausage meat.

Not looking grateful in the least he went to fetch his firelock and stick it in his belt.

Its Wild Wright who will turn you into sausage meat said he and I'll be there to see it done.

Wild Wright has run away to New South Wales.

Wild Wright's waiting for you at the Imperial Hotel in Beechworth he's heard what you been saying about Dummy.

When I heard this the very blood in my veins must of secretly changed its nature turning dark and calm where it were previously such a painful froth. I helped the little creature walk down his horse which hadnt run so far after all. But even before he left my sight I had forgot him my thoughts were all about Wild Wright of how I would punish the mongrel for my ruined life.

Mr Edward Rogers were the publican of the Imperial Hotel and even if I knew him both by sight and reputation I were most surprised to learn he had any knowledge of me whatsoever. Yet my horse had not drunk his 1st mouthful from the trough when the man himself come down to greet me.

Ned Kelly said he.

Edward Rogers said I.

Though shocked that a mick had used his Christian name he recovered quickly and took my sticky sap stained hands as if they was the Duke of Gloucester's.

Now heres the thing Ned said he and his manner were most regretful. We can't have brawling here I won't permit it. Isaiah Wright is a customer of mine and I'm sure theres a way you can settle this like gentlemen. Edward Rogers would not release my hands he turned them over to examine my knuckles handling me as tenderly as the Chinese herbalist who lays my ma's hand upon his velvet pillow.

I aint got no plans to fight him here.

You miss my meaning said the licensee his eyes blue and most excited though for what reason I could not guess. Its brawling that causes the difficulty said he although the Marquis of Queensbury now that would be another matter.

I never heard of any marquis and I said so.

Don't you follow London Prize Ring Rules?

We draw the line in the dirt its what we call the scratch and if you call that brawling its what I intend doing to him.

Thats bare knuckles?

If you'll send him out I don't need to even step inside your pub.

Edward Rogers stroked his beard.

I'm sure you know my reputation.

I knew no more than he wore a 3 pce. suit in the midst of summer.

You know I'm a great one for sport I'm for the quoits & the skittles & the cricket & the wrestling doubtless you heard it were me who got up that cricket match against the English circus did you see that?

I did not answer he did not care he took me by the elbow and seemed intent to push me down the lane beside the pub he were a rich man 20 yr. my senior so I did not wish to disobey but I pointed out that my horse had not quit drinking.

Dennis he called give Mr Kelly's horse a feed of oats.

A boy led my horse up the street while I were bustled in the opposite direction Mr Rogers bashing my ear without relent. I believe you know a lad named Byrnes said he you fought him at the Oxley Show. You beat him in 12 rounds I hear he is a co religionist of yours.

Thats Joe Byrne I reckon.

Isaiah Wright is a mad bugger of course you must know that. He's also got the weight advantage but Joe Byrne says I must not count weight too much in your case. Now come round here for I want to show you what I am proposing.

Walking back past the hotel rubbish bins the dunnies and the chook yard we finally come to a grassy plateau below which were Spring Creek.

So heres a spot what do you say? What could be 1/2 as nice for a proper fight between 2 gentlemen?

Well said I its very private.

That were the most simpleminded thing I ever said but Edward Rogers did not so much as blink.

Would August the 8th be agreeable he asked thats next week.

I said I were pleased to comply. As I were departing I seen Wright's great ugly phiz through the open window of the public bar he held up his thumb suggesting that I sit on it. Though I did not take up the provocation I were surprised he didnt come running after me. We both waited the entire week to have that fight for my part I never thought of nothing else except how much better I would feel once I knocked the b————r down.

By the time I arrived in Beechworth on the 8th of August the crowd were so large the Imperial could not contain it. Joe Byrne met me at the door escorting me to the residence upstairs where Mr Rogers awaited me with what appeared to be a green silk handkerchief.

Here said he throwing the item to me.

It were a pair of ladies' scanties or so I thought.

These is your boxing trunks.

As he moved across the room towards me I seen through the window the full extent of this mighty crowd some standing some seated in dining chairs all gathered round the grassy plateau.

Rogers took the silk trunks from my hand and held them against himself but if he were intending to make the garment appear more manly then he failed. He looked a poon.

I fight in what I come in I declared.

For God's sake this is the proper kit for London Rules. Wright is wearing some the same.

Thats his own affair I aint fighting naked.

Mr Rogers clucked his tongue looking mournfully down upon the assembly.

It aint naked he said its just bloody ignorant. Are you not proud to wear the colours?

It were only then I realised they had hung green & orange ribbons round the ring. To tell the truth I had forgot Wright were a proddy.

Come on son said Rogers you must show the colour. What are you wearing under your shirt?

He had his damn fingers at my shirt undoing the buttons I pulled away.

Long Johns he exclaimed thats the shot.

No!

Oh yes said he thats the very thing.

At that moment I heard a mighty roar Wright had come dancing out into the lawn 1/2 naked he had boots on his feet but he were barechested with no garment but a pair of orange silk shorts. He had legs like adjectival fenceposts big ugly looking knees and when he pranced around the ring I were shocked to see my mother Ellen Kelly occupying the best seat in the house. Wild performed in front of her swinging his fists and showing off and I were dismayed to realise the bulk of him the breadth of his shoulders his arms like thighs I had not made this picture on my brooding lathe.

Modesty were not the point no more I removed my clothing except for my long woollen combinations I pulled the green silk shorts on top. Though I felt a real dill what other choice were there?

Joe Byrne seemed amused but when I caught his eye he quickly developed a very sombre cast.

Very well said I lets do the b————r.

On my way out the door I were informed that fighting barefooted were not permitted so I accepted a pair of slippers 1/2 a size too small I didnt care.

In a light rain we came out past the chook house Wild Wright were sucking on an orange but when he saw me he spat it out and stepped up to me.

You're a dead man said he striking me across the head a mighty blow it knocked me down sideways I heard my mother crying foul foul foul I staggered to my feet in time to see Joe Byrne kicking Wright away. Eddie Rogers and my sister Maggie was holding my mother by the arms.

Blood someone shouted 1st blood.

As the liquid seeped into my eye so the scratch were made in the earth and the fight officially begun.

I do not recall nothing about the fight but it has been 50 times I heard Joe Byrne tell the story thus as follows.

We thought you doomed and rooned the minute you walked out past the chook house and Wild delivered that great sidearm to your head and you was on the floor before you even stepped up to the scratch. It were a proddy pub so no one give an eff what happened to a mick they planned to drink your blood. Wild had heard you had been mocking Dummy and now he were for the kill.

Wild cut your eye and your ma were screaming blue adjectival murder when Wild come in again he didnt even wait for you to rise. I barely knew you at this time but anyone could see that this blow werent fair I hollered for the referee but Eddie Rogers were both referee and bookmaker and he had all his money on Wild Wright. I were your only picker-upper so I judged it were against the rules for me to punch which is why I kicked Wright in the knees. Jesus! You should of seen Wild's eyes he could not believe my cheek the crowds was going mad your ma were barracking me and the fight had not even begun.

Rogers made the scratch with his walking stick and both of you faced off across the line. You already had blood running down into your eyes. Wild had an inch or more in height and he had the weight he were the Fancy of the proddy punters of that there is no adjectival question.

Wright were as effing mad as a snake there were nothing he would not do to win he were the strongest but if the truth be told he were a mite slow and clumsy.

Rogers dropped his spotted handkerchief and then it were on you struck 3 blows in fewer seconds. Wright staggered back on his heels and you should of heard the proddies screaming to see their mighty hero fall it were an effing war. Old Rogers had organised green and orange ribbons thinking it would be a certain victory for the Orangemen. Your ma were 1/2 beside herself shouting to the crowd that her son would deal with them as well. In the middle of the fight you grinned at her that brought some colour to her cheeks. When you strolled up to Wright you was still grinning at your ma then you knocked the b————r down as easy as if he was a sleeping cow.

Bill Skilling nearly wet himself he were so pleased he picked up your ma and shook her in the air.

Wild were trying to rise he knocked his pickerupper away and come back to the scratch. You got inside his reach again but this time he collected you underneath the chin and as your jaw clacked shut you fell but your eyes was still wide open. The pair of you went down together though you were up the 1st.

Wright's weakness were his speed yours were your reach. In the 4th round you aimed a mighty blow at his bull neck but failed the length whereupon he struck you an adjectival whack across the brow. You fell.

Round after round it went with 30 sec. rest when either party was knocked down. The rain picked up but no one went inside. Soon you both needed the assistance of your pickerupper and you was heavy in my arms your woollen singlet were sodden with rain or sweat I don't know which and Wild Wright were faring not much better. I never saw men so weary.

Eddie Rogers circled the 2 of you with his hands behind his back his nose stuck forward squinting like you was a balance sheet and he didnt know if he were rich or bankrupt.

Wild Wright come at you with his arms extended straight moving them up and down like an Eldorado battery he meant to crush you to the earth. You were watching him very wary indeed.

After you had ducked his punches 3 or 4 times Wild hollered to the mob that you was yellow. Dummy were pushing in and out of the crowd and now he begun to make an unholy din. This brought your ma back into it and she were screaming at you to kill Wild Wright.

The fight were slow the grass long since tore up and stirred to mud by this time and you were both bogged down in a heavy sort of punishment. When I picked you up your hands was a mess of blood and snot slimy and slippery like a beast just skun and slaughtered. Soon the wind came up and with it a dose of soaking rain Wild looked stooped and crumpled but to you the rain seemed a refreshment.

Wild were now slow and heavy while you was fast you hit his head he fell you hit his eye he fell again. The proddies' cheering become fainter Dummy were whimpering but your mother looked very pleased sitting bolt upright beneath Bill Skilling's umbrella her hands folded in her lap.

Wild's pickerupper had to carry his man to the scratch but he done no more than stand there swaying.

You said Now we're square.

Then you emphasised them sentiments with a punch that straightened Wild's spine and sent him crashing to the ground.

A blind man could see Wild Wright were done as a dinner but his pickerupper were a proddy so he dragged his hero's body to the scratch and lifted him up all 16 stone of him. Bill Skilling were crying for you to top him off but you only pushed and Wild Wright fell down most thoroughly defeated.

Then a great howl come from the crowd and Dummy broke into the arena to take a swing at you but his eyes was mad with disbelief and terror. He lay upon his brother fully clothed down in the mire and no one dare go near him.

Tom Lloyd were there that day also Bill Skilling and your ma and Maggie I didnt know Steve Hart at the time. Having placed no bets we had no winnings but we escorted you through the streets of Beechworth straight to Ryan's Hotel. On that day you was Jesus Christ Almighty even Father Duffy come to worship you.

As a result of winning the fight I become what is known as popular which were even worse than being hated as a traitor though the conditions was in many ways identical. Now every drunken fool thought he must fight the Great Champeen and take away his crown.

There is no pleasure in fighting either drunks or pimply boys and I resolved to live very quiet indeed I done my labour at the sawmill drawing my weekly wage and keeping from the pubs and racetracks you can ask my workmates they will tell you what a retiring chap I were. This does not mean a complete hermit many is the happy hour I spent with Tom Lloyd as we bought and sold horses but everything were on the up and up and I maintained the receipts of every beast we purchased. I had also made a friend of Wild Wright though he were soon arrested for Receiving and earned 3 yr. in Beechworth Gaol.

Joe Byrne come calling as well and once he realised how peaceful I were living life he brung me tobacco and when I said I didnt smoke he give me a book. If you seen Joe Byrne in a Beechworth pub you would never take him for a scholar you might note instead his restless limbs his wild and dangerous eye it could cut right through you like a knife. This same Joe Byrne sat me down on a log and opened up his book his hard square hands were very gentle on them pages.

Shutup Ned and listen.

So were I introduced to John Ridd the hero of the book called LORNA DOONE. I sat on a slippery debarked log at Killawarra but my eyes was seeing things from centuries before I were witness to a mighty fight between John Ridd and another boy as soon as John won he discovered his father were murdered by the Doones.

John Ridd lost his da at the exact same age I lost my own. He were a champion wrestler but tired of hearing about it often longing to be smaller. So even before I met with Lorna herself I liked this book as well as ice cream ipso facto it is proven that Joe Byrne the so called CRIMINAL were a better schoolmaster than Mr Irving who taught me how to make the ink without the pleasure of its use.

In 2 blessed yr. of peace I read LORNA DOONE 3 times I also read some Bible and some poems of William Shakespeare. I had no interest in the world outside least of all my family. While George King prospered as a horse thief I would not go near Eleven Mile Creek. It were not until the spring of that year I opened my eyes sufficient to see what had become of my brother Dan and what happened then I will tell you at another time. It were the end of my quiet life that is for sure.

24 Years

Eighty unbound quarto sheets of medium stock. Heavy foxing, stains and water damage, but still very legible.

Much of the material concerns an alleged slander by Mr Whitty relating to stolen stock. Dan Kelly's changed character described, also his conflict with Constable Flood and the ensuing flight to the Wombat Ranges, where an outlaw gang incubates. Some background concerning Steve Hart's transvestism. Kelly's meeting with Fitzpatrick and his introduction to Mary Hearn, certainly the M.H. of Parcel 2. Mrs Kelly's hostility towards Mary Hearn and the author's explosive response to George King's earlier behaviour. Pages describing the shooting of Constable Fitzpatrick are much revised by a second hand reliably presumed to be that of Joe Byrne.

What with babies & husbands to keep Mother busy Dan had to grow himself up alone & soon found a 2nd family of young men they was known as the Greta Mob. He now travelled the dusty plains in a great noisy crowd he drank and he smoked though I don't know how he paid for any of it because it is a fact he never worked for wages. He certainly could not afford to dress himself and he wore clothes previously abandoned by myself. Sometimes he persuaded Maggie or Kate to take up his cuffs or shorten sleeves etc. but as one year led to another they was ever more out of temper with him and by the time I come to pay attention my brother had become a scarecrow.

It were payday I were on the upstairs veranda of O'Brien's Hotel giving Tom Lloyd £2 which was owed for the servicing of certain mares. Soon we heard a drumming of hooves then a great mob of riders racing down the main street from the direction of Moyhu they pulled up outside the pub with much hooing and hahing the horses was snorting and whinnying the riders dressed very flash like desperadoes their hat straps beneath their noses and coloured sashes round their waists. Their mascot were none other than 16 yr. old Dan Kelly they had provided him a new red sash to wear round his middle.

As I watched from above my brother slid off his saddle and fell like a raggy doll into the dirt then a great cheer went up Good on you Dan good old Dan.

The tight faced boy saluted his admirers by throwing up violently in front of them. I ran down stairs and found him spitting and cursing and weaving round the road.

Then he saw me.

Kelly versus Kelly cried he roll up Kelly versus adjectival Kelly now.

If he was promoting this fight to keep his mates' interest the effort were wasted for in the time it took for him to draw the scratch his companions had walked their horses into O'Brien's yard.

To see him spoiled and abandoned it broke my heart.

I come towards him with Christian intentions but as I arrived at the scratch he swung a punch I easily ducked it but he irritated me & I clamped my hand firmly on his bony shoulder to escort him down the road. I had planned walking to old Mrs Danaher's house that were safe territory for us but as we passed the Police Station he slipped out of his coat and begun ducking and weaving it were a very stupid place for such a dance. Not 10 yd. away I could see a pair of highly polished boots resting on the veranda rail. Hall had been transferred but a successor were now lurking.

I can thrash youse Dan shouted come on come on.

He suddenly swung and I blocked him gathering him by his scrawny wrist. Shush I said and I saw the copper's boots withdraw into the shade. The traps is watching.

You b————d cried he what do you care what happens to me? Why don't you eff off back to your adjectival sawmill?

Fearing we was both in danger of arrest I got his coat over his head and backed up against a gum tree he were soft and squirrely like some big slippery fish.

I heard Cons Farrell call something then Sergeant Hogan come out the door and stood surveying us with his thumbs tucked in his braces. Fatnecked Farrell were running his hand through his ginger hair he made me think of a hotel cat with its tail swishing back and forth.

What is we doing here says Dan.

Shutup you just wait.

Mum's the word said my brother turning his drunk attention to the sugar ants moving in and out of the untidy bark after a while he began to slowly unwind his sash.

O Ned said he I'm such a fool.

It took a moment to realise he were not apologising for his attack he were upset to see his precious sash were soiled with vomit. Now he unwound the whole 6 ft. of it he were as weepy as a girl with a gravy stain on her ballgown. I told him I would wash the damn thing if that would make him happier.

You've got a girlfriend he sneered.

Observing Cons Farrell's broad grin I pulled my brother to his feet and guided him along the street.

I see said Dan thats why you won't come home you finally got yourself an adjectival tart.

Shutup.

You got a donah.

You know I aint got any girl Dan.

True said he your ma is your donah as everybody knows.

Shutup.

Hubba hubba Mamma is your girl.

The traps behind us was enjoying this conversation it would be spread round the township by the morning.

You got a grudge against George cause he married your girl.

The coppers dropped about a chain behind us but that was close enough to hear my brother declare George King a better horse thief than I would ever be.

When I jabbed him in the ribs he put his vomit mouth against my ear. Don't panic cobber they didnt hear.

Button your effing lip.

He put the mouth back on my ear I did not like the slippery feel of it. Said he George can duff an effing mob of 20 horses without effing touching them. The b————rs follow him.

I drew away but my little brother were as persistent as a hungry kitten.

George King has stole 500 horses and never been in adjectival gaol not even the effing lockup.

Not caring what George King done I marched my drunk brother up through Mrs Danaher's orchard leaving the smirking Constables to go back to their roost so then we cut across Horan's pasture which brought us back on the road beside the pub.

I told him Dan had to keep away from the mob and get himself some occupation. Though his crow black hair was falling in his eyes I know he were listening v. careful and so I offered to take him in as a partner dealing horses with me & Tom Lloyd.

Ned?

Yes Dan.

Lend me 10 bob will you.

I should of knocked him to the ground instead I opened my pay envelope and give him a 10/– note.

Don't pee it all away give some to your mother.

It were the 1st time he smiled at me all day. Thank you Ned thank you very much you'll have it back before you can say Jack Robertson.

I watched him lurch up onto the veranda to join his mates his long sleeves flapping his trousers dragging in the dirt a great cheer issuing forth as he entered.

These mates of his all talked a certain way and although their mouths was foul they was not criminals just young lads galloping to and fro to kill the time but from that day it were clear to me and Tom that the squatters would not tolerate my brother's friends for long.

In a very bad year even the richest farmers was cutting down saplings to feed their stock they was pressed hard themselves and so harsher than usual to their poor neighbours. Through his connections in government the squatter Whitty had been permitted to rent the common ground and as a result a poor man could no longer find a place to feed his stock in all the drought stricken plains. If you set your horse grazing beside the govt. road it would be taken by Whitty's drones and locked away in the pound. I have known 60 head of horses impounded in one day all of them belonging to poor farmers who was then required to leave their ploughing or harvest and travel to Oxley and when they got there perhaps they didnt have money to release them & so they would have to give a bill of sale or borrow money which is no easy matter.

By this time there was men so enraged by these abuses that they put the squatters' oats under the torch in revenge but I continued my labour at the sawmill keeping my head in the ground like the proverbial ostrich until they finally charged Dan with having stole a saddle. I will not say he never stole a saddle but on this occasion he were innocent and so I returned to the Greta Police Station to defend him.

I begun to furnish Constable John Farrell with the explanation of why my young brother should not be charged but he interrupted when I had hardly started.

The police are sick of your criminal activity.

Whose activity mine?

No one else is present.

You must of confused me with someone else.

Are you Edward Kelly of Greta? He opened THE POLICE GA-ZETTE that proved I were wanted for the theft of a mare which were property of Henry Lydecker selector.

I said I never done it any more than Dan stole that saddle he should leave the poor people alone and look instead how the squatters made a game of the law getting the best land for themselves. I pointed out how Mr Whitty had used dummying and peacocking to illegally gain his holdings on the Fifteen Mile Creek.

O I suppose we are picking on you he sneered. At that time I didnt know the policeman were Mr Whitty's son in law.

As a consequence of this false accusation against me I lost a day's wages while attending Oxley Police and another day's wages when the case were brought to court in Benalla where Mr Lydecker swore I never took his mare. Of course they had no choice but to acquit me.

I were grateful to Mr Lydecker for his words on my behalf and when I found a wild scrub bull I roped it and brung it to him as a gift. Whitty heard about this bull and of course decided that if a Kelly had give away a bull then it followed the bull must be stolen furthermore the legal owner must be Mr Whitty. I heard from many people I had stole this bull and would soon be charged for it.

I continued my work at the mill never knowing what day I might be summonsed. No charge were laid.

When Dan come to trial I took the day off to go with him to court. After he were declared innocent we went to the Moyhu Races where Mr Whitty were pointed out to me he were in the company of R.R. McBean and others.

I introduced myself.

Am I meant to know you said he looking at me like I were nothing but a tinker.

O you must know me Mr Whitty. I were very polite.

No said he I don't know you at all.

When the coward rudely turned away I continued speaking. But I hear you're saying that I stole your bull.

Whitty revealed that wild mad eye you see the 1st time a brumby feels a saddle on his back. You were misinformed Kelly.

O I don't think so Mr Whitty.

He then admitted he lost a bull which were later found but he had never blamed me for stealing it. He said his son in law Cons Farrell told him Ned Kelly had stole the bull then sold it.

I was happy to have cleared my name but next week I learned that Whitty were now accusing me of stealing a mob of his calves. I could of taught him a lesson then but did not.

Finally our mares in foal strayed onto the common land so the mongrel Whitty impounded them. Now Tom and me had fed them horses at great expense paid for the stallion and otherwise invested considerable funds. When Whitty locked them in the pound I decided to show him he did not own this earth. I didnt burn his oats or nothing all I done were break the lock at the Oxley Pound and take back what I legally owned this did not seem a crime to me not then or now.

The very next day my brother Dan were ambling peacefully through Oxley township he were dragged from his horse by Cons Flood then frog-marched into the laundry of the Police Camp where the cowardly Flood threatened to plunge his face into the boiling sheets. The same Cons Flood that seduced our sister Annie now tortured my young brother until he pleaded for his life he scalded his arm he thrust his govt. revolver against Dan's empty belly saying he would arrest him for stealing horses from the pound.

Dan pleaded he were innocent.

Said Flood I will see those mares back in the pound by tomorrow morning or there will be an adjectival war with you the 1st to fall. Then he set Dan loose.

I did not know it yet but this were to be my last day of paid labour it were noon which is dinner time at the sawmill so I were sitting with my mug of tea while the cook laid out the tucker table that is a sheet of canvas spread upon the ground. I saw a mighty cloud of dust and at its lead were my young brother he come galloping right into the yard scattering bark and dirt across the fresh baked yeast bread there are few greater offences in the bush.

I rose to greet him steering him and his mount away from the meal but even before he spoke I could see his injury not only on the arm which were already red and blistered but also the eyes. All the bluster had been leached away it were a dreadful thing to see.

He explained his injury also reported Flood's threat and I wondered who could be so stupid to think they could hurt my family without no fear of justice. Dan were my little brother flesh & blood I sat him on a log to dress his burn with butter then fetched a slice of yeast bread spreading it thick with golden syrup and finally I give him a good feed of lamb stew.

At 5 o'clock I handed in my notice at the sawmill then we set out to the one place on earth we could rely on. Heading south we rode straight past my mother's selection all them dead and ringbarked trees was the grave of honest hope. That night we slept rough by the Four Mile Creek that is deep in the folds of Mr McBean's Kilfeera Station where our horses still found grass no matter there were a drought in all the world outside. The next day we moved invisibly across the squatter's rolling land he couldnt see me he didnt know I were a serpent inside his arteries a plague rat in his bowels.

By noon we cut the Magistrate's last barbed wire fence then we come into unselected land the smell of the explosive eucalyptus growing stronger and stronger. We climbed all afternoon through giant dry forests of mountain ash but it were not till night that we finally heard the water running through the damp grass of Bullock Creek. In the moonlight I could see a silver field of bracken on its edge were Harry Power's old bolt-hole there were now a fallen limb across its roof. The bark were severely injured but the old burlap cribs was strong enough to take my brother's sleeping body. All night my mind turned the lathe I would not leave Dan until I had him fit but when that day come I would teach his torturers they could not steal our stock and threaten our families without suffering the consequences.

The Wombat Ranges is a rough steel wedge driven into the soft rich lands of Whitty and McBean & having entered through the Magistrate's property now 2 wk. later I departed alone through Whitty's Myrrhee Station. The drought were hard on this country but the squatter did not have to punish it the way a small selector did so all his acres was a contrast to my mother's where the grass were eaten to the roots. By Fifteen Mile Creek I come upon a pair of very well fed shire horses glistening in the moonlight also any number of healthy thoroughbreds some of them mares with foal nothing could be more different from the state of the stock when I arrived back home the following day the dairy cows' ribs was showing I counted 5 dead sheep their eyes picked out by the crows.

I give my 1st cooee from behind the cowbail a 2nd when I come in view of the hut.

After a few minutes my mother stepped out of the shade of the veranda raising her arm across her eyes.

What do you want she asked for I had not been to visit since the celebration of her wedding that were more than 2 yr. previous.

I want to see himself.

He's in Benalla at the Doctor's.

I jerked my head towards the sorrel mare which were standing very foul tempered in the paddock. Whats his horse doing here then?

The sorrel can't be rid she's got the splent.

I dismounted stepping up onto the veranda as my brother in law Bill Skilling appeared at the doorway. Now now Ned says he but when his eyes shifted in alarm I turned to catch my mother rushing at me with a piece of 4×2 which I swiftly encouraged her to drop. She begun clutching me with her bandaged hand I have seen likenesses of mothers plump and soft their skin glowing with the luxuries of cream and roast beef but my mother's hands was large and dried like roots dug from the hard plains of Greta.

Don't hurt him cried she I could not bear another loss.

It is Whitty that will have the loss said I and told her how they tortured Dan and stole my horses. It is time they felt a little pain themselves.

Don't do nothing she said you go back to work.

I've given up my job Ma I have come to steal them horses like you wanted.

My mother give a queer little howl and then she were in my arms completely I felt her poor hard body wracked by sobs.

I never meant to put you in harm's way I don't want you stealing nothing.

Shush shush said I it were only as I held her that I knew how deep I loved her we was grown together like 2 branches of an old wisteria.

What can I do for you Ned?

George King stood at the corner of the hut with his carbine at the hip his finger on the trigger but from that position he could not hit a wombat's arse and I could of knocked him down at least I thought so.

Young Dan's been blowing you can make a mob of horses follow you he says you learned it from the savages in Arizona.

George showed me his big white teeth. You reckon that is blowing do you Ned?

It is a knowledge I have need of George.

My mother said they had some spare money she would rather give it to me than be the cause of me being lagged once more.

I told her money were not my concern I meant to impound the squatter's best fed horses.

I aint got no time for this malarkey said George King what is it you want?

Mr Whitty's got a big mob out the back of Myrrhee they look like they been eating pretty well.

George smiled again but it were nothing soft or friendly. Ellen said he go put the kettle on.

I noticed how my mother obediently did the Yankee's bidding and this sickened me but it were not my business so him and me walked over to the horse paddock where we leaned against the rails staring at his lame horse a while.

When I come here Ned I were prepared to be your mate I would not marry your ma until you was out of prison. You could of been my partner then but you as good as told me to shove it up my blot.

True enough.

If you want to pinch a few of Whitty's ponies you don't need my permission.

I want to take a whole adjectival mob of them.

Ask Dan and Jem to help you. Or Tom Lloyd.

I don't want no one getting scalded for what I do I want you to teach me what you learned from them savages.

He didnt say nothing so we stayed at the rails looking at his mare trying to chew the bandage off her leg. After a while my mother called from the hut door that the tea were made.

Very well said George at last we'll do this one job together we'll borrow 50 horses from Mr Whitty in a night.

We can take them into the Wombat.

No we'll run them up across the Murray into New South Wales we'll cut the proceeds 1/2 and 1/2 now go on I can see your girlfriend has got your tea for you.

He climbed into the paddock I gone back in the hut to sit at the old table with my mother.

You won't be at war with George no more she said her fingernails all broken her knuckles swollen from her labours.

I held her hand against my cheek.

He's a good man George said she.

I could not say he werent.

I knew horses all my life but it took a Yank to show me what a contrary bugger the horse can be if you go towards it then it runs off if you turn your back it cannot keep from following. George King needed no mare or stallion or oats or whip or halter to start them horses walking he needed nothing but himself and he drew them away from the plains of Myrrhee and Kilfeera using nothing more than their own curiosity. I never seen such a picture as this previously there was 50 thoroughbreds swinging along in that easy canter their heads down all in single file trailing George King's Arab up into the ranges.

Never having been a thief before I were surprised to discover what a mighty pleasure stealing from the rich could be. When it come the squatters' turn to suffer they could not bear their punishment they was immediately screaming like stuck pigs calling public meetings about the outrage while all the time I lived on their back door more than once sitting on my horse to watch McBean eat tea & when his dogs was going wild he could do no more than stare out into the wild colonial dark. He did not own that country he never could.

Soon others was drawn into the ranges to be with us at Bullock Creek they come not to avoid honest graft the opposite when you stayed with me and Dan you would leave your grog behind and work beside us from dawn to dusk thus in the middle of that wilderness we cleared the flats and planted crops. We was building a world where we would be left alone.

Joe Byrne is now reported to be a Depraved Criminal well the 1st thing he done at Bullock Creek were construct a sluice for gold in other words he begun one of them Secondary Industries the government is so keen about. O he were flash his mood cd. swing back and forth like the tail of a cranky horse but you could say the same thing of the sainted Mr Whitty. Joe brought along Aaron Sherritt they was mates since birth at night they slept beside the fire curled up like cattle dogs upon the earth also they had a queer and private way of conversing they said THAT PLACE & THAT COVE & THAT THING and only they knew what it meant. They sat by the fire smoking their BLACK SMOKE they gone as mellow as 2 old Chinamen and very even in their temperaments.

I were most surprised one morning to see Steve Hart had found his way to us he were the horrid thing who had previously worn a dress and now I found him sitting on his horse surveying our achievements in the wilderness.

Nice horses.

I threw a stone & hit his gelding on the rump it reared and started.

Well eff you he cried I have ridden 2 adjectival days to be here Dan's my mate you well recall.

Well now you can ride 2 adjectival days back and if I get any visits from the traps I'll know where they got the information & I'll come find you wherever you are hiding then I'll break your skinny little neck.

You think I'm a sissy but I aint.

I don't think nothing about you.

Well I'm Steve Hart he said my horse is effed and I aint eaten in a day.

With that the bandy little thing dismounted it were disturbing to see his confidence out of proportion to his weight and age.

I aint a sissy he repeated.

I had a fascination about him I suppose and when he announced he would put his horse in my paddock I did not prevent him. It were a fine bay mare long necked fully 16 1/2 hands & v. strong I couldnt see how a boy that age would get the money for an animal like that. The saddle were an old fashioned Hungarian it were very worn and cracked I kept my hands in the pockets as he lay it across the fence.

I'm a Lady Clare Boy he said.

I pushed my hands deeper in the pockets.

Wisely he come no closer I'll tell you what I am said he.

That were a door I did not wish to open I told him we would have a cup of tea and then he could depart.

Why I tolerated them secretive and fervent eyes staring out at me through the smoke I cannot think it is a wonder I did not evict Steve Hart that day or the next for he quickly revealed himself a pesky talker full of assumptions about horses and history and every subject from the defeat of O'Brien to the correct way to plait a greenhide whip.

Joe Byrne were the scholar amongst us many is the poem he wrote the song he sang but Joe were inclined to be quiet in his opinions unless riled. By contrast you would think Steve Hart were a Professor to hear him on the state of Ireland blah blah blah rattling off the names of his heroes Robert Emmett & Thomas Meagher & Smith O'Brien he never seen them men but he were like a girl living in Romances and Histories always thinking of a braver better time.

Joe and me occupied the waking world we knew our hard circumstances was made by Whitty and McBean who picked the eyes out of the country with the connivance of the politicians and police. Against their force all this queer boy's daydreaming were no defence at all his Irish martyrs couldnt get us decent land not even remove our cows from Oxley Pound. The following morning I told him he had better leave.

He aint a bad little fellow said Joe Byrne.

He talks too adjectival much.

Theres some of it is educational.

He don't vex you?

He aint doing no damage said Joe besides he's company for Dan.

So I give Dan and Steve 5/– packing them off to Benalla for oatmeal and potatoes thank God to have a little peace.

3 days later I were butchering a kangaroo beside the creek stripping back the fur to reveal the shiny tight blue belly when I heard the crack of a breaking stick. Living in that valley were like inhabiting the insides of a banjo that noise were like a gunshot and I immediately detected 2 riders threading their way through the stripy shadow of the mountain ash. At 1st I thought it were Kate and Maggie then the front woman passed into the full sunshine and it were Dan he had been absent only 3 days and now he were wearing a bright blue dress his face blacked from ear to ear. Behind him come the smudge lipped culprit Steven Hart.

My brother and the strange boy rode directly up to me their horses stood less than one yd. away I tore out the kangaroo guts and threw them down into the dust I commanded Steve Hart to climb down from his horse.

Dan obeyed on Steve's behalf and he had a stupid grin about his coal black phiz as he smoothed down the rumpled dress it were bright new satin the label still hanging from its breast. When Dan held out his hand to me a single drop of blood formed in his palm like a saint in a Holy Picture then Steve Hart reached out his paw and I could see they had both sworn some oath together. Steve Hart's eyes was bright and secret I dragged him off his horse and threw him down. He scrambled to his feet.

You aint got no reason to hit me.

I roared at Dan to get the dress off.

Steve Hart ordered Dan to disobey he told me he could make an explanation but I said to shut his gob then turned on Dan to demand where they got the dresses and how much they paid. He answered they come from Mrs Goodman's in Winton he confessed they had stole them and for that mighty stupidity I kicked him up the quoit.

Hart sprung at me though I caught his wrist with one hand and slapped him down very hard with the other when he rose his fuzzy lip were bleeding his eyes was filled with tears. I told him I were leaving the camp and expected him to be gone when I returned.

I left the 1/2 butchered kangaroo for whatever man or beast could use it then I collected the dresses immediately setting off for Winton I were hoping to arrive before charges was pressed against my brother. After hard riding and a bad night's rest I come into the township and made my enquires and were directed to a broken backed cottage on the high ground above the Seven Mile Creek this were the residence of Davis Goodman hawker it were built in the middle of a wagon graveyard with spare wheels rusted springs and bits of timber over which was scattered the droppings of ducks it were a most distinctive odour. I untied the bundle and carried it up to the house.

My Cuban heels was hardly on the veranda before the door creaked open and a big bosomed woman with a lot of red hair and creamy white skin asked me what I wanted. I told Mrs Goodman I were returning her husband's merchandise but as she were inspecting the contents of the bundle a policeman appeared suddenly at the door.

This is him she cried arrest him Fitzy.

I told the Constable I had not stolen nothing.

You're all adjectival Kellys cried the woman whats the adjectival difference it all goes in the one pot.

And which adjectival Kelly is this asks the trap kind of humorous.

I am Ned Kelly.

Whereupon much to Mrs Goodman's consternation and my own

considerable surprise the policeman seized me warmly by the hand. My brother has give me written orders to take you dancing.

Jesus Fitzy cried Mrs Goodman wait a mo.

The Constable ignored her. I am Alex Fitzpatrick he said and you are the cove what knocked the bark off my brother John at the Police Commissioner's in Melbourne. You ate roast beef through the night in Richmond Barracks.

Roast lamb.

Thats right and you will have a jar with me this very adjectival night.

Fitzy this b————r is a thief.

Shutup Amelia said Fitzpatrick lets look at them dresses.

With that we entered Mrs Goodman's front parlour where a great deal of liquor and a 1/2 eaten leg of boiled mutton were in evidence and Cons Fitzpatrick opened my bundle to poke around with his whip lifting one dress then the other I thought him very like his brother he had the Devil in him.

Now heres a nice one Amelia.

Thats worth 2 adjectival pounds.

Heres another.

Thats 3 guineas.

O the Constable winked at me now Mrs Goodman has moved onto GUINEAS.

I said I only come to return the dresses I had no money for further purchase but Fitzpatrick handed them to Mrs Goodman saying she should put them on to show us how they looked again I were surprised to see her retire meekly behind a screen & Fitzpatrick poured me a sherry I would rather have had the mutton as I had not eaten for the best part of 2 days. He said his brother often spoke of me.

Soon enough Mrs Goodman appeared in a bright red dress it had a very large bustle her good temper had returned she told me I were a handsome lad I should dance with her.

Go on cried Fitzpatrick take a turn.

Mrs Goodman come towards me smiling her arms outstretched but I were shy and couldnt dance and when she lowered her arms I seen I had insulted her.

Mr Kelly is not here for dancing said Fitzpatrick he's here for shopping.

Mrs Goodman then showed us several other dresses from her stock but from this point she were sullen and again thought me her enemy.

Very good says Fitzpatrick now you can wrap up the blue and the red both. He had a way with him I never seen in another man insulting the woman even as he charmed her. Mrs Goodman presented both parcels to Fitzpatrick then told him she were sure he would pay his bill.

O yes I will give it to you double.

O you will will you?

Yes both front and back.

I begun to make my excuses thinking to find a feed and bed at Eleven Mile Creek but Cons Fitzpatrick winked at me saying I would either find a dancing partner of my liking or else go to the lockup the choice were mine. We stepped out into the dark and left Mrs Goodman rejected in her house I know for a fact that it were on account of this rejection that she later charged Dan Kelly and Tom and Jack Lloyd with Intent to Rape and Breaking and Entering and Stealing. Thus THE BEECHWORTH ADVERTISER wrote it up:

> In the neighbourhood of Greta for many years there has lived a regular Gang of young ruffians who from their infancy were brought up as rogues and vagabonds and who have been constantly in trouble and on Sunday we learnt that though it is but a short time since some of them have been released from gaol where they have been serving sentences for horse stealing a little game with which they are thoroughly au fait they have again indulged in their pranks.

It is more or less true about the horse stealing but there is no mention of how I earned Mrs Goodman's enmity you will notice that true & secret part of the history is left to me.

Every poor farmboy knows that Beechworth is the place for dancing you would not put the township of Winton in the same division so when the Constable and I ambled our horses along the middle of the dark & mucky road beside the Seven Mile Creek I said we must postpone that particular pleasure to another date.

Come on old man can't you hear the waltz playing?

There were no music other than what were made by a cowbell down on the floodplain but Dan's fate were in Fitzpatrick's hands. When we come upon the deep wagon ruts which is named Benalla Road the trap leaned his grog sour mouth towards my ear whispering I deserved an official commendation for returning the dresses to Mrs Goodman.

I had no clue what a commendation were but when the policeman steered his horse towards Benalla I had no intention of abandoning him.

I seen all the official memorandums said he they all come across my desk y'know.

Memorandum were more Greek I didnt know.

I seen all the memorandums agin you Ned Kelly but now I have a different type of information to lay against your name.

What is that I asked v. alarmed.

What is that he cried so loud he spooked his gelding into a short bolt. What is that he said and seemed to forget what he were about to say. This is in confidence he finally announced but I am going to be the Sergeant in Benalla bye and bye so then you'll have a mate who knows you Ned Kelly. You won't be just an adjectival scoundrel in a memorandum do you follow me?

I don't.

O Christ man I am John Fitzpatrick's adjectival brother I'll look out for you and your brother too.

How do you mean look out for?

No charges for the larceny of them dresses how's that for a start?

Then I knew my 2 day ride were worth it every inch & mile I shook his hand with great relief.

Now he cried catch me if you can.

Were there ever trap like him? Not in my experience. He shot off at a canter through the trees and though my mare were weary she always had great heart and now stuck behind the gelding in and out the gums under the death dealing branches over the crabholes the full 8 mi. We thundered across the Broken River Bridge and into Arundel Street right outside the cells where I had previously suffered but Fitzpatrick had no interest in the law he were quickly dismounted he untied Mrs Goodman's parcels then tethered his horse at the rail of the bootmaker's on the opposite side of the road.

What about some water for the horses?

Directly Ned directly.

I followed his excited footsteps as he rushed through a gate up onto the wide and dark veranda knocking loudly and uttering a cry I have heard so often from the other side.

Police open up.

The order were rapidly obeyed and there come a female voice atop Fitzpatrick's laughter as the pair of them tumbled into the house. A lamp were quickly lit revealing our hostess as a smiling sturdy woman with her hair done up in a kerchief as if for bed. She produced a tray of liquors which Fitzpatrick drunk from thirstily.

2 much younger ladies soon come into the room if they had been sleeping they give no sign of weariness their eyes was bright & their hair were coifed. One were a tall pretty blonde very jolly and bosomy she immediately begun waltzing with Fitzpatrick though there were no music none at all.

The 2nd girl could be no more than 5 ft. tall but her beauty were much finer more delicate her hair were the colour of a crow's wings glistening it would reflect the colour of the sky. Her back were slender with a lovely sweep to it her shoulders was straight her head held high. When she come into my arms she smelled of soap and pine trees and I judged she were 16 or 17 yr. of age.

I confessed immediately I could not dance and she said she would teach me and she fit into my arms as light as a summer breeze. Her eyes were green her skin v. white as it is with girls not long off the boat from home and she and her friend begun to sing and sway it being too late to play the piano Dee Dah Dee Dah.

She said her name were Mary Hearn and she had come from the village of Templecrone just this past year she said I were a marvellous student did ever anyone learn the steps so rapidly? I were suddenly more happy than I had ever hoped to be.

Having been 2 days in the saddle I now wished out loud I had a clean shirt and had combed the burrs out of my hair but she said I shouldnt worry for her own da were a blacksmith and farrier back home so the smell of horses made me most familiar and she lay her glossy head against my chest and we danced around the room with Mrs Robinson sitting in her chair knitting a long pink scarf.

No matter what skullduggery and death Fitzy later caused no matter how great a coward & liar he proved himself I still believe he never wanted no more than this in life and when he danced with that bosomy Belinda at Mrs Robinson's there were no malice in him.

We all collapsed out of breath on the pretty sofas they was uphol-
stered in expensive velvet with red & yellow roses in panels at the back
and even little cloths to keep the hair oil from staining.

Then Fitzpatrick brought out them parcels and the girls was excited
and wondering what could be inside although they knew very well of
course.

As the whole world now understands Fitzpatrick were a very poor
policeman but he might have worked in a haberdashery and made a honest living off it. He presented one dress to Belinda while I give the other to
Mary Hearn and both girls cried out in happiness Mary kissing me on
both my cheeks.

The girls departed to try on their gifts so Mrs Robinson brought out
the cold leg of lamb cutting us great slabs I were very hungry but knew I
must attend to my horse who had not been watered yet. Coming back
inside the house I heard my name called out Ned Kelly Ned Kelly.

I followed the call along the passage it were very dark I come around
a dogleg and there I found an open door and Mary Hearn standing in
candlelight she were holding the back of the dress together with her
hand.

Ned you'll hook me up.

She turned and took her hand away the dress sliding from her to the
floor she tasted like butter shortbread I told her what a sweet & pretty
thing she were and she put her hand across my mouth and buried her
face into my beard.

My daughter I cannot guess how old you are so I ask you not to read
no more until you have children of your own even then perhaps you will
be like me you will not wish to see inside your parents' door. But do not
burn this or destroy what follows I will want it for myself to remember
what a joy it were to fall in love.

Then we was playing what they call THE GAME you never knew so
many hooks and buttons and sweet smelling things we took them off her
one by one until she lay across her bed there were no sin for so did God
make her skin so white her hair as black as night her eyes green and her
lips smiling. She were a teacher with a mighty vocation pulling and dragging when I took her she were slender and strong as a deer her breasts
small but very full she threw back her head offering her pale throat to me
I run her to ground I took her breasts took them in my mouth sucking &

suckling I didnt know whose milk I stole but she were crying out and holding my hair it were the best thing that happened to me in my life.

We lay close together afterwards and smiled at each other and it were only when her babe awoke that I were upset. I had not known she were the mother of a child and I were ashamed to have acted thus.

Leaving well ahead of dawn I set off back across the rich flats heading up towards the distant Wombat Ranges they was beyond sight of the streets of Benalla. 2 days later I turned down beside Bullock Creek I were not prepared for what I seen.

Dan and Steve Hart had blazed a ferocious track up a gully along a ridge then down a hillside filled with wombat holes I should of been angry that Steve were still in residence but were I not only 24 yr. old with a new present handed me by Mr McBean who generously donated a mare named Music to my care? Over 16 hands she were square backed with a good barrel we was soon very tight together she knew how to oblige my every wish. No sooner was we arrived from our long journey but she could feel the excitement in the air she would not miss no challenges so in a mo I were galloping her along the flats leaning from the saddle to pick up a handkerchief between my teeth. I hurdled cockatoo fences whilst kneeling on her back and performed a dozen such acts of derring do and yet there were not one instant of this time I could forget that slender girl with her little baby. I desired her so very badly I had little time to think of Steve Hart I lay sleepless in my crib at night wondering what sort of coward would abandon a young Catholic girl to such a life of shame.

Next day I said I were taking the gold dust to the Assay Office in Benalla I didnt care if the others believed the lie or no.

On a cold frosty dawn I appeared at Mrs Goodman's house in Winton there were a child already out of bed throwing food to all the ducks but it took a long while for her father to hear my knocking. I told him I wished to buy a dress from his missus.

He informed me Mrs Goodman were still in bed but I could help myself he brung me inside and I seen the same mutton still sitting on the table with the addition of a snotty boy eating porridge from a bowl. A great number of dresses was thrown carelessly upon a sofa and amongst them I found a red one with sequins on its front. Davis Goodman claimed its price were £3 I offered £2 he could take it or leave it. He said he would take it so I give him the money then set off through the blustering cold wind to Benalla thence across the bridge and down to Arundel Street.

The very moment I come round the corner Mary Hearn stepped out to fetch the milk she were wearing a bright yellow cotton dress and for the 1st time I feared the baby's father were at home. When she seen me I tipped my hat as if just passing but her face lit up she didnt care who were watching her run down the steps and I lifted her up kissing her on the lips in broad daylight. All this occurred no more than 20 ft. from the court-house where I were 1st arraigned but so does life swing like a river cuts its banks in the boil of flood. I were a frightened boy no more.

Sir says she what brings you here of a cold morning?

I set her down she were lithe & slender moving from one foot to the other in a kind of jig. So this is love I thought.

I brought a wee present.

You did did you said she smiling all the time.

I did.

You want to give it to me?

I aint wrapped it yet.

O why go to all that trouble when you only take the paper off?

Inside the house it were dark and cosy as a swallow's nest I were pre-pared to kiss her again but she were v. busy flitting here to there attending to her tasks. Having swept out the firebox of the stove and laid the kin-dling she now put the match to it.

I asked where were the babe.

O he's a fierce little sleeper don't you worry. She ran a spoon across the top of the milk skin you didnt need to be a dairy farmer to see it were v. good milk there is no equal to the river flats at Benalla. Here she says taste the cream.

She put the spoon in my mouth then she stole the creamy milk back from me.

Whats this said she?

She had felt the gift bump against her so I said she might as well unwrap as crush it. Her lips were full & wide & very nicely shaped I never saw the like of her before she were so wonderfully familiar.

The kitchen were very dim and the kindling native pine so it were catching in the firebox with many small explosions. Mary took the gift from inside my shirt brushing it against her cheek the way I seen my mother touch a red rose to her face.

Silk she exclaimed then let the dress drop against her it were my flag I couldnt think a single thought nor see anything other than herself and I picked her up to hold her close against me. She were a gazelle although I never saw a gazelle she were a foal I carried her around the kitchen 1/2 drunk in happiness she had that dear Irish smell of homemade soap & ashes in her hair I loved her so I told her.

The kindling were all blazing she laughed happily but had yet to load the firebox and place the milk upon the stove. Lifting her even higher I kissed her throat and she moaned and I lifted her higher still I put my lips against her bodice.

Parting with reluctance we set the split wood in the box then she poured milk into a copper pan her hands was trembling. I stood behind her my arms around her waist waiting for the milk to simmer she swayed and hummed a little song about a girl who dreamt of great white horses.

I told her I had never imagined marrying anyone but now I could imagine what a peaceful life a man might have she turned towards me and I saw her eyes gone dark and serious. She put her finger against my lips.

Don't never talk like that you must not.

I begged her pardon she put her arms around my neck and kissed me further not only lips and eyes but also beard and moustache I were pleased I had washed my hair and beard in Ryan's Creek.

Soon as the milk come to the boil she poured it into a bowl setting a muslin cloth across the top then she checked the firebox and reduced the draft. I asked her would she like to try her dress and escorted her along the wide dark corridor towards her room. Her baby were asleep in the middle of the bed a fine fair haired boy with red pouting lips and chubby legs and she lifted him ever so gently placing him in an open drawer then drawing a blanket over him.

Her yellow dress were now dark & wet with mother's milk and what I wanted I wanted right or wrong I do not know if it were a sin or not a sin but we was both v. happy and lay in bed that morning long.

When the Clerk of Court opened up across the road my calm and tender Mary lay warm against my chest I were listening to Mr Grieves the bootmaker next door and I heard each tack he hammered then presently her babe awoke and I watched her feed him from them breasts which was all the more miraculous for their tidy size. The sucking baby lay his hand upon her chest he should have a father to look after him and it were then I got it into my head that I would make application for that post.

Soon as we heard the household stirring Mary said she must set to her chores Mrs Robinson were her employer after all.

I asked your mother when next I could see her. She said I would have to wait until Friday week this were almost 10 days in the future I rode back to Bullock Creek not knowing how to pass the days.

The 1st warning were not the gunshots but a tradesman's cart abandoned one wheel sunk into a wombat hole the name O'Reilly painted on the sides. This violence had struck not long before and although the horses was gone the dung were still fresh though no longer warm to touch. Some large and heavy object had been dragged from the cart cutting a great yellow gouge through the sedge & bracken to a stand of wattles at which point it become a juggernaut crashing through the barrier and breaking saplings 1/2 way along their length.

I were riding towards the injured wattles when I heard a carbine bark and next come the snap of a pistol so I slipped off and crawled through the sedge the air were ripe with the fruity odour of BLACK SMOKE or OYOUKNOW call it what you will. At the edge of cleared land I witnessed our camp in huge upheaval my Arab having leapt the fence were heading back across the creek I never seen him again my thoroughbred mares was all in a state of great excitement whinnying and racing round the yard.

Steve Hart had my Colt .31 he were blazing away bang bang bang firing murderously at the hut.

I had no idea who he were intent on harming I ran towards him but once I was in his range he shouted and the door to the hut swung open and out strolled Dan & Joe Byrne & Aaron Sherritt they might have been walking out of church so indolent and pacific did they seem. Joe bestowed on me a queerly sweet and happy smile but his interest were in the door which had taken all the fire now he kneeled before picking dreamily at the splinters with his knife. I were very confused and angry most particularly at Steve Hart who I had ordered to depart some time previous.

Then a strange voice says Would you happen to be the Ned that I am waiting for?

I beheld a big fat old Irishman he were seated on a log behind me. Though I never seen his lardy face before it were clear from the particular muscles of his forearm he were a blacksmith. This log he now straddled had been surrounded not 2 days before by bracken which were now all trampled flat. Between the log and creek was a set of bellows and the scattered remains of a forge. All this I noted in a moment also that there were a 2nd log that must of been used as his anvil for it were very burnt. Lastly a great rusty ballast tank with 1/2 its side cut out.

I asked who the hell he were.

He said he were John O'Reilly and he could see I were not happy. He also were unhappy and would remain so until he were paid the transport of the ballast tank plus the steel in the said tank also the cost of his labour for cutting the iron plate to fit the inside of the cabin door. He said he never did nothing on the cross before but THE LITTLE CROPPY BOY had bailed him up at the village of Tatong tempting him with a good plump poddy calf he promised to butcher for him. He were a widower said he and his 7 offspring was staying at present with his sister in Winton all of them was hungry otherwise he would never of give up this ballast tank so cheap. In any case he had seen no cattle since Ryan's Creek outside Tatong merely a great number of fancy horses in this very camp he noted them most particular.

I told him our stock was legally obtained and he would be paid as promised.

When I started for Steve Hart he anticipated me coming out to meet me offering back my Colt .31.

Now don't say nothing yet said he.

Holstering the pistol in my belt I told him he had disobeyed my direct order.

No I went a day along the track.

Then?

Then a great opportunity presented itself.

Yes said I the opportunity to betray our camp to this adjectival blacksmith.

Betray you he cried his eyes suddenly brim full. Why I'd rather burn in adjectival Hell than betray you and at this he threw his hat upon the ground. O Jesus you don't remember who I am.

No I don't.

When you 1st set eyes on me I were 8 yr. old.

You're mistaken.

No I aint you was the runner for Harry Power and you brung my da sufficient cash to make the rent o yes you did Ned Kelly then you done it twice more each time when the government was about to seize our land.

I had no memory of this at all.

Near Wangaratta said he then provided a list of all the places he had spied me in the intervening years the race courses the ploughing contests he seen me whip Wild Wright and lately he heard I were stealing horses from under Whitty's nose.

I come to join your gang. There aint much of me he said but what there is is very good.

I couldnt help but allow myself to admire his pluck.

I'll help you anyway you wish said he.

There aint no gang son.

You are the Captain you give an order they obey.

Everyone but you it seems.

I would never of come back except I saw a way to assist you and your door is armour plated as a consequence.

But look at that old blacksmith Steven Hart look at his lardy old face and his droopy adjectival eyes then tell me you don't reckon he won't be happy to provide my whereabouts to Whitty.

I thought of that so I bound pennies across his eyes. I warrant the old b————r don't know where he is.

And his payment?

It is a poddy calf thats all and how I make the payment is my concern not yours.

You ever duff a poddy calf before?

He hesitated.

Killed a beast?

I give him my hand and word said Hart.

I told him he were relieved of this obligation. Joe and me will manage the poddy calf said I and we will butcher and salt it down if that is what your man desires. Then when all is done you fix them pennies on his eyes and see him and his meat home to Winton. Then you can piss off to your beloved da in Wangaratta and the pair of you sing your rebel songs and tell each other stories about Meagher and O'Connell but don't come back here Steve. There aint no gang.

I would help any way you wish.

I'm obliged.

I could write a coffin letter to Mr Whitty I can make them very edifying.

No.

You think I am a sissy but thats something I can explain.

No you can't and you must excuse me for I have business to attend to.

Whatever you wish to call it black smoke or yen pok or oyouknow the substance were a tonic for Joe's character. Grog made him fierce & angry but the smoke turned all his movements as slow and gentle as butter melting in the sun. While he bled the bull calf I went to find a rope to raise it on a gallows for the butchering but when I come back the dead beast were already on its back with a small hole cut into its brisket. Joe winked and fitted a sharpened stick into the hole and lo the creature were neatly propped up leaning a fraction to the side.

No need for rope old man.

In a single long and lazy movement he had the skin off one side then he turned the carcass and propped it on the other to complete the exercise. Then with an axe he sundered the middle of the brisket from whence the tail were slit by a knife. There were never any sign of rush or urgency but within 20 minutes the carcass were cut into 4 pieces and Joe were wandering off to see Aaron about a little bit of THING or so he named it.

I called the younger lads to help deliver the bounty onto the blacksmith's cart but the old Irishman then announced he never travelled in the dusk for fear of bushrangers. He could not be persuaded out of our camp until morning when Steve & Dan & me must tote tongs & hammers & bellows out along the valley to his abandoned cart we then must line its floor with green leafy gum branches and lay the clean meat on top and cover it with wet bags then we must harness his horses and bind the pennies to his eyes. Even then we was a long way from being quit of him.

I put Steve Hart behind the reins this time I would personally escort the boy away.

Say goodbye I told my brother Dan for you won't be seeing Mr Hart no more.

It were v. difficult country for a wagon we had a long day getting as far as Tatong. When we begun following the rutted track beside Kilfeera it were only our 2nd morning and already the meat were on the nose. At Hansen's selection we purchased salt to preserve it as best we could.

At midday we caught sight of a solitary mounted policeman and I immediately commanded the blacksmith to remove his blindfold which he done with great eagerness tho when he seen the copper cantering towards us he tried to tie the pennies on again crying out he would be arrested he had done no wrong. I advised him shut his gob but he were in a panic even as he obeyed.

Steve Hart remained round shouldered and very still on the bench seat I give him my Colt .31 telling him to shoot the blacksmith if he did not behave.

Cons Fitzpatrick approached and begun to circle round my sweaty mare. Whats all this then Kelly?

Sir cried the blacksmith let me answer.

I seen he were waddling urgently back along the track towards us his blindfold pulled back up over his left eye while his right hand clutched the britches he had previously unbuttoned for his comfort.

Fitzpatrick had his back turned to this vision splendid but I seen Steve Hart aim the Colt and heard the hammer strike the nipple thank Jesus I give the boy an empty gun.

He's shooting me cried the blacksmith.

Shutup said Fitzpatrick turning to ride past Steve Hart who had already slid the useless weapon in his pants. It were the flies that attracted the policeman's interest they was gathering above the stolen meat as thick as priests at a wedding feast. When Fitzpatrick circled twice around the cart he leaned down to inspect the bumpy hessian bags the flies rose in a cloud to meet him.

At ease said he.

Steve Hart had already done time in prison he put his feet obediently astride his arms behind his back.

Not you cried Fitzpatrick I'm addressing the adjectival flies then he burst out into a great gale of laughter. The blacksmith saw the situation was more complicated than he had imagined he smiled at me uncertainly.

Well done said Fitzpatrick trotting back to me. Blessed if they aint the best turned out flies I ever seen.

That sent him into another laughing fit. Steve Hart were mortified by the joke against him but then it turned more serious and Fitzpatrick loudly announced he wished to interview me about horses stolen from Kilfeera Station and I accompanied him a chain or so away into the shade of a big old river gum while Hart stared nervously in our direction.

I asked Fitzpatrick did he have a warrant and in answer he leant confidentially towards me and tapped his beaky nose.

Theres no adjectival warrant you sap I'm still drunk I spent the night with old McBean now theres a man who can put away the piss.

So where is you headed?

Eleven Mile Creek as chance would have it.

Then you're going in the wrong direction.

Fitzpatrick removed a compass from a leather pouch but seeming unable to concentrate he tucked it away and smiled at me companionably. I am in love said he.

That adjectival blacksmith is listening.

Eff the blacksmith he can't hear nothing but what do you think of my information. I don't give a damn what no one says but I still need your particular blessing old man.

Who are you in love with?

I told you.

You did not.

It is your sister Kate as I said its very queer that we should meet out here a 100 mi. from nowhere when I've been thinking of you all week long.

But it were even more queer to think of Alex Fitzpatrick laying his sour moustache upon Kate's 14 yr. old mouth every bit as appetising as seeing Harry Power's ugly feet sticking out the bottom of my mother's bed.

Excuse me Sir called the blacksmith if you are arresting this gentleman can I go on now?

O Ned whispered Fitzpatrick she's so fresh & spirited she has such a pretty set to her neck don't frown at me old boy you come and see how I behave with her. He pulled out his compass. Aint it north east from here?

It were due north but that were not the point I told him we was heading for Benalla.

At this Fitzpatrick abruptly swung his horse away acting in an officious way towards the blacksmith who he directed to drove his mob of blowflies to wherever they belonged or he would have him on a serious offence.

O thank you said the blacksmith you're a fine man Sir could I enquire your name?

Eff off said Fitzpatrick.

Yes Sir.

What about me asked Steve Hart.

I'm taking Ned Kelly in to Benalla said Fitzpatrick you may accompany him if you wish.

I tipped Steve the wink but he were not soothed.

What are you effing lagging him for said he Ned Kelly is a better adjectival man than all your family combined.

Do you want to come in with him yes or no? It will be no problem for you to share his cell.

The boy stared back in silent misery.

Then eff off said the Cons.

Hart mounted the buckboard beside the blacksmith he did not look at me but as he flicked the reins his slumped body declared all his shame and the cart slowly pulled away towards the rainclouds in the north.

You won't come with me to see your sister asked Fitzpatrick.

Not just now mate.

You're set on Benalla?

I am indeed.

You know you're an adjectival fool he said peevishly removing his compass once again. You should of consulted me before you fell for that woman.

I could say the same about you and my sister.

Mary aint the girl for you Kelly I know her character I wrote to my brother just yesterday I told him I feared I done you a very bad turn when I made the introduction.

This were all water off a duck's bum to me I knew it were the ignorance that sort of male is prey to.

You don't know my character Alex.

You always think yourself top dog said he then waited as if he had asked a question. You think yourself the better horseman he suggested.

When I did not answer the erratic fellow dug his heels into the gelding's flank and he were off I admit he sat him very nicely there were never daylight seen between him and the saddle though he drove his horse so hard he might of killed him. 3 hr. later I found him waiting near the Broken River bridge the poor animal's flanks all wet with sweat and blood from his military spurs.

You are an adjectival fool he said then rode away again.

It is a generally accepted fact that a man once lagged by coppers will be abandoned by his mates this is not cowardice but common sense for the traps are always on the hunt for so called KNOWN ASSOCIATES who will be well advised to stay as far from the town as possible. Steve Hart knew this but didnt care and once his blacksmith were delivered to Winton he headed directly to Benalla Police Station. Informed I were not known there he thought them liars so he loitered on the street outside waiting for the time when I would be marched from the lockup to the courthouse.

Meanwhile I were a free man sitting happily with your mother on Mrs Robinson's veranda the spring had now come on the jasmine tumbling from the front fence in great white fistfuls as fragrant as a young girl's handkerchief. On Sunday early we went to mass for me it were the 1st time in many years and when the priest heard my sins he said I must get married and I told him I would attend to that immediately. That afternoon I paid 2 quid to rent a fancy sulky from Davis Goodman he were a mighty robber but no one else were doing business on the Sunday then I drove the sulky out to Eleven Mile Creek to show my beloved and her baby to Mother. I had no fears about the meeting were not Mary Irish and Catholic and very agreeable in her manner?

My mother received us inside the hut she made the scones she poured the tea I cannot say there were outright rudeness but that afternoon she repaid me for my behaviour with her beaux. She and George King sat in their chairs stiff as boards they never looked at Mary until she stood to leave.

Very nice to have met you said my mother it were a branding iron laid upon my heart.

On our way back to Benalla I saw the tears flow down Mary's pretty cheeks when I asked would she marry me she asked What about your mother's feelings I said my mother could go to Hell.

That night I took my good news to Fitzpatrick at his boardinghouse he said only an adjectival fool would marry Mary Hearn I demanded what he had against her but he dared not say nothing to my face. After I left him Fitzpatrick wrote a long letter to Mary its reason as badly tangled as Blind Freddy's fishing line but the gist of it were he loved me like a brother and would punish anyone who deceived me.

The following morning when I was sleeping Mary discovered this edict folded inside the handle of the milk billy she were so frightened by what she read she didnt even take the milk inside but gathered up her skirts and rushed down Bridge Street to the police stables. At that hour she saw no one save Steve Hart who were very cold & hungry but still maintaining his watch outside the lockup. Not knowing his connection to me Mary ran past into the stables where she wept and begged Fitzpatrick not to ruin her chance of happiness. What pleasure did it give the so called LADIES' MAN to see this beautiful woman's face contorted & wet with tears her lovely milky skin were crumpled like the letter in her hand.

Why are you so cruel to me she cried she could not see his face hidden in the shadow of the horse's flank. What have I ever done against you?

Tell him the truth Mary.

He will kill someone if I do.

You have my word as an officer Ned Kelly shall not harm you.

Its not me he'll hurt Fitzy.

This give the b————r pause to chew on his moustache looking Mary up and down. Who will he hurt Mary he finally asked and she turned her clear green eyes directly on himself.

Me?

I do not know.

Well girlie if you won't tell him the situation then I will undertake the duty for you.

Please Fitzy I beg you.

But his eyes was cold as he put his foot in the stirrup. You will tell him what you have hidden from him and I warrant he will take it calmly.

Steve Hart recognized Fitzpatrick as he come galloping out the stables like an adjectival mad thing and it is well known the policeman continued at this rate all the way to Winton where he visited the aforementioned Davis Goodman receiver hawker perjurer and from this lard bucket he purchased a small envelope of white powder and under Fitzpatrick's instruction Mrs Robinson made a glass of fresh lemonade loading it with honey before stirring in the drug.

Willie wagtails danced on the fence while my slender dark haired Mary give me the lemonade and watched me drink it.

When she took my hand hers were so clammy I asked if she was well. Dear says she I cannot marry you if you do not know the father of the child.

You told me it were a Mr Stuckey.

Mr Stuckey has another name.

O who is that?

He is also known as George King.

I heard the hateful truth but continued talking like a kangaroo will take those extra hops before it falls. Did George King promise he would marry you?

I knew he were married to your mother.

O God I groaned how could you let me take you to visit?

You wished it so much how could I refuse?

O they must of thought me such an effing fool.

They thought us both great fools dear.

Her sweet young face were deathly cold all joy abandoned. My hate for George King were deep and black as hard & cruel as a pike I should of killed him the day I come home from Pentridge he were wearing that yellow pullover my mother knitted I knew him then for what he were.

The chambers of my heart filled with melted steel the truth pushed like fire through my arteries and I roared out loud and jumped up to my feet. The drug had made my legs turn soft as dough.

Sit down dear.

I had no voice but threaded my way through the familiar house all the way to the back veranda where my saddle and bridle was waiting on the rail. I were staggering like a drunk and as I tried to lift my saddle I heard Mary call for Fitzy this made no sense at all.

It were very hard going down the steps towards the bootmaker's paddock but my mare were coming to meet me at the stile.

Where are we off to Neddy asked Fitzpatrick I didnt see where he appeared from.

Home said I.

Not today Ned.

He had handcuffs I took a swing at him but he got me in Hegan's hold he could never have succeeded had I not been drugged. He got my arms behind my back and told me he admired me more than any man he ever met I felt the shackles pinch which were pretty much the last thing I remember before waking in the cells next morning.

Cons Fitzpatrick come to call in the stiff necked company of Sergeant Whelan. I acted like I never knew him and I could see him much relieved he pulled in his gut then read his lies against me in a baritone it were alleged I rode a horse upon a footpath it were alleged I had been intoxicated I couldnt recall doing none of them things but had a very distinct memory that George King had dishonoured my mother and my fiancee.

It seems my character had become so altered overnight that an army were needed to contain me it now assembled on the garden path. The crowding of these traps caused me to step on Sgt Whelan's lettuce for which crime Cons Lonigan struck me in the kidney. Next I endured officious language from my so called Friend he bawled the prisoner should march left right left right.

On Arundel Street left right left right I seen a different category of friendship it were bandy little Steve Hart his clothes in a poor state after 2 nights in the street but his black hair were combed very flash parted in the middle with a curl on either side. With him was Tom Lloyd these 2 lads begun barracking the police together Steve could not contain his outrage at my fate. When he stooped as if to pick up a stone Whelan immediately called for the bracelet to be fitted to the Prisoner.

I called to Steve to put down his rock I reminded the dome headed Sergeant he had arrested me previously for Highway Robbery and I give him no trouble on that occasion. Today I were charged only with riding a horse on a footpath but Fitzpatrick had his bracelets out and were coming at me. When I brushed the coward aside my mates begun to cheer me and I walked on freely towards the court my head held high.

Good on you Ned you are a better adjectival man than all them cowards put together etc.

I begun to cross the street but Lonigan ordered me to halt and when I did not pause he leapt upon me from behind. Spinning on my heel I knocked the mongrel to the earth.

As the bootmaker's door were wide open I sprinted through it but the back door were padlocked Lonigan come at me and I brushed him off then Fitzpatrick caught my boot and tore the sole and heel clean off. He begged me cooperate so I sent him cooperating against the wall the boot-maker fast retreating his wig all crooked his tacks stuck like doll's teeth in his mouth. Then Lonigan come from behind seizing my bawbles he crushed them in his filthy hands while Whelan began to lay his fists into my kidneys the traps was yapping like fox terriers about me but I would not be still I carried them around the shop banging them into the walls.

A miller appeared calling out the police should desist they done so. They should be ashamed he said he were a fair sized fellow in a well made suit with a broad and honest face he asked would I permit him to apply the handcuffs I said I would seeing how he asked me so politely. When he enquired would I accompany him to court I went peaceful as a lamb but I did not forget about George King or the sentence I would pass on him as soon as possible.

Steve Hart & Tom Lloyd followed me inside where Mary were already seated that made 3 pair of eyes full of sympathy for my condition but it were only the 4th that I paid attention to I refer to George King's off-spring. Doubtless I were mad but when I looked down from the dock the baby seemed to glare at me with his father's cold blue eyes.

Then it turned out I had severely misjudged the miller's character for he were the Magistrate. Fitzpatrick then give his evidence against me and the damn miller found me guilty of Drunkenness and Disorderly Con-duct and Assault he fined me £4 and also 5/– for damage to Fitzpatrick's clothing then the mongrels took me down to the cells once more.

Mary Hearn saw Steve & Tom counting the pennies in their pockets she told them to follow her to the Bank of Australasia where she with-drew her savings then the 3 walked to the Police Station and give it all away to the government.

When I were brought to meet my benefactors I hardly seen them noticing only that baby's eyes and the way he curled his lip at me as if he already knew the penalty I would do against his blood. It were then I learned the child's name he were christened George as well.

I had to wait while the receipts was issued it begun to thunder and by the time my mare were splashing down the boggy track to Eleven Mile Creek it were hailing hard. I forced my brave Music through the pain I had my .31 Colt stuck in my belt and my .577 Enfield rolled inside my oilskin coat it were better my powder were dry I didnt care about my cold and shivering skin.

As I come alongside Halloran's house the hail stopped and the sun emerged and from that govt. earth there rose a fragrant mist. I spied our neighbour Bricky Williamson running across the paddock when his boot fell off he did not stop but continued clump footed through the mud. Thinking he were going to warn George King I dug my heels into my mount and galloped across the back of Halloran's block then jumped the high 4 rail fence thus approaching my mother's property from the south. Even before I come around from behind the cover of the cowbail I seen something were wrong for a wedgetail eagle rose into the sky the crows squalling with fury round its mighty wings. In the middle of the yard George's sorrel mare lay dead & mangled a 2nd wedgetail had its head buried in its gut. The mare were destroyed by a shotgun in both head and heart thus opening a great greasy feast the big kidneys was 1/2 gone already and a line of shining blue intestines led from their natural place towards my mother's hut. The eagles feasted the crows attacked. I unwrapped my Enfield and approached the hut on foot. Everything were still.

I burst into the hut finding nothing but a great deal of grain spilled over the table and 3 rats gorging on it.

I called King's name and something moved beneath my mother's bed I cocked the rifle.

Come out you coward.

It were only George King's issue 3 yr. old John and 4 yr. old Ellen I ordered them tell me what had happened but they would not budge their eyes was glistening like baby possums in the dark. Under the other cribs I found nothing only a 4th rat which were in great distress lying on its back and dying like a blowfly.

I come out outside looking up in the peppercorn in case he climbed it thence to the veggie garden where I discovered my da's old shotgun laid across the path my mother sitting on the top step of the stile. She were rocking the way you see the old women do at a wake her big veined hands rested on her belly. When she turned around her eyes was sunk her nose seemed grown she gone completely grey in just one day.

He bolted said she I could not stop the b————r.

I picked up the shotgun it were well warmed.

But I stopped the adjectival horse she said and noting the way she continued holding her hands against her belly I realised she were with child again she were too old for this having lost 4 teeth while pregnant with John King now her cheeks was cleaving to her gums. I put my arm around my ma feeling only bone no flesh no hope she said her hut were damned it had never escaped the stinky man's curse and she would burn it to the ground she didnt care what crockery she lost.

I knew there were no curse on anything except that put on us by the police and squatters. I went back inside to fetch her a glass of brandy and observed King's tankard missing from its hook also a scalp he claimed to have took off a red Indian. I brung the brandy back to my mother but although she did not refuse the drink it brought no colour to her cheeks and her eyes saw nothing hopeful.

She said the years she spent with George was a curse for added proof of it she pointed to the irises she had planted round the borders of the hut I thought her mad to find even the flowers a cause of misery but then noted a movement and realised it were a rat. Soon I seen there was many they was running around in great distress standing up and waving their paws.

She had poisoned the rats dealing with them better than any rat charmer but she saw their death as proof of the curse by now she were too emotional for me. I prayed one of the older girls would come to help me but Maggie were now married to Bill Skilling and Gracie was nowhere to be seen. Sometime in the late afternoon Kate returned I will never forget the contrast she made to her mother her large dark eyes her shining long black curls. Kate coaxed her frightened 1/2 brother & sister out from under the bed it was her who found Gracie hiding at Halloran's.

Her children tried to persuade their mother back inside but she were ever a stubborn woman none could change her mind. At dusk I fetched Maggie who brung a big pan of baked lamb also a brandy bottle so we all of us ate beneath the peppercorn tree and that night my mother slept at Maggie's.

Next day Bricky and I buried George King's horse it were night by the time I returned to Mary Hearn she were nursing her baby in Mrs Robinson's kitchen her back turned towards me.

Hello said I.

No reply.

Hello my dearest.

She wd. not look at me. Where were you?

I said I needed to build a new house for my mother I mentioned nothing of King but when she put her baby to her shoulder the child stared at me with his departed father's cold blue eyes.

Fitzpatrick come to Mary Hearn begging her to speak to me on his behalf he said he only gaoled me because he loved me but Mary would never forget the threats he had made against her she were a mere 5 ft. tall and v. slender but she backed the big booted policeman off the veranda he tripped and stumbled on the garden path. Don't never come back here again you vermin scab.

I don't think Mrs Robinson will want to hear that.

O don't make me tell Ned what you just said.

But Ned were the knot at the middle of a tug of war at Eleven Mile Creek I were labouring each day to construct a temporary shelter for my mother this were what you might build to keep the rain off your hay no more than 4 posts with cross bracing on 3 sides some ironbark rafters with bark lain down then saplings lashed on top. When that were complete I commenced the new hut and my mother were very happy with the progress. Every nail driven made her back straighter her eyes brighter her only complaint were that I continued to depart as the sun went down. Finally I asked Mary to camp with me beside the creek but she said my mother hated her. Mrs Robinson then announced she needed £2 for Mary's room I found the money but I did not reveal my domestic situation to my mother just the same she smelled another rat.

Some sheila no doubt said she looking towards the home paddock where the cows was as usual all massing at the gate. She loved her horses but she never liked a cow I know it.

You know it aint just some sheila. I brought Mary out to visit I think you must recall.

Must I now? Gracie get them cows into the bails.

I don't reckon you would forget.

She snapped her head around bringing her hard eye to bear on me. Ah yes I know the one she had herself a child off a married man.

Thus troubles rushed towards us like white ants hatching on a summer night in Benalla there were a knock on Mary's window and a man calling Ned Ned Ned it woke us from our sleep. Mary whispered it were Fitzpatrick I must not answer but raising the sash I found the policeman in a dreadful state he were very drunk & wretched declaring himself the most miserable man alive for he had lost my friendship. He fell off the veranda into the hydrangeas I rescued him then took him walking down the centre of the muddy midnight road me in my underwear him in his uniform he wept profusely he said he only lagged me to prevent me doing murder to George King.

It were one in the a.m. before I had calmed and forgive him but it were nearly 3 hr. more before I had pacified my Mary who were in a fierce rage against Fitzpatrick she revealed he had one girl in Frankston another in Dromana and refused to make an honest woman of either one. She could not appreciate what it meant to have a policeman as a friend but we Kellys was so constantly oppressed by Flood & Hall & Farrell that Fitzpatrick were of great value not least to my mother who were once more running her shebeen.

At Eleven Mile Creek I were framing out the bedroom when Fitzpatrick arrived in mufti announcing he wished to spend his day off assisting me he had brung his own tools his chisels was worthy of a cabinet maker. He carefully unwrapped a very good long plane and this we put to work immediately.

In Benalla that night Mary and me was laying in bed we heard footsteps on the veranda. Here comes that lying devil said she.

But it were Steve Hart he were wanted by the police for having stole a saddle we hid him on the floor then in the morning I sent him back to Bullock Creek. I promised to see what could be done to have the charges against him dropped.

How could you do that feat asked Mary are you a squatter suddenly?

I'll see what can be done.

You've been talking to Fitzpatrick.

No I aint.

3 days later Fitzpatrick were again at Eleven Mile Creek I asked what he could discover of the charge then spoke very favourably about Steve's character. Fitzpatrick promised he would enquire but explained he come on a more pressing matter a charge sworn against Dan Kelly by Mrs Goodman alleging Breaking & Entering & Stealing plus Intent to Rape.

I knew Dan had not been in the district so could honestly pronounce this a lie Fitzpatrick could see I told the truth this were the advantage of our friendship.

Said he Even Sgt Whelan knows she's lying. He has written a memorandum to Melbourne saying he is set on getting Mrs Goodman and her husband sent down for perjury. Whelan don't want Dan at all so here is how we get him off. You bring your brother to the station so he can give himself up.

And why would I do that?

So he will be found not guilty and Mrs Goodman can be punished.

We walked to Bill Skilling's hut where Mother & Kate & Maggie & Bill all took part in the decision. When Fitzpatrick finally departed we all agreed he were a good man and Dan would be well advised to do as recommended.

Next morning I told Mary I had to visit my brother then I paid Mrs Robinson sixpence for a few cold potatoes and a mutton sandwich. It were wild & blustering spring weather I set my face against the gale heading once more on the long familiar journey to the Wombat Ranges through the rich dirt of Kilfeera up Ryan's Creek and into the wild unselected country when my nose smelled those tossing trees I knew this were my haven my one good inheritance off old Harry Power he give me land like a Duke to his older son for every track and ridge I were obliged to him.

At Bullock Creek in the damp dripping dawn my brother Dan agreed to do what I asked of him he were very frightened of prison but donned his oilskin and set his hat low on his eyes then Steve and me accompanied him down through the Wombat towards the plains.

The evening we come into Benalla it were still raining the Broken River running very high. Steve and me witnessed Dan Kelly surrender himself bravely he were taken to the cells by candlelight.

As Fitzpatrick had promised the case soon were brought to court with Dan acquitted of all serious charges but then the adjectival Magistrate cleared his throat and as a kind of afterthought he give Dan 3 mo. for Damaging Property.

When the sentence were pronounced my brother's eyes sought mine he were but 16 yr. old a grubby boy with dirty fingernails his black hair plastered flat upon his head. Dear God he winked at me it broke my heart to see him taken down. That were the end of my friendship with Constable Alexander Fitzpatrick.

This took place in 1877 the government were in crisis there was no funds for gaols or judges' pay so when Dan got out of prison in February he were suffering badly his clothes hung off him his eyes was dull his skin had scabby sores from hunger. He come to find me in Arundel Street where I were still resident I told him he should stay away from the settled areas as they was infested with police who now would lag anyone to justify their own employment.

Dan returned to Bullock Creek where he soon were joined by others including Joe Byrne & Aaron Sherritt they was finding the police in their own district as agitated as bull ants. When Fitzpatrick come knocking on our door one March evening I were packed and already on the way to Bullock Creek before he broke into the room.

The warrant against me were for the theft of Whitty's horses but 4 weeks later the police issued another against Dan Kelly & Jack Lloyd on the basis of evidence that they RESEMBLED the people who sold some of Whitty's stolen horses.

So were the hornets stirred on Easter Sunday Cons Lonigan following my mother back from mass in Benalla. I don't know who he thought he might arrest there but he were disappointed having to assist in the birth of a baby girl.

We was our mother's sons we come like the 3 Wise Men to welcome the baby to the world Joe Byrne were of our number. It were just on dusk the birds was fidgeting in the trees they might of benefited from the pipe on which my mate were sucking. His entire life were about to be decided but he sat beside me on the blind side of the hut wrapped up in the fruity smell of yen pok. Opium is alleged to dull the senses but it did not prevent Joe recognising the boots thumping on my mother's front veranda.

Cops he warned. Fitzpatrick.

I never even heard the horse. You sure its him I asked.

Joe didnt move but his pale blue eyes observed me remove the little Colt revolver from my belt.

Aint there a warrant out for Dan he asked.

For him and me said I charging all 6 chambers then sealed each with grease before placing the weapon carefully inside my belt. By then Joe's eyes had drifted away he were watching the sweet smoke rise and cling like cobweb on the darkening walls.

I cursed him softly and moved around to the south side of the hut where I could see my brother through a window. He were still as a rabbit staring at his fate i.e. Cons Alexander Fitzpatrick. As I watched my mother put in her teeth then spoke to Gracie who run out the hut returning a moment later followed by her sister Kate.

I seen Fitzpatrick pull my sister roughly onto his knee that were the last adjectival straw as far as I were concerned I showed myself plainly at the door.

Off I ordered.

Although he must of seen my gun the policeman disobeyed he patted my little sister's hand. As for my mother she ignored the outrage opening her oven door and withdrawing 2 loaves of crusty bread on a long handled shovel.

Get my sister off your effing lap.

Fitzpatrick sighed You see what I must tolerate from those whom I protect?

You must not worry none said Kate my brother will be nicer when he hears we're to be married.

O you silly tart I cried he cannot marry you.

Fitzpatrick pushed her from his lap I seen his hand go round his revolver mine was already on the Colt.

What game is this he asked.

You're spoken for already you mongrel.

That got the ma's attention.

He's engaged to one tart he's got another pregnant in Frankston.

My mother never hesitated she raised her shovel and clouted Fitzpatrick across the head his helmet fell he stumbled drawing out his .45. I fired the .31 hitting him in the wrist his revolver clattered to the floor.

The new baby screamed and Joe Byrne come in the door his pupils the size of pinpricks he had my father's old shotgun aimed at Fitzpatrick more or less. Little John King scuttled under the bed bum 1st. Kate had run away and were moaning behind the curtains of her crib. I ordered Joe to put down his gun and get the children over to Maggie Skilling's.

Bricky Williamson took one look at Joe then volunteered to take the kiddies he departed with babies hanging off him like an old sow running with her piglets sucking on her tits.

Fitzpatrick were trying to wrap a handkerchief around his bleeding hand he cringed from me. It aint like it seems said he.

Shut your mouth cried my mother I saw she had taken possession of the police issue .45 which she were pointing at the treacherous Fitzpatrick her hands was covered in flour her jaw were set her eyes alight with the power of her mighty will.

You spoiled my girl you b-----d.

Fitzpatrick seemed surprised to see her take issue on this point.

I'm very adjectival tired of whining cheating men my mother said she cocked the pistol with her big flat thumb it were wrong of me to let the last one go.

Fitzpatrick then begun to cry he said he were a wretch he knew it but he swore before God he never would report us if we only let him live. Snot ran out his nose gathering in his whiskers he were an abject creature which won him no pity from my mother she spat on his head screaming that Annie were buried beneath the willows that were one daughter already dead from a policeman's pizzle. I seen she might just shoot him.

Give me the weapon Ma.

Her hair were 1/2 unpinned her eyes was strange. I moved v. slowly extending my hand towards the .45 but even as I secured the cold hard barrel I knew I could not predict my mother.

Now let it go Ma.

Her mouth twisted downwards. Do it careful said I or you'll have me beneath the willows too.

At that her mouth collapsed issuing a dreadful cry she begun tearing at her hair. I took the revolver's deadly weight as she rushed out into the night I could hear her bawling echoing down around the creek you never heard such grief it contained Bill Frost and George King all them lost children every loss and hurt she ever suffered it would wrench your guts.

All around Fitzpatrick were people he had betrayed there was Dan & me & Kate whimpering on her bed there were more pain in that hut than any of us could bear I removed the shells and give his weapon back.

If you have read Cons Fitzpatrick's sworn statement you will not know of our kindnesses to the snivelling cur. Joe poured him rum I cut the bullet from his hand then dressed the injury and when he finally departed our hut he stood in the doorway thanking me with the following speech Joe Byrne were able to write it down so I submit it here as evidence.

FITZPATRICK: I have to say you are as decent a man as ever I met and I want you to know that I know you saved my life tonight and I didnt deserve my life to be saved I am very sorry to have lost your respect for there is no man's respect I would rather have.

Once he had gone Joe recorded the following exchange.

E. KELLY: What did you think of his speech?

J. BYRNE: May he be roasted on hot iron the b−−−−−d is going to shop us all.

So did it come to pass.

The Murders at Stringybark Creek

Bank of New South Wales letterhead, 42 sheets of medium stock (8" × 10" approx.). Some water damage.

Manhunt following shooting of Fitzpatrick. Evidence that the police expected the fugitives apprehended fatally. An account of the gunfight at Stringybark Creek and Kelly's often repeated claim that the gang acted in self-defence. Confirmation that Dan Kelly was wounded by police fire. Auron Sherritt's role as scout and supporter. Many attempts to cross the flooded Murray River, then a daring crossing of One Mile Creek while it was under police guard.

Once our mother returned to the new hut she would not leave it she sat by the fire drawing shapes in the ashes I could not persuade her to flee though it were clear she were in serious trouble she had threatened a policeman.

You don't want to be in prison Ma.

You don't know what I want.

All my life I had stood by her when I were 10 I killed Murray's heifer so she would have meat when our poor da died I worked beside her I were the eldest son I left school at 12 yr. of age so she might farm I went with Harry Power that she might have gold when there were no food I laboured when there were no money I stole and when the worthless Frost & King closed round her like yellow dingoes on a chained up bitch I sought to protect her.

Leave me said she go save your brother I made my bed I'll lie in it.

No said Dan it were me the b————r come for.

Go she said fiercely for Jesus' sake let me live with what I done.

Kate were howling in her bed Dan were most distressed he tried to hold his mother's hands you aint done nothing.

She wrenched herself away I've been a fool she said I've been as big a fool as any mother could ever be.

She pushed Dan firmly towards me. Look after him said she he were a lot of trouble getting born don't let him go to waste you hear me?

Yes Ma.

You hide him from the traps you hear I'll stay with Katie.

Many is the time I have imagined those final moments in the gloomy hut Kate bawling on the bed my mother kissing us both on the cheek.

Go said she my soul's within you.

Next day we boys was far away and safe enough despite the warrants sworn against us for Attempted Murder we was in places where we could not be found. It were our people at Eleven Mile Creek who suffered. A warrant were issued for Maggie's husband Bill Skilling who had been 4 mi. away in the presence of witnesses. Bricky Williamson done no more than carry the children to safety but on the basis of Fitzpatrick's lies he were charged with Aiding and Abetting Attempted Murder. This same charge were laid against our mother and as I had left her undefended the police took her and the baby as easy as plucking mushrooms in a cow paddock. The pair of them were took to Beechworth Prison.

And there Sir Redmond Barry waited for her like a great fat leech hiding in the bracken its only purpose to suck the living blood it were the same man who wished to hang the rebels at Eureka the same man who sentenced our Uncle James to death for burning down the house. When we heard he were to be the Judge we sent word through Mr Zinke we would surrender if Barry released the mother & babe but the great man thought us less than dog manure beneath his boots. Word came back he planned to teach a lesson to us so called LOUTS.

In response I pledged to do the same for him.

Kate were now denied to Fitzpatrick for all eternity the cowardly policeman next slunk down to Arundel Street bearing the gift of an embroidered dress for baby George it were 9 o'clock on a Monday night and mother & child was both asleep but that were nothing to Fitzpatrick he knocked against their window pane ordering Mary to dress the boy in the new garment immediately. Well and good he were too dangerous to disobey so Mary done the dressing then lay George in his cart wheeling him out onto the veranda.

Of course Fitzpatrick had no interest in a baby and once he struck a match and frightened George to death he declared himself very bored by all the bawling. The thing he wished to know were did Mary need assistance he worried how she might survive now Ned Kelly were a hunted man.

Mary would of liked assistance to pull his beaky nose but said she had a little money saved with the Bank of Australasia.

This were a most intelligent defence and it blocked him for a moment but then he come back asking if she had had her bank interest entered by the clerks.

She didnt know she told him. Who ever would?

Show me your savings book said he them clerks is scallywags sometimes they forget to write in the interest and that suits the bank believe
me they make 1/2 their profits from forgotten interest.

Mary were not going to show him no road but he were insistent looking at her so hard she could feel the hatred his eyes glistening like a dingo
in the dark.

I'll show you when I find it Fitzy I can't think where I've hid it then
baby George begun to cough. Now said she I must put this little chap
back to sleep inside.

No no not yet I haven't examined him properly.

Mary prepared herself for one more match light inspection but then
Fitzpatrick said excuse him he must use the dunny. When he finally
returned all his passion for the baby were forgotten and he sat himself
down in the rattan chair stretching out his legs.

I have a secret he announced.

I shall put George down to sleep said Mary then I'll hear it.

You'll hear it now said the trap I have talked to the Stock Protection
Association and the members are more than happy to assist you.

She laughed she couldnt help it. If them squatters know my name its
only because they heard I were a slut.

They'll think you the Blessed Virgin if you help them catch Ned Kelly.
She felt his mouth brush against her hair it were then she knew he were
even more loathsome than she had previously thought. No Fitzy she said
I could never do that.

Not even for your baby's sake?

She begun to shake so hard she could not speak. Fitzpatrick stretched
himself out further in her armchair he struck a match. I took the liberty
said he then she seen he were holding her blue bank passbook. Fitzy! You
was in my room give that to me.

I reckon I'll keep this Mary I'm sure you don't mind.

She could not imagine why he would want her passbook but she
recognised them cruel eyes in the match light. O Fitzy why do you
hate me?

He blew out his match the dark air were acrid with sulphur. I don't
hate you girlie but any Magistrate could look at this passbook and see you
cannot support this child he is Endangered as we say in law.

He were threatening to have her baby removed into an orphanage she
would kill him 1st.

Very well she said I'll think about your offer.

Yes he said coldly you can call at the Police Station before noon tomorrow.

The minute he departed she knew she must flee she picked up the cart and carried George to her room then she dressed him in singlets nighties jackets shawls as many garments as she could fit one atop the other his arms and legs as stiff as broken limbs in plaster of Paris and he were crying very loud.

While Mrs Robinson's pianola played the Sailor's Polka she rolled her own few possessions in a scarf and wrapped this inside a woollen cardigan. Then she changed her mind and tucked these items all around the baby bearing him along the passageway the floor were shuddering beneath the heavy tread of a RESPECTABLE squatter's boots.

She set her burden down in Arundel Street and pushed the cart through the windy dark towards the crabholed road that led to Eleven Mile Creek.

She prayed Almighty and merciful God who hast commissioned Thy angels to guide and protect us command them to be our companions from our setting out until our return to clothe us with their invisible protection to keep from us all danger of collision of fire of explosion of fall and bruises. Even when the moon appeared in a chasm of clouds it were no comfort but a frightening apparition the clouds were lowering and angry north of Benalla the wind begun to blow and with it come a fine needling rain that stung her face. She removed her coat and lay it across her babe as the rain blew harder & heavier she were drenched to the bone. For a Kelly this were no bad night but for Mary a severe ordeal. She were afraid of Chinamen of blacks of swagmen her heart were beating as loud as a horse's in her ears.

At dawn your Aunt Kate saw a strange poor woman come limping down the track from the direction of Greta in the darkness your mother had already missed the Skilling Williamson and Kelly huts she now were doubling back her feet cut & blistered but her rattled baby were blessedly asleep.

O God have pity cried Mary they cannot force me to betray him.

Though Kate never knew her relationship to me she brought your mother inside and when they had both reassured themselves that George were not damaged by his adventure Kate bandaged the stranger's feet with vinegar & brown paper then she learned who she were also the crimes Fitzpatrick had done against her.

You're home here lovey said my sister safe as with your own own people dear.

Redmond Barry put on his lambskin then sentenced our mother to 3 yr. for Aiding and Abetting the Attempted Murder of Constable Alexander Fitzpatrick he further ruled she could not keep her baby with her he were a cruel and heartless b—————d his time will come.

The Wombat were steep & twisted deep gorges bounded by almost perpendicular ranges yet it did not feel safe the location of our camp were known to more people than were right. 1st come Aaron Sherritt with his wooden box of opium or oyouknow. Next were Jimmy Quinn then Wild Wright who said in explanation that he had been mooching around Finch's saddlery in Main Street Mansfield. Moss Finch were a closelipped old b————r he never talked to no one Wild Wright least of all for he were well known as a troublemaker in the town and not above a little thievery. When Moss Finch seen Wild drifting through the long oily shadows of his shop he were straight onto him.

What can I do you for Isaiah?

Well you could buy me a jar of porter Mr Finch.

Ah but you know I don't drink Isaiah.

It aint you we was discussing.

It were just banter Wild never had no hope of a drink he were bored and looking for some person or item to amuse him then it come to his attention that old Moss were sewing up a very long strip of hide into a belt or strap he could not see exactly what it were.

Whats this adjectival thing?

Ah look out now you've dropped the buckle.

Wild set the buckle on the work bench. Who would need a 25 ft. long belt?

The silence what followed offended him he always were v. sensitive. It's a pulley belt he suggested.

Still Moss did not answer.

Whats this effing thing for? Wild's voice were rising ever ready to imagine others thought themselves above him.

Put it down Isaiah you know I've got a family to feed I aint got time for playing games but by the time Moss had finished speaking Isaiah Wright were pushing his face close against his own.

I think you better tell me what its for Finchy.

Here said Moss impatiently digging into his apron heres a bob go have a drink if that will calm you down.

Well that done it. Never in the whole history of Mansfield had Moss Finch ever been known to buy a drink for no one.

Wild pocketed the money. Tell me what it is 1st.

Very well Isaiah its what they call an undertaker.

O yairs said Wild in the way bush people do meaning please continue.

Yes thats what they call it.

What does it do?

Lord help me what does it sound like it does its for carrying a body its for strapping a dead man to a packhorse like I said its an undertaker now get out of here and let me finish. Moss picked up his lump of dirty yellow beeswax running it up and down his thread the wax were crisscrossed with deep dry furrows.

Who are you making that for Mr Finch?

That aint none of your business Isaiah.

O come on Mr Finch I never done nothing against you did I?

Moss said that were not the point yet it were clear to him that Wild had not asked the question idly.

Never hurt you in any way never borrowed your horse or nothing.

Moss looked at the beeswax closely as if them crisscross lines was holding some secret information. All right said he I am making this for Sgt Kennedy now go and leave me.

Kennedy is planning on killing someone?

Moss Finch turned on him his eyes very fierce.

Why Jesus Christ cried Wild they're going to kill the Kelly boys.

That were what Wild cantered 30 mi. to tell us. Thus we imagined our undertakers the leather straps lay fully revealed like giant tapeworms nestling in our guts all our lifetimes growing larger every day. No one cooked that evening we just sat staring in the fire watching the sap sizzling out of the big green logs as the dark come down it were the young lads who concerned me most. Steve and Dan squatted side by side sipping their billy tea they was brave hiding their feelings in the darkness of their hats.

When we had ate a can of sardines and was all rolled up in our coats for the night it were Joe Byrne who spoke. His voice were grey & scratchy as when he were out of oyouknow.

He said he were going to America or Africa the sooner the better the future were clear to him. You don't mind Ned he asked.

I don't mind.

You fellows could come too we could go across to Gippsland and get a boat from Eden. They won't think to look for us in Gippsland they'll be watching the crossings of the Murray River. Ned?

He won't go said Steve.

Why won't I?

You won't leave Mrs Kelly he said and he were right.

In the morning Joe were feeling crook so he did not depart he stayed the next day too complaining about his legs & guts. He didnt say nothing but I knew them leather straps was in his dreams as well as mine.

3 days passed and he were still in residence when Wild Wright come cantering back down the track like bad news looking for its mother. That b−−−−−d Sgt Kennedy cried he.

I moved to take his horse by the bridle so as to lead him away from the others but Steve & Dan was already beside him their dread written clearly on their downy faces.

What news mate?

Wild untied his bowyangs then loosened the girth. They've got an adjectival Spencer boys he took off the saddle handing it to Steve.

What have they got asked Dan.

Get us a cup of water will you Dan said Wild.

For a moment I thought Wright were being considerate of Dan's feelings but he waited for him to return before saying That b−−−−−d Kennedy has borrowed a .52 calibre Spencer repeating rifle.

Which Kennedy?

Sergeant Kennedy Dan.

Jesus.

He got a shotgun from the priest and a Spencer off the Woods Point gold escort said Wild them effing traps are intent on doing damage to you b−−−−rs.

Jesus.

Whats a Spencer asked Dan but no one answered the Spencer were a modern machine of war.

Well heres the thing said I they can't shoot us if they can't find us. I were trying to make a joke of it but Joe gave me a v. hard look indeed.

As Wild finally departed he made us the present of a lump of lead stolen from the roof of the new Mansfield Post Office. Steve then fetched the kettle so we could mould new balls but even so he must of known we had no chance against a Spencer.

I took young Dan for a walk down towards the creek I told him that while Joe were leaving us it were safer for him to stay by me. Harry Power and me were hid at this place many a time no one never found us.

I wouldnt adjectival leave our ma it aint just you.

I never said you would Danny.

Don't call me adjectival Danny.

Dan.

You called me Danny in front of them its an effing baby name.

Dan then.

Thanks Neddy he grinned then tried to knock my legs out from under me he were a funny little weasel I wrestled him onto the ground like you would a kangaroo dog. As we rolled around in the dust I seen his dirty grinning phiz all my life we had been locked like this I would not let him die. Our hut were our defence but now I looked at it I recalled how 1st I knew it at 14 yr. of age when I thought it weak & blind.

No one's going to find you here said I then I called to Joe asking would he scout with me. He hesitated but then saddled up we headed towards Toombulup which is the way the cops would bring their undertakers from Mansfield. Soon we come up on a knoll on a soak on a long ridge and in the soft sandy soil Joe saw something which made him whistle. Eff that said he it were the tracks of 4 police horses plus the packhorse which would carry our bodies back into the town.

We rode on in heavy silence another hour or so then the whistle came again.

Eff this heres more traps.

My dear daughter I will not lie to you I were very afraid when we seen that 2nd set of tracks it seemed certain our hiding place were now betrayed. This later party followed along a kangaroo pad to the old gold diggings at Stringybark Creek it were the creek next to Bullock but one.

As we turned for home I knew Joe were thinking he had been a fool he should of left us while he had the chance. He were a hard man he were known as Snake Eyes and Bullet Eyes but them that named him thus had not looked into them eyes to see a 24 yr. old staring down the barrel of his own destruction.

When dark come we easily located the police they had made their camp in the obvious clearing on Stringybark Creek at the point where the butts of 4 fallen trees met at right angles building the fire right in the niche of the X made by the trunks. Their blaze were so big they was all lit up like actors on the stage and whatever they was arguing about tomatoes or their cultivation them murderous firearms was always slung ready on their shoulders their eyes fixed forever upon the dark. I recognised Cons Strahan and Cons Flood judging them v. foolish to illuminate themselves so brightly.

It were a place of echoes every snapped twig an event so when a branch crashed down behind us 2 of the traps jumped up immediately their rifles aimed into the night. Who's there! Stand there! etc. etc. Without knowing it Strahan had his gun pointed directly at my chest but the Sergeant with the repeating rifle never moved he laughed at the 3 Constables. What a lot of Nervous Nellies.

Strahan slowly lowered his gun so Joe & me moved back into the speargrass retreating quiet as warrigals towards Bullock Creek. I could still hear Cons Strahan on the subject of tomatoes again the Sergeant's mocking laughter.

Soon as we rounded the spur Joe spoke urgently into my ear You see that Sergeant's adjectival repeater mate? I smelled Joe's smile it were a sardine can peeling open in the dark. Thats the effing Spencer he said I put my hand across his mouth telling him to shut his hole. O thats a beautiful thing that Spencer. I punched him in the chest but were very pleased to see him laughing in my face for Joe Byrne when happy were a mighty force. I told him I would buy him a damn Spencer once we was out of our dilemma.

Why buy apples when they're growing on the effing tree?

Shutup it is 2 of us vs. 4 of them and all we have is the carbine and Harry's old .31.

Theres 4 of us as far as I can count.

Dan's not in this.

You aint his adjectival nurse so if you want to protect him then get the little b————r a decent gun.

He's got a gun.

Come on damn it Kelly we'll surround the b-----ds. If we don't get them weapons now we deserve to die.

He were not wrong yet I couldnt bring myself to that next step in my life so we returned to Bullock Creek still undecided.

That night Joe shared the lookout standing beside me on the ridge above our camp. An hour or so after midnight the wind changed to the south it came in long hard gusts the bush hadnt got a good shaking in a while so now the deadwood were falling around us while a great bank of cloud blocked all the moon and stars.

In the chill of morning I fancied I could smell the rain and my mind went to Melbourne Gaol where the water must be thundering on the tin roof above my mother's cell. I had failed to protect her I vowed I would do better with my brother Dan. I thought very sentimentally of him through the watch but the moment he were awake the little b----r were a thorn in my side tugging his long sleeves over his grimy mitts and cursing me for leaving him to sleep all night. His hair were wild his face smudged with charcoal it were adjectival this and adjectival that. The lorikeets & kookaburras was fighting their foreign wars above us they couldnt wait to get stuck into it again. Steve Hart stood silently beside the armoured door he were very flash with a bright red sash his hat strap adjusted as was his custom only later did I realise he were dressed for battle.

I cuffed Dan and told him to wash his face he began to pout but when I told him to come and investigate the traps his mood immediately repaired.

Wait a mo he said just a mo.

He run to the creek when he returned his face were washed his hair combed his sleeves damp but neatly rolled. Next he set his hat and when he was satisfied with the angle he produced his precious sash from a back pocket. It took a while to tie the cummerbund to his satisfaction but finally he wrapped his poor fowling piece in a blanket and was free to trail me upon his horse.

This were the hour my mother woke to face her prison day I don't know if she thought of me but I thought of her as her 2 sons followed the waters of Bullock Creek in the direction of the police. It were melancholy country much abused by miners we tethered the horses on the flat of Stringybark Creek coming the last 10 chains on foot we found only Cons

Flood & Strahan present at the camp. Thus did the odds turn in our favour.

I sent Dan back for Joe and Steve then lay amongst the speargrass spying on Cons Flood at the fire as he dropped a handful of tea into a billy he swung it around then set it down. Strahan had just called smoko when I heard my mates sliding through the speargrass soft as brown snakes I seen Joe's hot excited eyes then made the sign to Steve Hart to stay down.

It were now or never I crossed myself rising quick from the speargrass with my .577 Enfield in my hands. Bail up! Stick up your hands.

Cons Flood turned to face me as Joe Byrne come out of hiding. Throw up your hands he bawled he were holding a broken stick rolled in a blanket of course he had no gun.

Flood slowly put up his hands but Cons Strahan begun to run away. Joe screamed Bail up you b—————d.

Joe had no weapon and I were covering Cons Flood so that made Cons Strahan my brother's man but Dan could not bring himself to fire.

When Strahan dived for the cover of a fallen log Joe Byrne jerked his stick in rage shouting at my brother Shoot the b—————d now or he'll pink you.

Strahan popped up from behind the log his carbine raised. I squeezed the fateful trigger what choice did I have?

The air were filled with flame & powder stink Strahan fell thrashing around the grass moaning horribly. I took the .31 Colt from my sash then run to Flood but it werent Flood it were a stranger who raised his trembling hands. Don't shoot don't shoot don't shoot.

I told Dan to cover the b————r whoever he were then hurried back to Strahan the poor b—————d were shot dead through the right eye blood washing down his livid face this were the ripe fruit of Constable Alexander Fitzpatrick.

I approached the other Constable with my gun trained upon him it were clear he anticipated his own death his eyes was bulging and though he stood his ground I seen the waxy terror in his face he were a good sized man over 6 ft. with pleasant features a square black beard. I said I were sorry to have killed Cons Strahan and tried to have him understand I wouldnt harm himself.

You're Ned Kelly?

I am.

It isnt Strahan you killed said he its poor Tom Lonigan.

But I knew Lonigan from our fight in Benalla. That aint Lonigan said I the Constable looking at me v. baleful. It is Tom Lonigan he said and you have made his wife a widow the poor beggar has 4 children. I said I were very sorry but Dan cried out Lonigan had asked for it and were a silly b————r for firing on us.

On the ridges the mountain ash gleamed like saints against the massing clouds but down here the crows & currawongs was gloomy their cries dark with murder. Ned it is the same silly b————r who tried to pull your balls off in Benalla.

Shut your gob I told Dan but my little brother had witnessed the blood pour down the dead policeman's cheek and settle like muck in the tangle of his beard he did not show his distress but hooted like a schoolboy. I seen he had commandeered Lonigan's Webley and were concerned he would do someone an injury I therefore ordered him & Steve Hart to collect all the police guns and empty them of shot & powder. Steve avoided my eye but he obeyed.

Dan begun to tear apart a loaf of yeast bread that had been left cooling by the fire he offered some to Joe but Bullet Eyes couldnt find the Spencer and were in a savage mood he had no friend in all the world.

Dan were wolfing down the bread laughing and talking his mouth full his trouser cuffs unrolled around his boots and dragging in the mud. My thoughts come slow and heavy.

You aint Flood I said to the Constable.

My name is McIntyre.

Well Mr adjectival McIntyre said Joe Byrne where is that effing Spencer friend?

The repeater? Scanlon has it.

Who might he be?

Him and Sgt Kennedy have gone out looking for you.

To effing shoot me don't you mean?

No we come to apprehend you.

It were with a sort of dread I saw Joe smile he would now be my mate to death but there were something hard & cruel I never seen until this day when he brought the barrel of his brand new Webley within an inch of the policeman's nose.

You are a liar.

McIntyre began to answer but Joe cut him off.

Shutup I want to see them undertakers I heard so much about.

I don't know what you mean said McIntyre and I can still see the small deadly twist that answer produced in Joe's mouth. To prevent a bad thing happening I come at Joe stretching my left arm towards the Webley and speaking his name but this were as stupid as petting a fighting dog and he pistol whipped my arm.

Eff off he snarled it were not personal. In his eye McIntyre had planned to truss his body like a dead roo then carry it blood dripping flies buzzing along the ridges down the valleys into Mansfield.

Show me them undertakers he demanded.

No I assure you.

When McIntyre stepped backwards Joe kicked McIntyre in the knee it were the exact same kick he once give to Wild Wright. McIntyre cried out stumbling as Joe pushed him at gunpoint towards the tent. There was discovered ammunition & ropes & axes laid on a groundsheet but also the 2 straps Moss Finch had worked in Mansfield they was displayed very shipshape coiled tight 2 ft. across. Joe dragged them into the clearing the stink of linseed oil rising up like funeral parlour flowers amongst the bush.

Joe picked up a small axe and McIntyre thought his end were come he stepped backwards falling into Dan.

Joe I cried.

My mate looked at me as at a stranger.

You touch him I said I'll fire.

Joe raised the tomahawk in his left hand then brought it crashing down upon the leather belt crying out the word c--t with every chop until the shining hateful thing were cut in pieces too small you could not use them to tie up your pants. Joe spat upon the ground he were panting and pale when finally he looked at me again we was both v. embarrassed about what had transpired.

McIntyre sat suddenly his head held in his hands.

We had paid the price we might as well procure the merchandise so we waited for the other 2 police to bring us back the Spencer. Lonigan's dead body lay beneath sheets of bark but we stayed away from him. On the valley floor it were gloomy and threatening rain but the damned flies was buzzing like a summer's day excited by the blood for me it is the sound of death forever. Soon Stringybark Creek would be the most famous stream in all the colony but no one could imagine such a forlorn place they couldnt see the dead black wattles or speargrass with no nourishment to offer.

At the end of the long afternoon we finally detected our hunters returning from the north following the creek not slowly neither. But I knew the path were narrow so they wd. be compelled to arrive in single file.

Hsst lads here they come.

We fell into the places we had planned Steve crawling into the police tent with McIntyre's shotgun and Dan and Joe slinking back into the speargrass. I lay behind a log near the fire where McIntyre obediently sat on the same log so his mates could easily see him when they rode into the camp.

I heard the 1st horse blowing then I ordered McIntyre to stand and speak he done so.

The Kellys are here. You are surrounded.

Very amusing were their answer.

No no throw down your arms.

I waited too long for as I gained my feet I seen the 1st policeman's hand were at his revolver it were Sergeant Kennedy.

I fired a warning shot then Joe & Dan & Steve all come running shouting. The 2nd policeman were Scanlon he spurred his horse forwards firing at me as he done so. My gun responded and Scanlon lurched onto his horse's neck and lay there motionless. The Spencer clattered to the ground then Scanlon's body followed it were lifeless as a bag of spuds.

Events continued without relent Dear God Jesus it were a sorry day. Sgt Kennedy jumped off his horse firing and McIntyre set to running though he were no threat he were intent on stealing Kennedy's horse. He fled back up towards the track to Toombulup.

Kennedy took one more shot at me then looked around when he seen his horse were gone he retreated into the bush. I picked up the Spencer but it would not fire it were heavy and foreign its mechanism a mystery to me so I threw the cursed thing away. Ahead of me in the deep gloom of the untidy scrub I could see the blue of Kennedy's uniform.

I called I would not hurt him but he were gone leaving his deadly modern cartridges fallen on the ground. I loaded my .577 Enfield juggling the powder flask & ball & cap as I pursued him.

What he were luring me towards I did not know I tracked him by broken twigs and crushed leaves down onto a boggy little speargrass flat & there he were just 2 perches in advance of me I held my fire.

The ridge on our left flattened and around its apex we were almost at German's Creek where the cunning b————r suddenly dropped down into a miner's trench.

I called out to him Surrender I will not harm you. There were no reply the bush suddenly v. quiet except when I begun to move again my boots making the most appalling din the sticks cracking and exploding. I crept back up the ridge hoping to look down into the trench where Kennedy was hid.

Instead he jumped out from behind the tree not 3 yd. before me his pistol flashed my Enfield answered. I got him in the armpit he ran crashing wildly through the scrub and I followed calling at him to surrender as I measured off my powder and dropped in my ball ramming it home with no time for wadding. He wheeled round raising his arm to shoot but I fired 1st.

Curtains of bark hung from the trunks like shredded skin. As he fell I ran to where he lay wide eyed & crumpled then taking possession of his gun I discovered nothing more lethal in his hand than a mass of clotted blood. He had been trying to surrender.

He were shot in the chest and losing a great deal of blood from the wound in his armpit. I knew he were finished so I went to make him comfortable but there is no ease in death.

Ah my poor wife said he I must write to her. Get me my notebook.

He were in great pain I pulled his notebook from his breastpocket it were very bloody but I tore some pages that was unblemished and give him a pencil. When he finished writing I told him I were very sorry more sorry than I could ever make him know. You are a brave man said I.

He sighed and said he were a fool that his wife just lost a boy 11 mo. old little Thomas now she had the grief of losing a husband as well. He told me about his little Tommy how he were a fine strong boy they never thought to lose him he had the grandest smile. He were continually breaking off his narrative for he seemed to be suffering very much and who could bear to look upon him so? Not wanting him to linger alone in such agony I quietly reloaded my gun.

He wished to talk about his little boy again weeping frankly at how he missed him every minute of every day.

I then said soon he would be with him.

Sgt Kennedy looked up at me sharply. You have shed blood enough said he.

I fired and he died instantly without a groan.

On this day of horror when the shadows of the wattle was gluey with men's blood I could not imagine what wonder might still lie before me. We lads come down across German's Creek into Bullock Creek driving the police horses before us we now had 4 rifles & 4 Webleys and Joe rode with the Spencer slung across his back. As for me my skin were sour with death.

A friend arrived I will not say his name but thank God he didnt come a day early or else he would of been branded a member of the so called KELLY GANG. He and I had wanted no more than land a hearth to sit by in the night but he seen us in possession of the police horses and knew that dream were gone to smash.

The rain begun sprinkling on the dry earth I wished it could wash away my sin but it come on the cold breath of the Southern Ocean there were no forgiveness there. I told my friend I hoped he would get some good grass from this rain he gave me a folded wad of banknotes having sold his stallion for me I asked would he take the money to Mary Hearn.

Harry Power led me to that hut when I were no older than Steve or Dan. This here is Bullock Creek said he it won't never betray you. But it were a dead blind place I knew that at 15 yr. of age it were like a beaten dog cowering in the shadow of the hills. All night I had bad dreams very confused I saw Kennedy raising his hand to surrender and me shooting him again & again. In the grey dawn I ordered the boys to set fire to the hateful hut I were glad they never asked me why for I never could have said. As the rain grew heavy we dragged logs and sticks in through the open door there were flour and cans of sardines we kicked them to one side what was we thinking? There was nails & horseshoes but it seems we didnt need their burden. The sky were still dark when we brung the burning torch inside our haven the armoured door swung open useless to protect us.

Steve Hart began to sing some mournful song in the old language I told him to be quiet we would write our own damned history from here on.

It were not until the hut were burning that Dan revealed he had a bullet wound from Cons Scanlon he said it werent so bad a scratch but I seen how he held his reins in his left hand and by the time we crossed Kilfeera Station he were hunched over and his teeth was chattering. We imagined the armies of vengeful traps already on our heels not knowing Cons McIntyre had come unhorsed and were hiding in a wombat hole. Grim daylight of the 2nd day showed the smoke rising from my sister's hut but I would not place her at risk for Harbouring so we skirted farther eastwards all this time Dan looking very bad.

The rain begun in earnest it come down like leaden buckets broke in 1/2 and the clay soil so dry & eager its thirst were slaked easily as a kitten. The runoff were soon a yellow sheet the bark & sticks made dams then broke apart and sailed down into the gullies. The mild level country creeks was now dragging fistfuls from their own banks and as we pushed our mob of horses over the Oxley flats the world were walled & ripped apart by water.

We was making our way towards the mighty Murray River thence the colony of New South Wales not fleeing but retreating. Before we could ford the Murray we had to cross the Ovens River before that we must ride 30 mi. through countless streams swamps and bogs arriving at the Ovens on the 3rd day around 2 o'clock in the morning. We could hear the roar of the river rocks and logs bumping the pylons in the dark though the bridge itself appeared unflooded.

Dan were looking very ill indeed so I ordered Joe Byrne to knock up the landlord from Moon's Pioneer Hotel and get some brandy he must pay the full tariff I said we was not thieves. Joe let out a very bitter laugh striding towards the dark hotel angrily slapping his whip against his sturdy thigh.

After the grog arrived Dan drank and vomited then we pushed on across the bridge but the flood had claimed the road on the other side so we was forced upstream until Taylor's Gap when we finally drove the 4 police horses & the 2 packhorses into the flood.

The current here were v. swift with Dan not steady in his saddle I therefore mounted behind him as we swum across together he were still the little nipper cursing me so violently he made me laugh. It were here my copy of LORNA DOONE were ruined also Sgt Kennedy's message to his wife for when I dried the paper afterwards nothing were writ on it no more.

Coming back downstream into the dismal rainsodden hamlet of Everton we knocked up an old man in a nightgown Coulson were his name. I counted out the full price for what we took telling him my name so he could tell Ned Kelly were no thief.

Up in the high ranges west of Beechworth we finally rode into the scrub on the hill above Aaron Sherritt's selection. We fired off 8 shots and sure enough Joe's childhood friend trotted up the hill on a bay mare he walked around us silent examining the police stock I could see his troubled eyes study their brands they was clearly marked VR.

I asked had he heard any news about us but as usual he looked 1st to Joe.

Whats the story cobber?

Joe shook his head I could see Aaron were most offended by his silence yet wouldnt turn to me for information.

Whats the story Dan? The boy were all waxy skinned and hunched over in his saddle he couldnt answer neither. Then Joe offered up the Spencer repeater from its holster but Aaron could see VR stamped on its stock he would not touch it.

At last he looked my way saying I might follow him if I liked.

We soon was riding single file along the path the hill were becoming v. steep he took us round the shoulder of Native Dog Peak. Here we finally come to a clear piece of ground where horses was lately kept you could see the worn earth the clear scars on the trees where they had been eating bark. Joe wd. attend to the hobbling he said.

Aaron escorted me and my brother down the hill along a kind of footpath high above the precipice Dan were leaning on me heavily but soon the way were too narrow for the pair of us.

I'll carry you.

I can effing walk. He teetered but I got my arm under him with the rock to the left of us & thin air on the right he were yelping like a puppy before we come around a corner and to my great relief we found a cave.

I propped him up against the wall. I said You'll be all right Dan.

What you going to do?

Aaron straight away begun to light a fire.

No said Dan the traps will see the smoke.

But in all this rain the smoke were no danger so once the fire were well established I passed Dan the whisky bottle. Eff that said he and pushed it away his eyes was on the branding iron Aaron had lain upon the coals.

I squatted in front of him.

Do I have to?

You're a Kelly I said.

I wish I werent.

After we waited Joe came in to announce the horses was hobbled. Steve Hart sat with his arms round his knees staring into the fire I wonder if he wished he were not a Hart that his daddy hadnt filled his head with all them rebel stories.

Reckon we're ready said Aaron removing the hot iron it were a little straight line brand commonly used to change a C into an E. I helped Dan take off his shirt the wound on his right shoulder were raw and red the pus was pooling in its center. Aaron asked were he ready but Dan drew away.

Then Aaron gone into the back of the cave to fetch the yen pipe he sometimes shared with Joe.

I don't want that Chinky ess it makes me puke.

Suit yourself said Aaron setting aside the pipe to pick up the glowing brand once more.

I want my brother to do it.

Suit yourself.

When Aaron give me the iron Dan turned to face me holding out his right hand and I took it like I were walking him across the creek to school.

Ready?

Eff it he said and I lay it exactly on the wound. The smallest sound came from his lips his eyes rolled back in his head. The poor little b————r smelled like a sausage in the pan.

There were a great commotion in the night I heard the girlish voice 1st it were damned insistent but I couldnt make out who she were nagging. It were raining hard outside I could see her agitated shadow in the weather back and forth like a fruit bat lost in the storm.

You are a blessed tragedy she said as far as I could judge she were no more than 12 yr. old. You was always a larrikin said she well I can't complain I knew that of you but this time you have turned yourself into as great a tragedy as ever walked. And I always thought your mother hard on you.

My mother is an adjectival cow said Joe Byrne suddenly very loud.

Don't she cried I aint going in there.

Come on my sweet.

It smells awful something's dead. Don't pull at me Joe I aint a heifer.

But for all her protests she did what were requested they passed along the wall behind my head her wet skirt brushing my face.

No road Joe I won't.

Its a blanket he said firmly its clean enough.

They was quiet a moment then he struck a lucifer and the light of a small spirit lamp illuminated the far end of the cave.

I wanted to get home to you Bessie. It just werent so easy as it sounds the traps was hunting us like dogs.

I kept my eyes closed but did not need to look to know that this were Bessie Sherritt i.e. Aaron's sister.

Joe it werent you they was hunting.

You don't know adjectival nothing Bessie said he and I smelled the sweet odour of opium he must of got from Aaron.

Joe that aint correct it were Ned Kelly shot Fitzpatrick. Tell me if I lie.

Well he sighed its too late now any road.

Isn't it true but my own da's a policeman?

That were in Ireland long ago.

Its still the English language he read me out the warrant it says DAN KELLY AND NED KELLY it says OTHER MEN UNKNOWN. No one is calling for Joe Byrne they would name you if they wanted. You don't have to run nowhere you can just tell the truth.

Them b————rs will know me soon enough.

They'll know Ned Kelly she said desperately its him who done the murder. Its him and Dan they listed in the GAZETTE.

Sssh said Joe.

No I will not ssh said she. Wake up wake up you shan't be hanged. Aaron won't allow it he can protect you in this thing.

He must of done something for she gave a sharp little cry of pain and then Joe snuffed out the lamp. You tell him not to effing meddle this aint for him.

In the dawn Bessie Sherritt were gone and Joe were as calm & neat & rested as if nothing had occurred. It were him who made the tea who buttered a bandage for Dan's shoulder who assisted Steve and me to carry our provisions back to the horses. I saw the girl Bessie standing at the edge of the clearing she didnt own no coat so her dark hair were soaked her dress all sodden on her skinny little shoulders she were staring passionately at Joe.

Friend of yours I asked.

Joe shook his head. Come to America with me old man.

She's your donah don't deny it.

No she aint.

You didnt shoot no one Joe I'll write a note and swear it.

You can swear any adjectival thing you like it won't make no difference. He yanked the girth and waited for the horse to let out its breath before tightening it another notch. You can write until the effing cows come home but we killed 3 coppers and they won't be happy till they pay us back. Come to America with me.

I looked at the girl standing shivering her arms crossed in front of her little bosom. She's your donah Joe.

I'd rather kiss the effing Banshee.

Looking at the object of his derision I seen a poor girl shivering in the rain but Joe's pale eyes was seeing a darker dream than mine.

If I stay here don't you see I'm dead?

I don't know if it were fear or opium but something had turned his sunburnt face as hard and slippery as a china bowl. It were not my place to argue with him over a woman but I were a man with 4 sisters & a mother & as we left I rode right by poor Bessie I give her a friendly nod. In response her eyes drew back into her head and her lips pursed and a mighty wad of spit come at me.

It were a very small deposit on the capital that would soon be offered to the Mansfield Murderer.

To escape the police there were no choice but to ford the Murray River into New South Wales although the word river gives a poor picture of the sight that met our eyes in the district of Barnawartha. The Murray is a maze of swamps and billabongs but in flood you cannot know what can be crossed till you try & try we did for 3 weary days attempting one place then the next driving the police horses up into swamps and lagoons until the water grew too swift and deep.

God did not see us the waters would not open and no matter how hard we pushed the Murray would not part nor the rain relent. Every time we returned to the banks the brown tide had risen higher than before marooning unmilked cows on islands their udders swollen their painful bellows echoing across the dull insistent waters.

Finally we come to a miserable bit of drowned land mostly wattles & reeds all inundated and beyond this some big old red gums and here the current become so treacherous you could see it from the way the fallen trees raced down the river their crowns rolling over and over lifting water like a paddle wheel.

Dan sat with his hand on his wounded shoulder watching thoughtfully. Steve Hart were close beside him hunched over on his horse with the brim of his hat low on his eyes.

Very well said I then we will head back to Aaron's. I looked to Joe but he held out his hand as if to say goodbye.

It can't be crossed Joe.

He looked out across the dreary tumbling waters. I should of pissed off long ago said he without another word he spurred his horse out into the reeds the water were high on the horse's belly it floundered and then rose then plunged down once more.

Catch me he cried his voice were far away but when the horse rose a 2nd time it were clear he had located a spine of submerged land which he now were following like a miner does a vein of gold. Suddenly the river were very shallow only to the fetlocks of his mare. This was sufficient for Dan he gathered in his mare getting ready for the plunge.

Look hissed Steve suddenly.

I seen a large milled log sweep in front of the rider he were on the edge of a deep & dangerous channel.

Not that. Look behind.

I turned to see a dreadful apparition a large bunch of mounted men emerging from the bush they was perhaps 1/2 a mile to the south. The details was blurred by rain but it were clear they was the police an adjectival army of them come to avenge their dead.

Joe had not seen them yet he'd spurred his mare into the channel she were swimming bravely on. The police trotted out across the grassy plain that separated the bush from the flood. As Joe rose from the torrent to join a stranded heifer on a muddy island he were about 100 yd. out in the stream thus easily within range of a Martini Henry.

Steve were leading Dan and their mounts deeper into the flooded wattle scrub behind a bit of hillock from where he hissed at me.

I could not drag myself away from Joe he were in mortal danger but now witnessing his undertakers approach he brought his horse up on its hind legs so it pranced. He walked it backwards that were normal in a circus but very unusual in the middle of the Murray River.

Come on Ned.

I were beholding an act of courage it made the flesh stand on my arms. A hateful roar went up from the police I heard the drum of hooves it were like the Picnic Cup. A rifle shot whistled overhead I hurried down into the flooded wattles where the 2 boys was already bickering.

Get your adjectival head down said Steve.

I don't want to get my powder wet.

Don't worry about the effing powder.

O yes I see you're keeping your gun dry.

Look look you silly b————r Steve cried plunging his pistol under the muddy water. Does that satisfy you now?

We was interrupted by a blast from out on the river it were the prancing horseman firing his Spencer at the sodden sky.

Halt the traps shouted you're under arrest.

Shoot the b—————d called another.

The murderers was almost next to us the air above our heads were rent with explosions we ducked then felt the water push its icy fingers up our ears. When I surfaced Joe were off again he were swimming to America his horse in the middle of the flood with a great stretch of brown water ahead and no island in sight.

Of course not one of them traps had the courage of a so called HARD-ENED CRIMINAL they poked around the bush a little but never so much as got their boots wet. They left us by 3 o'clock that afternoon we was dripping wet and certain our mate must be washed upon a bank the mud running from his nose like some drowned calf. Dan's lips was blue I changed his dressing then we all dried our firearms in melancholy silence.

We sat on our horses watching the flood slowly rise until it were dark even afterwards we continued our watch although Steve were sure Joe must be drowned and Dan would guarantee he got away. We remained without a fire to warm us and not until almost the next day was we rewarded by a murmuring above the suck and wash of flood it were a prayer a litany this human voice talking in the night. They would leave their adjectival mate it said they would ride away and leave a fellow. Well eff them for a mob of effing this and effing that.

We found a single rider poking his way very slowly through the dark eff this and eff that it were belligerent Joe Byrne. To a man we was most pleased to have him back which don't mean we didnt barrack him a little asking him how were America and was the girls as pretty as we heard.

We was dead men now he answered we might as well accept the fact.

John King 3 yr. & Ellen King 5 yr. & Gracie Kelly 13 yr. all come shrieking in the hut to hide beneath the bed. All this I know from Mary Hearn she thought it were a game until she saw their pursuers was 2 big moustached officers their heavy pistols drawn.

Out cried the traps. Bail up!

Their munitions was .45 Colts but the policemen didnt feel that were sufficient for their safety and the larger of the pair now snatched Mary's baby from his cart and held him as a human shield.

Little George begun to scream and wave his fists. His mother wrapped her blanket about her and come to rescue him but the officer jabbed her in the belly with his Colt.

Drop your guns he cried.

Sir she cried there aint no guns in here.

Don't lie to me shouted Supt Brooke Smith we know Ned Kelly's here. He ripped off her blanket revealing what she would not wish to show no man.

Sir cried she the baby is falling. It were true the babe were slipping from the trap's grasp but fear can make a big man deaf and Inspector Brooke Smith were in Holy terror that I were hiding in the hut he thought his end were near.

Come out Kelly you'll be shooting children if you fire.

O give my baby back Mary cried she darted forward but were knocked away she had no more power than a plover squealing around a raided nest.

Go on cried Smith get out the brat is in my care. So saying he got a knee up under George's bottom a firmer grip around his chest.

Mary thought she were about to have her baby confiscated by the government. O do please return him to me Sir.

Brooke Smith swatted at your mother in reply it were to Kate he spoke. See all the men I have out there today? I will have as many more tomorrow and when I find your brothers I will blow them to pieces as small as the paper in our guns.

Sir I beg you he's just a baby I am taking care of him very nicely as you see. I'll show you my saving book if you would like.

Are you Kate Kelly?

Don't tell him nothing said Kate.

My name is Mary Hearn Sir I have broke no law and neither has my son.

The name of Hearn meant nothing to the Inspector but the other officer were Detective Michael Ward a much more diligent and dangerous creature altogether. This is Kelly's child he announced.

Good grief exclaimed Brooke Smith. Look how the little demon curls his lip.

Mary pushed forward but it were too late the crooked Ward had taken the baby in his own custody.

He has the gripe Sir thats all it is.

If you're a clever girlie smiled Detective Ward you'll tell me where its daddy's hiding.

And suddenly with no warning he tossed the baby into the air.

Christ said Brooke Smith.

Ned aint the father Sir don't hurt him.

Liar said Ward throwing the baby again it were far too rough George's head snapped back his mouth flew open.

O I curse your seed cried Mary.

Ward's grin failed him.

I curse your unborn children said Mary her blood were icy cold her eyes as black as coal. May your children come to the straw with feet like toads and eyes like snakes.

Silence!

You will be like a blackfellow with no home to turn to. Your wife will lie with soldiers. You will wander the roads with sores & weeping warts.

Detective Ward were white and waxy as an altar candle.

Halt cried his partner or I'll fire.

Mary were just a girl of 17 normally v. meek & polite in manner her skin still unspoiled by the colonial sun but now her mouth were thin and straight. Then may you get red and scaly skin upon your private parts.

I order you cried Superintendent Brooke Smith & discharged his pistol through the roof.

That were the moment George's eyes changed colour Kate will attest to that. One moment they was blue the next a yellow brown the colour of a ginger cat. In the heat of the furnace metals change their nature in olden days they could make gold from lead. Wait to see what more there is to hear my daughter for in the end we poor uneducated people will all be made noble in the fire.

We determined to return home to Greta even if the ground were crawling with policemen we could safely get tucker and dry clothes but when we got back to the Ovens River at Everton it were running 8 ft. higher than when 1st we crossed.

I'll lead youse across said Steve this conversation took place at night in the flooded main street there were a dog behind the butcher's shop throwing himself against his chain the horses was spooky requiring all our attention so we circled and chivvied while discussing what we was to do.

Ned said Steve we'll go across at Wangaratta.

Joc had been very sour and glum since his failed attempt to swim the Murray he spoke sarcastically to him. Did it slip your mind theres a railway line to cross or did you fancy you could jump the effing packhorses across a 4 rail fence?

Shutup.

Well said Joe you can forget the railway gate its locked.

We don't need no gates said Dan theres a railway bridge at Wangaratta.

The traps will have it guarded Danny.

Jesus Christ don't call me effing Danny.

Ned said Steve I can get us under the railway bridge Ned.

Don't listen to him Ned.

And what were you proposing Joe?

Shutup said Joe I'd go upriver to Bright we'd cross there easy as you effing well know.

Thats 30 adjectival miles.

You're such a lazy b-----d Hart you'd rather ride 8 mi. and get lagged at the end of it.

Shutup about being lagged we won't be lagged.

How can he get us under the railway bridge when the effing river is in flood?

I'm not the one who thought he could swim the Murray.

Keep your voice down.

Theres a rock ledge underneath the bridge said Steve flood or no flood I've crossed there all my adjectival life.

I heard a squeaky window rise up in its sash.

Turning to Steve Hart I reminded him Wangaratta would be full of traps they would show us no mercy if we failed in our attempt.

You have my word I will get you through.

Very well said I we're off to Wangaratta.

We drove the free horses before us walking them until we cleared the township then set off cantering through the dark up the empty main road from Everton to Tarrawingee thence to Wangaratta arriving around 4 o'clock our mounts all but ruined by their exertions.

Through grey early light & drizzle we come down through the sodden town 2,000 citizens was sound asleep our horses' shoes as loud as cannon in my ears. Riding down to where the railway crossed One Mile we saw the mongrel creek were running a banker so Joe Byrne begun immediately to curse at Steve. You silly mutt you effing clift we should have gone to effing Bright etc. etc.

Shut your gob I ordered Joe he spat but were too busy keeping the driven horses together to argue.

Steve tipped his hat to Joe and grinned I'll see you in America he said then persuaded his horse down into the current. He promised an underwater ledge we could only pray there were one. A woman were watching from a house across the street when I saw the way she looked at us I understood we was recognised and even in that grey and watery light it were clear I were reviled a murderer I took the plunge the water were exceeding high and deathly fast my horse begun to blow in fear but the ledge were true & we scrambled beneath the railway line and out the other side.

Come on you b----rs we been spotted.

We was pushing the poor horses very hard making for the Warby

Ranges while the witness Mrs Delaney went puffing up the hill to wake up Supt Brooke Smith and his army of police.

It is only 5 mi. from Wangaratta into the foothills this is hard & gnarly country unloved by squatters and relegated to the poor but Harry Power's apprentice knew its dried dugs its swollen knuckles he had been taught its every twist and gully. Now the Warbies folded themselves around us like a mother and we slept protected by them whose names I cannot say in places we may yet require again.

PARCEL 10

The History Is
Commenced

Bank of New South Wales letterhead, 64 sheets of
medium stock (8" × 10" approx.). Creasing, foxing,
staining.

*Of particular interest for the dual motives for the
history's composition. Mary Hearn's response to
the reports of Stringybark Creek murders. The
author's response to fatherhood. His faith in a
parliamentary enquiry. Mary Hearn's recollections of transvestism among the Irish peasantry.
An explanation of Kelly's refusal to flee when
it was possible. His trial by a jury of his peers.
This parcel also contains two annotated pages
from* The Melbourne Argus *in which that newspaper's account of the Euroa Bank robbery is
quibbled with.*

2 days later Dan & me was on our way to visit our sister Maggie we approached Eleven Mile Creek like blackfellows in the night. There were a 1/4 moon some fast moving cloud permitted sufficient light to show the familiar bosom shape of Bald Hills. Behind them we knew 20 police was now encamped each one sworn by secret oath to avenge their dead companions.

Everything at home were devastation the dark shadow of my mother's 1st hut looked damned forsaken. Closer still were the hut I built so she might escape the stinky man's curse though the arresting traps had dragged her from it anyway. We knew this 2nd hut also abandoned but as we passed there were a ghostly yellow light flickering beneath the door. I reined in my mare.

Come on said Dan lets go.

The hair on my own neck were upright when I come beneath the peppercorn tree but through the 8 pane window I seen a female figure walking back and forth a saucepan in her hand. When Dan plucked at my elbow I shrugged him off. From the saucepan rose a cloud of dense yellow smoke though I were more concerned with that crow black hair that white skin and in my confusion imagined it were my mother unexpectedly made free. I felt a bolt of joy the weight of worry lifting off me.

Ma I shouted.

Jesus Christ moaned Dan please lets go.

But the woman heard my cry she turned and to my shock it were Mary Hearn.

Its Ned I called.

Shutup shutup Dan begged Jesus Christ do you want the whole effing police force to know you're here?

Mary Hearn come out on the veranda. Is it you she whispered.

It is.

It aint safe said she.

I looked to Dan he sighed and drew his Webley. As he turned to keep the watch I entered the hut it were filled with sulphur smoke little George lay in his box upon the floor his face very red & shining his yellow brown eyes staring at the candlelight.

What ails the little one?

Mary did not reply.

Why are you by yourself all alone?

I don't bother anyone here I can keep the smoke up to him all the night.

Did you read about me in the newspapers Mary?

She moved a little to her left so she were in a direct line between me and her child.

Mary I would never kill no one unless I had to.

She shook her head.

They would of shot me if I didnt shoot them 1st.

She tried to smile. I prayed for you said she.

I shot them fair and square Mary.

She starting fossicking on the high shelf where the demijohns of oils & turpentine was stored she produced a scrap of newspaper and by peering v. close I seen there were a drawing of a demonic kind of man.

Read it.

The author of this so called LIKENESS were not content to show my natural imperfections he must join my brows across my nose and twist my lips to render me the Devil the Horror of the Ages these engravings in the newspaper was made by a coward who never had his beasts impounded or his family gaoled on the evidence of perjurers his only useful trade were to persuade the people to hate & fear a man they never met.

This aint me.

Read the write up Ned then tell me it aint you.

Her arms was wrapped like chains around her chest I couldnt leave her in this state I were detained like a locust in a web. The headline said MURDER OF POLICE AT STRINGYBARK CREEK. I don't know who wrote it but he made us Irish Madmen. I had mutilated Sergeant Kennedy he claimed I had cut off his ear with my knife before murdering him. Moreover I had forced my 3 mates to discharge their pistols into the bodies of the police so all would be guilty of the crime the same as me.

I heard Dan's heavy boots upon the veranda the door swung open. I can see their adjectival fires behind the hill he pleaded.

Advise me if you see them coming.

O Jesus Ned lets go now.

But all the love & light in Mary's eyes were cold as ash in the morning grate I could not leave.

You go Dan I'll follow in a while.

You know I aint leaving without you.

I won't be more than 5 minutes said I then returned to Mary. You think I done them things they say?

O Ned I don't know what I am to believe.

Well I will tell you what I done and then you judge you don't know what them police is like.

Your mamma dragged my da's chair up beside George's box there she sat with shoulders rounded waving the smoke about him. I am a man a man that loved her & my body yearned to comfort her to touch her skin but instead I talked.

I began with Fitzpatrick and Kate telling how that event had played out much like she predicted then I described all that happened until Kennedy received his mortal wound poor Dan it took much more than 5 minutes it were nearly dawn when I finished & the light were wet & grey as drowning. At that dismal hour I heard the cry Mopoke Mopoke it were no owl it were my brother.

Snuffing the candle we both come out onto the front veranda and there we seen the undertakers smudged as charcoal in the rain an army of invaders riding round the flank of our familiar hills. As Dan were hurrying towards the creek I turned to follow but Mary Hearn touched my hand what bliss what torture she loves me yet she loves me through the drizzling rain.

If you will lead men you cannot be away from them no more than from a dairy herd or to put it another way when no rooster is present the cockerels will grow their combs till they're red and flapping across their beady eyes for once their leader is absent they exercise their own judgment setting plans in course they would never dream of if their Captain were up front.

I did not forget neither my men nor my mother in her cruel Scientific gaol but I am guilty of neglecting both while setting the fire back blazing in the eyes of Mary Hearn. I returned with Dan to sleep in our hiding place in the Warby Ranges but didnt talk to no one I were so very tired then at noon I were shook awake to be informed a big party of men were riding in formation across the plain below. This was a larger number than were hid behind Bald Hills but as they seemed headed towards the township of Winton I went back to sleep. No need to write the name of the family that harboured us only that they lived a hard life in the rocky foothills of the ranges they were no better than they should be they knew what it were to have the police harassing them the squatters squeezing them enclosing all the common land for private use.

Waking at dusk I found the friend's family spreading newspapers around the floor and table. In this little hut it were usually hard to find sufficient paper to wipe yourself but now it were a rat's nest of ENSIGN and ADVERTISER and ARGUS there were no smell of cooking only of the cold black ink. The baby had torn the front page of THE MEL-BOURNE HERALD but not so bad I couldnt see my name. Mr Donald Cameron had asked the Premier the question WHETHER HE WOULD CAUSE A SEARCHING ENQUIRY TO BE MADE INTO THE ORIGIN OF THE KELLY OUTBREAK AND ALSO THE ACTION OF THE AUTHORITIES IN TAKING PRELIMINARY STEPS FOR THE ARREST OF THE CRIMINALS. He said he had information that POINTED TO THE CONDUCT OF CERTAIN MEMBERS OF THE POLICE FORCE AS HAVING LED UP TO THE MANS-FIELD MURDERS. This were the best news in many a long day. I never heard of this cove Cameron previous but he were neither blind nor stupid he understood we was driven to the deed that the law was scandalous in our pursuit.

But there were more than this to hearten me Mr Berry the Premier had answered him THAT IF RELIABLE INFORMATION WERE TO REACH HIM THAT DIFFICULTIES WERE INTERPOSED BY WANT OF PROPER ORGANISATION AMONG THE POLICE HE WOULD OF COURSE INSTI-TUTE AN ENQUIRY.

Well look at this lads I said heres a go.

Joe's eyes was sick & fluey. Politicians he declared.

So?

So it don't mean nothing said he and in exchange for my HERALD he give me the front page of THE MELBOURNE ARGUS where I read we was all declared outlaws who could be shot on sight and was entitled to no more mercy than a rabid dog.

You can believe this one he said this is most reliable.

The 2 boys looked from him to me their faces stretched like drums waiting to see what I would say.

I have a mind to talk to this Cameron cove said I.

And how asked Joe would you manage that?

I'll tell you in the morning lads. I give Joe back his ARGUS and retrieved THE HERALD and from this I tore the write up concerning Cameron.

You aint going back to Eleven Mile?

Its my neck said I.

Its your adjectival pizzle cried Joe Byrne as all 3 turned from me to hunch around the papers. Daughter forgive me when I confess how little thought I give for their agony I were a man in love I left them alone to drink in all that poison ink.

1/2 an hour later I were Romeo himself riding through the gap above Glenrowan the night sky a deep royal blue and the outline of Bald Hills clear above it. There were no sign of police fires but my Juliet were very tense as she took my hand and squeezed it there were no kissing. When she pulled out a chair I sat down not knowing what she had in mind though the table were unusually clear of dishes and on its clean top a sheaf of paper were stacked alongside a Post Office pen & a bottle of red ink labelled PROPERTY OF KATE KELLY.

Dear said she I would be very pleased if you would write down what you told me previously.

Which part of it?

Why every part.

O I aint no scholar Mary you know that.

Well if you truly love me you will do it.

What were I to say that I never learned my parsing? All I could think were to lay with her one last time I were mad as a dog and didnt care the traps was meanwhile humming like a hive of bees not 400 yd. away.

The whole of it?

From the time Fitzpatrick tried to marry Kate. That part.

I reckon I know what you plan to do with it said I.

Ah but do you? Is that true now?

The life were in her eyes again.

You think said I we should send it to this Cameron cove?

But she never heard of Mr Cameron MLA when I showed her the cutting from THE MELBOURNE HERALD she put her hand upon my wrist.

Write it down dear said she then come to bed.

She begun to brush her long black hair I needed no more encouragement than that. The 1st page were rapidly accomplished then the 2nd and 3rd. Oftentimes Mary come to read with her cheek pressed against my ear I do not boast when I say I felt her moved to tears sometimes to exclamations of anger she said there were not a soul alive who could read these words and blame me as the papers did.

It will persuade Mr Cameron?

It would persuade anyone.

For one long night this chaste dance did continue sometimes the dogs barked and soon after midnight there were a great alarm when Kate & Maggie found 2 policemen crouching behind the pigpens but mostly there were no greater upset than a night train crying in the distant dark the old people say it were the trains brought the famine to Ireland well they brought the coppers to Benalla together with artists ready to sketch my bloody corpse.

When finally I completed the death of poor Kennedy I give Mary everything I had writ & she removed the blue ribbon from her hair so it fell down around her neck and shoulders but she would not let me kiss her yet she bound all my words tying them with the ribbon like you will see the clerks do in Benalla Court I am sure it is the same in Parliament. Then she carried my chair so it were below the shelf that holds the demi-johns as noted and she placed the roll behind the turpentine.

There she said alighting carefully to the floor.

She come to me and then we kissed.

Will you post it in the morning?

We will make a copy for Mr Cameron she said but even as she spoke she took my scabbed hard hand placing it ever so gently on her belly.

And I knew before she said the words I knew that it were you in there I were very pleased I kissed her on the neck and on the mouth I smelled her fine dark hair and kissed her bright black eyes.

It is for him I cried thats why you wished me to write it. Its for him!

Or her she said she were smiling and crying.

Or her my love.

So when our daughter comes into the world she will always know the proper story of her da and who he is and what he suffered.

You may wonder why her speech did not make me gloomy it were clear that your ma were certain I would be murdered by the government and that you would never know what man I were. But it werent nothing to do with death at all it were its very opposite you was my future right away from that moment you was my life.

Thus were I drawn into this occupation as author for once the letter were completed I immediately commenced a 2nd to Mr Cameron which labour kept me absent from the boys I were not there when the trouble come bearing down on them out of the scrub but will tell the story just the same.

The traps is on you lads cried our host his braces was broke he held up his britches in one hand hauling Steve's saddle and bridle with the other hopping pigeon toed across the muddy yard.

For Jesus' sake they are at the swamp go boys they'll lag us all.

Joe's gelding & Dan's mare was in the yard but neither one had nothing more than head stalls both was scatty v. excited by all this uproar. Dan were in the outhouse Steve tossing knucklebones with the littlies but now the alarm were called he run directly into the Friend's hut. The Missus was hard of hearing not to say stone deaf she were sitting at the table skinning rabbit. Steve said nothing to her ripping back a curtain she had hung across her roughnail cupboard he pulled out her Sunday best a dainty little dress of black & orange lace on its bosom was many flowers of strange description. With no apology or explanation Steve tore himself inside it fierce and brutal as a goanna with its head inside a chicken. Tugging the hem over his muddy moleskin knees he strapped his hobble belt around the middle then wedged in 2 short barrelled Webley pistols.

Out in the yard the husband were crying to his brood Run children run go run away they'll lag us all.

The mother never heard this she were gobstruck staring at Steve Hart large fat tears sliding down her ruined cheeks.

By herrings she whispered thats my dress.

As Steve kneeled by the fire there were the loud ripping noise of fabric when she heard it she made a little cry. I'm sorry Missus said Steve scooping up ash some of it were dead and some of it were still alive he rubbed it heedless on his face & hair crying out eff and ess when the embers burned him.

You godless mongrel said the Missus.

Then Dan run in from the outhouse and the woman watched in horror as Steve sent her blue town dress flying across the hut it were caught by Dan in the doorway.

No please she pleaded but my brother's eyes was dead as stone he begun to don the garment.

By the laws the Missus suddenly cried by the laws I'll injure you severely.

She were no weakling she were broad of shoulder and substantial in the chest and once she armed herself with a splintery stick of firewood both boys retreated she were very fast indeed.

The traps is coming Steve explained but she chased the unnatural looking pair out the door calling all those curses Irish women use when they wish not to offend their Saviour. Salvation seize your soul sorrow take you but there never were a Holy Writ against club swinging so once she had gained the yard nothing could inhibit her. Each time Dan tried to get into her dress she set upon him and to the muddy injury he had already done the item she added bright red blood.

As Dan withdrew from her blows Steve called to him Gird yourself. Where he stole a word like that only the Lord knows but Steve Hart were a magpie. Gird yourself! Dan got the dress over his head then turned and come charging at the Missus or so she thought.

I told youse the Missus cried to her husband as she fled I told youse he'll murder us all. She veered away towards the gully in the direction opposite to her fleeing brood one of which were later found wandering by the railway at Glenrowan.

Dan ran back into the hut also set to black his face by some recipe previously concocted with his mate but he had the brains to pour water into the ashcan. When he come out again into the muddy daylight he raised his filthy fist at Steve in wild salute.

We is the Sons of Sieve cried he. Dear daughter it is Sieve not Steve although it is off the latter that he must of learned it.

Joe Byrne meanwhile had mounted his horse he were in a very savage mood having decided to take as many coppers as he could before expiring but he had managed to slide no more than one cartridge into the Spencer when he were stopped short by the sight of Steve & Dan.

What the eff is this he asked but in the confusion of the moment he accepted the ash paste when it were offered urgently smearing it across his face.

We are the Sons of Sieve.

All the normal questions & profanities was prevented by our host he brung 2 saddled horses to Steve and Dan.

Bad cess on you boys said the furious old fellow. Harry Power never done nothing like this to my missus he were an adjectival friend to us.

Joe Byrne were confused he looked to Steve.

We is the Sons of Sieve.

O be off with you cried the old man you is an adjectival disgrace to bushranging I hope you effing die.

After a dangerously short ride this strange party come to a large flat grey rock high on a hillside here they could lay on their stomachs and watch the gathering of the undertakers 200 yd. below. Beyond a stand of white gums there were a flat clear area of grass it were here the army had gathered it had grown more heads than the Hydra now there was 30 men all armed to the teeth. Dan recognized Superintendent Nicolson the one who had arrested Harry Power but far more alarming was 2 blackfellows now in conversation with the Supt.

Niggers hissed Steve Hart I aint afraid of niggers.

Shut your hole said Joe still confused & discombobulated by the dress but for discussion on that topic there werent no time. What you is calling niggers is black trackers that one old b————r is more dangerous than 20 effing Spencers.

They've no adjectival hope of reading our tracks you take my word for it.

Joe shook his head indicating what a waste of time it were to argue with a sissy boy but Steve insisted he said that swamp is all churned up by beasts therefore it follows the tracks cannot be read.

Listen to me girlie it don't matter if a herd of wombats done their business them blackfellows can track us all the way to himself's place.

Well we aint there so it don't matter no road.

Is there nothing in that noggin fool? Ned will be there they'll lag him the moment he arrives.

No matter how strange Steve looked how slight and weak he were never nervous of offering an opinion not even to a man bent on a maniacal war. No they won't said he.

Joe already seen 2 traps were laying a sheet of canvas upon the grass a 2nd pair were breaking fallen branches beneath their feet.

They're having an effing picnic.

Soon there were a merry fire and much tucker were produced. Clearly the blackfellows received no invitation to this feast and soon they retreated into the bush beside the swamp.

Joe Byrne now fed 5 cartridges into the Spencer's cunning mechanism. There were no noise except what is made by a modern brass munition being levered into the chamber of a Spencer. We have to bag them blacks said he.

No one argued now he ordered that Steve take the horses behind the hill he were obeyed. When he told Dan to ensure his Webleys was both loaded my brother done so. Then Dan and Joe set off down the hill walking v. bandy legged on the sides of their boots so as to make less noise. Dan were sick at heart thinking there were no choice but murder.

Before too long they left them rocks & box trees entering the white gum bush the ground here were a cold & clammy bog. Dan followed Joe Byrne through the forest of peeling trunks lifting the hem of his dress with his left hand holding his Webley in his right it were a poor weapon accurate at most to 20 yd. Soon he heard the loud voices of the police then suddenly they was arrived at the deadly place.

Their knees was brushed with bracken fern the bark hanging from the trees like tattered skin already blasted in a war. Ahead they clearly seen the party of traps and even closer was 2 blackfellows sitting on their haunches amongst the stripes of dark & light. The older one were talking very quietly in their queer tongue the younger one replying only a word or 2.

Dan and Joe closed in very careful the snap of twig or leaf could give them away the boss tracker squatted in a mote of sunlight he were a sturdy old fellow with a tweed coat white moleskins a pair of knee high boots police issue. As Dan and Joe neared they could now make out the apprentice in the shadow a skinny young warrigal v. natty in tweed britches and blue shirt. At the same time Dan and Joe come upon him he reached the pitch of some complaint but what that were they couldnt understand.

Joe Byrne stepped out of the shade and the boy went quiet.

Nothing were said but the blacks rose slowly to their feet.

When Joe Byrne jerked the barrel the old man held his hands up in the air and his apprentice done the same tho it were an action obviously new to him.

You read them tracks to the police uncle Joe whispered.

The tracker shook his head.

You sure uncle?

The old boy knew the score immediate. Nothing here boss he whispered back I swear by Jesus them tracks all belong to cattle.

You tell them police fellahs there aint no tracks in here.

Them b————rs get by very good without me boss you watch them.

They give you tucker uncle?

The old man shrugged.

You know my name uncle?

I reckon you Ned Kelly boss.

You know what Ned Kelly does to traps uncle.

Yes boss but I not a trap boss I not one of them Queensland b————rs I aint hurt nobody.

Very good said Joe though he didn't know what Queensland b————rs was or what that meant. No more were said. The trackers sat down on their heels again the boys retreated back in amongst the shadows.

Them trackers was good as their word they never said nothing not then or even later they led the police away in the opposite direction straight back towards Eleven Mile Creek. Believe me this were no favour to your father.

Late that night the boys rode through the gap at Glenrowan. Once they descended onto the plain at Eleven Mile Creek they watched the hut for a good 2 hr. before they begun cautiously to approach. Finally Dan burst through the door and were distressed to discover it not only empty but abandoned to the rats.

Having previously received intelligence of Supt Nicolson's approach I had already loaded Mary and George into a spring cart and with Maggie riding ahead as a scout we had set out along the meandering tracks threading through the river gums to Moyhu. Here the letter were posted to Mr Cameron that done we hurried onwards soon passing through the townships of Edi and Whitfield. When the moon rose Maggie turned home I then drove Mary & George all the way across the grey and white plains to the upper King River that is the doorway to the high country you will recall from the lesson I learnt off Harry Power. At dawn we safely made camp a mile or so from the Quinns. Cooked meat were delivered and the spring cart disposed of where it would not raise suspicions.

That same yellow dawn the boys had reached Moyhu securing a safe camp on Boggy Creek both parties remaining hidden through the day.

At dusk I saddled the cart horse a quiet old mare named Bessie I set Mary and her sick baby on her back this were no way to be either a mother or an outlaw but we had vowed never to be parted from each another. As the moon shone on the King Valley we begun to poke slowly up a spur on the western side of the King after the ridge were attained we proceeded south towards the mountains I were always in front leading Bessie by a rope but this were scratchy country & a great ordeal for Mary who would be no horsewoman even on McBean's rich river flats.

We was in love as never before though it were certainly no time of bliss with the undertakers upon us your brother George v. sick indeed. We cantered into the valley near the Buckland Spur and once I located the old miner's hut we both spent all our time trying to make the little fellow well. We had ridden all night but there were no rest the baby's breath turning very bad and nothing settled on his stomach but would come back up accompanied by a deal of mucous. I woke the magpies with my axe cutting notches into the trunk of a mighty stringybark I got myself high enough to make a good harvest of eucalyptus leaves. Then with whatever was useful in the miner's tip I constructed a eucalyptus still as in easier times I made one for poteen. To light a fire were a danger but this distillation would do the boy much better than the sulphur smoke.

By evening of the 2nd day his breathing were less troubled & at dusk I dropped a gum & peeled sufficient of its bark to make a most effective curtain. Thus we could permit ourselves a lighted candle. We ate cold mutton and once George slept I told Mary she too should rest and I went outside to keep watch over my family. My Colt were in readiness 6 percussion caps snugged on the nipples my charged .577 lay across my knees. Many hours passed but it were not until the dew begun to fall that I heard hooves amongst the river rocks I cocked the carbine's hammer and held my fire.

3 riders come threading through the ti tree scrub. Thank God it were my mates delivered safely. Joe Byrne led the way into the clearing Dan's gelding were very meek pushing his nose right into the mare's tail and then Steve come hard behind. I could see no faces nor clearly distinguish Dan's garment which I took to be a smock.

I called to Mary through the open door We got company.

She had been asleep but now come rushing to the doorway with the candle in her hand. Lifting this light she revealed a scene worthy of the Theatre Royal it were blackface men in dresses. I begun to laugh but then I heard her body fall & found her laying in a cold and muddy puddle by the door. She had fainted dead away.

Steve entered the hut like the Dame in the pantomime. Mary opened her eyes she never asked what happened or why she woke up back inside the hut nor did she smile or laugh or point at the dress. Instead she up and at him she ripped at his empty bosom and tugged at the yellow flowers around the lace.

This won't solve nothing she cried.

Steve squared his shoulders and hooked his thumbs into his hobble belt but his eyes was filled with wild confusion.

Lay off said he retreating one more step. Mary were 6 in. shorter but now she invaded the territory he abandoned plucking at the dress until the lace tore in her hand.

It is Molly's Child you think to make my Ned?

This made no sense we knew no Molly but Mary's pretty face were scratched from her nightriding it give her a wild & desperate kind of look.

Get off me cried Steve his eyes asking would I help him but I were more confused than him.

Steve then pushed Mary in the direction of the hearth saying Fetch me a adjectival cup of tea why don't you.

I would of punished him immediately but the slippery little Jesuit squirmed away. I caught his arm then seen Mary had chose to obey him she picked up a dirty tin pannikin slopping it full of cold black tea.

May it turn to adjectival poison in your Molly mouth.

Joe Byrne laughed to see Steve so disadvantaged by a woman but in a moment this become an ugly snort. He sunk down on the bench behind the splintered table and remained deep in shadows his brawny arms folded across his chest.

Ned if you won't say it then I will.

I advised Joe not to say nothing he would regret telling him Mary were as good as wife to me.

It don't matter she must not talk to Steve like that.

I would of dealt with him as well but Mary laid her cool hand upon my wrist.

Are you Joe she asked him butter would not melt in her mouth.

Bullet Eyes sized her up. It aint your place said he at last.

You are wrong she said this place is mine and Ned's.

Jesus eff me cried Joe Byrne.

Shutup I said there aint no one standing watch and there is horses all around the hut.

Though Joe were a mad b————r he could turn sensible at the drop of a penny he come outside with me as did Steve & Dan. The horses was in night hobbles they could hardly move so we released them and walked them down to the King and there they finally watered. No one said a word about what had taken place inside we talked quietly about the police the black trackers the 2 boys saying nothing of the dresses they was wearing.

When the animals had drunk their fill I led man and horse alike to an old holding yard a mile further upriver. Me & Harry Power had built it 9 yr. previous. Then I dispatched young Dan to keep lookout on the slope below the hut and sent Steve back to watch over Mary. All were now peaceful or so it seemed but when Joe and me brung home the firewood I was most annoyed to discover no food upon the table and your mother once more backing Steve Hart against the wall.

If you are the Son of Sieve what is you the son of? Can you tell me? Or must the priest ring the bell for you to give the correct response?

Steve were a man ready to die in war but also a boy he didnt know how to fight against an older sister. Its Ireland he offered.

Ireland is it continued Mary. Had she been a male she would of known to let him off the hook but she didnt realise Steve were already cowed. Well says she I'm sure you is nothing worse than a colonial lyre bird copying anything it hears.

Now fair go Missus you must not talk to me like that.

O said Mary her shoulders was so straight & slender I am sure it is a fine brave boy you are. I am sure you aint one of them murdering cruel b—————ds who make Ireland such a Hell on earth.

If she had been a man this was the moment at which Joe Byrne would up and hit her and even were she the size of a shire horse he would of dropped her and kicked her in the throat for good measure. But now all he could do were stare balefully at me until he could bear his own silence no more.

Well whats this bloody dress Joe cried at last or is it some effing secret?

Its what is done in Ireland Joe said Steve sitting down beside him.

Joe seemed to wish no more affiliation with the boy in the dress than with the harpy woman. God Jesus help me said he.

Its what is done by the rebels insisted Steve as I'm sure you heard your own da relate. Its what is done when they wish to scare the bejesus out of the squatters.

In all my life entire this were the 1st time I ever heard that secret revealed. Mary come to the table and sit opposite Steve.

There aint no squatters in Ireland Steven Hart.

The knights then its just the same.

Knights?

The knights cried Steve the adjectival Queen of England for your information.

Then do you see. She paused.

What should we see Joe asked her coolly.

Mary lit an extra candle & the light washed up her long white arms and across her scratched and lovely face. You are Joe Byrne? She wedged the candle into a knothole in the table and now were clearly revealed the other deep knot I mean the fury in Joe Byrne's forehead.

Then you should know Joe this costume is worn by Irishmen when they is weak and ignorant.

Doubtless Joe could not believe his ears. We is all adjectival Irish here his voice went lower hers went higher in reply. I am ever so sorry to go against you Joe Byrne but you are colonials. I am the Irish one and it is the truth I am telling when I say I have seen many men in dresses before today.

No one commented.

Mary then took a cup of sugar & a spoon she rose from her seat to carry the service around the table. Steve hesitated to accept the gift then took 2 spoonfuls and stirred his pannikin in silence.

If wearing sheets & masks & dresses were such a powerful remedy said she well then Ireland would be a paradise on earth and all the Kings of England have burnt in Hell. Do you Steve Hart wish to turn the people against my Ned?

We is 4 men Joe interrupted 4 men what has the whole damn country trying to murder us theres £1,000 upon our heads there is 30 traps wandering the plains with authority to shoot us dead on sight. My guts is bad my marrow is hurting the last thing I need is to have lessons in this business from a tart.

If you steal from the poor selectors began Mary.

God save me cried Joe she's worse than an effing solicitor I hope she don't cost as much.

Mary handed me her sugar bag I returned it to the table then took her by the arm.

Come dear I said I took her by the arm.

I won't shutup Ned I'm sorry but I will do you all the great favour of telling you what uniform these boys is wearing.

Dear God thought I even a murderer does sometimes deserve a holiday but as I thought it Mary begun the tale with Joe Byrne sitting in judgment on her his hostile yellow eyes examining her.

Your mother stood in the middle of the hut with her hands clasped in front of her a scratch on her cheek had begun to bleed.

My da she said he were a blacksmith in a village by name of Templecrone you never heard the name don't worry Steven Hart you talked about them knights well in this part of Donegal there were a Lord and he would sometimes leave a horse with my da for shoeing and then neglect to collect it until he were good and ready the poor blacksmith bearing the cost of feeding & stabling.

There wasnt no knight but there were Lord Hill and one morning he left behind an uncommon horse he were a gelding very high and handsome jet black in colour. The white blaze upon its forehead were exactly in the shape of the map of Ireland everyone remarked on it.

When nighttime fell no one come down from the so called GREAT

HALL to collect Lord Hill's horse my da grumbled O it were an imposition O it were a liberty but I noticed he give the beast molasses with its oats so I knew he loved that horse he couldnt help himself.

It were winter so the light went early much earlier than it ever does in Benalla. In Templecrone it were pitch black by 4 o'clock of the afternoon and on this one day there were a great storm out in the Atlantic & a fisherman were drowned the winds terrible loud and bitter. It were me who heard the knocking on the door at 1st I thought it were the wind.

But here was men in dresses.

They was the Sons of Sieve said Steve Hart but your mother would not be distracted. I were 6 yr. old said she and they was big men all their faces was blacked and one of them were a great lanky galoot he had a mask. They was each man holding burning faggots and the high wind were making them flare up high and wild licking towards the fringes of the thatch.

Get your da said the leader his voice very stern but still I imagined it were some prank like is practised by the strawboys when they put on the dresses or the sheets going from house to house on Halloween or May Eve and you must do what they say or else will have some trick played on you. Behind the men in dresses were a larger mob though being only 6 yr. old I were not afraid not at all I fetched my da and I tried to stay close by him to hear what favour the men would demand or trick they would threaten but then the da pulled me back into the house shutting the door behind him when he stepped outside.

We was a big family 7 girls and me the middle one. It were bath night and since my ma were no more a housekeeper than me today I knew one child would not be missed so I put on my slippers and my mother's shawl then crept outside to see what fun & games would now take place.

The whole crowd of men had pushed into the stables by the time I arrived and my da already persuaded them to put out their faggots for he had a mighty fear of fire he had lit his own lanterns at his personal expense. There was 5 horses stabled on that particular night but Molly's Children and their friends was all gathered around the stall of one and of course it were that tall black gelding property of Lord Hill.

I can tell you very particular how the men was dressed though all was not dressed the same. 6 of them wore dresses these was for the most part garments their wives would of happily give away they were sewn and patched and torn our village was poor enough but no woman would have use for these dresses not even to tend the pigs. All the men had black ash or coal painted on their faces some had been most mindful to cover every skerrick of white skin the rest was pretty careless. There were one had a mask made out of the feathers of a wren or many wrens a fierce looking thing I would not have recognised its owner excepting he wore his wife's dress so I knew it straight away. He were the tenant on a strip of land out on Thinglow Road in truth it were not so hard to name the others.

My da knew the men too but he did not speak to them familiar and though they was sober he talked to them like they were very drunk and might take offence at the smallest thing.

Now boys said he now I'll be fair with you. If hat you have then hat he'll wear I'll not say no to that.

I wondered what hat this might be then one of the men got down in the stall to secure a top hat on the horse's head it werent a proper hat it had been made particular for a horse. The poor beast didnt like it and went to shaking its head the effect so very comic I laughed myself.

There Lord Hill said the man. He called the horse LORD HILL although his name were MERCURY.

Then another chap produced a sack from which he took a kind of crimson blanket with a white cotton border in other words it were made up to look like the cloak of a Cardinal or Lord. My father permitted this raiment to be laid upon the beast.

Ah Lord Hill said the 1st man what a Lord you is to Lord it over us.

Ah Lord Hill said another this land is our land it is not yours to take and give. What say you to that Lord Hill?

Even if Mercury answered to the name Lord Hill he could not of course say nothing. One of the men jumped down into the stall he had what is called a twitch a loop of rope which is put round a horse's lip and when its turned the animal cannot easily move its head so now he fitted this device and twisted it.

We know what an adjectival twitch is Joe Byrne says.

Answer me you b—————d said the man you can say whatever you like. Of course the horse said nothing how could it?

Very well said the man then you is to be put on trial and we'll see how well you like that.

The men in dresses now all jumped down into the stall like spiders dropping from a tree. Being farmers they was swift & skilful they soon got more ropes around the poor creature than around Gulliver if you ever heard the story. The horse found himself so tightly bound he could move no more than a fly in a web but his big dark eyes was full of fear I thought it a prank but I do believe poor Mercury had seen his fate he knew no good would come of it.

Then they took a knife and a long stick.

Mary stopped.

I do not like to say it.

No one encouraged her we all was horsemen staying v. quiet to think of this horse so cruelly tormented though still wondering what would happen.

They done to the horse what they dare not do to its master. The stick were sharpened to a point then hardened in the fire and the man with the wren mask thrust it in the horse's belly.

O Jesus cried Dan he had just come in to be relieved from his watch.

O yes said Mary fiercely they stuck it in a good foot deep and when it come out there were a portion of its gut attached like to a crochet needle.

The b–––––ds said Joe Byrne.

My da then jumped into the stall.

Joe slammed his fist against the table all the metal pots jumped in the air.

My da seized the stick from the wren man and tried to break it over his knee but then all the men in ugly dresses leapt upon him they dragged him outside the stall and in the high alley of the bay they thrashed my da they struck him on the head and shoulders with the stick threatening they would do the same thing to him as they done to the horse.

My Mary were now crying trapped inside her horror like a bird inside a church I couldnt reach her no one could. Her da were left bleeding in the dirt she said she would of gone to him but she feared they would bring the dreadful stick to him so she stayed in hiding. She heard grown men blame the horse for taking their common land they said the proof were having Ireland on his head and they demanded of the poor beast why they should not take Ireland back from him. Much horror the girl saw and heard the horse were shrieking horribly.

In the midst of this cruelty her father saw his pretty dark haired daughter lying curled up in the shadows. Then he rose up with a great roar and swept her into the house and there barred the door and when it once were locked he gave the girl to her mother.

What more happened Mary didnt know only that for a long time that night the wind were not high enough to blunt the wailing of the horse.

In the morning when she woke there was soldiers all round the house and she seen the grand Lord Hill come dressed as for Parliament a powdered wig upon his head. The children wasnt permitted out of doors but nonetheless she observed the remains of the horse being loaded onto the cart it were sickening to see the butchery done to it.

The white blaze were later found in the house out on Thinglow Road the tenant were Michael Connor he were convicted of Swearing Oaths and Theft of Property then he and 5 other farmers were hanged in Donegal.

My da were a United Man said Mary but he give evidence against them all and I will tell you boys if you wish to ride around in this costume the people will not love you. You must ease their lives not bring them terror.

Joe Byrne set down the cup and walked out into the night.

That night inside the hut beside my Mary I were restless my beard hot & itching my limbs as agitated as a threshing machine what horrible visions assaulted me e.g. what were my father doing with that dress in the tin trunk and to what purpose. That is the agony of the Great Transportation that our parents would rather forget what come before so we currency lads is left alone ignorant as tadpoles spawned in puddles on the moon. Laying on the damp floor of the miner's hut I smelt the smoke and ashes of your mother's hair she were a sweet young girl she were a stranger from an ancient time.

Joe went to keep his watch & then Steve returned to stretch out upon his oilskin coat. As written he were a little fellow but he had a blacksmith's snore and once his organ begun to play I pulled on my elastic sides and went out into the air. I were well accustomed to the bush at night but this one were like a nightmare all the black gum trees looked alien and monstrous. Joe Byrne were amongst them somewhere.

At night every river has a secret twin a ghost of air washing above the living water down towards the sea I arrived at a flat white gravel bed where our shallow creek joined the river and there I felt the cold air on my cheek and with it an unholy smell it were poor Joe Byrne he were afflicted by the diarrhoea. He were silent in his agony a contrast to old Harry Power who would moan & thrash & curse the heavens for his pain.

Are you crook old man I asked when he come down to the river. I couldnt see his eyes but his teeth grinned white.

I'd give my bawbles for a pipe said he A little oyouknow would fix me up. He were still smiling but his voice were hard as a spoon rattling in a metal cup.

I had no opium but I did have news to comfort him I told him the letter to Mr Cameron were posted.

This give him no relief the opposite it set him off on a furious bout of leg scratching. O we'll all be pardoned now said he I'm sure they'll set your mother free.

Well perhaps they will.

O Christ Ned do you know who this Cameron fellow is? Do you know what sort of house he lives in?

I read what he said in Parliament.

Yes he is an effing politician.

Yes thats what they have in Parliament.

And you think a politician will defend the likes of us? We are weevils in their flour.

What is the matter with your legs Joe?

It aint my legs mate its my effing neck. You should of come to me about that letter I don't mean no offence but when Cameron sees your writing he'll think us even worse than what we are.

He would of said more except a spasm took him and for a moment all he could utter were eff and ess. If Cameron were a horse he said at last you'd see he were swaybacked and short necked you'd never effing look at him.

It were in the paper Joe you read it too.

You is a very clever bloke Ned save you don't know a rat's arse about politics.

And you aint read my adjectival letter mate.

O Jesus he cried bending over his guts were exceptionally bad O Christ you're impossible. I got to go he said then stumbled through the ti tree scrub to find a private place.

When the last troubled smudge of Joe were swallowed in the bush I removed my boots I left them on the bank and picked my way through the water out to the larger boulders. Finally I found a flat white rock it were wide but narrow enough so I could lay down and drop my arms and let the river run briefly across my wrists. The story of the poor horse had laid a greasy pall upon me now the cold mountain stream were like a poultice drawing out all the ancient poisons I filled my hat with water pouring it across my head it smelt of earth & moss same as the flesh of a river trout. The clouds was light but queerly yellow on their edges as they moved across the ageless constellations.

I woke in bed next morning to discover Mary sitting over me the baby in her arms. It were still too early for any birds except a solitary robin in the scrub beside the hut. You must leave me here she whispered I replied there were no choice we all of us had to keep on moving.

His fever is too high he cannot travel.

I did not speak roughly but in the leaden light I firmly removed baby George from her arms carrying him out of the hut down under the twisted black ti tree past the wet dresses which Dan or Steve must of washed in the middle of the night the garments was spread like catfish skins upon the river bank.

What are you doing?

We are going to cool him.

At my command she got down in the freezing water then I un-wrapped the steaming baby from his shawl it were a shocking vision he had always been a hefty wombat but now his ribs was prominent his skin the colour of lamb fat in the river water.

O the poor darling she wailed as I baptised him holding him under his arms in the mountain water O dear Jesus it is a cruel thing to have a baby in this country.

I paid no attention to her keening for I knew this were exactly how our mother cured our fevers so now I passed the patient back to her then filled my hat and give him another dose onto the head.

It will kill him she cried her eyes was pooled with tears. O Jesus help me what will I do? The baby's eyes was sunk his protest against the icy water were as weak & thin as paper.

I had no wish to torture a child but could not let my boys be captured and would never abandon this woman and baby unprotected in the bush.

By the time we come back to the hut it were clear he were much cooler his lips was blue so Mary wrapped him in the shawl then all 5 of us squatted round him looking down to see if he might improve. The boys was never short of an opinion but in this case all was silent. They didnt wish to be nabbed on account of a baby yet they was not cruel and it were jittery Joe who dipped his finger in water and put it in the baby's mouth. If the fingernail were dirty George never minded he sucked it very hard. That very moment we clearly heard the sound of a horse or horses splashing through the river crossing.

Traps cried Dan then Joe violently jerked back his finger from the baby's mouth. George of course begun to bawl Mary cooed at him but she were too slow for the circumstances so I licked my finger dipped it in the sugar bag and stuck my finger in the sucky mouth. The baby's silence were as valuable as life itself.

Joe urgently racked a shell into the chamber and slipped out the door Steve were after him but messy Dan waited till now to fumble with his powder flask.

Come Mary I said I'll put your finger in the sugar too.

But Mary cared only to hold her child and neglected the sugar. So my sugar finger must remain inside the mouth as we crabbed together with the baby on my left hand and my .577 cocked in my right. We edged beside a narrow tributary to a place where tall swordgrass covered the stream and here Mary lay down as in a grave & when I looked in her frightened eyes I knew we could not live like this no more I could not have her follow me as the wives followed their husbands into war in olden days.

A fright of blood red parrots flared & swept through the khaki forest.

Ahead of me some 20 yd. Joe jumped out from behind a grasstree he sprinted towards the river the Spencer in his hand. Racing after him I wondered would I ever lay eyes on my wife again then I seen Steve and Dan rising cautiously from behind a fallen log my ears was filled with my own crashing footsteps I ran through knee high bracken.

A single rider were now clearly visible through the scrub I stopped to raise my Enfield but then he kicked his horse forward and I seen it were Joe's mate Aaron Sherritt. In his hand he held a small wooden box and it were towards this that Joe Byrne ran & I saw what I must of known before. He were both slave & lover to the Chinaman.

. . .

I did not like Aaron he were always whispering in Joe's ear seeking out Joe's eye making mention of this place & that time neither one the rest of us could ever know. The minute he come into our camp he took Joe down to the river where the pair of them indulged in the contents of that Chinese box and smoked their pipe and pickled their bodies with celestial taint. When he come back Aaron's mocking mouth were smiling at us like he knew things he would not tell. And yet and yet and yet I cannot fault Aaron Sherritt he were as tough as nails a mighty bushman.

It were thanks to Aaron's information we knew a small fire might be risked in the hut's old fireplace and his gift of bacon & eggs could now be cooked. Mary sat alone on the single bench us men leaned against the dusty log walls smoking pipes & roll ups while Aaron poked peacefully at his frying bacon describing to us the various parties of armed police Captains Commissioners & Superintendents all the most important actors in the colony was in search of us daily racing from hut to hut along the roads across the open plains.

Aaron pulled a battered MELBOURNE ARGUS from his back pocket it were still a shock to see my name so famous. Aaron drew our attention to a squib it showed the Police Commissioner holding a dead possum with all his men arranged behind him as if they had slain a mighty lion the scene were set inside a settler's hut and a mote of light streamed through a hole in the bark roof illuminating the dead marsupial. The engraving made no sense till we learned of the raid on the Sherritt family's hut at Sebastopol this is now a famous story perhaps you heard it. Imagining he'd found the Kelly Gang's headquarters the Commissioner let off a shotgun as he entered and so not only scared the pants off Aaron's brother Jack but blasted a hole in the bark roof and killed the ringtailed possum. The caption to the drawing read A SAD CASE OF MISTAKEN IDENTITY.

For a change the ARGUS had no cartoons of Superstitious Mick or Ignorant Bridget the Irish maid instead the pictures was of the coppers their point being they did not have the brains to find the Kellys. Here is one from MELBOURNE PUNCH I paste it down upon the page.

> *Whipper (who has never been beyond Keilor Plains):* "I say, aint it shameful they don't catch the Kellys? Why don't the police jump on their horses and ride 'em down?"
>
> *Snapper (who has been as far as Dandenong):* "No sir, you're

wrong—quite wrong—strategy, sir—strategy's the thing—wait for 'em behind a tree!!"

After the Commissioner departed from the Sherritts' he led the charge onto Joe Byrne's mother's property interrupting the old dame's milking. Aaron had a long lazy jaw and laughing hazel eyes he told this story particularly to Joe he done it very comical performing Mrs Byrne's Irish curses and Commissioner Standish retreating backwards from the bails and standing in a cow pat with his nice clean boots.

All Joe's pains was gone he laughed but I began to see the storyteller did not really like me laughing too. I never thought Aaron very clever but always a good natured chap though today I observed a calculating quality about them merry eyes. Soon he abandoned his funny stories asking Joe to keep an eye on the bacon and do it like at Hodgson's Creek whatever that meant. Can I have a word Ned?

His mouth were still making a smile but he didnt look at me till we come to a sandy patch beneath the ti tree. Here he squatted as a bushman will do then broke a stick and for a moment I believed he intended to draw a map.

Well he said I see you is very adjectival jolly.

I asked him what were eating him.

I aint talking against you.

You aint said nothing yet.

I got to be honest mate everyone knows the b————rs will get you in the end everywhere I go they're offering money for information. I want to keep Joe's spirits up but only a fool can't see how this will end.

I thanked him for his confidence though my sarcasm were wasted.

You should let go of Joe mate said he smiling.

I aint holding him Aaron.

He don't deserve this punishment he didnt kill no one yet as you well know.

I am sure Joe will go if he wishes to.

You have a power over him Ned he don't deserve this outcome.

What outcome might that be?

You know he said but he couldnt hold my eye.

Is that to mean that I deserve it Aaron?

Seeing he could not answer I set back off towards the hut.

Theres something else he called I seen he were holding out an envelope. Thinking it were Cameron's reply I grabbed for what I thought an envelope but it were just a pale green square of paper speckled like a plover's egg. I asked him what it were but he only shrugged.

Unfolding the paper I seen nothing but the words NED KELLY it were the slow hand of an individual not fully confident of their education. Where is this from?

But I already knew the answer.

It is reckoned to be from your ma.

I seen how Ellen Kelly had secretly laboured upon that scrap and it pierced my heart that NED KELLY should serve not only as name & address but must carry all the weight of shame and subjugation teeming in her breast. Them b-----ds would not give her paper she must of stole it & pencil both & when she were sent to walk back & forth alone in the yard of Melbourne Gaol she tied her message to a rock and threw it into the rockyard thus did young girls write love letters to their men.

Prison is a hard place the souls within it murderers or worse but them 2 words was carried by some unknown person to someone else unknown there were no gain to it only risk but even the lowest of them prisoners knew what were done against my mother were UNFAIR. The Queen of England should beware her prisons give a man a potent sense of justice.

One Monday morning Maggie come out of Mr Zinke's office in Beechworth and there was waiting a hawknosed old lag with his brows pushed down hard upon his eyes he asked were she Maggie Skilling and give her the paper when she affirmed it.

Maggie soon passed the scrap to Aaron who handed it to me and the demand made of a son by them 2 words were clear. Now of course it were no single man standing in between me and my mother not only Bill Frost or George King but also the Governor the Premier & the Police Commissioner & Superintendents Nicolson & Hare and below them all the great pyramid of serfs Fitzpatrick & Hall & Flood nearly 100 of them to be defeated.

Telling Aaron to go back inside I cogitated by myself in the dank little clearing beside the King the ti tree scrub was hung with flotsam from the October floods the earth was moist with rotting bark scented with mud and eucalyptus. In that fragrant chapel with God as my witness I swore an oath that if Mr Cameron's character were as Joe Byrne had warned and if he did not soon release my mother then I would burst the prison walls asunder and take her back myself.

· · ·

As Aaron departed he done me the disservice of leaving Joe deep in useless dreams I told the boys they was to guard him and Mary and the baby
while I went to find something for the dinner pot but that were not the
truth I were set to devise a stratagem equal to my vow.

When I left the camp at Sandy Flat even the clouds seemed party to
my confusion and for much of the day they hung low above my head the
colour of dirty wool. I had not the least idea of where to look or what to
do and even my horse showed pity treating me like she would a woman
or a child. She were so sorry she refrained from pigrooting when I
mounted.

All day we poked along through the maze of wild ridges me talking to
her while her ears flicked back to listen but she had no better idea of what
I should do next.

How I wished for a better man a Captain to advise me. My own father
died when I were 12 yr. old the only boss I ever had were Harry Power and
once I seen his feet of clay I left him far behind or so I thought. Yet as this
dismal cloudy day wore on I finally understood I were still the apprentice
and Harry were the master I were still following his rutted track. It were
on account of him I knew this were a blind gully and that were the best
spur to get me to the humpback ridge. Your Ignorance he called me when
teaching me the secrets of the Strathbogies the Warbies & the Wombat
Ranges. If you know the country he said then you will be a wild colonial
boy forever.

This were untrue as were proved by his own arrest and incarceration
in Pentridge Gaol but this were his path I loyally followed and if I pushed
along the Buckland Spur till dusk why I might end up in Harry's bolthole
on the cliff above the Quinns and wake tomorrow morning with Supt
Nicolson crashing on me like a grey box in a storm.

I reined in my mare but there were a patch of loose shale & she
propped & slid with the crupper hard around her tail as she steadied on
the ledge below. Beyond this precipice were a mighty sea now ridge after
lonely ridge rolling all the way to Mount Cobbler and in this wild and
roiling landscape I finally seen the truth.

The bush protected no one. It had been men who protected Harry
and it were a man who betrayed him in the end. Harry always knew he
must feed the poor he must poddy & flatter them he would be Rob Roy or

Robin Hood he would retrieve the widow's cattle from the pound and if the poor selectors ever suffered harassment or threats on his behalf he would make it up with a sheep or barrel of grog or fistful of sovereigns.

Harry were not captured because the traps suddenly learned his trails and hideouts he were arrested when he put a lower price on his freedom than the government were prepared to pay. The sad truth is the poor people's love is cupboard love and all it took was £500 for the police to be led directly to his secret door.

Harry can be excused he never heard his own blood price but ours were advertised in every paper it was as well known as the price of stockmen £1 a week and drovers £40 a year the Kelly Gang were worth £800. I aint no scholar as I said but the arithmetic were simple we would muster £8,000 and scatter it around the district like water on the drought bare plains. This good news I brung back to camp but I were away too long it seemed too many hours had passed since Joe's last smoke he now were sneezing & his nose were running and his good mood were all gone and he were once more out of temper with the world.

Kelly you are adjectival mad he cried slamming his fist onto the splintered table I will not effing do it I'm damned if I will I've gone too deep already.

In the silence that followed Mary quietly lit the lamp and once the yellow light washed up the cobwebbed walls it shone into Joe's beard and I seen that flaw to his looks that harelip hidden deep in the shelter of his fair moustache. I will not rob a bank he said.

What are you frightened of asked Dan they are going to hang us anyway.

He were a brave little b————r but I got his pimply beak and twisted him off his chair and down onto his bony knees I promise you I cried I promise all of youse that you will not be hanged.

You'll not be hurt cried Mary she hung the lantern off the hook above the table. Not one of you brave boys will be harmed.

That's very comforting said Joe Byrne are you a witch?

Mary put her nose against the baby's head but her eyes never left Joe's glare. You have my word she said.

Joe were famous as a ladies' man in Beechworth he brought them gloves or stole them scarves there were nothing he did not know of how to make a woman happy but now he were pale and sick he had no charm. You're barking mad he told my wife.

Shutup I told him.

You are both mad you too Ned you cannot break your mother out of Melbourne Gaol.

Well he never said he could cried Mary.

Yes but thats what he's thinking. I know him girlie he loves his ma like nothing else.

Ned tell him you don't think that Ned.

He couldnt do it said Joe not if he robbed 2 banks not if he had £100,000.

Don't tell me what I'll do Joe Byrne.

We've spilled their blood the only hope is California O Jesus he cried eff you Kelly just let me go.

I pursued him outside the sky were dusk white above the black umbrellas of the gums Joe Byrne had mighty thighs & calves he were noisy as a wombat crashing up the scrubby hill he were cursing eff and ess I followed him for 50 yd. the sticks was snapping like baby ribs beneath his angry boots. Then come a thick silence.

Even if you got a ship I called you'd have to grease the Captain's palm also pay your passage Joe where else would we get the money but from a bank?

I aint afraid of dying he said at last then I made out his lumpy shape he were sitting on a stump or rock or fallen tree.

This plan don't call for dying.

I won't kill I have enough bad dreams already.

Or killing neither.

A long silence from us while the kookaburra gave its last call for the night.

Just let your ma serve out her term it aint so long. We both done as much time in prison and it hasnt killed us yet.

But I were not prepared to debate with him about my obligations they was no less to my mother than to him. I took a noisy step or 2 towards him and he backed away. Go back to Aaron but don't whine like a yellow cur.

I aint leaving said the maddening b————r don't you know why?

I did not answer when he spoke again there were a tremor in his voice. Ned you are as good a man as I ever known. He come through the dark putting his clammy grip upon my arm. I am your mate he said thats my bad luck.

He were Aaron's mate I thought thats worse luck still. We walked to the hut no one spoke until our eyes was naked in the candle light.

I'll tell you what I'll do for you he said I'll go to Benalla and inspect the bank.

He'll inspect some opium I thought.

You don't have to come back Joe you could send word.

Thank you Ned he said engaging himself urgently with his tobacco pouch.

Later while he saddled his bay I stood waiting in the blue night with Steve and Dan. Joe said we soon would know how the bank were guarded and the most profitable day to rob it I did not expect nothing of him now. When he mounted he done the unusual thing of leaning down to shake my hand.

Don't kick no one in the knees I said.

In the bawbles more like it.

I waited until the soft clomp of the hooves could be heard no more then I also parted from the youngsters it were me towards the hut Steve and Dan to keep the 1st watch of the night together.

Inside the hut I could hear George's snotty milky breathing I were melancholy.

Dear asked Mary.

Yes?

I have been wondering if grumpy Joe is so mistaken. Why should we not all sail to America?

O Jesus Mary we have no money Mary we have to rob the bank to get the money if we are to get away.

But when we have the money dear?

Well 1st we have to rob the bank Mary there aint no avoiding it.

This were the moment our misunderstanding begun I were not ready to discuss how the money would be used I were thinking only how to rob the bank without the boys being killed. But your mother had travelled many miles beyond that place she already had the sea spray on her cheeks.

I been wondering said she exactly what experience do you have of robbing banks.

I think I know well enough how to rob a bank.

O forgive me she said I never knew it were something you done before.

You must not let Joe worry you I reckon I can rob a bank.

She come to join me at the table. I wished to hold her in my arms to run my fingers down her slender back to place my hands across the curve of her stomach.

And how would that be she asked. It were such a clear straight gaze she had.

I didnt think bank robbing were an art of much interest to women.

It is a subject that is become more than 1/2 interesting to me. For instance would you be planning to stroll in the front door?

I fancy thats as good a door as any other.

And would you rob the bank when it were locked or unlocked?

When it were unlocked.

Unlocked?

That don't suit you Madam?

I certainly would not arrive when the bank were open said the surprising girl. I never would wish to have the difficulty of dealing with customers as well as the tellers.

O would you not now?

I would go after 3 o'clock when they were tallying the take then I would knock at the door and have a cheque with me that I needed urgent to be cashed.

Mary I said you must of robbed a bank before.

I have a baby in my womb said she that I would like the pleasure of seeing upon her father's knee.

You understand I have an obligation to my mother?

Indeed I do and to me as well.

That I do.

You should expect the manager to have his pistol handy.

I will knock at the door and the mongrel will shoot me dead?

Well that certainly is the danger at Benalla where old Patrick McGrath will know your face don't you think? And Philips who drank with us and Fitzy that night at the Bridge Hotel he's still head teller but I were thinking Ned are you known at all in Euroa?

Mary it were you showed me the drawings in the papers they'll have seen them in Euroa too.

Then the Euroa bank will be expecting the Devil not my handsome

Ned. Let me trim your beard you get yourself a nice suit from Mr Gloster and anyone will see you is a darling darling man they would think you was a squatter. The tellers would have to open the door if you had a cheque to cash.

And would you not come to the door for me my Mary?

I would cross the world for you. She come around the table and then she took my scabbed and callused hands and placed them carefully upon her.

Dear daughter you know I never had no proper education at Avenel I would have to be there with my sixpence each Monday morning except when my father were in the lockup and then my mother must be granted a CERTIFICATE OF DESTITUTION. From the time we went to Greta I had no school at all so there are much better educated men than me to write the story of our robbery and you may study this account as a fair example. Yet not one of them scribes was sufficient for your mother's taste as you will note from her comments on the sides. Heres my cutting and theres your ma she sits watch on these sentences like a steel nibbed kookaburra on the fences in the morning sun.

The Morning Chronicle, December 11, 1878

The Sticking Up of Faithfull's Creek Station

The homestead of Faithfull's Creek Station is three miles along the railway line from Euroa and only a stone's throw from the railway line itself. Shortly after noon on Monday one of the employees of the station, a man named Fitzgerald, was sitting down to dinner in his hut when a bushman sauntered up to the door, and taking his pipe out of his mouth, inquired if Mr McCaulay, the overseer, was about. Fitzgerald replied, "No, he will be back towards evening." The bushman said, "Oh never mind, it is of no consequence."

Fitzgerald continued to eat his dinner, but the door of his hut was open and he had a clear view of the bushman beckoning to some persons in the distance. As Fitzgerald was finishing his dinner he saw two very rough looking characters join the bushman. They were leading four very fine horses, in splendid condition. There were four bays.

3 bays and a grey

The bushman then proceeded to the homestead.

He was very handsome, over six ft. tall, built in proportion

Mr Fitzgerald's wife was, at that time, engaged in household duties in the homestead kitchen. The old dame was considerably surprised that a bushman would enter with no invitation, she asked him who he was and what he wanted. He said, "I'm Ned Kelly, but do not be afraid; we shall do you no harm, but you will want to give us some refreshments and food for our horses, that's all we want."

Mrs Fitzgerald immediately called for her husband who duly arrived. His spouse introduced him to the bushman, saying, "This is Mr Kelly, he wants some refreshments and food for his horse." By this time Kelly had drawn his revolver and Fitzgerald, knowing him to be the Mansfield Murderer, said, "Well, of course, if the gentlemen want any refreshment they must have it." Ned Kelly then entered into a conversation with the Fitzgeralds, making very particular enquiries about the number of people employed at the station. To all questions satisfactory answers were given.

While this was going on two other men, one of whom is now known to be Dan Kelly, were busily engaged in feeding the horses. A fourth man was standing at the gate, evidently keeping watch.

Kelly then took Mr Fitzgerald to a building used as a storehouse and locked him inside, all the time making assurances that no harm was intended to anybody. As the station hands came up to the huts to get their dinner they were very quietly ordered to bail up and were marched into the storehouse and locked up with Fitzgerald, no violence being offered them as they went quietly.

3 of these men knew E. Kelly's good character for many a year

Later in the afternoon Mr McCaulay, the overseer, returned from his rounds and when crossing the bridge over the creek he noticed with some surprise that quietness reigned about the station. As he neared the storehouse he heard Mr Fitzgerald call out from the building, "The Kellys are here. You will have to bail up." He did not believe this but then Ned Kelly came out of the house and, covering him with his revolver, ordered him to bail up. McCaulay, without dismounting, said, "What is the good of sticking up the station? We have no better horses than those you have." Kelly then repeated that he wanted food and refreshment; he also added that he wished a place for he and his men to sleep.

Still McCaulay did not believe it was the Kelly gang, but when Dan Kelly came out of the house he recognised, he said, "his ugly face" from the portraits previously published in this newspaper.

D. Kelly has clear blue eyes, strong cheekbones, a strong and handsome face

McCaulay then said to the Kellys, "Well, if we are to remain here we may as well make ourselves as comfortable as possible, and have our tea." He led them back into the homestead. The Kellys, however, were very cautious. They took great care that some of the prisoners should taste the food first, being afraid poison might be administered to them. Nor would all four of them sit down at once. Two of them had their meals while the other two kept watch until relieved. It was just as the second pair finished Mrs Fitzgerald's Mutton Stew, that the cry went up there was a new arrival, a hawker with his wagon and two horses. This was Mr Gloster,

On time to the minute

who has a shop in Seymour, but is in the habit of travelling about the country with a general assortment of clothing and fancy goods.

Ned Kelly called out to him to bail up, but Gloster did not see the danger and went about unharnessing his horses as was his normal custom. Daniel Kelly immediately raised his gun and was about to fire when Ned Kelly prevented him doing so. McCaulay also called out to Mr Gloster he should bail up or there would be blood shed. Gloster, who appears to have been a pretty obstinate fellow, took no notice of the threats of the Kellys or the entreaties of the overseer and so continued about his business. Ned Kelly put his revolver to Gloster's cheek and ordered him obey or he would blow his —————— brains out. At this point quite a drama was enacted in the dusty yard and it was only by the endeavours of Mr McCaulay that Kelly was prevented from shooting Gloster. Dan Kelly was eager for blood, as he expressed a strong wish "to put a bullet through the —————— wretch." Gloster was then locked up in the storeroom and the four ruffians then proceeded to ransack the poor man's cart where they each provided themselves with a new outfit. As luck would have it the fit was very good

A strange coincidence indeed

and the four soon made bush dandies of themselves, helping themselves freely to the contents of the scent bottles which they found among the stock.

E. Kelly wore a blue sac coat, brown tweed trousers and vest, elasticsided boots, brown felt hat

Before going to bed for the night, the Kellys opened the door of the storeroom, and let the party out for a while to get some fresh air, but at the same time keeping their revolvers in their hands and watching their prisoners very closely. While they were all smoking pipes together, a friendly conversation took place. Ned Kelly said, "I have seen the police often and have heard them often. If I had been a murderer I could have killed them any time I chose." He spoke a great deal about his mother whom he continued to insist had been unjustly imprisoned and her newborn baby cruelly taken from her. He gave the clear impression he would give himself up if the government would release his mother.

Not true. He never said this. He will give himself up on no account.

DESTRUCTION OF TELEGRAPH

Having locked up their prisoners for the night, two of the gang went to sleep, while the others were keeping watch. Early next morning they were all up, and breakfast having been taken of, one of the gang was sent by their leader to render the telegraph wires unfit for use. There are wires on both sides of the line. On the west there is a single line belonging to the railway department, while on the opposite side are four lines used for the general business of the colony. These are sustained by light iron poles. In order to destroy the railway telegraph the earthenware insulators were broken, and the line fell to the ground. A great deal more damage was done, however, to the other lines, as the ruffians took some stout limbs and smashed seven or eight of the cast iron poles, and then twisted the wires into an inextricable maze. The Kellys appeared to be very uneasy when the trains passed up and down the line. The passengers were plainly seen from the homestead looking at the broken telegraph wires. It was not until afternoon, however, that a train stopped and a man got out. He proved to be a line repairer sent down from Benalla to see what was wrong. As soon as the train passed out of sight the man was made prisoner and locked up inside the storeroom. When this was done, Ned Kelly went to Mr McCaulay and asked him to write a cheque for him on the National Bank of Euroa. This McCaulay bravely refused to do,

He was at no risk and he knew it

but in searching the desk Kelly found a cheque for £4 and some odd shillings. He said this would answer his purpose well enough. The gang now prepared to make a start, Kelly saying they were going into the township, and that everyone including Mr McCaulay would have to be locked up during the gang's absence. One of the gang, a man named Byrne,

A loyal brave friend who would not depart the colony until all concerned could set sail together

was to stay behind as sentry over them, and in order to secure their quietness one of the prisoners was taken out and kept covered by Byrne's rifle. The clear intimation was that if any of the party attempted to escape this man would be shot.

The ruffians then left the station, Ned Kelly driving a spring cart, Dan Kelly driving the hawker's cart, the third man accompanying them on horseback.

ROBBERY OF THE EUROA BANK

The bank was closed at the usual business hour, 3 o'clock, and at a quarter to 4 o'clock the two clerks, Messrs Booth and Bradley, were engaged in balancing their books, while Mr Scott, the manager, was in his room close by. A knock was heard on the door, and Mr Booth asked Mr Bradley, who was nearest the door, to open it and see who it was. On the door being opened a bushman presented a cheque for £4, saying he wanted it cashed. He was told it was too late, and he then asked to see Mr Scott the manager. Mr Bradley said it was too late for that day, as all the cash was locked up. The man then pushed his way in, saying, "I am Ned Kelly." He was immediately followed by another of the gang, a young man wearing a grey striped Crimean shirt and new lavender tie, and both men drew their revolvers, forcing the clerks to go to the manager's room which was just behind the banking chamber. As soon as they got in Ned Kelly ordered Mr Scott to go and tell the females in the house what visitors they had and to bring them back.

No. First, E. Kelly requested money, was given £300 in cash and told there were no more—a lie, as E. Kelly knew.

Thus was soon assembled Mr Scott, Mrs Scott, her family of five children, Mrs Scott's mother, two female servants.

She flirted with him, a married woman. She thought him very handsome, better than her own husband that was clear. It was her that found the key to the safe and give it to E. Kelly. Afterwards Mrs Scott never did stop saying what a polite and dignified gentleman Mr Kelly was, she did not have much luck with the husband of her own. He was a short bald-headed little fellow.

[Several lines here obliterated completely.]

After some little delay and hesitation Mr Bradley handed over the keys,

A lie, as is proven above, it was the Missus give up the key

and Kelly then proceeded to search the strong chest. He took all the money and notes out of it and placed it on the counter, there was about £1,900 in notes and £300 in gold. Ned Kelly then went outside and brought in a small gunnybag, into which he stuffed the notes and gold. Turning to Mr Scott, he said "You have a buggy in the yard. You had better put a horse in it as I have to take you all a little way into the bush and the buggy will be more comfortable for the women than the carts we have."

Mr Scott said his groom was away, and Kelly thereupon went outside and harnessed the buggy himself. The whole party then went into the back yard where the hawker's wagon was standing. Mr Booth, Mr Bradley and three of the children were put in the wagon in charge of Dan Kelly. Mrs Scott and her mother and the two other children and one of the servants were placed in the manager's trap, which Mrs Scott was ordered to drive. The other cart was driven by Ned Kelly and in it was placed Mr Scott and one of the servants. Thus did the gang steal not only the bank's gold but twelve people, driving them out of the main street of Euroa, which was very quiet on account of there being a funeral in the town that afternoon.

And whose idea was that, I wonder?

They drove rapidly to Faithfull's Creek Station. Here the women were allowed to go on to the house, and Byrne, who had been sentry, allowed the captives to come outside.

At about a quarter to nine the ruffians prepared to head back into the bush, but before doing so they locked up the entire party with the exception of McCaulay. Kelly directed him to keep the prisoners for three hours longer, and at the same time impressed on him that the gang would be in the vicinity, and if he let any of them free then he would be held responsible for it. Kelly and his mates then rode off in the direction of Violet Town.

A WARNING IGNORED

The particulars at hand show not only that the offenders have performed a daring exploit, but also that they feel themselves masters of the situation.

So they were—and are!

That they have outwitted the police is obvious, and until some explanation is given, the public cannot fail to hold the opinion that the outrage should have been easily prevented. It has been stated in the press more than once that the gang would in all probability stick up and rob some bank, and thus good warning was given to the authorities. There are 100 members of the police force exclusively engaged in hunting these criminals, and while their performance is giving cause for jubilation in certain quarters, respectable citizens can only look upon their failure with despair.

At Faithfull's Creek we was tried before a jury of our peers you would not know it from the papers.

There was 12 men taken captive and Joe Byrne were by my side to guard them we was all squeezed into a slab hut 20 ft. × 12 ft. which were normally used for holding tools & provisions. It were a hot still night the men was busy on the harvest but this year they was using a mechanical reaper & binder that had some trouble with its innards and that were the overseer McCaulay's complaint that I were causing more trouble than the adjectival reaper & binder. It were McCaulay who took the best seat for himself a rack toothed old iron skeleton of ancient patent thus he lounged in the corner until I kicked him out saying I were the overseer now many is the secret smile this provoked amongst the men.

The so called MISTER FITZGERALD normally occupied that seat but he did not complain he had known me all my life. Old Snorer were Fitzgerald's nickname he were a mate of Harry Power & Billy Skilling and had a well earned reputation for finding the laziest job on any station. When his seat were taken Snorer found a corner atop 2 bags of chaff and there he stayed the night sleeping v. loud & comfortable indeed.

Jimmy Gloster the hawker were another prisoner he were still playing his pugnacious part acting as my mortal enemy.

Peter Chivers were a posh spoken labourer with big muttonchop whiskers he were called the Moth because if you lit a lantern he wd. appear he were often in Mother's shebeen but no one feels natural sympathy for a murderer and in this there were no difference between the Moth and them that only seen my likeness in the newspaper. There were also present a cockney mechanic for the reaper & binder name of Leeves and 6 casual labourers from the Wimmera it were very clear none of them relished the prospect of being locked up with the Mansfield Murderers.

There were also one fellow very broad of shoulder with his hair parted down the middle his moustaches waxed his eyes fixed on me from the minute I come in the hut and while his mates was all concerned about their comfort for the night he done nothing more than lean against the wall to stare. When everyone were settled when even the reaper & binder mechanic had been granted a place to sit it were the man with the waxed moustache who spoke up very bluntly.

What reason did you have to murder them men at Stringybark Creek?

I asked his name he said it were Stephens and I might as well know that he had been a trap himself.

I told the cove it were me alone that done the shooting and Joe Byrne now leaning against the door with 2 pistols in his belt had at that time no more lethal weapon than a stick.

The men all turned as if expecting Joe to support my claim but he give a smile like Riley's dog and dug his hand into his pocket from which he brung some string & a lump of beeswax.

I told them the traps come into the bush with a Spencer repeating rifle & Webley pistols and they had brought long straps specifically made to carry our bloody bodies back to Mansfield.

The men was very still & attentive but when Joe turned his interest to the 2nd pocket their eyes followed. Now he calmly lit the reed in a pannikin of tallow and they observed him place it carefully in the middle of the floor. Once the light were steady he held up a piece of leather no more than 4 in. in length.

This is a souvenir of that very strap said he.

There were no sound save the skurr of a native cat out in the darkness.

It would be no evidence in an English court but that little piece of undertaker had a mighty effect upon our jurors some was so disgusted they did not wish to touch it others examined it v. close for what information I did not know. Stephens were not swayed he said it were easy to imagine the police would be afraid of me for I already tried to kill their colleague from Benalla.

Do you mean Fitzpatrick?

Yes Fitzpatrick.

Snorer then took the stand so to speak. He didnt swear on nothing but admitted to the company he knew me man and boy he said Ned Kelly would never miss his target so if he had wished to kill Fitzpatrick then Fitzpatrick would be dead today. As Ned Kelly had shot the Constable in the hand then he would personally warrant that is where Ned Kelly meant to shoot him.

Stephens turned on me with a most dubious expression.

Not wavering from his judgment I said Fitzpatrick promised to marry my sister but were revealed to have 2 fiancees already in production.

And so you shot him said Stephens his tone sarcastic.

No my mother were upset so she hit him.

So then you shot him?

No the mongrel drew his Colt .45 there was children in the hut and I judged the lesser risk were to shoot the hand that held the gun.

And then he tried to arrest you and you resisted?

No he apologised for his character and we dressed his wound and then he rode away saying he wished to be my friend if you knew Fitz-patrick you would believe me.

O I know him.

And what is your opinion Mr Stephens?

Stephens sighed then wiped his hand across his face. It is well known he is a mighty fool.

Joe Byrne caught my eye.

And that were why the police come to ambush you asked the mechanic. On this cad's evidence?

Yes said Joe they boasted to Ned's sisters they would scatter his brains across the bush.

So thats what lay behind it said Chivers. They came to kill you and you killed them instead?

Well I had nothing but a stick said Joe smiling regretfully. I don't see what I could of done.

We had nothing decent to protect ourselves I said all we wanted were their weapons. We never wished them dead.

The b—————ds shot to kill said Joe you see that is the problem. I doubt any of you gents would of permitted them to have their way.

The hut were quiet again but for the sound of the train passing in the night. I looked around at the men one by one I asked what they would of done if they was in our boots.

They give no answer though the softening in attitude was definite.

And what would you do about my mother I asked. She is imprisoned for Aiding and Abetting Attempted Murder which were neither attempted nor murder in the 1st place.

Again no answer.

Her baby is taken from her I said and they did not answer. And here is the thing about them men they was Australians they knew full well the terror of the unyielding law the historic memory of UNFAIRNESS were in their blood and a man might be a bank clerk or an overseer he might never have been lagged for nothing but still he knew in his heart what it were to be forced to wear the white hood in prison he knew what it were to be lashed for looking a warder in the eye and even a posh fellow like the Moth had breathed that air so the knowledge of unfairness were deep in his bone and marrow. In the hut at Faithfull's Creek I seen proof that if a man could tell his true history to Australians he might be believed it is the clearest sight I ever seen and soon Joe seen it too.

It were late when the men begun to sleep Snorer were up on his chaff bag earning his good name. When the lights was doused you could see the stars through the chinks in the bark roof it were then I asked Stephens what an enquiry would do if such information were put before it. He said there was many bad politicians in the Parliament but Mr Cameron were a man of principle.

A letter would be read Joe asked you think this Cameron's dinky di?

O yes indeed.

You think an enquiry would be a possibility?

By Jove I believe they would have to call one if they heard what you told me.

Thus Joe took from Stephens what he would not accept from me and this my daughter will explain the story in the newspaper relating how one of the so called OUTLAWS come into the homestead late at night and were seen by the women to be labouring over some document all through the long hours until dawn. It were Joe Byrne that wrote the 2nd letter we sent to Cameron it were very eloquent and strong.

The effect on him were tonic in the morning he werent scratchy there were neither sneezing nor mournfulness about him. On this day we robbed the National Bank in Euroa & as my stratagems was realised step by step Joe smiled more and more. Oftentimes he laughed or caught my eye. More than once he whispered in my ear that Mrs Scott the bank manager's wife had become my great admirer. He were very polite to her also to her husband he did not neglect to show the piece of undertaker.

I do believe it were Joe who rallied Scott to our cause if not entirely then sufficient for the bank manager to tell a reporter that with regard to the conduct of the gang although domineering in giving their orders no attempt at violence or roughness was made on any of the hostages.

It were also Joe Byrne that begun the display of flashy riding prior to our departure we showed them what Wild Colonial Boys could do we demonstrated riding the like of which were never seen before we galloped laying longways on our horses' spines our feet at their tails and our noses in their necks and sometimes reclining with our feet upon the neck.

And lo they did applaud us with their eyes bright their faces red bank managers & overseers & ex policemen they stood in the scorching sun and cheered us that were a development we never hoped before.

PARCEL 11

His Life at
25 Years of Age

Brown wrapping paper cut to 40 rough pages (4" ×
8" approx.), then crudely bound with twine. Title
page has a large hole along the gutter not affecting
any text.

*The author acknowledges the gang's notoriety is
growing at the very time that the newspapers
refuse to publish Kelly and Byrne's letters. A misunderstanding between Kelly and Mary Hearn,
and a suggestion that the police and postal
authorities conspired to prevent the delivery of
important letters. Also contains a newspaper
clipping from* The Jerilderie Gazette *reporting
the gang's daring capture of that town, together
with Kelly's detailed explanation of his motives.
In both tone and handwriting these latter pages
of the parcel attest to the outlaw's growing anger
that he should be denied a national audience.*

The government were filled with men of alleged dignity and high distinction so it were a severe embarrassment they lacked the brains to arrest a gang of men so meanly educated. The papers reported Steve Hart's nose were hooked or Dan Kelly had a squint but this could not diminish the fact the government had lost control of an entire slice of territory and they could not account for that to themselves or others.

It were the police who come up with the explanation of our great popularity. According to them there was thousands of Kelly sympathisers throughout the North East and this were why no one could arrest us. We was being fed and hidden by a great army of friends.

As you know this were my ambition but at this stage I were still widely known as the Mansfield Murderer and far from popular. We done Euroa on December 11th. On the 4th of Jan. the police arrested 21 men on no other charge than that they knew Ned Kelly or was related to him or had shared a cell in prison. Some of them imprisoned was my real friends including Wild Wright & some I only ever spoke to at a family wedding others had stopped being my friends after Stringybark Creek for instance Jack McMonigle he had sent word he did not wish to see my face now I were a murderer. But then poor Jack discovered what it were to be slandered & perjured & he were handcuffed & herded on to Benalla railway station & shoved into a box car like he were nothing but a daggy sheep to be transported up the hill to Beechworth Gaol & held there on remand. The entire colony cd. see this were unfair we was being ruled by warders there were no more justice than in the days of yore.

No word yet from Cameron MLA tho he must by now of read 2 letters a rough one from me & an educated one from Joe. Through January the harvest were continuing but on 21 farms the men was absent from their labour thus did the police earn themselves lasting enemies while making us enduring friends. Now the Kelly Gang become Agricultural Labourers and many is the haystack we built. As Dan were now a rich man he complained bitterly about his servitude but through the long hot days of early Feb. I made sure we all done our share. In these 2 mo. we established permanent welcomes throughout the North East we had more holes than the Moyhu rabbits.

I had hoped to net £10,000 from Euroa but the actual amount were £2,260 this were still a mighty sum I give this currency to Joe Byrne thanking him for his friendship & loyalty I told him I were not his warder he cd. go to America or anywhere he liked.

Joe lay his hand upon my shoulder he said I were his Capt until death & he give me back the currency saying he might take just £65 so his mother cd. settle a bill & another £20 so Aaron cd. pay the government the rent on his selection. When he said this I were ashamed I ever thought him less than what he were.

£1,975 remained to us. Money enough for dresses for the girls new saddles for our mates we was happy to get Jimmy Gloster out of debt and reward B. Gould for other services. Mrs Griffiths a widow were able to bring back her daughter who had been compelled to work as a servant in Tasmania. When we had alleviated these & other hardships we still had £1,423 a fortune except we now had the personal responsibility to liberate not only my mother but them additional 21 men in prison. We engaged Mr Zinke in their defence.

The Victorian police was naturally v. free in offering blood money it were not only A. Sherritt we permitted to accept their bribes. We cd. look down from the Warby Ranges and see the plumes of dust rising off the plains and know the police was actors in a drama writ by me.

Mary had witnessed us come back to camp after the robbery our open shirts ballooned behind us our weary horses splashed by creek crossing matted with dust & sweat & torn by prickly scrub but we was all triumphant. Steve Hart kissed Mary on the cheek Joe Byrne picked her up & swung her round & round & told her that her husband were a General now he were the greatest adjectival man alive.

When the newspapers wrote Ned Kelly were handsome I took no notice of their puffery I were waiting on for the news from Cameron although MLAS must be busy men I knew our letters must aid his case in Parliament. I were not so simple as to think I wd. be excused my crime but every day I were prepared to hear my mother had been set free.

I paid very close attention to the newspapers but it were your ma who purchased the scrapbook I suppose you have it in your possession now it is a most distinctive green with a stamp on the inside to say it were made by Parson's Printery in Benalla. In this Mary soon began to paste reports from far & wide she would not tolerate a lie or error but must correct it in the margin some news she also copied out by hand doubtless imagining that volume in a bookshelf in a distant happy time.

WILD WRIGHT *(to Judge Wyatt): You will not get the Kellys until Parliament meets and Mrs Kelly is let go and Fitzpatrick lagged in her place.*

JUDGE WYATT *(remanding Wright once more): I am sorry I would give you fair play if I could.*

I need give you no evidence that your mother were our 1st and best supporter ahead even of my own brave sisters. It were she who hid our money who dug it up when it were being decided who would receive what amount she were very particular we should use it wisely counting the notes & coins into an envelope so people was given what they needed no more no less.

I were waiting for the Parliament to meet but much else occupied our minds and bodies now very busy with both harvest & police we was moving constantly from place to place. In all this your ma were not abandoned by the Kellys she will tell you if you ask her that she went with Kate and Maggie into Benalla where they bought themselves handkerchiefs & scarves they did not care to explain to the shopgirl why they should pay with handfuls of sixpences.

Them girls was most resourceful no trap could follow if they did not wish it so on a hot clear day 3 weeks after the Euroa robbery Mary & Kate drove up in a spring cart to the back of Kilfeera & there found me camping comfortably on 15 Mile Creek. Kate unloaded corn beef & tea & sugar while your mother come to me down by the creek a great pile of newspapers bundled in her arms. Her face was covered with a veil to keep away the flies I could not see her eyes or mouth.

The Parliament?

For answer she lifted the veil to kiss me.

The letter?

That Cameron has received your letter said she it is all reported as you'll see. But her manner were strained and once I opened up the papers I soon learned all the editors had been shown my letter by Cameron but NOT ONE WOULD PRINT MY ACTUAL WORDS instead they was like snotty narrow shouldered schoolteachers each one giving their opinion on my prose & character. Throwing their garbage to the ground I were v. angry to be called a CLEVER ILLITERATE PERSON by that rag THE MELBOURNE ARGUS another paper said I were filled with MORBID VANITY this were a gross offence against justice the colony being ruled like Beechworth Gaol. I kicked the papers apart and would of ripped them with gunshot were it not for fear of revealing our location to the traps.

Mary took my hand & kissed it she held my face and stared deep into my eyes. Dear said she it don't matter no more.

She led my hands down onto her stomach. Said she Our baby will read your letter dear.

But I were in a rage she could not comfort me my words had been stolen from my very throat.

Your mother asked would I like a nice walk which should of surprised me for she didnt like the heat but in truth I were not paying great attention to your mother but stewing in my own juice and plotting what revenge I would take upon them higher ups who so oppressed us all.

I'll stick up an adjectival printery I said I'll print the adjectival thing myself.

She took my arm then together we walked the hill the grass brown & glassy beneath our feet.

You neednt stick nothing up no more you have got all that you require.

Except justice.

You have me she said laying her head against my shoulder why could that not be enough? You have me & yr. baby & you have your friends & more than £1,000.

I said she did not reckon the expense of being an outlaw. We walked further up the hill till we found a single gum tree and there sat down in its thin shade watching a wedgetail eagle circling in the sky above.

I explained to her the money would soon be spent it would not be cheap to have my mother released from Melbourne Gaol.

But now you can give your mother what any mother wants for her child.

And what might that be?

His safety.

You aint saying I should run away?

The best deed you can do your mother is to go as far as you can from harm's way.

You don't know me said I & were very offended she should think me such a selfish coward.

Is it true do you really love her more than me?

It aint the same.

They won't never let her free Ned you must accept that no matter how you love her. She were convicted in a court of law.

I told her she did not know of whom she spoke she could not imagine the hardships Ellen Kelly had endured.

She will not die in gaol but you will perish if you remain in the colony.

If they won't release her I will take her then by force.

But you promised to buy our passage once the bank were robbed.

I cannot abandon my mother Mary you know that.

Then what of me?

What of you?

I have waited for you to rob the bank but I will not wait to watch you die.

Don't cry please Mary.

I am not crying I will not cry. We have £1,000 and we must use it as we both agreed.

You have misunderstood me.

No when your mother is released she can join us in California and I will care for her forever I will wait on her & make her broth even if she spits on me & calls me a tart. When she is an old lady I will be her nurse & slave but I will not remain here & wait for them to murder you I cannot do it.

But they cannot catch me Mary they can't even find their way along the public highway.

You promised me.

You are my life entire said I but now her face were closed like doors I could not open no matter how hard I hammered. They will print my letter then you will see what happens the Australians will not tolerate a mother be gaoled for no offence.

No one will ever print your letter she shouted.

Then like I said I will print the adjectival thing myself. But she were already walking down the hill.

Come back I cried but she did not turn her head held high she seemed a girl no longer but a stranger cruel & proud. I squatted on the dry summer grass for that moment when she wd. relent. I glimpsed her pretty white ankle as she climbed through McBean's barbed wire fence then she disappeared into the scrub and when Kate drove the spring cart round from behind a stand of wattles your mother were in it and I called out her name but it were caught on the wind and blown back in my throat.

I did not know she abandoned me till the week had passed my sister Maggie discovered £200 in £5 and £10 notes amongst the dregs of the last supper there were no clue if the remainder were still buried or if Mary had took it with her. She were the only one that knew its hiding place.

Hell's curse to her. This I thought and worse besides it does not mean I did not love her the very light of my life were stolen away my baby vanished but I remained at my station that is the agony of the Captain if rats is tearing at his guts still must he secure the freedom of his mother and all them men in gaol. I fought with everyone I were in torment from all sides then next week a telegram were sent care of Kate from Port Melbourne WILL WAIT 5 DAYS 23 NOTT STREET.

The air in the North East were hot & still as a baker's oven the white ants flying around my beard crawling in my ears & up my nose I were the monitor once more making fresh ink from McCracken's powder nothing give me no relief but the ceaseless labour with my pen I wrote 30 pages to your mother explaining why I could not yet depart they was dispatched by post to 23 Nott Street.

The threatened 5 days come and went I could not bear to be inside my skin. The boys was filled with pity but when night come they was weary from hard days working in the shadeless paddocks they snored like bullockies in the stinking hot nights I wrote another letter 58 pages long this one for the attention of the government if I were ignorant & unlettered as is claimed then so be it but I made known the earliest days of my life showing the history of the police and their mistreatment of my family.

My letter to Mary were returned ADDRESSEE UNKNOWN the police done this I know my mail were tampered with. On the same day come a tearful letter from Nott Street she was in torment not having heard from me she were sailing to San Francisco. To Hell with all traps I hate them. Everything I had they took from me.

On the 7th of February 1879 the Kelly Gang rode to Jerilderie to renew our cash reserves from the coffers of the Bank of New South Wales. My 58 pages to the government was secured around my body by a sash so even if I were shot dead no one could be confused as to what my corpse would say if it could speak.

It would be hard to find so much as a Chinaman who has not heard how the Kellys controlled Jerilderie for an entire weekend. Personally I read in 6 different newspaper accounts that we planned it better than a military campaign. Well it is no good having a dog & barking too so I will stick this one cutting down for you but please imagine my feelings during the events here described. My 58 pages was pinching & cutting me I could feel them words being tattooed onto my living skin.

The Jerilderie Gazette, Feb. 16, 1879

The Kellys at Jerilderie

It appeared that Ned and Dan Kelly called on Saturday night at Mrs Davidson's Woolpack Inn, where they had a great many drinks. Ned Kelly entered into conversation very freely with the barmaid, informing her that they had come from the backblocks of the Lachlan. They asked a number of questions of the barmaid respecting Jerilderie. Ultimately the conversation turned on the Kellys. When the strangers asked what did the people in Jerilderie say about the Kellys they were informed that the Jerilderie people thought them very brave. The barmaid sang, by way of amusement, "The Kellys have made another escape." After several more drinks the Kellys engaged two beds, and said they would take a ride into Jerilderie and return again.

THE ATTACK
After midnight on Saturday the police barracks were surrounded by Ned Kelly, Dan Kelly, Hart and Byrne. One of the gang shouted out— "Police! Police! Get up, there is a great row at Davidson's Hotel." Con-

stable Richards, who was sleeping in a room at the rear, got up and went in the direction of the sound. In the meantime Constable Devine had got on his trousers and opened the front door. The two police were then confronted by Kelly, presenting two revolvers saying, "Hands up, I'm Kelly," and in an instant the other outlaws came up with their revolvers.

The two policemen being secured, they were guarded by two of the gang while the other two compelled Mrs Devine to go with them (in her night-dress) and show them where the arms etc. were stored. They kept strict watch till morning, when they locked the police in the cells, and kept sentry over the premises on Saturday and Sunday night.

On Sunday morning Mass was celebrated at the Courthouse, distant 100 yards from the barracks, and as it is usual on these occasions for Mrs Devine to get the Courthouse ready for the service. About 10 a.m. she did so, but was accompanied by Dan Kelly.

During Sunday the blinds of the barracks were all down. The two Kellys dressed out in police uniform, and during the day frequently walked from the barracks to the stable.

During the time the police were locked up Ned Kelly conversed freely with Devine about the shooting of the three Constables, and stated that Kennedy fought to the last, but he denied he cut off his ear. Kelly asked Devine if there was a printer in the town; that he wanted to see him very particularly, as he wanted him to print hand-bills and a history of his life. Kelly also read to Mrs Devine several pages of what he wanted printed, but Mrs Devine could not remember anything about it on Tuesday.

Kelly also told Devine that he intended shooting him and Richards,

I would never kill them but it were essential they obey

but Mrs Devine begged them off. Ned Kelly said that if Devine had not left the force in a month he would return and shoot him.

On Sunday night Edward Kelly again rode up to Davidson's Hotel where he had a great many drinks,

If 2 be a great number then he does not lie

and entered freely into conversation with the barmaid. He stopped at the hotel until midnight, when he returned to the barracks. During

Sunday night two of the gang would sleep while the other two kept watch, and so on until morning.

On Sunday the revolvers were cleaned, every bullet being extracted and the weapons carefully reloaded for the dangerous work of the next day, which, we are glad to say, terminated without loss of life. Early on Monday morning Byrne brought two horses to be shod, and Hart bought some meat in the butcher's shop. A little later Byrne went into one of the shops and bought a number of articles.

THE SURPRISE

No one in the town had the slightest idea that the Kellys were in Jerilderie. Several persons saw Ned and Dan Kelly, dressed in police uniform, in company with Constable Richards, coming down the town about 11 a.m. on Monday, but had not the slightest idea they were the Kellys. They were taken for fresh police, and certainly from their outward appearance they looked to all intents and purposes like Constables, more especially since they were seen with Constable Richards.

The townspeople could not realise the idea that the Kellys were here until they saw the telegraph poles being cut down, and Ned Kelly walking into the front of the Telegraph Office, revolver in hand.

Shortly after 11 a.m. Ned and Dan Kelly, with Constable Richards, entered the Royal Mail Hotel. Poor Richards was compelled to introduce the Kellys to Cox, the landlord of the hotel, and Ned Kelly explained that he wanted the bar parlour for a few hours, as he was going to rob the bank and intended to fill the room with any townspeople who happened along. The astonished Mr Cox himself was the first prisoner placed in the room, and for the next hour everybody who came to the hotel was marched into the same room till it was crowded. Then Byrne was despatched to the bank to fetch over the staff of that institution.

BANK TELLER LYVING'S NARRATIVE

About 10 minutes past twelve on Monday morning I was sitting at my desk in the bank when I heard footsteps approaching me from the direction of the back door. I at first took no notice, thinking it was the manager, Mr Tarleton. The footsteps continued approaching, when I turned round on the office stool and noticed a man. I immediately accosted the fellow, who looked rather stupid, as if he had been drinking.

He were stone cold sober of course he were acting the part

On asking him who he was and what right he had to enter the bank by the back way, he levelled a revolver at me, answered that he was Kelly, and ordered me to bail up. The fellow, who afterwards turned out to be Byrne, ordered me to deliver up what firearms I had.

Young Rankin then came in and Byrne ordered us both to come with him to Cox's Hotel. Here we met Ned Kelly who asked for Mr Tarleton. We then went back to the bank but could not find the manager in his room.

Ned Kelly then said to me, "You had better go and find him." I then searched and found the manager in his bath. I said to him, "We are stuck up; the Kellys are here, and the police are also stuck up."

Byrne then got Hart and left him in charge of the manager, who was subsequently taken over to the room where all the others were kept prisoner.

Ned Kelly then took me to the bank. He said, "You must have £10,000 in the bank here." I then handed him the teller's cash, amounting to £691.

Kelly asked if we had more money, and was answered "No." Kelly then obtained the teller's revolver, and again requested more money. He then found the treasury drawer and insisted on it being opened. One of the keys was given to him, but the manager had the second key and so he could not open it.

Byrne then wanted to break it open with a sledgehammer, but Kelly brought the manager from the Royal Mail Hotel and demanded the key. The drawer was thus opened and the sum of £1,450 was taken out and placed in a bag.

Kelly then took down a large deed box. He then expressed his intention of burning all the books in the office. The whole party then went into the Royal Mail Hotel. Daniel Kelly was in the hotel, and Ned Kelly took two of the prisoners out to the back of the hotel and burnt three or four of the bank books.

Now the bank were robbed but this were not the main purpose of my visit I come to Jerilderie determined to have 500 copies of my letter

printed this would be a great profit to Mr Gill the editor of THE JERIL-
DERIE GAZETTE.

Up to that day Gill's only importance were to make public the price
of cows in calf and so called GENERAL SERVANTS I come to elevate him
to a higher calling. HE WOULD PRINT THE TRUTH THEN MY MOTHER
WOULD BE RELEASED FROM GAOL. As soon as Ellen Kelly were reunited
with her 9 mo. old babe I would be free to follow Mary Hearn and once I
found her I would never let her out of my sight again I would walk on hot
coals or cross the River Styx if need be I would cry a go and leave the
banks & government alone.

By far my most important business in Jerilderie were to seek out
Mr Gill so once the bank were safely robbed I retired into the strongroom
to change out of my policeman's uniform. When lacing my boots I heard
men's voices in the banking chamber they was crying Who is there and so
I come to educate them. I were most amused to see a fat old pig he must
of weighed 18 stone. At his side were a long thin streak of bird manure he
had a bald head his bony chin 1/2 hid beneath a large moustache.

I am Ned Kelly said I then watched the power of fame suck both
men's eyes until they bulged identically. I raised my revolver and the fat
cove turned to run I called I would shoot him in the arse his prize possession. The fat one baulked the thin one bolted but as the telegraph lines
was cut I were not very much concerned.

I bet you is a Justice of the Peace I said to the remaining prisoner I
would lay 100 quid on it.

I have that honour Sir.

And your mate Jack Spratt is a JP as well?

No Sir.

What is he?

O that is Mr Gill the editor of our newspaper.

The only man in Jerilderie I wanted and he were now escaping up the
centre of the dusty road. I am going to shoot you I told the J.P. I were v.
angry & chased him back into the pub.

Joe Byrne then quickly trailed me out into the hot and empty street
but Gill was already vanished. Joe were eff and ess he were most annoyed
on my behalf.

Thats where the b-----d is hiding Ned.

He indicated a wide verandaed building its nose were sticking out
into the street where it did not belong. The sign said JERILDERIE

GAZETTE we went straight to it but it were a ship abandoned the skipper & sailors taken to the boats. On the bridge we found racks of type alongside a shining black patent press.

Damn it Captain we will print it ourselves.

Since Mary's departure Joe were steady as a rock he had a wooden box of yen pok which he smoked in fair to moderate quantity there were nothing he would not do to assist. Said he Don't you worry mate I'll get that teller from the bank he reckons that he's got the School Certificate.

5 minutes later he escorted Mr Lyving into my presence I ordered him to set my letter into type. He were of a tall & manly build but when he took the compositor's board from Joe his hand were shaking he peered blindly at the slugs of type and I understood he could not read them back to front no more than I could.

Don't get yourself upset I'll find the adjectival printer.

Joe Byrne departed the township on horseback he knew the importance of the document. I held my gun on Mr Lyving spelling out the required letters so he could find them faster but it were no good he were a dunce. The clock struck 4 with no more than 20 words having been completed. I were upset I confess it and I was loudly persuading the teller to increase his labour when a plain trim woman arrived at the flywire door. Behind her stood Joseph Byrne red as a perch the sweat dripping off his nose.

I got the wife said he.

Mrs Gill come through the door when she saw Mr Lyving she sucked in her breath and clucked her tongue.

I said I wished a urgent job of printing done.

She didnt hear me but begun to rouse on poor Lyving saying her husband would be in an awful temper when he heard he been fiddling with his fonts.

Mrs Gill said I.

It takes a 5 yr. apprenticeship to learn to set the forms.

Mrs Gill we need a urgent job of printing done.

Then tell him leave the fonts alone said she. If you give me the copy my husband will print it for you when he returns.

I don't have a copy its the only one.

It is called the copy even if there are no others now give it to me please for I have a cake in the oven and it will burn if I am long away. What is the name asked she picking up a receipt book off the counter.

It is Ned Kelly.

Whether she were deaf or daft I do not know but my name had no effect on her. How many pages are there Mr Kelly?

58.

Locating a stub of pencil she licked it. Received from Edward Kelly said she 58 pages of copy.

She were very diligent I will say that for her she had to know how I wished the pamphlets stitched & bound all this wrote on the receipt. She said she would require a 5 pound deposit so I give it to her and she wrote down that I had.

Now said she you must give me the copy.

I could not believe it said Joe Byrne the Captain gives her all his pages. It were bail up your money or your life so the old bitch robs Ned Kelly and he give her all his golden pages.

That were Joe to a T he never saw no good in anyone.

The Jerilderie Gazette, Feb. 16, 1879

The Kelly Gang's Departure from Jerilderie

Prior to his departure, Kelly went into McDougal's Hotel. At this time the bar was crowded with strangers. Where they came from, and where they went afterwards, no-one knows, but there cannot be any doubt that the gang was assisted here on Monday by their "sympathisers."

At the hotel Kelly shouted and paid for drinks. He said that he had a great many friends—and if anyone tried to shoot him it would be quickly revealed who was on his side. He said "Anyone could shoot me, but if a shot was fired, the people of Jerilderie would swim in their own blood."

On taking leave, Kelly removed two bottles of brandy, which he paid for. Before he mounted his horse he said he would take his own life before he would allow the police to shoot him. He added that he was not afraid to die at any time, that all that he had on his conscience was the shooting, in self-defence, of three —————— unicorns. A short time after this Kelly got on his horse, and with Hart galloped off, singing "Hurrah for the good old times of Morgan and Ben Hall!" the strangers giving a cheer.

The outlaws went on the Deniliquin Road a short distance, but suddenly wheeled around in the direction of Wunnamurra, joining Byrne and Dan Kelly about a mile from town, the last two men having charge of the money taken from the bank—which was securely fixed on a spare horse.

2 weeks later I come to collect what were due & owing Jerilderie were dark as we walked the horses along an echoing lane between a grain merchant and the GAZETTE building. If there were a police guard at the GAZETTE he had gone to bed so Joe and me stood in our saddles & climbed on the veranda roof. Twice my spurs clattered on the tin roof but Mr Gill & his Missus didnt wake until the blue flare of Joe Byrne's lucifer shone through their lids.

Its him said Mrs Gill he's in.

By then I had my gun against her husband's bony skull he werent going to run off this time.

Give me your gun Mr Gill.

Gill pulled at the sheets like reins.

No gun said he.

I retrieved the police issue whistle from the nail beside the bed. Hand over the adjectival gun I'm sure they give you one.

His bony jaw were set his eyes was bulging it were his wife who reached beneath his pillow & the husband watched with angry eyes as she delivered a Webley revolver into my care.

Gill blurted he had not printed my document.

Then you shall do it now said I and stuck the Webley in my belt.

I cannot God help me its not my fault.

Mr Kelly said the snubnosed woman here is your £5 please take it back.

Listen Missus you get your old man out of bed and tell him to print my letter or I will spread him like dung in a paddock.

O have mercy Mr Kelly we give your letter to the police.

I were stricken wordless Joe Byrne spoke in my place You are very effing brave Missus do you understand how brave you are? She shook her head watching fearfully as Joe Byrne drew the curtains shut.

Do you know how long it took our Captain to write that letter how he laboured to put the facts down right?

The government has possession of it now she cried aint that who you wrote it for Mr Kelly? It has gone where you intended it I'm sure.

Joe turned up the wick on the lantern and with the bare room now brightly illuminated there were no disguising the fury in his eyes. This were a poisoned man his bowels was set hard as black cement and Mr Gill now understood there were no shield between himself and punishment he folded his hands in his lap waiting for the worst.

Doubtless he considered himself a brave fellow to face the Kelly Gang but he were a coward to his trade as printer he were honour bound from ancient time to let the truth be told but instead he give it to its enemy. He were stupid as the government itself if he thought I could be stopped so easy.

Ned said Joe you was a fool to trust these people.

O no Sir no he werent Mrs Gill begun to cry to beg me not to kill them I told her if she read my letter she would know I were no murderer. As for her husband he were no more than a child breaking a spider web and the same web will be spun again tomorrow I could not be silenced.

I imagined myself v. calm but Joe later told me the pupils of my eyes had turned an unholy red. Goodnight said I or so I'm told then turned and walked out of the window.

That night the Kelly Gang made camp by light of rain & lightning strikes and while the boys lay quiet as dogs wrapped up in their coats I sat with my backside in a puddle my oilskin above my candle & my paper.

I begun again they could not prevent it. I were the terror of the government being brung to life in the cauldron of the night.

Conception and Construction of Armour

Brown wrapping roughly cut into 30 rough pages (4" × 8" approx.), but unlike Parcel 11 these remain unbound. Considerably torn and stained. Text mostly drafted in lead pencil but some in blue ink.

A belated celebration of his daughter's birth. Winter in the high country of the Great Divide. The lineage of the Kelly armour is proven to be modern rather than mediaeval. An account of how the armour was made.

It is one thing to toil with your pen another thing entire to do it while you fight a war. In the autumn of 1879 I tried to once more write the 58 sheets stolen from me by the Gills I tore up pages then begun again by flooded creek by light of moon and when I had made such a mess my brain were addled I returned to this splashed & speckled history you now hold in your hand.

I had boasted I were a spider they could not stop me spinning but that were in February and by the end of March I had to admit I could not repeat what I previously done. My Jerilderie Letter were lost forever.

My daughter if I make mistakes of grammar now do not think yourself grander than your father but bear in mind the circumstances of composition in the autumn of 1879 Supt Hare & Detective Ward was always on our heels also those black trackers from Queensland was murderous demons they already butchered many men before they caught the scent of us.

April passed then come the chilly rains of May we rode at night & slept by day all the while enduring such inconvenience as diarrhoea fever thrown shoes faintheartedness the flattery of spies & known informers.

The June frost were early but there were still no word from Mary Hearn and Ellen Kelly were still interred inside her sunless cell no matter what vow I took. Ned Kelly were the most feared & famous outlaw in the colony but I cd. not get my mother an inch closer to her freedom.

I had abandoned the letter to the government. I would of give up this very history too but I knew I would lose you if I stopped writing you would vanish and be swallowed by the maw. I see it now I were 1/2 mad but each day I wrote so you wd. read my words and I wrote to get you born.

By the 2nd week of June I knew you must be arrived but no word come there was only frost & silence the southerly winds brought the lonely chill off the mountains at Bright & Mount Beauty. Dan caught bronchitis I lay my pen aside at last and bound up the pages in a parcel. When I tied the ribbon a great sadness entered like a worm into my heart.

On June 20th of 1879 we come to collect our supplies as previously arranged riding down from the bush to the back of the village of Strathbogie as we followed the frosty cowpads down towards the shanty I had the sight of a young woman running across the wintry white she were dressed in a black coat a bright blue hat and as she run she waved.

Have you noticed how fair weather brings ill news? This were a beautiful bright morning with all the paddock sparkling with frost the butcher birds lined up on the fence their pretty singing filled me with foreboding.

Telegram cried my sister Kate.

I trotted to her side her nose & ears was red but her bright green eyes was shining she were not afraid. Telegram she cried again then give it to me.

It is addressed to you Kate.

Yes but its for you.

My hands was freezing the paper v. warm for it had lately been steamed open then glued back the paste were still not dry. What is it?

Read Ned read the thing.

DAM AND FILLY AT PASTURE IN SAN FRANCISCO FEED IS PLENTIFUL.

It is her?

It is indeed.

My daughter it were you. You was born. You was in a foreign land but safe at your mother's breast I roared like a bull my breath burst forth & froze in that clean Australian air. Galloping in a circle round the paddock then a figure 8 I stood astride the mare one legged my pistols in my hands and all the boys stared they thought their moody Captain were finally insane.

He is a da called Kate.

Then what a show of riding they put on to welcome you and what a knees up promptly followed even if the porridge were still bubbling in the shanty pot.

The Kellys are here. Barefoot boys ran through the frost a girl on a Timor pony set off to bring the word these was our friends. Our hard won money flowed like wheat from a broken bag.

The police was in all the hills & towns about but the country were not theirs they had not the least notion of the celebration which now spread like yellow gorse across the hills. Joe Byrne sang Rose O'Connell and his great baritone echoed out across the paddocks even the daggy sheep even the wall eyed donkey heard that you was born. Steve danced a jig in the middle of the track he were nimble & pretty as a pony. Dan were quickly drunk he wrote your name upon his hand then swore an oath to sail and bring you back to where you did belong.

These was your own own people girl I mean the good people of Greta & Moyhu & Euroa & Benalla who come drifting down the track all through the morn & afternoon & night. How was they told of your birth did the bush telegraph alert them I do not know only that they come the men the women with babies at their breast shivering kiddies with cotton coats their eyes slitted against the wind. They arrived in broken cart & drays they was of that type THE BENALLA ENSIGN named the most frightful class of people they couldnt afford to leave their cows & pigs but they done so because we was them and they was us and we had showed the world what convict blood could do. We proved there were no taint we was of true bone blood and beauty born.

Through the dusk & icy starbright night them visitors continued to rise from the earth like winter oats their cold faces was soon pressed through doorway and window and even when the grog wore out they wd. not leave they come to touch my sleeve or clap my back they hitched great logs to their horses' tails to drag them out beside the track. 6 fires these was your birthday candles shining in 200 eyes.

There was spies amongst them that we must accept even the best merino must have its dung & dags but I wd. be no more muzzled by spies than by cowards like Mr Gill. The words must be said and say them I did beneath the dazzling Milky Way the skies spilled like broken crystal across the heavens. Upon a bullock dray I stood I never planned my speech or understood its consequences and when it was done I didnt even remember what I said except the government must deliver the innocent from gaol or else I were provoked to show some colonial stratagem. I had no idea what that might be but spoke the truth it would be worse than the rust in the wheat in Victoria or the druth of a dry season to the grasshoppers of New South Wales.

The spies & fizgigs heard me they shook in their traitor's boots. 2 days later the police struck again arresting my old mate Tom Lloyd the news-papers called him my loyal lieutenant and for that lofty crime he too were remanded to Beechworth Gaol.

Having once more brung down the wrath of the traps on our supporters I thought it wisest to disappear from their districts for a short while.

Taking Aaron Sherritt for a scout we journeyed to the shepherd's hut up on the Bogong High Plains you will recall I said the walls was papered with words and pictures from THE ILLUSTRATED AUSTRALIAN NEWS they was tattered like old skin and very yellow often gnawed on by the mice.

Aaron stayed for 2 nights flattering me that I were of colossal strength and I should be the ruler of the colony etc. he had a gormless wheedling smile he were more annoying than the rats inside the walls I were v. pleased when he returned to his selection.

Soon there were heavy snow and our different scouts was sometimes unable to provision us and we was therefore reduced to eating a beloved horse but for a while we remained safe from the attentions of the world.

It were during them winter storms we begun studying the paper on the walls my LORNA DOONE was long ago ruined in the Murray so there were not a great deal else to read but the news of 18 yr. before. The previous incumbent must of been a Yankee every page he pasted were about their Civil War I were often disappointed to find the outcome of a battle eaten by a mouse. I read from the floor to 6 ft. of height then constructed a kind of hurdle so as to get up under the rafters I come across the badly damaged likeness of a ship called the Virginia the south-erners had clad it all with iron there were another ship the Monitor its bridge were like a tower forged of steel 1/2 in. thick an ironclad monster with a pair of 11 in. guns like the nostrils on a face. O that a man might smith himself into a warship of that pattern he could sail it to the gates of Beechworth & Melbourne Gaols. Blast down the doors. Smash the walls apart. No munition could injure him or tear his flesh he would be an engine like Great Cuchulainn in his war chariot they say it bristled with points of iron and narrow blades with hooks & straps & loops & cords.

Steve Hart come to read beside me on the hurdle I told him this is what them Mollys should of worn yes this were the very seamstress he needed for his dresses. He were very taken by the fancy but Joe were out of opium he lay brooding on his cot and didnt hear me.

Are you sick old man?

Joe just rubbed at his legs but when Dan joined us upon the hurdle he suddenly had a great sarcastic spasm asking how we knew we was so effing safe to stand there reading.

I reminded him there were 2 ft. of snow outside.

He swung himself out of the crib and pulled on his boots he said we was all simpletons we had no idea of the forces brung against us.

Steve made some mild remark for which Joe pulled him off the hurdle and offered to break his teeth and soon after he got on his horse and rode away.

5 days later he returned his nose bright red from the cold his beard covered with frost & icicles. He wished to speak in private but I said he could speak freely before Steve and Dan so he begun to curse me saying I were the village idiot easily gammoned by Fitzpatrick or Harry Power or any knave who smiled at me. I was betrayed he said and did not know it.

And who is the traitor?

Perhaps its me he said. His eyelids was almost shut but there were such a fury visible he looked 1/2 mad. Perhaps I have been offered my life in exchange for yours.

Who could offer that?

Superintendent Hare.

You talked to him he nabbed you?

Not directly.

Aaron is the go between?

Joe sat down heavily upon the hurdle his face seized in his hands. O Jesus Ned he moaned I'm sick he looked up at me with his bloodshot eyes the icicles & frost was melting his beard were matted like a sorry dog.

Aaron sets out with the police tomorrow night.

Sets out for where?

He swayed so far back upon the hurdle I reached out to steady him but he chopped my hand angrily aside.

For here said he.

There was silence in the hut as we all saw what had occurred.

You done the right thing mate.

O I wish to God I were not your adjectival mate he cried I don't want what lies ahead.

Dan were sitting in front of the fire with his back to us but now he stood his bright eyes shining from his dirty face this were a boy no longer but a Kelly burnt and hardened by the fates.

Shut your hole he said you are our mate we won't let you suffer.

I seen the future said Joe every adjectival night I see the things that happen in my dreams.

It aint you thats going to suffer its effing Sherritt he's a dead man now.

You wouldnt understand you mongrel he's my mate he's trying to save my life.

Shutup I snapped at them I were the Captain and it were time to cease this endless bicker. Removing a piece of paper from my britches I lay it before Joe's poisoned eyes.

What is it he asked and turned it upside down.

It is the pattern for the ironclad man.

Who is he asks Joe.

He is you said I he is a warrior he cannot die.

It were Steve Hart who pointed out that the necessary material grew plentifully upon the land it might be as easily plucked as the pippins in Mrs Danaher's orchard. He asked the riddle what strange crop is it that a poor man can harvest from the paddocks of the Greta district the fruit is steel 1/4 in. thick.

The answer were the mouldboards of the farmers' ploughs.

So while the traitor Sherritt led Hare & Nicolson to the empty hut on the Bogong High Plains our mate Joe Byrne come with us back down to Greta he were sworn loyal till the death but I seen a better future now and there were no death involved.

As soon as we was in our home district I ordered Steve & Dan bring in the crop of steel that may sound easy if you never wandered round a 1/2 ploughed paddock on a rainy night. Thus did the dragon collect its scales each morning more iron were lying in the muddy shallows of the Eleven Mile Creek.

On my mother's own selection I made the templates for the 1st ironclad suit I used fresh peeled stringybark just as women use the paper for a dress. I promised Joe he would not die and I made the 1st template to protect his sturdy body cutting the sheets of bark to allow his big arms play then I fashioned a flange to give protection at the shoulder.

This won't never work said he.

Joe were sick so I didnt mind his complaints I used a lump of charcoal like a tailor uses chalk I traced the shape of a mouldboard it would take 2 cultivators to make the chestplate 2 more for the back. For his head I made a fort like the turret of the Monitor I made a thin crack so he might observe the destruction of his enemy no gun could hurt his tortured heart.

By the time this 1st exemplar had been decided we had 7 mouldboards collected so the girls loaded 6 cwt. of charcoal onto a dray then delivered it behind Bald Hills. Here we set up our forge beside a little creek for anvil needing no more than the river gum we lay across the stream its cool water washing the timber all the while.

The British Empire has steam & factories & thousands come to toil each day carrying out its orders it cannot imagine what we colonials have in store. We required no steam only a heavy hammer a chisel a punch also 3 pr. of tongs which we easily forged ourselves. The most difficult element were the labour it required all 4 of us and a full day from dawn to dusk. It were hot as Hell & twice as thirsty our bare arms and chests was tortured by pinprick burns each time we hammered the scale flew up as thick as grasshoppers and when day's end come we was freckled with small wounds but we had achieved our 1st Monitor and while the crows squalled & the parrots looped their lacy flight across the brittle paddocks we lowered 1 cwt. of wet steel onto Joe's shoulders.

It won't work he said but I placed the helmet on his head and it fit him perfectly.

The 3 of us stood back in silent veneration as the Soldier of Future Time turned his back to walk with steady tread there were a slight squeak from the cockplate swinging from its wires did ever such machine of war tread upon the earth before? It marched slowly & silently to the rise a mighty black shadow painted against the pale evening sky we seen its inky arm rise & point directly at his head.

There were a powder flash a loud retort the turret jolted sideways by the blow. Joe Byrne had shot himself in the head he fell onto his knees and as we run up the hill his hands lifted the helmet and in the last cold light I could see his eyes.

Shutup he said.

I stood before him speechless.

Shutup he said shutup it works I grant you.

Joe were a very tough nut but not the only one next day I ordered Maggie and Kate to bring additional recruits. The British Empire had supplied me with no shortage of candidates these was men who had had their leases denied for no other crime than being our friends men forced to plant wheat then ruined by the rust men mangled upon the triangle of Van Diemen's Land men with sons in gaol men who witnessed their hard won land taken up by squatters men perjured against and falsely gaoled men weary of constant impounding on & on each day without relent. Maggie & Kate led these troops to secret places and once they had swore their oath upon my Bible we showed them why they need no longer tremble before the law. We wasnt men with pikes no more and would not repeat the tragedies of Vinegar Hill or the Eureka Stockade.

Throughout the spring & summer certain farmers did secretly construct their ironclads in the quiet gullies of the North East you might hear the lyre bird imitating the ching ching ching of the hammer striking blows. Them suits was made and buried in the soil awaiting resurrection.

I wished only to be a citizen I had tried to speak but the mongrels stole my tongue when I asked for justice they give me none. In the autumn of 1880 I were forced to compose the following coffin letter 7 of us sat round a rough table we manufactured 60 copies which Maggie and Kate mailed to farmers and others including Aaron Sherritt.

ORDER EFFECTIVE NORTH EASTERN VICTORIA IN THE TERRITORY BORDERED BY THE MURRAY RIVER IN THE NORTH ALBURY BRIGHT MOUNT BUFFALO AND MANSFIELD TO THE EAST THE GREAT DIVIDING RANGE TO THE SOUTH. WESTERN BOUNDARY MADE BY THE ONE JOINING ECHUCA AND SEYMOUR.

Any person residing in the above territory who aids or harbours or assists the police in any way whatever or employs any person whom they know to be a detective or cad also those who would be so depraved as to take blood money will be outlawed and declared unfit to be allowed human burial. Their property will be either consumed or confiscated and them and all belonging to them exterminated off the face of the earth. The enemy I cannot catch myself I will give a payable reward for. I wish them men who joined the Stock Protection Society to withdraw their money and give as much more to the widows and orphans and poor of Greta district where I spent and will spend again many a happy day fearless free and bold.

I give fair warning to all those who has reason to fear me to sell out and give £10 out of every £100 towards the widow and orphan fund and do not attempt to reside in Victoria but as short a time as possible after reading this notice depart forever. Neglect this and abide by the consequences which shall be worse than the rust in the wheat in Victoria or the druth of a dry season to the grasshoppers of New South Wales.

I DO NOT WISH TO GIVE THE ORDER FULL FORCE WITHOUT GIVING TIMELY WARNING BUT I AM A WIDOW'S SON OUTLAWED AND MUST BE OBEYED.

Edward Kelly

We all assisted in making fair copies of the letters but it were only Steve who drew each coffin very particular it were a well honed skill of his. Sometimes he added a picture of a bleeding knife sometimes a skull & skeleton.

Joe Byrne however would have none of these things added to Aaron Sherritt's letter he took it away by himself and I cannot know what he added exactly but when he were finished I seen he covered the whole other side he had a lovely hand he were famous for it even as a child. Joe & Aaron was friends from earliest time they sat side by side in desks at the Woolshed School they fought Chinamen together they duffed cattle they was locked in cells they lain together by the campfire like dogs under the vast & ancient sky. I observed how carefully he blotted the words and how finely he addressed the envelope but never read them words and only after it were posted did I get any inkling of the threat contained therein.

Aaron will leave now said Joe you mark my words.

O I don't think so.

O yairs he aint stupid I have told him we will be compelled to kill him if he don't depart.

Several weeks passed then Dan come back into camp one night he announced he had intelligence that Aaron were sleeping in the caves above Joe's mother's hut he were sharing quarters with a party of police.

Well I'll be damned said Joe he must not of received my letter.

O he cannot shutup about your letter everyone in the Woolshed Valley can recite it word for word.

Then why aint he departed?

When Dan answered I am sure he spoke the truth it is not the kind of thing he would make up.

Aaron says he plans to shoot you and eff you before your body has grown cold.

Then he is a dead man said Joe Byrne he has just decided.

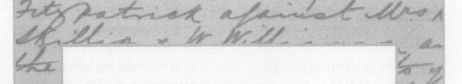

PARCEL 13

His Life at
26 Years of Age

7 pages (12" × 14" approx.) all being the reverse side of advertising fliers for a horse auction held by Geo. Fisher & Sons, Wangaratta, on 7 May 1880. Acidic paper now in very fragile condition. Entirely in lead pencil, the small hand betraying some urgency in composition, but this parcel is most remarkable for the two roughly excised pages of *Henry V* attached by rusty pins to pages 6 and 7.

A frank account of the murder of Aaron Sherritt and Kelly's correct assumption that the police would respond post haste. Details concerning the occupation of Mrs Jones' hotel at Glenrowan and the kidnapping of the schoolteacher Curnow. On page 7 the manuscript is abruptly terminated.

I did not wish Aaron Sherritt's death though he were a traitor he would of seen me hanged as soon as look at me. For Joe Byrne it were a different matter the root were deep & violent I cd. no more touch it than his beating heart.

On a winter's night the moon were full a red haired German by the name Anton Wick come walking home a 1/2 mi. from Sherritt's hut he were apprehended by 2 large men they was Joe Byrne & Dan Kelly their chests much increased in girth by the heavy armour hidden underneath their oilskin coats. Wick knew Joe all his life but he were of alarming size now his face were painted black he had become a machine of war. Dan Kelly put the bracelet on Wick ordering him to come knock on Sherritt's door.

Wick warned there was police inside the hut.

We do not give an eff were the reply.

Wick stumbled along the track his hands behind his back Joe Byrne said nothing Dan knocked upon the door.

Its Wick open up.

What do you want?

I am lost. This were a weak excuse as Wick lived so close he could of seen his hut from Aaron's roof.

You silly mongrel. Aaron Sherritt come into the night and saw the twin holes of the shotgun his oldest friend were holding in his hand.

Who else is there he called and while them brave policemen cowered beneath the bed Aaron heard the small cry issue from Joe's lips it was very quiet an exhalation the noise a boy will make when caned upon the hand. It were almost the last thing he heard.

. . .

Moonlight shone on the centaurs Dan Kelly & Joe Byrne their iron helmets were strapped to their saddles as they galloped down the centre of the public road straight through the Beechworth Chinese Camp where Joe purchased a little of what he fancied it looked like nothing more than waxy brown plum jam.

The same cold moonlight shone in the bush behind Glenrowan where me & Steve Hart was helping each other into our ironclad suits it also shone in Marvellous Melbourne flooding through the high window of my mother's cell.

At Domain Road the bare branches of the English trees made shadows thin as handwriting upon the Commissioner's walls. This historic night were so bright even if Commissioner Standish had extinguished every lamp nothing could escape my intelligence he were my creature now I knew his heathen rug his billiards table I knew the smell & appearance of his friends and when the Constable come knocking on the Commissioner's door I did not have to be there to know what the message said.

The Kellys have struck they murdered Aaron Sherritt our informer.

The Commissioner thought he were the servant of Her Majesty the Queen but he were my puppet on a string he ordered the Special Train as I desired he summoned the black trackers and called for Hare & Nicolson who thought themselves famous as the capturers of Harry Power they never imagined they would be captives in a drama devised by me.

At about the hour the police horses was brought from Richmond Depot to the railway yards me & Steve Hart was attending to our stratagem at the township of Glenrowan we was rousing the plate layers James Reardon & Dennis Sullivan from their tents beside the line.

I informed them that through abuse & tyranny the police had forfeited the right to the land also therefore the rails upon it. We escorted them along the track and through the Gap and where the rail curved we ordered them to remove 2 lengths of rail which they done with great reluctance. The rails was thrown down the steep embankment with 9 red gum sleepers still attached.

Last night I seen my dear old mother in a dream who knows how such things happen her cell were so clear I could of drawn a map there was 2 grey prison blankets folded neatly on the shelf a Bible and prayer book on a rickety white table. Mother sat waiting for me on her crib her palliasse were folded as required.

You come for me she said yes I said they are forced to give you up. I seen how she had suffered this last year her eyes had retreated her lips was eaten from within her hands so large & knotted you could see her nerves like baling twine beneath her glassy skin. I see Mr Irving finally made you the monitor she smiled. Looking down at myself I seen the ink on my hands & up my arms it were bleeding down my shirt & moleskins.

I spilled it I said tho I did not remember having done so I were surprised that I must be back at Avenel Common School. You put that sash on she said do you hear me. It were 7 ft. long & fringed with gold I had nothing to be ashamed of Mother and me walked side by side along the catwalk I looked down to the ground floor where there were much smoke and destruction many policemen was lying dead.

The front gate of Melbourne Gaol were shattered and in its opening were that ironclad Monitor its 11 in. gun pointing up the nave of the prison but the sea were lapping across my boots all Russell Street were washed away.

Beside the railway line at Glenrowan is a little pub run by Mrs Jones it is in her best room where I now sit on the eve of battle. Our ironclads is stacked against the wall 3 of them in burnished metal the 4th is Steve Hart's painted with black & orange flowers in a pattern of his own invention. The walls are whitewashed hessian the ceiling calico the table I write on is made from cedar it wd. suit Napoleon himself.

Beyond a thin partition is my hostages most of them will be revealed tomorrow as my volunteers. There is another category of prisoner I refer to Police Constable Bracken & Stationmaster Stanistreet they have that self righteous look that is common in men like warders who will never be fined or imprisoned or dismissed from their positions in the colony. I were at the railway crossing on Saturday afternoon when a 3rd hostage come towards me. He didnt know yet he were a hostage but he were identifiable as such from a great distance with his darting eyes and his beard so soft & blonde it wd. be better on the head of a doll.

And you must be the schoolmaster said I when he drew his buggy up beside me at the railway gates.

How did you know?

O I wd. recognise you anywhere I thought you are that prim & superior fellow my mother must stand before in her threadbare dress she must beg to have me educated.

He knew me without introduction I could see he were fascinated to look so close into my eyes. He descended willingly from his sulky he were a cripple he walked with his heel high when he seen me looking at his one thick boot he held my gaze.

My name is Curnow said he his pale blue eyes was shining like a girl's.

In his left hand he were carrying a thick book I took it from him and seen it were the plays of Shakespeare.

Do you object to a man reading he asked.

O I sometimes read a book myself said I then asked him were this one any good.

O yes he laughed as if I wd. never know what of I spoke I were an oaf in muddy boots tracking across some oriental rug. O yes it is very good I cd. of slapped him for his insolence instead I ordered Dan escort him into custody at Mrs Jones' hotel.

Later I were back here in my quarters writing as quickly as I cd. there were a knock upon the door and lo it were the little cripple with his book I told him he might enter. His big bright eyes looked everywhere about him taking in the ironclads but it were my inkwell that he lingered on the most.

I see I interrupt you at your labours.

His face were so strange & proud his head too large upon his narrow shoulders where it wobbled side to side as though all his mighty thoughts was a weight too great to carry.

I asked which play he were reading.

It is about an English King he said but as he spoke he looked at all my papers spread across the desk and he were almost cross eyed with curiosity as if he seen a dog standing on his hind legs and talking.

Mr Kelly you give the appearance of an author.

I did not answer it werent his business.

He craned his neck towards me. Is it a history you write?

I said THE ARGUS called me a clever ignoramus I were sure a schoolteacher would hold the same opinion.

Mr Kelly said he there is a novel called LORNA DOONE I don't suppose you know it.

The name jolted me back to the Killawarra sawmill and that gift from Joe Byrne. Shutup and listen he had said.

I told the teacher I read it twice and wd. of read it a 3rd time but my copy turned to mush when we crossed the Ovens River.

I read a lot about you Mr Kelly but I never heard you was a scholar. Let me remind you how LORNA DOONE sets out. Then the strange little cove balanced himself on his crippled crooked legs and held his book of Shakespeare across his heart and closed his eyes and from his great head he dragged out the following words of R.D. Blackmore. AND THEY WHAT LIGHT upon this book should bear in mind not only that I write to clear our parish from ill fame but also that I am nothing more than a plain unlettered man not read in foreign languages as a gentleman might be nor gifted with long words save what I have won from the Bible or master William Shakespeare whom in the face of common opinion I do value highly.

Curnow opened his eyes and smiled at me.

IN SHORT he quoted I am an ignoramus but pretty well for a yeoman.

Then speaking in a more normal voice he said Mr Kelly it is no bad thing to be an ignoramus for if Mr Blackmore is an ignoramus then you and I wd. wish to be one too. And at this the fellow folded his big white hands in front of him and shifted the weight of his head to the other side of his shoulder.

Let me read your history Mr Kelly he begged.

It is too rough.

It is history Mr Kelly it should always be a little rough that way we know it is the truth. He continued in this vein and finally I relented of a page. It were many a long year since I stood before a schoolteacher & even tho I had 3 guns stuck in my belt & had the power to take away his life it were v. queer. He read the page then lay it gently upon the table and I waited in some temper for his judgment.

It is very damned good said he.

It is rough I know.

It is most bracing & engaging given the smallest of improvements it could be made into something no Professor would ever think to criticise.

I said I knew the fault were with the parsing.

Parsing pah cried he it is a simple matter if you let me assist.

We do not have the time mate.

It would take no time Mr Kelly no time at all.

There's 500 adjectival pages.

I could do it in a night said he if I were in my house with my books about me.

Then Joe Byrne entered & ordered the teacher to depart Joe asked what the eff I were doing talking to that fizgig for he had taken a fierce set against him from the start.

O he is for us anyway he is a cripple he can't do us no harm.

Jesus Ned aint you the one who give his copy to that cow in Jerilderie said he & in the lantern light I seen his awful eyes.

You need another pipe old man?

No and your brother is drinking too much already he said everyone is adjectival boozing what will happen if the train comes now? Its too late I can feel something has gone wrong.

Another knock upon the door it were that schoolteacher once more he put his finger to his lip & hopped towards me.

Situation you should know Mr Kelly he whispered.

Eff off you spy said Joe thrusting his Webley in his soft white neck.

The teacher turned his velvety eyes upon me I ordered Joe withdraw his weapon then Curnow held a finger to his pretty lips. Mr Stanistreet has a gun. I fear he will use it on you.

Thus did the strange little insect prove his friendship tho Joe Byrne's hard & suspicious cast of mind werent bending. I said eff off he said and pushed our informant out into the bar returning alone in a moment with a new pistol in his hand. So were the stationmaster's Colt confiscated but Joe give the teacher no credit. He told me for my information that his ironclad were no good it already cut & blistered him upon the horse he were damned if he wd. fight in it for he couldnt see to shoot straight.

Then so help me God poor old Joe begun to weep he said it were wrong to murder he wd. go to Hell for certain.

Suddenly I noticed it were v. quiet out in the bar they was listening. Tapping my finger to my lip I whispered the hostages should be encouraged to perform some entertainments.

Joe blew his nose and turned away. As I walked out into the bar he were staring out the window his own face looked back at him its black eyes full of dark & fearful imaginings.

As Mr Zinke wd. say time is of the essence daughter please excuse this scrawl.

The hop legged teacher call'd I shd. let him visit his home to fetch his special shoes he cd. not dance w/out them.

I joked that I wd. never let him escape so easy.

O I do not wish to miss this night he sd. then he put down his book & come to sit beside me. He were handsome & repulsive I cd. not take my eyes off him.

He—most people think the police have it coming to them.

Me—you are a v. uncommon schoolteacher Mr Curnow.

He—O I'm sure you know my opinions are quite usual in the colony.

I let him off the dancing but once he propped his twisted self against the bar I order'd all shd. sing a song including himself.

1st Mrs Jones' little boy sang Colleen Das Cruitha Na Mo & then Steve sang The Rising of the Moon & then the voices join'd 1 × 1 even our volunteers on the hills cd. hear them as they watch'd the shining railway line.

Next I commanded the teacher he must stand & sing a song to class. He were such a proud strange creature every eye went to him he hobbled to the centre of the room standing with his hip jutted queerly out to hold his big book steady.

He—I have no song.

The people—sing sing.

He—but here is a little something suitable for the occasion.

To my horror he ripped 2 pages from his lovely book & then declaimed from them aloud he were a little milksop but when he recited he were reveal'd to be pure currency.

Here is the very words he spoke I pin them to the page as tore directly from his book.

he which hath no stomach to this fight,
Let him depart; his passport shall be made,
And crowns for convoy put into his purse.
We would not die in that man's company
That fears his fellowship to die with us.
This day is called the feast of Crispian:
He that outlives this day, and comes safe home,
Will stand a' tiptoe when this day is named,
And rouse him at the name of Crispian.
He that shall see this day, and live old age,
Will yearly on the vigil feast his neighbours,
And say, "Tomorrow is Saint Crispian."
Then will he strip his sleeve and show his scars,

And say, "These wounds I had on Crispin's day."
Old men forget: yet all shall be forgot,
But he'll remember with advantages
What feats he did that day. Then shall our names,
Familiar in his mouth as household words,
Harry the King, Bedford and Exeter,
Warwick and Talbot, Salisbury and Gloucester,
Be in their flowing cups freshly remembered.

I do not know where that deep voice came from for the teacher's normal manner were light as a reed bt. now he read to us his eyes afire his face that of a soldier by my side so did the priests rise up beside the common people in times of yore.

Those what listened sat on floor or table they wasnt well schooled it werent their fault but many cd. not write their names. Their clothes was worn the smell of the pigpen & the cow yd. was both present but their eyes burn'd with the necessary fire.

Constable Bracken were scowling but amongst the other faces there were astonishment for even if the meaning were not clear they cd. see a man of learning might compare us to a King & when in the middle of the poem Dan & Joe come back in from the night then all eyes went reverently to those armour'd men. Them boys was noble of true Australian coin.

This story shall the good man teach his son;
And Crispin Crispian shall ne'er go by,
From this day to the ending of the world,
But we in it shall be remembered;
We few, we happy few, we band of brothers;
For he today that sheds his blood with me
Shall be my brother; be he ne'er so vile,
This day shall gentle his condition:
And gentlemen in England, now a-bed,
Shall think themselves accursed they were not here,
And hold their manhoods cheap whiles any speaks
That fought with us upon St Crispin's day.

When he finish'd there were a moment of silence & then Mrs Jones let out a great hooray & all the men was clapping & whistling & the little cripple were alight I pick'd him up & sat him on the bar he give me the 2 pages from his book.

He—a souvenir of battle.

Me—but you will do wt. you promised?

He—regarding your history? O I couldnt do it here Mr Kelly. I wd. need to take it to my house. I wd. need my books about me.

He waits. No time

The Siege at Glenrowan

THOMAS CURNOW *had entered the dragon's lair, the benighted heart of everything rank and ignorant. He had danced with the devil himself and he had flattered him and out-witted him as successfully as the hero of any fairy tale, and now he carried the proof, the trophy, the rank untidy nest of paper beneath his arm. These stained "manuscripts" were disgusting to his touch and his very skin shrank from their conceit and ignorance and yet he was a man already triumphant. He had ripped out the creature's bloody heart and he would damn him now to hell.*

He hurried towards his buggy. His legs would not work, they had never worked. He could not dance or run. He could only hop and limp and when he did so quickly, like this, it sent shooting pains up into his thighs and buttocks. He hurried through the cold clear eucalyptus night and as he came around the south east corner of Mrs Jones' hotel he overheard his character discussed.

That teacher is a liar, he heard Joe Byrne cry. —He is a f-----g fizgig. Let me pink the b----r, Ned.

Shut-up, said Dan. I hear a whistle.

Shut-up, said Steve Hart. It's coming.

Dear God, let not the train come yet. Curnow dare not hurry and therefore took his horse and buggy home at a slow and easy pace. There were mobs of men sitting amongst the dark trees, he felt them watch him, felt their dull and resentful unlettered eyes. Dear God, let them not murder him.

At his cottage behind the schoolhouse he tapped on the door but his wife would not withdraw the bolt.

For God's sake, woman, let me in. It's me, your husband.

Once she had admitted him she did not wish to let him go. She clung to him and wept.

No, no, Thomas, they will kill you.

Good Lord, Jean, there are hundreds of policemen on their way to death.

What will happen to me? she cried.

It was then he heard the whistle of the train, and he thrust the rat's nest of papers into her arms. He snatched up a candle and his wife's red scarf.

He ran as best he could, down the gully beside the schoolhouse, then up the embankment to the railway line which had always been there waiting for him. And there it was, the head-lamp of the locomotive, the rails gleaming like destiny itself.

The entire colony was cowed by Ned Kelly but Thomas Curnow lit the candle, and while the frail flame flickered in the hostile air he held the red scarf in front of it and he stood in plain clear view of whomever would take his life.

The locomotive loomed, all steam and steel, and as the brakes screamed and the steam gushed he screwed up his face waiting for the bullet in his spine.

What is it? called the guard.

The Kellys, he cried.

And he had done it. It was history now. In a few minutes the train would return to the station and disgorge its living cargo of thirty men and twenty horses. He had saved them all. As he hurried home to his cottage the noise at the station was terrific, men shouting, horses rearing and plunging from the vans. Thomas Curnow heard them as he knocked urgently on his cottage door and was admitted by his tearful wife.

. . .

In the confined space of Mrs Jones' best room the members of the Kelly Gang now donned their armour, clanging chests, bumping heads, gouging Mrs Jones' cedar table as they searched for carbines, pistols, ammunition. Of the so-called hostages only one took this easy opportunity to escape and by the time Ned Kelly came back into the bar to extinguish the lanterns and douse the blazing fire, the long-bodied short-legged Constable Bracken was sprinting through the bush. He fell down the ditch and scrambled up the other side, then he hurdled the fence which separated the shanty from the railway line.

Bracken rushed out of the darkness. —The Kellys, they're here.

He was bug-eyed, unshaven, out of breath. He pushed his way onto the crowded chaotic platform but the Melbourne police did not know him, and they were occupied with unloading fretful horses. No-one would pay him any attention.

Meanwhile Ned Kelly stumbled through a different crowd, inside the darkened shanty. He found the hallway, then the skillion. He emerged into the night air, walking with the slow dream-like gait which was the necessary consequence of the one hundred and twelve pounds of armour hidden beneath his long oilskin coat. His grey mare was waiting and he mounted with some very considerable difficulty and then ambled his horse two hundred yards down the track towards Glenrowan station. The police paid the curious horseman no more attention than they paid to Bracken, whose plaintive voice could be heard amidst the confusion of men and horses.

Where is the senior officer? Where is he?

Ned waited until Bracken had finally found Superintendent Hare, then he turned back to the shanty.

. . .

As the police climbed the fence between the hotel and the railway line, three ironclad men awaited them in the dark shadow of the front veranda. The tallest of them, Joe Byrne, raised his rifle.

This f-----g armour. I cannot b----y sight my rifle.

Shut-up, they'll hear you.

The police hurried through the open bushland not bothering to take cover. At the point where Superintendent Hare finally paused, there was nothing separating the two parties but a small revolving iron gate. They were thirty yards apart.

Where is Ned? Dan Kelly whispered.

I'm here, boys. The older Kelly took up his place in the centre of the veranda and raised his Colt revolving rifle.

And here's your grandmother with her big iron nose. So saying, he fired.

Immediately, Hare fell.

Good gracious! he cried. I am hit the very first shot!

And then the cold night was suddenly ablaze with gunfire. The gang held back in the deep shadow of the veranda, all except Ned Kelly, who stepped out into the moonlight and took steady aim.

Fire away, you b----y dogs. You can't hurt us.

No sooner had he said this than a Martini-Henry bullet smashed through his left arm. He grunted, turned, and then he felt the second shot rip like a saw-blade through his foot. He turned and retreated to the hotel.

. . .

In the first minute the police fired sixty bullets and in the following half hour they held their fire for no man or woman, child or outlaw, and when they did finally relent for a moment the night air was rent with a high dreadful shrieking. They had shot the boy who had sung "Colleen das cruitha na mo."

Thomas Curnow, sitting at his desk four hundred yards away, put his hands across his ears.

What is that? his wife asked.

Nothing, nothing, go to bed.

Oh dear God, what have you done? Those poor hostages.

They're not hostages, said Curnow, they are there because they're with the Kellys. They're as bad as bandits.

But now she was the one trying to go out the door, already tying the red scarf around her neck.

It's a child, she said. Are they shooting children now?

Thomas Curnow limped across the room, and angrily pulling the scarf away from her, he burned her neck and she cried out with pain.

God help you, girl, don't you see, everyone is for the Kellys? You were born here, Jean. Have you no idea what class of person you are dealing with?

You coward, she cried. They're shooting children.

Me a coward? Oh dear Lord, who have I married? A coward is it? Then who saved those policemen while you were weeping in your bed? Go to your room.

What's that?

Shut the curtain, it is a Chinese rocket. It is some kind of signal from the Kellys. You had better pray there are enough police to win the day.

Another fusillade echoed round the valley and she came to him and took his hands.

Oh Tom, what have you done?

What I have done, he said, is become a hero.

. . .

For a day and night the shanty had been a lively jolly place, but it was not suitable as a fortress. The outer walls were one board thick, the inner ones no more than paper and hessian, so now the hotel offered no more protection than a Sunday dress. The bullets penetrated so easily and so often that those inside could do no more than lie upon the floor and pray.

When Ned Kelly limped back inside it was pitch black and the air was sour with cold wet smoke. The air was rent with the screams of young Jack Jones. Hell itself could not be worse.

Ned, stop them. They're murdering us!

I will.

He walked once more to the front door and was greeted with twenty rounds.

I'm hit, cried a voice in the back room. God save us all.

Jack Jones shrieked, the bullet had broken his hip bone and penetrated deep into his gut. A man pushed forward in the dark, the howling boy in his arms.

Get out, Kelly, damn you, let me through.

Ned Kelly stepped aside.

It was the labourer, McHugh, and he stood in the open door holding a white handkerchief in his left hand while he grasped the injured child in his right.

Don't fire, you mongrels, it's a child.

Help me, cried Jack Jones.

The place is full of women and children! Stop firing!

There was one more shot but then silence, and McHugh walked out the door. Mrs Jones followed. Immediately two shots rang out and she slumped to her knees, her hand to her head.

I'm shot! she cried.

But it was only a graze, and she was able to crawl back along the floor and lie behind her bar and there she remained, whimpering for her child.

No-one spoke to Ned Kelly in this time but he did not need to have his responsibility pointed out. He could not protect these people against the police, nor could he protect himself. It seemed there was no machine ever invented that could protect these people from the forces God had placed upon the earth.

Is that you, Ned? cried a voice from the hallway.

Is that you, Joe? Come here.

Come here be damned. What are you doing there?

Come here and load my rifle. I'm cooked.

So am I. Dear God, I think my leg is broken.

As Ned walked towards the voice he could feel the blood pooling in his boot.

Leg be damned, Joe, you've got the use of your arms. Come with me and load my rifle, come on, load for me! I'll pink the b———rs! Hare is finished. We'll soon finish the rest.

We've done these poor b———rs an awful harm.

Well, we ain't lost yet.

Joe Byrne did not answer.

Where are you? Ned began to kneel and then his leg collapsed, he fell heavily. Immediately he began to crawl forward, scraping the heavy steel cock-plate noisily along the floor. —Here, load my rifle. Joe?

With his good right hand he found Joe Byrne's hand but it was limp and bloody as a freshly skinned beast.

Joe?

He pulled himself closer and propped himself against the wall. In the darkness he located his friend's nose and mouth, then placed his hand across them. The beard was soft and wet, the lips were warm against the palm but all that fretful breath was still.

Oh Joe, I'm so sorry, old man.

Another hail of bullets ripped through the dark hotel, splintering wood and breaking glass and causing the hostages to raise their voices in shouts of anger.

Shoot them, Ned. Stop the b———rs!

I will, I will.

He wrenched himself violently to his feet and stumbled back along the hallway into the bar.

Dan? Steve?

He opened the door to the front room where he had, a short time before, confidently laboured on his history. At that time he would see his child again. At that time he would release his mother. At that time these people would occupy their own land without fear or favour, but now the world was a filthy mire and mess.

Dan?

They're gone, said a voice in the darkness.

Not shot?

Your brother and his mate have left us. You must stop them cops, mate, you have to stop them now for they are murdering us.

I will.

He stumbled out the back door and into the early dawn.

Intending to draw the police fire onto himself, he mounted his horse, although with considerable difficulty. As he rode down the police flank, he heard gunfire from the front veranda. He twisted painfully in the saddle and then he realised Dan had not left at all. He and Steve Hart were standing side by side on the veranda of the shanty blazing wildly at their foes.

He had no strength. His left arm was useless. He began to swing down out of the stirrup but fell hard onto the ground. He walked painfully towards his brother, no longer deigning to take cover or hide himself. He hammered the butt of his revolver against his chest to let Dan hear him coming to the rescue.

I am the b ----y Monitor, my boys.

But he was not the Monitor, he was a man of skin and shattered bone with blood squelching in his boot. The Martini-Henry bullets slammed against him and he was jolted and jarred, his head slammed sideways, yet he would not stop.

You shoot children, you b ----y dogs. You can't shoot me.

He fired, but he could not see to aim. He roared and raised his revolver and struck it against his chest, the blows ringing with the distinctiveness of a blacksmith's hammer in the morning air.

Dan! Come with me, Dan. I am the b ----y Monitor.

But between him and Dan there was a small round policeman in a tweed hat standing quietly beside a tree. It was plump little toads like him who had fed off the Kellys for ever. He might as well have been Hall or Flood or Fitzpatrick, they had become the same.

Ned fired. Then the man dropped on one knee, raised his rifle and fired two shots in quick succession.

Ned never heard the rifle fire but the first blow hit his right leg and he was on the ground before he felt the deeper sharper pain of the second hit.

My legs, you mongrel!

And then they were on him like a pack of dingoes. They ripped him, kicked him, cried that they would shoot him dead, and even while their boots thudded on his armoured chest he saw his little brother standing on the veranda. He was a Kelly, he would never run.

. . .

Ned Kelly would be spared the sight of Dan's empty useless armour which was raked from the ashes of Jones Hotel on Monday afternoon. It was his sis-

ters, Kate and Maggie, who would be left to fight the police for possession of the two black and bubbled bodies which had been found lying side by side in the burnt-out hotel.

"The scene at Greta, when the charred remains of Hart and Dan Kelly were carried by their friends, was perfectly indescribable," reported The Benalla Ensign. "The people seemed to flock from the gum trees. They were some of the worst-looking people that I ever saw in all my life."

. . .

Thomas Curnow, meanwhile, was escorted by six policemen directly from his cottage to the Special Train and from there he was taken to Melbourne, where government protection was provided him and his wife for four more months. This was curious treatment for a hero, and he was called a hero more than once, although less frequently and less enthusiastically than he might have reasonably expected.

If this lack of lasting recognition disappointed him, he never revealed it directly, although the continuing, ever-growing adoration of the Kelly Gang could always engage his passions.

What is it about we Australians, eh? he demanded. What is wrong with us? Do we not have a Jefferson? A Disraeli? Might not we find someone better to admire than a horse-thief and a murderer? Must we always make such an embarrassing spectacle of ourselves?

In private, his relationship with Ned Kelly was more complicated, and the souvenir he carried from Glenrowan seems to have made its own private demands upon his sympathy. The evidence provided by the manuscript suggests that in the years after the Siege of Glenrowan he continued to labour obsessively over the construction of the dead man's sentences, and it was he who made those small grey pencil marks with which the original manuscript is decorated.

12 page pamphlet in the collection of the Mitchell Library, Sydney. Contains elements in common with the handwritten account in the Melbourne Library (V.L. 10453). The author identified solely by the initials S.C. Printer: Thomas Warriner & Sons, Melbourne, 1955, the year following Thomas Curnow's death.

Death of Edward Kelly

COLONEL REDE, *the Sheriff for the Central Bailiwick, was attended by Mr Ellis, the Under-Sheriff, and presented himself at the door of the condemned cell punctually at 10 o'clock to demand the body of Edward Kelly in order to carry out the awful sentence of death. Mr. Castieau, the Governor of Melbourne Gaol, had some little time previously visited the prisoner, and seen his irons knocked off; and the necessary warrant being presented by the Sheriff, he tapped at the door, and the prisoner was made acquainted with the fearful fact that his last hour had arrived. All this time Upjohn, the hangman, who was officiating in this horrible capacity for the first time, had remained unseen; but upon the door of Kelly's cell being opened, the signal was given and he emerged from the condemned cell opposite, now occupied by his first victim. He stepped across the scaffold quietly and, as he did so, quietly turned his head and looked down upon the spectators, revealing a fearfully repulsive countenance.*

The hangman is an old man about 70 years of age, but broad-shouldered and burly. As he was serving a sentence when he volunteered for this dreadful office, and as that sentence is still unexpired, he is closely shaved and cropped, and wears the prison dress. Thick bristles of a pure white stick up all over his crown and provide him a ghastly appearance. He has heavy features altogether, the nose perhaps being the most striking and ugly.

As this was Upjohn's first attempt at hanging, Dr Barker was present alongside the drop, to see that the knot was placed in the right position. Upjohn disappeared into the condemned cell, and proceeded to pinion Kelly with a strong broad leather belt. The prisoner, however, remarked, "You need not pinion me," but was, of course, told that it was indispensable.

Preceded by the crucifix, which was held up before him by the officiating priests, Kelly was then led onto the platform. He had not been shaved or cropped, but was in prison clothes. He seemed calm and collected, but paler than usual, although this effect might have been produced by the white cap placed over his head, but not yet drawn down over his face. As he stepped on the drop, he remarked in a low tone, "Such is life."

The hangman then proceeded to adjust the rope, the Deans in the meantime reading the prayer proper to the Catholic Church on such occasions. The prisoner winced slightly at the first touch of the rope, but quickly recovered himself and moved his head in order to facilitate the work of Upjohn in fixing the knot properly. No sooner was the knot fixed than, without the prisoner being afforded a chance of saying anything more, the signal was given; and the hangman, pulling down the cap, stepped back and, withdrawing the bolt, had done his work.

At the same instant, the mortal remains of Ned Kelly were swinging some eight feet below where he had been previously standing. At first it appeared as if death had been instantaneous, for there was for a second or two only the usual shudder that passes through the frame of hanged men; but then the legs were drawn up for some distance, and then fell suddenly again. This movement was repeated several times, but finally all motion ceased, and at the end of four minutes all was over, and Edward Kelly had gone to a higher tribunal to answer for his faults and crimes. The body was allowed to remain hanging the usual time, and the formal inquest was afterwards held. The outlaw had requested that his mother might be released from Melbourne Gaol and his body handed over for burial in consecrated ground. Neither of these requests were granted, and the remains were buried within the precincts of the gaol.

Acknowledgments

I wish to thank Paul Priday and Sam Carey, who accompanied me on my initial research trip to North Eastern Victoria; Laurie Muller and Richard Leplastrier, who were my companions and instructors on a later visit; and Esmai and Ken Wortman whose trust in me I have attempted to honour in these pages.

I owe a particular debt to these books: John McQuilton's *The Kelly Outbreak,* Kevin Passey and Gary Dean's *Harry Power: Tutor of Ned Kelly,* Henry Glassie's *Irish Folktales,* Keith McMenomy's *Ned Kelly: The Authentic Illustrated Story* and Ian Jones' *Ned Kelly: A Short Life.* Of these, it is Ian Jones I am most particularly obliged to. It was to his works I turned, almost daily, when I was lost or bewildered or simply forgetful of the facts.

Many other people were helpful. Peter Smalley, Kevin Rapley, Diane Gardiner, Roland Martyn, Roy Foster and Evan Boland all led me towards information that had previously eluded me. Joe Crowley acted as my research assistant in Australia. Terry O'Hanlon applied a stern eye to matters agricultural. Sharon Olds and David Williamson read late drafts of the manuscript and contributed useful and constructive criticism.

I laboured for four exhilarating weeks in collaboration with my editor Gary Fisketjon, whose green spiderweb annotations (delivered daily by messenger from midtown Manhattan, or Franklin, Tennessee, or Adelaide, South Australia) sometimes precipitated a storm of silent debate but always, day after day, page after page, resulted in a tighter, truer, better book. Who says there are no great editors anymore?

Finally, my greatest debt is to my wife, Alison Summers, whose clear literary intelligence and flawless dramatic instinct illuminated and clarified a work that at times threatened to swamp and drown me.

A Note on the Type

This book was set in Minion, a typeface produced by the Adobe Corporation specifically for the Macintosh personal computer and released in 1990. Designed by Robert Slimbach, Minion combines the classic characteristics of old-style faces with the full complement of weights required for modern typesetting.

Composed by Creative Graphics, Allentown, Pennsylvania

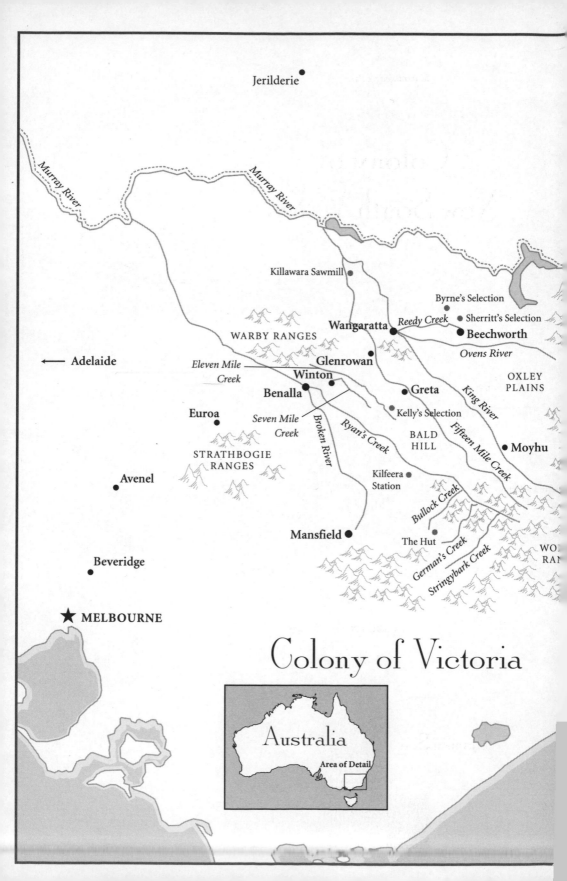